I0754776

By Richard K. Morgan

No Man's Land

Thin Air

Thirteen

Market Forces

TAKESHI KOVACS NOVELS

Altered Carbon

Broken Angels

Woken Furies

A LAND FIT FOR HEROES

The Steel Remains

The Cold Commands

The Dark Defiles

NO MAN'S LAND

NO MAN'S LAND

RICHARD K. MORGAN

NEW YORK

Del Rey
An imprint of Random House
A division of Penguin Random House LLC
1745 Broadway, New York, NY 10019
randomhousebooks.com
penguinrandomhouse.com

Published in the United Kingdom by Gollanz, a member of The Orion Publishing Group Ltd., London.

LIBRARY OF CONGRESS CATALOGING-IN-PUBLICATION DATA
Names: Morgan, Richard K., author
Title: No man's land / Richard K. Morgan.
Description: First edition. | New York: Del Rey, 2026.
Identifiers: LCCN 2025022253 (print) | LCCN 2025022254 (ebook) |
ISBN 9780345493156 hardcover acid-free paper | ISBN 9798217095094 ebook
Subjects: LCGFT: Fiction | Fantasy fiction | Novels
Classification: LCC PR6113.O748 N6 2025 (print) | LCC PR6113.O748 (ebook) |
DDC 823/.92—dc23/eng/20250626
LC record available at https://lccn.loc.gov/2025022253
LC ebook record available at https://lccn.loc.gov/2025022254

Printed in the United States of America

1st Printing

First US Edition

BOOK TEAM: Production editor: Jocelyn Kiker • Managing editor: Paul Gilbert • Production manager: Sarah Feightner • Copy editor: Faren Bachelis • Proofreaders: Debbie Anderson, Emily Cutler, Julia Henderson

Book design by Susan Turner

The authorized representative in the EU for product safety and compliance is Penguin Random House Ireland, Morrison Chambers, 32 Nassau Street, Dublin D02 YH68, Ireland. https://eu-contact.penguin.ie

No Man's Land is for Virginia

Companion in the Forest, Comrade in the Fight,
Country Girl Convert Extraordinaire.

The woods are lovely, dark and deep,
But I have promises to keep,
And miles to go before I sleep,
And miles to go before I sleep.

—Robert Frost

To hope's end I rode and to heart's breaking:
Now for wrath, now for ruin and a red nightfall!

—J.R.R. Tolkien

NO MAN'S LAND

PROLOGUE

HE CAME OUT OF THE FOREST AT DUNSANY CRAG AS NIGHT WAS falling, stood for a moment looking down into the dale. The evening sky above was bruising steadily to black. The winking lights of villages showed like clusters of votive candles across the valley floor. He heard a dog bark in the distance, the iron clank of a farm gate as it closed. He breathed deep, as if trying to catch a scent to go with these faint sounds of human habitation. He shoved the cut-down McCulloch trench gun into the leather sheath across his back. Relaxed for the first time in what felt like days. Faint hints of a breeze, spider-walking delicately over his face, almost warm. This time of year, late spring, trembling on the brink of summer, there was no real wind to speak of up here.

But the trees behind him rustled their branches noisily just the same.

They weren't happy. They didn't like what had been done.

He supposed they had a point. The scent of the *skogsra* was still on his fingers, green and musty as he lifted his right hand to his nose and breathed it in. Wry grin. Tree sprites were picky lovers, but nothing if not passionate once aroused. He was going to be sore down there for a while.

His own gratification aside, he counted it well worth the cost. The child drowsed peacefully in her blanket, pillowed on his shoulder, held firm in the crook of his arm. Little Ellie Furlough, brought out safe and sound, less than three full days from when her mother first begged him to help, and not a mark on her. He was proud of that, for all that most of the work had not been his own. Tree sprites were noted gossips; there was little enough in the Forest they didn't know about. After some ribald pillow talk, the skogsra led him straight to the sleeping child, and that was that.

Easy money.

There was a sheep track, unwinding down the slope beside the crag, indistinct in the gloom, but nothing his Forest-sharpened eyes couldn't handle. It should get him safely down into the rolling pastures below. Then it was just a matter of homing in on the nearest of the villages. He couldn't recall specific names for any of these places; he wasn't up this end of the valley that much. They tended anyway toward uniformity in his mind—modest stone cottages, quiet lanes and infrequent streetlamps, cozy inns and neatly kept market squares.

It didn't matter. A phone box, a taxicab, he was home and dry.

Behind him, darkness thickened through the Forest, as if massing for one last attempt to drag him back in beneath the trees. He grinned again, drew the blanket up an inch on the sleeping child's cheek. He reached up and touched the worn walnut butt of the McCulloch where it jutted at his shoulder—for luck, for comfort, hard to say which. He shook off a final reflexive shudder in the broad muscles of his back. Began a careful descent toward the soft beckon and gleam of the lights below.

HE FOUND THE PHONE BOX he wanted easily enough, tucked away in a gloomy corner of the village square, the iron lattice cubicle lit wan yellow from within by the light in its roof. Like most of its kind this close to the Forest, it had been stripped of all but the faintest flecks of paint. Naked iron—sign of the times. He dug out a coin, thumbed it through the slot, and hit the button. Asked the operator to put him through to the Erlsley exchange.

Niamh picked up on the third ring.

"Erl—" Throaty, explosive coughing, swiftly stifled. "Erlsley Bird Cabs."

"It's Duncan. I thought you quit the Craven As."

"So I did." The lie palpable down the crackly line, even through her soft Irish lilt. "Turns out the first thing that happens when you stop smokin' is this hackin' fuckin' cough comes right back. Had it all day."

"Thought you were going to the doctor, too."

She snorted. "Sure, I'm made of money, Duncan. It's just a fuckin' cough."

"All right. Listen, I'm out at"—he bent and peered out of the phone box, found the village sign—"Kettley Cross, looks like. I got her."

"You *got her*? That's—two days, Duncan! That's got to be some kind of record, is it not? How in the name of Mother Mary did you—"

"Believe me, you'll not want to know. Can you send someone?"

"Sure. Kettley Cross. Gonna be a while before they arrive; that's way out west. But I can get one of the Holden Bridge drivers to cover it for us. Anything he should bring? *You* need a doctor?"

"No. We're all good. Quick as you can, though."

"Oh, and here I was thinking I'd let it lie for a couple of hours. It's *me,* Duncan! You gonna wait there by the box?" She coughed again. Stifled it again. "Like I said, it could be a while."

"No, there's an inn across the street here, Man of Oak. Tell the driver I'll be inside."

"Got it." She rang off.

He replaced the black Bakelite receiver, looked at it pensively. Despite everything, scrying had never been his thing. He sometimes got flashes, had learned not to trust them too much.

But that cough sounded bad.

He shouldered his way out of the phone box, pushing the stiff iron hinges on the door with an effort, trying not to bump the sleeping child in the crook of his arm.

Maybe that was what distracted him, or maybe just the lingering concern about Niamh and her—

"Hoy, *Treefuckah*!"

Duncan whipped about, hand raised to the butt of the McCulloch at his shoulder. The insult had come crisp and clear through the evening quiet, but there was no disguising the otherworldly melodic chime of the voice. He took a careful step away from the iron comfort of the phone box, just enough room to draw the trench gun in a hurry if he needed to.

Because now, almost certainly, he'd need to.

High musical laughter, pattering ghostly across the deserted market square.

"And look at that—he can dance, too," said the voice. "Aren't we lucky?"

Huldu.

They were perched at random across the square, five of them, like man-sized roosting vultures made of moonlight and tinsel shards. He clocked and counted them with speed born of long, grim custom. Two on the drystone wall that led in from the lane; one on the driver's bench of a horseless dray parked by the Man of Oak—neatly blocking Duncan's way to the inn door; one on a low cottage rooftop; and one, as if to make a point, on the tall, brand-new sandstone war memorial cross in the center of the square.

It was the one on the cross who had spoken.

The one with rank, the one with the most voluminous glimmering robes hanging about his ivory-pale flanks. The one now grinning a thin-lipped, wolfish grin full of sharper-than-human teeth.

Duncan nerved himself up. Flexed the fingers of his right hand, preparatory.

Perhaps seeing this, the Huldu leader rose on his perch with a full-body shudder, sprang lightly down from the war memorial, and landed in a crouch. He straightened up in front of the engraved names of the fallen, adjusted his robes with mannered care—it was like watching someone wrap themselves in the emptied-out fragments of a thousand smashed kaleidoscopes. He squared his shoulders and slowly raised his head. Six foot six, maybe closer to seven. Muscled like an Olympic swimmer. Eyes like pitch with a tiny candle glimmering in the depths of each one, moonlight thrown back from the mirror black. The stare was meant to paralyze with fear. He ambled toward Duncan like the promise of death.

"You have something of ours there, I believe."

"Certainly do." Duncan reached up and cleared the McCulloch from its sheath—single unhurried pull, soft strop of it leaving the leather. He pointed the gun, one handed. "Small grape, unrefined iron load, eight balls. Where do you want them, Fae?"

The Huldu stopped dead. The grin turned upside down, the fangs gritted.

"That's better," Duncan said. "Now suppose you fuck off."

"We are five, Treefucker. And you are one."

"Makes no difference." Duncan willed his voice not to tremble. "I don't know how fast your pals are, but it won't matter to you. You'll be down and screaming with your guts torn out."

"Is that so, mortal?"

"Count on it. And I'll be sure and put the second shot right through your fucking skull. That's a stone promise. You want to die, *im*mortal?"

The Huldu shifted on their perches, exchanged glances with each other behind their leader's back. Something rustled among them. Duncan hoped it was fear. He could just about work the pump action on the McCulloch once without dropping Ellie Furlough, but if it came to a real fight . . .

The Huldu's leader hissed, like the world's biggest, angriest black cat.

"I don't think you realize who I am," he snarled.

"I don't care who you are." Duncan reaching now for the old rage, feeling how it fueled him, how it fed cold iron into his voice. "I hate your whole fucking species, pal. It doesn't matter to me which ones I send back to the Gray. And it might as well be you tonight, so *give me a fucking reason*!"

The shouted words hung in the air like smoke. And now he was shaking; he couldn't help it. Ellie Furlough stirred and frowned in her sleep, snuffled and burrowed closer into Duncan's shoulder. But she didn't wake. The Huldu leader's gaze glittered as it switched from his confrontation with Duncan to the toddler's sleeping face.

"Oh, you hate us, yes, how you hate us." It came out a sibilant whisper. "But I see that hasn't stopped you taking our culture when it suits you."

"This?" Duncan tipped his chin down at Ellie. "This is a curative, a resting glamour. Learn 'em from any woodswoman or witch in the county."

"Yes." The Fae leader's eyes seemed to kindle with tiny flames. "And where do you think your woodswomen found their magic in the first place? Where do you think they went, like bitches in heat, to suck and fuck and be paid in kind for their whoring?"

High chimes of laughter once again from the other Huldu, like shards of stained glass, falling and shattering. But Duncan knew a climbdown when he saw one. The relief coursed through him, hot as fresh piss.

He kept his face stone.

"That is none of my concern," he said.

"Well, this little *squealer*"—the Huldu reached out toward Ellie's sleeping head with one pale long-taloned hand; the hunger in his elfin face was terrifying—"was also none of your concern. And yet you saw fit to interfere and take her from us."

Duncan's forearm was starting to ache from the strain of holding up the McCulloch with just one hand.

"It's what they pay me for," he said.

"Pay!" The Huldu spat out the word. "Tree thief, in your whole pathetically short life, they couldn't pay you enough to cross *me.* You made a grave mistake tonight. You fell into a trap."

"You going to talk all night, Fae? Here she is. Come and get her."

Small silence and stillness in the air between them now—as if the whole village square and the confrontation in it had become a daguerreotype of times past, silvery and smudged and hung to be peered at on some drawing room wall. The Huldu leader drew in breath across his teeth. He shook his head.

"No. We've had our fun. For now. But mark this, tree thief—the next time someone asks you to set foot in the Forest and bring back some pretty little brat we took a shine to, understand that you are known and marked. That we have found you, and now our eye is on you. Your time is ending, Duncan Silver." The Huldu leaned in a little, the fanged grin came out again. "Or should I call you Master Duncan of Stac Dubh?"

The daguerreotype, bleaching out, protective glass shattering . . .

The mansion crashing into his mind—*blond sandstone Victorian grandeur, four stories tall with the cupola, neatly kept lawns and graceful sweep of gravel drive, architectural statement and testimony to an age now renounced. He sees the wooded rise of the Munro behind, the peak set against a torn and tarnished silver evening sky, a light on in the window of his third-floor room . . .*

It was an image so rock solid it could only have been summoned by glamour. Pulled hard from his memories by the creature in front of him, given fresh life in both their mind's eyes.

Like a storm wind howling through his head . . .

Duncan pulled the trigger on the McCulloch without a second thought.

PART I

FAE RISING

As the light faded and the haze deepened,
mystery crept nearer from every side.

—Lord Dunsany

ONE

THE ADDRESS WAS IN WEST ERLSLEY—THEY OFTEN WERE—IN A maze of run-down tenements and concrete walkways that stank of piss and the charred extinction of small conjuring fires. Pathetic remnants of bone and fur and feathers in sheltered corners, where the meager sacrifices had been made. Huldu runes scrawled across the stone in charcoal or daubed in blood. As far as Duncan could tell, most of it was gibberish. Certainly, there was nothing you'd call a functional spell anywhere on these walls. Here and there, he even spotted the odd piece of mathematical notation in the mix, though his math was not good enough to work out if it had any more coherence than the Huldu symbols it coexisted among.

None of which surprised him in the least.

In the trenches, he'd seen men cling to all and any systems of faith they could muster, some even distilling their own homegrown superstition, ritual, prayer, *whatever*—anything at all to give the illusion of control over the vast impersonal forces that brought them death on a daily basis. One soldier under his command in early 1915, Private Greaves, had carried with him a set of intricately whittled wooden figures that he would take out whenever he had leisure, set up in some configuration that evidently had meaning to him—though the configuration often changed—and would then crouch and whisper softly to them under his breath, like a mother soothing small children to sleep.

Greaves had taken some sour ribbing for this early on, but Duncan had ordered it staunched, and after that the other men left him alone. Later, when Greaves had proved remarkably long lived, given the action they'd all seen, a couple of the other soldiers from the company even started to gather round and join in with the ritual. They'd stand and watch diffidently while Greaves set out the whittled figures, wait until he gestured them closer, and then crouch with him, and begin. Their pooled murmuring would softly rise and fall in the lamp glow and gloom of whatever bivouac they'd lucked into. It managed to be both eerie and strangely comforting at one and the same time.

Now that he thought back, Duncan realized that there might have been something of Huldu slenderness and poise in those carved wooden figures. And he wondered belatedly what home Greaves had come from, what part of Britain, where such things might already have had currency, even back then. It wasn't something he'd ever find out now—Greaves died in the mud at Ypres, along with almost everyone else under Duncan's command at the time. The way he heard it later, a tank whose driver was addled on carbon monoxide fumes lost control nosing around a machine gun nest revetment. The tank veered, clipped and toppled three men, Greaves among them, then crushed them into the ground as it churned desperately in reverse. Duncan supposed the slender, whittled wooden figures met a similar fate.

Wake up, Duncan.

Stir of other figures now, blunt and hunched against the cold as they spilled across the concrete walkway ahead; clink as a boot caught an empty bottle and sent it skittering. The sound yanked him back to present concerns. He slowed a little, assessed the spread. It didn't look like much—local toughs, three of them, pinched pale faces under rain-damp hoods, bulky workman's jackets that made them look bigger than they were. Booted feet, stumbling a little with the booze or maybe just with sitting too long in the cold. Long-necked brown beer bottles, too loosely held to be weapons. WAR DEBT MALAISE, blared the headlines, ECONOMY STALLED, NO SOLUTION IN SIGHT FOR FOREST CRISIS. Fear, panic, exhaustion, unemployment spiraling steadily upward, and well, here's your result.

Duncan eased to a halt.

"Gentlemen," he said warily.

"Fucking Otherkin," one of them spat uncertainly.

Duncan couldn't really blame him. It was in the cut and weave of the hooded jacket he wore, the boots with their intricate tooled leather. For clients, he dressed to broadcast his trade, to sell how well he belonged in the Forest, and that look wasn't a million miles from all the cute and cheap and practiced signifiers the dress-up brigade pulled to ape the Huldu they'd mostly only ever met in the pages of novels and maybe the sepia-tone projector slides of a Russell Maynard Dalton lecture. To the young toughs' boozed-up eyes, Duncan looked the part. Wannabe Fae fuck pretender at large. Dilettante. An easy mark.

If they'd seen Duncan's eyes and expression and stance more clearly, they would have understood their mistake.

But it was a gloomy autumn afternoon in West Erlsley, glowering black rain clouds hung low and soaking up what little decent light was left in the sky. And these angry, idle young men were neither close enough nor sober enough to pick up on the details of the mess they were about to make.

"I'm looking for Umber Cottages," he preempted them. "This the right way?"

It stalled whatever they'd had in mind. They looked at each other, unsure. The biggest of the three swigged exaggeratedly at his beer. He lowered the bottle, wiped his mouth. Belched loudly. Gestured broadly.

"It's this way, yeah. But, uh . . ." Swaggering closer, visibly gathering courage. "You gotta pay a toll, like."

Duncan looked at him. "No, I don't."

The moment stretched, twanged, and snapped. The tough looked away.

"You'll want to let me pass," Duncan suggested.

Confused looks between the other two. They hadn't seen what the first man had, but they weren't too drunk to sense the shift. The lead tough stood reluctantly aside. Duncan moved past them with every appearance of casual amiability. He grinned at them, nodded. Later, sobering up, they would try to piece it together and fail, and bicker and blame each other. But Duncan's eyes would linger in all their memories, and each would privately understand that this was not a scuffle they could have won.

Meanwhile, Duncan made his way along the concrete walkway, undecided if he was happy to have avoided the fight or not. As ever, his rage simmered close to the surface. But something, some remnant of shame and regret for the mess with Ellie Furlough last spring, was enough to hold it down.

Just enough.

He took a couple of turns in the concrete warren, following the directions he'd been given, and shortly after that, he stumbled on Umber Cottages. It was one of the worst misnomers he'd ever seen—a short, ugly terraced row of two-story worker housing in cheaply finished gray stone. Raw concrete steps led up to wooden front doors with peeling black paint. Pokey little windows sat high up, like eyes peering myopically into a future printed too fine to read. The facades were modern—probably put up in the early days of Re-clearance, when it was still thought the advance of the Forest could be stopped, and thousands were drafted for the work—but already the stonework looked stained and tired.

Duncan found number sixteen and knocked. A wan-looking woman of about fifty opened for him, looked him up and down with narrow suspicion.

"We don't want none o' that," she snapped, in accents from somewhere a long way south of Erlsley. "She's to be left alone. G'ahn, or I'll call the bottles on yer."

"Duncan Silver," he said. "For Irene Rush. I'm expected."

From within the dimly lit spaces behind the door, something shrieked like a howitzer shell descending.

The noise froze the woman where she stood. Duncan nodded.

"Perhaps you'd better let me in."

She stood aside, wordless. Duncan ducked his head and stepped through into the hall space. The shriek came again, intensified. He tracked it to a side room, door solidly closed. He moved past into the living room. No gas in these premises, certainly no electric; what light there was came from hurricane lamps stood on the sideboard and main table, wicks cranked up, and a struggling fire in the grate. Shadows capered on the walls.

"Are you him?"

She sat coiled and wrapped in a shawl and nightgown in an armchair at the sole window in the room, staring out at what must have been the backyards of the row. Legs drawn up under her, one naked foot trailing from under the hem of the gown. Hard to tell in the dim light, but she seemed young. Pale skin. Long dark hair, left down and uncombed, he reckoned, for quite a while. There was a livid mark on one cheek where someone had struck her hard enough to break the skin. Glimmer of recent tear tracks she'd left unwiped.

"Aye, I'm Silver." He said it as gently as he could. "Like the pirate."

"Like the pirate," she repeated mechanically.

Speaking seemed to stir something in her. She turned in her chair to look at him fully, and it dawned on him that she was an attractive woman. The pale face framed in all that hair reminded him of someone—one of the actresses he'd had postcards of as a boy, perhaps. Ethel Warwick, tits out for Whistler, or maybe that American one he'd liked, Marie Doro. Fey, young, silk-draped things, all big beckoning eyes, leaves and flowers strewn through their hair.

"They say you'll go to the Forest, Mr. Silver?" Her voice was a dredged whisper, a husk. "They say you're not afraid?"

"A lot of men will go to the Forest, Mrs. Rush. Especially for the money you promise. Especially in these times."

She nodded, moved again in the chair. Both feet touched down on the floor, revealed long, shapely calves above. He saw that the gown was pricey—sheer silk, out of place in the stark tenement surroundings. Irene Rush had fallen on hard times, and maybe not that long ago.

She sniffed and cleared her throat, wiped the back of her hand over each cheek in turn to clear the tracks of her tears.

"Yes, I—I suppose you have seen service? You have passed through the fire?"

He tried not to grimace at the phrase. It was overly popular that year, much delivered from pulpits and lecterns and the benches of Parliament—*passed through the flames; baptism of fire; passage through the flaming rites of the War to End All Wars.* So forth.

"I was in France, yes. And Flanders, for a while."

"Then you are not afraid."

"Mrs. Rush, a man who goes to the Forest and is not afraid is a man who will not be coming out again. Try not to believe too much of what you read in the pulps."

The hard-faced older woman came and stood in the room with her back to the window. Arms folded, watchful, touching distance to her ward. He saw in her face that she didn't trust him any more now than she had when they had their misunderstanding at the door. He wondered how many like him they'd already seen, how much of their obviously dwindling funds they'd seen wasted with no result, how many shysters calling and slipping away with an easy grin. Demonologists, Theosophicals, Sword-and-Orbsters, all the sub-Blavatsky types and splinters, Woodsmen-who-weren't, fly-by-night witch and warlock fakes, Otherkin flimflam artists, the whole sad circus erupting into their lives one tawdry act after another . . .

Once again, through the wall from the room next door, the awful, downward hurtling shriek. The older woman's eyes moistened. He saw how Mrs. Rush flinched, how her hand rose trembling toward the livid mark on her cheek. Her gaze fell away into whatever place had stolen the strength from her voice.

"It won't stop," she husked—to him or to herself, it wasn't clear. "It just . . . won't stop."

He nodded. "In all likelihood, it has the Sight. It will know I'm here."

She looked at him again, then, as if for the first time. As if the whole thing had only now become real in her mind. It was a common enough moment among afflicted parents. Duncan took the snuff box from his pocket, crouched beside her to make himself less alarming.

"Look—Mrs. Rush, let me be honest. At this moment, I cannot be sure that your child has been removed to the Forest, or that what's in the next room is a changeling. But it certainly sounds that way. And there is an easy test. Here." He held out the snuff box. "Open this."

She took the box, struggled a moment with the ornate catch, then lifted the lid and peered inside.

"Iron filings," he told her. "Perfectly harmless. Touch them. You, too, please, madam."

The older woman looked at him mistrustfully a moment, then leaned in and put a finger into the box.

"Take a small pinch, please, both of you. Rub it onto your skin." He watched them obey him like sleepwalkers. "You'll agree it does no harm?"

They both nodded, like mechanical toys. He straightened up. "Good. Now, should I bring Miriam in? Or would you prefer . . ."

Mrs. Rush looked up at the older woman. The retainer pursed her lips and left the room.

"It's Mimi," Mrs. Rush said brokenly. "No one ever calls her Miriam."

Out in the corridor, Duncan heard a key in a lock, a door opened. The shrieking began in earnest. The woman came back, dragging a thrashing, flailing, diminutive rag-clad figure by one thin arm. It resembled nothing so much as a three- or four-year-old girl with similar features to Mrs. Rush herself, and it was clearly terrified of everyone and everything in the room.

"*Mama, Mama, no, don't let them,*" it wailed. *"Don't let them burn me!"*

Mrs. Rush dissolved in tears, buried her face in her hands.

"Mama, please, I'll be good, I didn't mean it, please, Mama, please, I won't—"

Duncan hissed a word of command in Skogurtal, and the creature blinked, then shut up as if its jaw were a sprung trap.

It was all the evidence he needed. Nothing human could be compelled in the Forest speech that way. But of course it would not do for the mother, and Duncan felt a tiny prickling sensation in his throat at that tenacity, an unquantified blend of joy and rage and loss that threatened to prick out tears in his eyes. He swallowed hard. Cleared his throat.

"Let me hold her," he said very gently.

And rapidly, before anyone could react, he stepped across and took the child by both thin wrists from behind, held the skinny arms apart. The older woman let go, startled. Duncan lifted the creature forward so it stood right in front of the mother. He felt how its muscles tensed and writhed, fighting his grip. He widened his arms, pulled seeming-Mimi into something resembling a crucifixion. Tears flooded the child's eyes, flooded down its face. It moaned and writhed.

But it no longer spoke.

"Mrs. Rush." Duncan, urgently now—this had to be done fast, while her fortitude lasted. "For your own peace of mind, I would like you to take some of the iron filings and gently rub them on this child's arm."

She stared at him, long moments in which he saw the truth finally breach the walls she'd built in her mind, erupt to the conscious level, where it could no longer be denied. She made a noise, a convulsive sob that wracked her whole body. But when she met his eyes again, he saw the change, the new determination to go with the knowledge she now would not deny.

She pressed her lips together, tears still welling up, still spilling down her cheeks.

But she did it.

She pinched up the iron filings in her fingers, reached out for the thing that looked like her daughter. The creature's muscles cabled against Duncan's grip. It kicked out, twisted and thrashed. Duncan grimaced, tightened his hold, and nodded urgently at Irene Rush.

"I'm sorry," she wept.

But she pressed the iron filings onto one thin arm near the elbow.

Duncan averted his eyes.

Flash-flare, magnesium bright, blinding in the dimly lit room.

The mother screamed, but it was lost in the high, ululating howl that broke from the child, and put every hair on Duncan's body erect. It was all he could do to maintain his grip, haul back and prevent the creature from kicking Mrs. Rush in the face.

A sudden reek of scorching stormed the room, made the two women gag.

Then acrid smoke, ribboning up off a wound that glowed moss green in the blotched and blunted vision the flare had left them.

Duncan wrestled the thrashing sprite back, away from the mother it had fooled.

"Your daughter is in the Forest," he said.

TWO

HE TOLD IRENE RUSH TWO WEEKS, BECAUSE HE HAD TO TELL her something. The truth was he had no idea how long it might take to locate her daughter. But in his experience, this was not what parents wanted to hear. They needed parameters for the agony. They needed the promise it would end, and soon.

"What should I do?" she asked in a firmer voice than she'd so far shown him. With the changeling dragged back to its room by the older woman and reimprisoned there, she seemed to have composed herself a little, gathered some fragments of previously unsuspected resolve.

"There's nothing you can do," he said truthfully. "You must understand, the Huldu are nothing like us. They are not a unified society, they're not even a unified tribe, especially not in this part of the country. These are not coordinated raids, authorized by some Faerie parliament or king—all that's a fantasy of the romances and the pulps and that bloody Maynard Dalton."

"I—I thought that Mr. Dalton . . . He is a—a psychical researcher, is he not? An expert on Faerie and the Forest?"

"Russell Maynard Dalton is a charlatan. A purveyor of sensationalist lies and half-truths for profit. Frankly, the man should be jailed for the false theories and conspiracies he spouts to the—" Duncan stopped himself, held down his temper with an effort. He'd been about to say *the needy and the credulous.* Dealing with the changeling and Mrs. Rush's tears had churned him up. He smoothed his voice out, played the expert. "There are some semblances of an ancient Faerie kingdom in the south and west of England, parts of Wales, that much is true. And something similar in parts of Scotland, some preeminent warlords here and there. But even these are remnants, rotted through with the centuries the Huldu have been in hiding. And here in the north of England, there is not even that. It's a mess of clans, sparring and squabbling, trying to fill the new forest spaces. Things are in flux. If I had to guess, Mrs. Rush, I would say the Unbinding has taken the Huldu almost as much by surprise as it has us. In the meantime, abductions like these are casual acts, whimsical, spur-of-the-moment impulses of passion or spite by beings we really don't understand at all. There's no obvious pattern, there's no rationale."

He saw the fresh, rising wave of horror in her eyes. He reached across the small space between where they sat, laid a hand softly on her arm. "But—there are ways for me to track Mimi's abductors, and we can expect that they won't have taken her very far. You must wait to hear from me. One day at a time, Mrs. Rush. It is the only way. And as I said, it will most likely take a couple of weeks."

His worst result for a successful rescue was nineteen days; he had no reason to think this one would take longer, and he guessed the mother, once reunited with her child, would likely forgive any overrun. Certainly anything up to an extra week.

And if he was gone much longer than *three* weeks in the Forest, well—in all likelihood he wouldn't be coming home at all, with or without Mimi Rush.

"Will . . ." She swallowed. "Will they hurt her?"

"No." Said with blunt conviction—because how could he tell her anything else, what purpose would it serve?—hoping he'd get the girl back before he was proven a liar. "Not intentionally, anyway. Not when she's so small. They will be fascinated with her, the way you or

I might be with a puppy, or perhaps a pet monkey you thought to train. But the Huldu are not consistent in their enthusiasms. They grow easily bored."

She shuddered. "How long do you think they have had her?"

"Not long."

It was a reflex, dismissive, the bare instinct to comfort, and Irene Rush saw through it like a pane of cheap glass. Her lips tightened. Duncan cursed himself. Hurried, stumbling, to limit the damage.

"That test with the iron filings? It tells us a lot. It works on the Huldu, and most of what they've brought back into our world with them. But the changelings are different. They're conjured to fit in with humans, to fool us. The sorcery is made with that in mind. It's a slow process, but give most changelings a couple of years and they lose almost all of their sorcerous attributes. In time, they will come to be almost as human as the children they were made to replace. Now you *saw* that reaction, Mrs. Rush. I can tell you with certainty that that thing in there pretending to be your daughter was brought into being no more than six months ago, probably much less."

"Six . . . months?" Something in her eyes—a trembling on the brink.

"I would say so. Is that when you started to notice the differences? The mood changes, the frenzies?"

"Mr. Silver, six months ago, we were not here, in Erlsley."

Oh, Christ on a fucking bike . . .

"We have had to move around, you see. For work. With my husband . . . gone, and the times the way they are. It has not been easy . . ."

She saw the look on his face, jarred to a halt.

He remembered the Thames snarl in the older woman's voice. "You were in London?"

"No, not—not then. We haven't lived in the capital for . . . some years."

"Where, then?" Trying to keep the snap out of his voice, because this was fucking . . . "How far from here?"

"A village called Dowgreave. It's—it's not far outside Macclesfield."

"Aye, I know it."

"I had clerical work in Macclesfield. For a while."

"And you came here when exactly?"

Glances between Rush and the older woman. "Uhm—about four months ago, I would say."

Macclesfield. Well over fifty miles from Erlsley, even for a south-southwest-flying crow. By Forest path, it was going to be more than half as much again. A lot of ground between, some of it still unfamiliar to him despite the years . . .

Come on, Duncan, get a grip. It's the same basic Forest either way. Maybe a couple of clan lines to be crossed, but nothing you haven't done before.

Still . . .

He drew a deep breath. "All right, Mrs. Rush, this part is important. Can you remember if Mimi—what you thought was Mimi—started acting out of character while you were still in Dowgreave? Or did it begin here?"

"I—don't know." Staring into the space between them. "She's always unhappy when we have to move. I suppose it started when we got here; but maybe just before, yes, in Dowgreave. When we were packing up. I'm sorry, I'm sorry, I don't know, I just don't *remember.*"

Voice muffling as she pressed her face into her hands and sobbed. Her shoulders trembled with the force of it. Duncan said nothing. The older woman glowered at him, put a tentative hand on the nape of her mistress's neck. He waited. The sobbing ebbed, the trembling seemed to ease . . .

Abruptly, Irene Rush lifted her face from her hands. Something new in her eyes as she looked at him now. A new iron in the voice as well.

"Susan, would you leave us alone for a moment?"

The older woman went on glowering at Duncan. "Ma'am, that's not—"

"It's fine, Susan." Mrs. Rush sniffed, like a debutante snorting cocaine for the very first time. Dabbed at her eyes with a ragged handkerchief from her sleeve. "Mr. Silver is an honorable man. Go to your room, please."

Susan's glare redoubled in intensity, clear warning for him in her eyes. But she gave way. She took her hand away from Mrs. Rush's neck, patted her awkwardly on the shoulder a couple of times instead, then swept past Duncan with a final murderous look.

They waited until they heard the door to her room open and close again.

"Is it more money you want, Mr. Silver?"

There was a defiant gleam in her eyes, something that went beyond tear sheen. Duncan shook his head.

"It's not the money. But the more of the Forest I have to cover—"

"I will do anything, Mr. Silver." Shrugging so the shawl fell away from her upper body, reaching to slowly unlace the top of her nightgown. "Anything at all to have my daughter back. Do you understand me?"

Her breasts mounded under the thin silk as she tugged at it. He could make out the dark ovals of the aureole around each nipple, the weight where they pressed forward against the garment. He thought of his boyhood postcards again . . .

But the women on those cards had gazes that beckoned coyly or burned with heated desire as they looked at you out of the lens. Availability by design. He looked into Irene Rush's eyes, saw nothing there but desperation and the gritted will of some animal willing and able to gnaw off one of its own limbs to escape the trap it was in.

He'd seen the same thing once or twice before, over in France when they passed through towns shattered by artillery or hamlets pillaged by previous waves of soldiers also passing through. Women who'd had everything else taken from them, offering up, with dead eyes, the only bargaining counter they had left in return for rations to feed a child or aged parent a few more godforsaken days . . .

"It's not the money," he repeated. "The money's fine. I don't need anything more from you, Mrs. Rush. But if I don't know whether Mimi was taken at Dowgreave or here, it does complicate matters. And that may mean more time. I'm sorry."

A shudder ran through her. She reached up to lace her nightgown again.

"No, Mr. Silver. It is I who should be sorry. I tell Susan I see an honorable man before me, and then I attempt to prove myself wrong the moment she is gone. Please forgive me."

He felt the hot surge of mingled joy and rage again, prickling at the back of his eyes.

"You are a mother," he said quietly. "You want your child back. Nothing you do to that end will ever need forgiving. Nothing, ever. Please remember that."

"Well . . ." She drew the shawl about her shoulders again. She pulled herself visibly back together, sat up straighter. "What must we do with Mi—with Mimi's . . . with the . . . changeling? While you are gone, I mean. I don't know if I—"

"Don't concern yourself," he told her. "I'll deal with that. All part of the service."

HE TOOK A FEW PAGES of notes after that, careful, probing questions that Irene Rush answered in a dead and distant voice when she could or simply shook her head when she couldn't. It didn't take long. Duncan thanked her, got no reply beyond a brief meeting of his gaze and a dutiful twitch of the lips. You could not have called it a smile. He left her sitting wordless in the chair, staring into space much as she'd been when he came in.

He met Susan in the entry hall and explained what he needed her to do.

She cracked the door on the imprisoning room, stony faced, and Duncan dragged the changeling out by one arm. It kicked and wailed and clung to handy bits of furniture, finally to the doorjamb itself, until he managed to tear it loose and get it out into the hall. Instant change of tactics—now it bared its teeth and flew at him, flailing, scratching, shrilling in his face like a lost soul. Duncan rode out the ineffectual attacks, then backhanded the creature savagely across the face to still it. Irene Rush had chosen to stay in the living room; she'd pretty clearly had enough for one day. But the blow was loud in the hall space, unmistakable, and he heard her stifle a sob in response. He sighed, dragged the dazed changeling to the front door. Susan held it open for him, stood aside, and handed him a folded cheque. From the way she looked at him, she still didn't like him much better than she had when he came in.

"It's orl the money we 'ave." She made sure he knew.

He nodded, dragged the changeling outside and down the concrete steps. It stirred as it felt the cold, began to weep and beg again for its mother—until Susan closed the door behind them, and then its noise making abruptly ceased. A change went through it, a complete unpicking of the motions and gestures and expressions that had made it Mimi Rush. It ceased to cringe and cry, stood up straight and poised. It cocked its head with preternatural, wholly adult aplomb, watched him out of suddenly unblinking urchin eyes.

"That's better." Duncan felt the ooze of blood from a scratch over his eye, thumbed it away, licked his thumb. "You want to live much longer, you shut up and do what I tell you."

Of course, changelings severed from their intended hearth and purpose tended not to live very long anyway. The spell-work saw to that. Listlessness set in fast, followed in short order by actual physical decline. Decay time varied, depending on the age and art of the Huldu who'd built the enchantment in the first place, how much effort went into the spell, and how long the changeling had been in place. The end result would always be the same. Dissolution was usually waiting a matter of days, at most weeks, down the line.

But this changeling didn't know that yet.

Briefly, he tried once again to imagine himself into what it must be like—called into being, fully formed as the simulacrum echo of some other, more important life; put in place of that being with nothing to hold you but a driven instinct to imitate the original and hide your own nature as best you could. Left forever alone among strange creatures, to fend for yourself and fit in, losing any faint sense of self you might ever once have owned.

And then to lose it all, to be cut loose from any purpose you ever had.

He shivered in the chilly air, sniffed. Papery odor of rain inbound.

"I'm taking you back to the Forest," he said roughly. "It's not far. You behave, we won't have a problem. You give me any trouble, I'm going to take another handful of those iron filings and grind them into your eyes. Are we clear?"

"*Fforessst . . .*" the changeling rustled, apparently to itself.

"That's right. Time for you to go home."

BACK BEFORE THE WAR AND what the Theosophicals now liked to call the Unbinding, it was a good couple of hour's brisk walk from the western fringes of Erlsley to anything you could reasonably call *forest.* Once you were out of town, bleak moorland was the norm, sporadically netted over with the crisscross of dry stone walls and drover's paths. The landscape came studded with outlying farms and sheep folds and shepherd's hides, the safe, monotonous roll of the terrain broken up here and there by occasional copses, lone ancient oak or yew or elm, and the odd squiggle of younger foliage tracking and shrouding the meander of a small river or ambitious stream. Open ground, easy to navigate, bracing to hike.

No longer.

The oak and yew and elm had bred back overnight, brought forth monstrous atavistic versions of themselves by the legion, taken back the land wherever humans were sparse. Those who'd been around when it happened—as opposed to overseas and getting shot at—reported the crack and boom and horizon-wide sheet lightning of endless thunderstorms, driving, drenching rain for weeks, unearthly rumbling, tearing, creaking sounds, night after night, making dogs skulk and whine, infants cry, and adults shudder. According to official record, it drove a small number of people gibbering insane. Some claimed to have seen the Wild Hunt thundering headlong amid the clouds, others the emergence of the ancient dead in ranks from fiery chasms torn deep in the land.

And so forth.

By the time Duncan got back from the abruptly aborted war in Europe, it was impossible to know how much of this might have been true. The weather had quietened, as if exhausted by the birthing it had done. The night skies were eerily clear and quiet. Any fiery chasms were long gone, or at least shrouded from the human eye. The dry stone walls and drovers tracks, the outlying farms, sheep folds and shepherd's hides—all had been swallowed up along with the moors. They existed now under the new forest canopies like the drowned ruins of some rural Atlantis—overgrown, brooding, silent. He'd seen them in his work, generally gave them a wide berth. Often they contained things you were better not having to see.

Whether a similar fate awaited Erlsley itself in the long run, along with all other human habitation across Britain, was something bookish experts in Whitehall and Oxford and Cambridge were apparently still debating. For now, the massive canopied ramparts of the Forest bulked and loomed and drowsed in the breeze, a scant half mile from where the cheap new housing on the city's western fringes gave out.

The Number 4 tramline went out that way.

Duncan rode the tram standing up, one hand looped in the safety strap overhead, the other clamped on the changeling's wrist. Muggy warmth belted out from the carriage heater, steamed up windows streaked with rain, spread the woolly, intimate smell of dampened clothes and human bodies around him. The tram was packed, people hurrying home from work or errands run, eager to get indoors before night could fall. They did an intricate, shuffling dance at every stop, as passengers got up to disembark, bumping and pressing and excusing themselves to each other as they maneuvered down the aisle.

The changeling stood quiescent at his side—altogether too much exposed iron and steel in the tram's interior for any kind of struggle to be worth the risk—and played to perfection the role of small child out with her rather stern father. They got the odd glance now and then, maybe the cut of Duncan's woodsman clothes, maybe just someone wondering where this poor little poppet's mother was. But the war and its dislocations had shaken family roles loose of their mountings along with everything else, and there was little sign yet that things would settle back the way they'd once been. People made do, and unusual tableaus just weren't that unusual anymore.

The tram lurched on the last curve before the turnaround at Rawbury. The changeling flinched as the motion threw it in the direction of the gleaming metal trim on the nearest seat. Instinctively, Duncan yanked it back to avoid the contact. It knocked briefly into him, regained its poise, said nothing. They locked gazes for a moment.

"Just watch yourself," said Duncan gruffly. "You can get hurt."

The tram rattled to a halt at the turnaround and people bundled out. Duncan broke gaze with the changeling, hung on to the strap, and ducked his head in a vain attempt to see through the misted windows. Rain striping the glass now in earnest. They got out onto slick gray cobblestones in the full horizontal bluster of it all, watched the other passengers tramp off with heads down against the weather. No one looked back. The driver gathered up his satchel and left the cabin, headed for the warmth of a cozy-looking break cabin built alongside the line. He nodded at Duncan, but said nothing. The door of the cabin opened onto cheery fire glow within, then swallowed him up. Boisterous male voices, right down at the limits of Duncan's hearing, nothing a normal man would have caught. He thought the changeling was listening, too. He jerked its arm.

"You're done with this world," he told it, switching to Skogurtal. "Let's go."

Beyond the rails and cobbles of the terminus, a muddy lane unwound up a rolling incline into the countryside. A waist-high dry stone wall tracked it on the left. On the other side of the wall were fields of rough grazing, rising to the piled and tangled remnants of the trees felled during the Re-clearance.

And beyond that—like some fantastical frozen tidal wave in autumnal shades—the Forest itself lay waiting.

THEY TRUDGED UP THE LANE in the gusty wind and rain, found a gap in the drystone that had once been barred by an iron gate. Duncan supposed it had been unhinged and removed to facilitate the carriage of felled timber down the hill and through to the town. Inured by the long Victorian dream of man's mastery over nature, the authorities had kept at clearing back the Forest for quite a while before realization set in—that the forces now at work in the land were beyond any human control. Whatever this change was, whatever it presaged, that splendid Victorian whip hand was lost. Between the freakish accidents and casualties on the cutting line and the unexplained disappearances by night, morale was already sputtering and spiraling down in flames, like a defeated Sopwith Pup Duncan had once seen die in the skies over the Somme.

But what really killed the Re-clearance effort once and for all was the demoralizing rapid regrowth the Forest could put on within days of a fresh cut.

Pushed hard, the logging crews found they could maybe make fifty to sixty yards a day into the encroaching tree line while daylight lasted—*no one* would work once darkness fell—though clearing the resulting mess afterward took far longer than the cut itself. Then, after a couple of days, the storms would roll in, bringing torrential rain and near dark conditions all day, forcing the crews to abandon all work and sit the weather out, grumbling and shivering and recounting apocryphal Forest horror stories in taverns and guesthouses nearby.

And when the skies finally cleared, the logged area was regrown once again, if anything, thicker and more impenetrable than before.

Duncan led the changeling into the fields, then up toward the dead tree line. It wasn't his preferred approach to the Forest. The felled trunks and tangled branches were a nuisance to negotiate, and reminded him uncomfortably of antitank obstacles the Germans had built at Delville Wood. As if, in their idiocy, men had attempted to destroy the invading Forest and ended up just furnishing it with a handy demarcation zone instead.

They reached the first of the toppled oaks and clambered up, the changeling proving preternaturally agile on bark surfaces once he let it go. For a moment they both stood atop the broad curve of the trunk, staring out over the yards and yards of similarly murdered and tangled-up trees and the living Forest beyond. The wind-driven rain came and striped them both across the face, gave the moment a wet immediacy in contrast to the dreary trudge they'd endured to get here. The canopies in the tree line tipped and shook and shivered. Duncan pointed at the motion.

"That's where you belong," he said flatly.

"Ffffforessssst."

"The Forest, aye." Duncan went to give the changeling a hard shove in the back, knock it off the trunk to the grass. At the last moment, something stopped him.

"In there," he said, pointing again instead, "somewhere, is the one who made you. Maybe you can find that Fae fuck. Ask them what they think you should do now."

The changeling swiveled its head to look up at him. He thought he heard vertebrae click and crack with the motion. With every passing minute, it looked less and less like the small child it had been spawned to replace.

"Siiiiiilvaaaa," it hissed.

"Aye, Silver." Brusque impatience now. "That's me. You tell them in there, I'm coming for the child. Silver is coming. Tell them I'm bringing the speaking iron. Tell them I'll cut down anything that gets in my way. Tell them if they've harmed her in any way—"

And then, like the *hiss/snap* of a camera bulb, firing and dying, he was suddenly sick of his own unrelenting rage.

"It's not your fault," he heard himself say, unaccountably with the faintest hint of a Welsh lilt. "You did only what you were made for. No hard feelings, eh? Just get going."

The changeling looked steadily back at him. Wet gleam in its eyes.

"Ffffffffeelingssss," it said, as if describing a decision it had taken, and then it jumped down to the turf below. It landed like a cat, turned on all fours, and stared back up at him.

Duncan pointed at the tree line again. "Get yourself under cover," he said. "This rain is going to come down hard. Get in the woods."

It looked at him a moment longer, then, like the flash of a fish belly in water, it whipped about and was gone, scuttling on all fours into the tangled chaos of felled and shattered trees. He lost it there, stood watching a minute longer, unsure why. He thought he caught a flicker of movement, saw it once more, clambering slickly up and over a jutting deadwood branch farther out, slipping instantly back down again.

But in the thickening rain, it was hard to tell for sure.

THREE

HE MADE IT BACK TO THE TRAM TERMINUS JUST IN TIME FOR turnaround. Grabbed a seat at the window and dozed with his head against the glass as the tram rattled back into town. Ragged, flash-lit dreams, fragments from the war, stalking his shallow sleep. Machine gun fire, screams and pleading eyes. A soft, Welsh-accented voice. And somewhere in there, little Ellie Furlough, falling terror-stricken into a hole filled with mud and rusted barbed wire and the rotted corpses of men still somehow moving and moaning in pain . . .

He jolted awake, a half dozen stops short of the city center.

On the other side of the glass, the rain appeared to have relented, and the interior of the tram felt abruptly stuffy and overheated. He shook off the dream, got out at the next stop, and walked the rest of the way to Skoldergate. Around him, the city shuttered and fussed its way toward end of day—lights in shops and offices going out, blinds going down, men and women with keys locking up and hurrying home. Along each street, the gallows-arm iron streetlamps took up the fight against the early dark.

Corner of Skoldergate and East Cavendish there was a brazier stand selling roast chestnuts. Duncan stopped to get a bag and chat to the big weatherbeaten Glaswegian who ran it, a marine color sergeant called Crammond who'd managed to mislay his lower left arm and eye on a beach at Gallipoli. The army had duly fitted him with a natty aluminum replacement built by some French-sounding firm working out of Hendon—De Soutier or something—and Crammond affected a black patch to cover the scar-edged void where his eye had once been. *Been ma leg,* he was known to comment to his customers, *coulda goan the whole hog and got masael a fuckin' parrot, too.*

"Awright, big man?" he asked Duncan, using his prosthetic hand to prod and stir the current scatter of chestnuts on the griddle. "Whit ye up tae?"

"Out to Rawbury."

"Oh aye—dumpin' trip, wiz it?"

Duncan nodded.

"That mean ye're goin' tae the Forest again soon?"

"Looks that way."

"Sooner you than me, pal. Work I wouldnae dae if ye paid me a fuckin' peerage."

Crammond's first job after demob, he once confided to Duncan, was with a Re-clearance crew working the fringes of the vast new growth now carpeting the ground between Loch Lomond and his native Glasgow. There was a big national drive to employ disabled veterans—your company could get the King's Crest for it—and the newly established Forestry Commission was no exception to the trend. For most of that first summer home, Crammond had made himself useful around the logging camps in whatever way he could; had even helped pioneer some specifically tooled limbs designed for Forestry work that were apparently part of a coming trend in the prosthetics industry. At the time, he viewed the Forest and the tales he'd heard about it with the same mix of skepticism and fascination most returning soldiers had. On the one hand, it seemed like a bunch of old wives' tales. On the other hand—well, *ye had the fuckin' Forest, right there in front o' ye,* newly grown and seemingly overnight. *Ye couldnae really argue wi' that, now, could ye?*

Since the trees were actually there, and no argument about *that,*

Crammond split the difference and just concentrated on getting paid to chop them down.

Then his new limbs started talking to him.

In ma heid, like. Tellin' me no' tae cut the fuckin' trees, leave them be, what did they ever dae tae me? These communications, initially soft and liminal, grew more insistent over time, and more violent; incitements dinning in Crammond's head, like teeth grinding on tin, to *jist stoap cuttin'*, turn his metal-and-leather appendage on his fellow workers, why not, and ultimately on himself. *Thought it wiz jist the fuckin' shell shock, ye ken? But then one day ah'm intae the tree line wi' this big sook oot o' Inverness, ah've got a limb on wi' this big fuckin' saw blade. And it turns, all by itself, that blade, goes to chib this teuchter in the neck. Fuckin' limb moved like it wiz alive. Ah fell over oan ma erse, wiz the only way tae stoap it, pretend ah tripped oan a fuckin' root. But ah saw the way that teuchter looked at me efter, and ah knew he knew.* By then, the disappearances had started. The men were hearing uncanny voices from deeper in the forest, a growing terror stalked the forestry camps after dark. *Whole fuckin' circus wiz comin' apart. Ah took oaff that limb and ah fuckin' walked. Literally fuckin' walked, man, right back to Govan.*

After that, like so many veterans with combat stress reaction, Crammond drifted. His neighborhood would not hold him, nor in the end would the wider cradle of Glasgow itself. Everything in the city just reminded him of what he'd been before the war, what he'd lost, and how there was no way back to any of it. The drift took him down to London for a while, some work that Duncan gathered was less than wholly legal or wholesome, then on to Birmingham for more of the same or worse, and finally to Erlsley, where he worked doors and dealt cocaine and mostly stayed out of trouble. Random collision with a chorus girl dancing at the Lyceum cemented him in place and, as the relationship blossomed, apparently gave him something approaching peace.

The hot chestnut stand followed soon after, mainly as a cover for more lucrative illicit activities. Against Crammond's expectations, it did quite well. Now he and his girl were ensconced in expansive furnished lodgings above a confectioner's over on Mitchell Street, and were making plans to actually buy the place. Duncan had been across there a couple of times, but he didn't make a habit of it. The girl, May, didn't seem to like him. Crammond once mentioned something about her coming from tinker stock, various aunts and grandmothers who had the Sight, and Duncan guessed that the gift had made its way down the generations. In which case, what she saw when she looked at him wasn't likely to reassure her very much.

Duncan held up his end of the blether with Crammond for a while, long enough for night to fully fall, then he took his paper-bagged chestnuts and headed off with their comforting heat held one-handed to his chest. Fifty yards up the street and across, Erlsley Bird Cabs was a beacon of yellowish light between shop frontages already shuttered and dark. A single car sat in the rank outside, a rickety-looking prewar Unic, one of its ornate head lamps listing visibly lower than the other. No driver at the wheel—he was in the office, chatting up Niamh.

"Broken down, aye?" Duncan asked, banging noisily inside. The door was sticking since last winter, and no one seemed disposed to do anything about it. "I'll come out and take a look at the engine if you want."

He knew the cabby—a wiry, weatherbeaten thirtysomething with powerful, work-worn hands, years of farm labor in his past, trench memories in his gaze. No one you'd choose to cross. But these days, the Forest trumped the trenches in all but the most extreme cases, and Duncan was a bigger man into the bargain. The cabby shrugged.

"Car's fine. Just on my way out for some snap, like. Takin' orders." He turned back to Niamh. "So you want owt bringing for you, hen? Butty or summat?"

Niamh shook her head, smiling a rueful smile. The cabby said something softly under his breath, grabbed his cloth cap off her desk, and crammed it on his head. He nodded at Duncan with measured defiance and walked out. The door banged behind him, the echo of the noise flew around the high-ceilinged room a couple of times. They watched through the window as the man bent and cranked his Unic to life.

"Could you try not to scare away all the pretty birds, Duncan?" Niamh, no longer smiling so much. "Sure, it's boring enough sitting in here without them being scared to talk to me, too."

"Him?" Duncan stared balefully out at the cabby as he climbed aboard his chariot and clattered away into the night. "He could have stayed."

She picked up the post from where it lay sheafed on her desk, shoved it at him like a challenge.

"For your information, Duncan Silver, I have a father and three brothers back in Galway for that paternal shite. That's why I left. Don't need it from you here as well, just because—" Her voice snagged on the last word, tore open into the hacking cough. She stifled it before it could get properly started, hurried into other conversation, voice tightened with the effort. "So how was the Merry Widow Rush?"

"Aye, it's a changeling." Leafing absently through the thin sheaf of envelopes, pretending not to notice the cough. "Dropped it off out at Rawbury."

"You don't sound too happy about it. It's a job, isn't it?"

"It's complicated. Rush moved home at least once in the last six months. Dowgreave, outside Macclesfield, before she ended up here. It's right on the fringes of the Forest. Been there a couple of times; it's risky country. The Huldu could easily have worked the switch while she was still living there. I'll need to talk to Garner, see if he still has his ear to the ground over that way."

"You want me to call him?"

"No, I'll do it. Garner's prickly at the best of times. You don't need that grief."

Niamh rolled her eyes. "I'm a big girl, Duncan."

Duncan grunted. The one interesting exception in the sheaf of obvious bills and circulars he held was a grubby white envelope with a Whitby postmark, addressed in a rounded feminine hand. He turned it over, saw the name on the return address, and grimaced.

Ellie Furlough's mother.

"This everything that came in today?"

"No, you had a drop-in, too. This fella." Niamh prodded a calling card across the desk at him. It was pricey work—embossed lettering, a stylized color crest, done in painstaking flecks of black and gold and green.

"Forestry Commission?" Duncan picked the card up, eyed it curiously. "That's a new one."

"Thought they'd been around since the end of the war?"

"Aye, but not coming to see me. What's he like then, this"—squinting at the name—"'Martin Hardy, Special Estates Management'?"

Niamh shrugged. "He's a Brit. Suit, mustache, forties; serious as fuck. Got an accent on him to match. The way he stands, I'd say he was ex-military, too."

"Who isn't these days? Is he coming back?"

"He asked if you would be so *keind*"—sliding into her upper-class English burlesque—"as to attend the commission's offices at Albion Place, tomorrow at nine. Tea will be served."

"You're making that up."

"Only the last part." She dropped back into her habitual Irish brogue. "You had nothing in the diary, so I told him yes. I've marked it for you."

Duncan hesitated.

"It might be paying work, Duncan."

It might. It might also be a run-in with someone from his military past that he could well do without. Reminiscence that could only open old wounds, questions he'd rather not put answers to. Besides which, he had an 1891 bottle of Port Ellen upstairs, gift from an overjoyed and very wealthy client last year, and it was long overdue for opening. The bad taste of Irene Rush's desolation sat in the back of his throat like dust, and the letter from Ellie Furlough's mother promised more of the same. He fancied a determined effort to wash it all away tonight. An early start tomorrow was not what he needed most.

"Duncan?"

"Heard you, Niamh. Loud and clear."

He unlocked the formal glazed door on the staircase against the right-hand wall, tramped up the six flights of stairs to the top, and let himself into his rooms.

. . . and do not doubt that we are eternally grateful to you for the return of Our Angel. We look only for some hopeful news on the future of her Condition, but no doctor that we consult can give any such assurance to us. Perhaps you, with your gathered Experience and Arts, may yet . . .

Duncan closed his eyes, pressed thumb and forefinger against the lids. He let the primly written sheets slip from his other hand and float to the floor beside his armchair. Nothing there that Mrs. Furlough hadn't written to him at least twice before over the last five months. Little Ellie, her angel, still crumpling to the ground like dropped laundry as soon as she heard any sudden, loud report, and then taking hours to wake again. They'd hoped that over the summer it might pass, but there'd been no improvement, and now autumn was here with its farewell to promise and light and—

He'd fucked up.

Behind his eyes, for the hundredth time, he saw the fight at Kettley Cross play out—

The Huldu leader leaning in, the fanged grin. "Or should I call you . . . Master Duncan of Stac Dubh?"

The mansion crashes into his mind—blond sandstone Victorian grandeur, wooded rise of the Munro peak behind, torn and tarnished silver evening sky, light on in the window of his third-floor room . . .

Like a storm wind howling through his head . . .

He pulls the trigger on the McCulloch without a second thought.

The trench gun belches smoke and fire, delivers the small grape load into the Huldu at sternum height and point-blank range.

Magnesium flash-dazzle in the space between them, like some angry newborn sun, flaring to life. The Huldu leader screams, goes thrashing backward like he's made of snakes, innards wreathed in green fire.

Hits the cobbled ground hard.

Duncan's eyes are already screwed mostly shut against the expected glare, but still his vision blotches and worms in purple and green and black. He scans for the others, ready to leap and spin. Yanks the McCulloch in close, left hand tight on the pump-action slide, arm awkwardly bent to keep Ellie Furlough in its crook.

He chambers the second shot. The spent shell jumps out and tumbles, hits the cobbles, rolls away.

On the ground, the Huldu leader twists and smolders and screams. Inhuman sounds. His acolytes move in, hissing, crouched low, watchful and poised. In all likelihood, they have Duncan bracketed. There's no way he can beat them all to the pounce.

He sees the option—a way out of the mess he's made—and grabs it.

Step in, angle down. The McCulloch pointed now at the Huldu leader's head.

"Your call," he shouts. "Get him to the Forest, pick the iron out of his guts, he might heal. You rush me and he dies, right now! So do some of you!"

And the instinctive assessment he's chasing turns out to be true.

These are not clan warriors, not canny, centuries-old skirmisher types. They're sycophants, courtiers, hangers-on. Young, unproven males.

They act accordingly.

They hesitate, they show him their fangs, they hang back.

On the ground, their leader screams. Skogurtal syllables, surfacing, sibilant and broken, from the heaving morass of his agony.

"I'm waiting," Duncan snarls.

Two of the bigger Huldu creep forward, more on all fours than upright. The unhuman gait, the bared fangs, the hatred in their faces is nightmare fuel for weeks to come. They grab at their writhing, groaning leader, get him under the arms. Drag him slowly back.

And the leader lifts an arm.

Hinges upward from the waist—Christ knows what it costs him in pain, what arcane strengths he pulls on to do it—and points one taloned hand.

Utters the curse.

IT TOOK DUNCAN A WHILE to work it out.

At the time, grinning high on the combat adrenaline of the moment, he'd thought he was the target and shrugged it off. He was pretty much immune to that shit, as far he could tell; had been for years. Go see the witch up on Crawgate, get it muttered over for offset, maybe even set some kind of minor offering at a tree altar in the Forest fringes to seal the deal. Worst-case scenario, it was going to be a rash of some sort or headaches for a couple of weeks.

But then Ellie Furlough's family threw a modest party to celebrate her safe return, some overjoyed relative clapped his hands loud, and little Ellie keeled over on the spot like a sniper victim at the parapet.

Duncan was there, guest of honor, glass in hand. The moment he saw the wean go down, he *knew.*

You fucked up, Duncan.

"You certainly did," he told the empty room around him.

He knocked back what was left of the Port Ellen in his glass, grimaced as the neat spirit went down. The bottle was on the floor by his chair, dark glass, ornate label, long neck. He reached down, hooked it up between his fingers by touch alone, poured himself another harsh measure. He got up with a convulsive effort, took his glass to the window. Peered out at the lamplit street below, the facades across the way and the march of rooftops away west.

You couldn't see the Forest from this far into town. But its presence haunted Erlsley just the same, hovered in the margins of thought, like the letter from Ellie Furlough's mother, discarded on the floor at his back, like the promise of the hangover tomorrow morning would bring.

He stared out across the rooftops and into the night.

"Come on then, you Fae fuck," he said softly. "Stop hiding behind little girls. I'm right here. Let's see you finish what you fucking started."

It was like an incantation in which he had no faith. Hollow, tinged with bitter desperation. The night waited impassive, unaffected, like an incoming tide piled up beyond the glass. He cursed again, a soft, indeterminate *fuck it* under his breath. Turned back to the room behind him, but all it held for him was the whisky and his rage.

He set about sinking himself, slowly and deliberately, in the depths of both.

FOUR

ALBION PLACE, AT THE HEART OF ERLSLEY'S BUSTLING MUNICIPAL center, looked pretty much the way you'd expect with a name like that. Proud Victorian facades in blond sandstone faced each other across a boulevard-width street. Big doors and porticos every thirty yards and tall sash windows on every floor bar the attic. Number 28 featured a grand porch held up by four smooth columns on a two-step base, and the Union Jack on an angled flagpole above. Twinned brass plates on the forward columns announced BRITISH FORESTRY COMMISSION EST. 1919 in cleanly graven, black painted letters.

The polished brass winked unmercifully at him in the morning sun.

Against all odds, the new day had come in viciously bright, with clear blue skies and what Duncan's father used to call a lazy wind—it couldn't be bothered to go around, so went right through you instead. Alerted to some of this by the slanting blades of sunlight through the blinds in his bedroom as he woke, Duncan wore a pair of smoked-glass sharpshooter lenses against the glare when he headed out. It got him some funny looks on the street—outside of movie stars, no one wore sunglasses this side of the Atlantic—but whether it did anything for his hangover, he couldn't honestly say. It didn't feel like it. The aspirin he'd taken when he got up didn't seem to be helping much either.

He went past the hard-gleaming brass, up the two steps, and through the double-width door under the portico, where he was greeted by a doorman and then a receptionist, who verified his appointment and led him on clacking heels across the marble lobby and up a sweeping staircase to offices on the second floor. Subdued bustle of coming and going in the corridor, in and out of rooms with doors left ajar. Men in suits, women in secretarial attire, carrying files or folded papers, here and there the cylindrical tubing of a map holder. They paused and stood aside for Duncan and his escort. Duncan glanced into one office, saw a small group of men gathered at a blackboard with a neatly chalked diagram across it. In another, dusty-looking antique tomes lay opened on a long table. The receptionist stopped, finally, at a handsomely varnished wood paneled door. Knocked and gave him a reassuring, if slightly quizzical, smile. He realized he was still wearing the sharpshooter lenses and fumbled them hastily off.

"Come!"

Exactly the cut-glass tones Niamh had described to Duncan the night before. The receptionist opened the door, ushered Duncan into a high-ceilinged space almost as big as his whole apartment. Turkish carpet on the polished wood floor, two sash windows almost twice the height of a man, ornate cornicing on the ceiling overhead. Sunlight poured into the room with a bright force Duncan could have very well done without.

"Mr. Duncan Silver," the receptionist announced.

"Thank you, Molly." Hardy came out from behind a large mahogany desk to greet him. "Perhaps you could rustle us up some tea. Have you breakfasted, Mr. Silver?"

As a safety measure, he had not.

"I'm not very hungry," he said truthfully.

"Just tea, then, Molly. Thank you." He waited until Molly had left. "Very pleased to make your acquaintance, Mr. Silver. Colonel Martin Hardy, at your service."

Duncan took the proffered hand, got a firm shake that wasn't trying to prove anything, and a smile to match. But the smile was quick, perfunctory, and above it, hard dark eyes measured Duncan's face with keen attention.

"Where did you serve, Mr. Silver?" Deceptively casual.

"Western Front. You?"

It was blunt to the point of rudeness. Among fellow veterans, you'd mention place names, battles, regiment. Hardy took the deflection with no more than an elegant raised brow. "Oh, like you—Flanders and France, for my sins. Coldstream Guards."

Another smile, this one wintry. The Guards had famously taken a pasting in the early years of the war. Duncan heard their officer ranks were all but wiped out.

"Must be a change." Duncan looked around at the office. "Forestry."

"Not as much as you'd think, really. It is, after all, another kind of war." Hardy gestured to an occasional table and a couple of armchairs, all drenched in the sunlight streaming through the tall windows. "Please, Mr. Silver. Take a seat. Take off your jacket, if you prefer. The tea won't be long."

They sat. Duncan couldn't make up his mind whether the warmth of the sun on his face made him feel better or worse. He left his jacket on. Hardy crossed his legs with officer elegance, placed clasped hands on his knee.

"Yes, as I say, another kind of war. With new enemies, and rules we have yet to learn. You, Mr. Silver, will know that more than most."

"Never thought of it that way." He honestly hadn't.

"Yet you'll agree that Great Britain is once more under threat, in all likelihood under a far greater threat than Kaiser Bill ever presented? Vast swaths of our country taken effortlessly from us, cities under siege, smaller communities all but cut off from each other in many cases. In the war, we were at least an island, with coasts we could defend. Here, the enemy sprouts, quite literally, from within." Producing a slim silver case from his jacket. "Smoke?"

Duncan shook his head. He'd never acquired the habit, even in the trenches.

Hardy arched the elegant eyebrow again, but he made no comment. He took a cigarette for himself, leaned forward to light it from a heavy onyx lighter stood on the table between them, then sat back and smoked for a moment or two.

"I'm curious to know," he said finally. "If you don't think of what we face as a war, what keeps you going back into the Forest as you do?"

"They pay me."

"Yes, I know that." Trickling smoke idly from his nose. "Quite highly, too, if the one or two cases I'm familiar with are anything to go by."

Best leave that one alone. If Hardy meant the business with Viscount Savin's son, or the Canning family mess, then he had levels of access Duncan didn't want to think about. And if not, well, then he was just fishing and fuck him into a muddy crater for that.

"My fees vary."

"Indeed. According to what, I wonder."

This hangover was going fucking nowhere. "What do you want, Colonel Hardy?"

"Hmm." There was an onyx ashtray on the table to match the lighter. Hardy leaned in and knocked ash off his cigarette. "Yes, they said you were blunt. What do I want, Mr. Silver? I suppose you might say I need to satisfy my professional curiosity. We live in times of smoke and mirrors, and cheap conjuring for effect. Séances and revenants and bloody fairies at the bottom of the garden—I assume you saw that asinine piece by Conan Doyle in *The Strand* a couple of years back?"

"Heard about it."

"Yes, well. As I say, times of cheap conjuring for effect. But I have no use for a cheap conjuror, and would like to spare myself the embarrassment of being seen to hire one in error. We are newly established here at the commission. It wouldn't do to jeopardize the faith being placed in us."

"And what faith is that?"

Hardy shrugged. "That we can hold back the darkness."

THE TEA CAME, PUSHED IN on an ornate trolley by a matronly woman with a pink shiny face. She parked beside the occasional table. Demure clinking of good china as the trolley rolled to a halt. Hardy nodded his thanks.

"Ah, here we are—Harrogate's finest. And cake, too! You are spoiling us, Mrs. Clifton! Thank you, you can just leave it for us." He beamed at Duncan. "Shall I be mother?"

He set about pouring for them, as if it were the thing he'd been trained for his entire life. Mrs. Clifton closed the door discreetly behind her. A stillness settled into the sunlit room.

"Tell me, Mr. Silver," Hardy not looking up from his task. Voice as careful as his gaze on the teapot and cups. The tea sparkled as it poured. "Did you ever see . . . angels? Over there, I mean. At the front? At Mons, perhaps? Or later, at the Somme?"

"No."

Hardy distributed teacups and saucers, milk jug and sugar pot. He served slices of the cake onto small plates and laid them out.

"I see. Did you perhaps encounter . . . other things?"

Duncan shifted impatiently. "I was not at Mons. And from what I hear, that whole thing was shite the church made up to boost morale. Ghostly bowmen, wasn't? The shades of Agincourt? Arrow wounds on the bodies of German soldiers?"

"I've heard that said, yes."

"But that's not what you're talking about?"

Hardy finished with the tea service, took his own cup, and cradled it between his palms as if for warmth.

"I saw arrow wounds not long after Mons," he said quietly. "And the arrows that made them. But those wounds weren't just on the Germans."

"No, I don't imagine they were."

"Arrows the likes of which I've never seen, before or since. Black and filigree silver, so they caught the light, as if the shafts had been . . . embedded with shards of crystal. When you looked at the fletching, it was thick, too thick for just feathers. It seemed to move. Like something alive, like . . . leeches attached to the shaft. And the wounds were . . ." Hardy looked up, manufactured a small, apologetic smile. "Well. No one wanted to touch those arrows."

He sipped some tea. Cleared his throat.

"The first time was a reconnaissance mission. Woods on a slope to the northeast of our position. The Germans had been scarce, considering what advances they'd already made. Command suspected a pincer movement, so we were detailed to sneak up there and take a look. I took eighteen men into those woods, Mr. Silver. I came back out with only two. What do you say to that?"

"I'd say you got lucky. Did you see what killed your men?"

"Not really, no." Tone matter-of-fact. "We had no frame of reference back then, you see, for what we were facing. We saw the bodies, German infantry, looked like a whole detachment had been ambushed. And while we were staring at them, the Huldu did for us, too. Corporal Timmons was the first. From the sound, I thought he'd been bitten by a viper. That was the arrow, of course. Made a hissing through the air. Timmons cried out, fell. Nobody knew what to make of it; we'd no experience to put it against. Timmons crawling toward us, screaming, we didn't spot the shaft at first. And then, when we did, I couldn't work it out. Looked like a swagger stick, caught up somehow in his battle dress. And by then, two more men were down. Someone—I think my sergeant—yelled *Archers*! It made no sense."

He gave Duncan the small, awkward smile again.

"We started firing into the trees. Blind barrage, completely hopeless. Someone tried to pull the arrow out of Timmons. He was still screaming, you see. And then so was the poor sod who'd tried to help him. Private Lamb—young lad, quite possibly underage when he volunteered. There were a lot like that. Anyway, he grabbed the arrow shaft and pulled. His hand came away ripped up and bloody, as if he'd hauled on a strand of barbed wire."

Duncan nodded. "Fresh elf-shot will do that, aye."

"We fired another barrage, very ragged this time. Timmons died, or at least he stopped making any noise. Lamb collapsed, weeping over his hand. More hissing; we saw the arrows coming this time, they seemed to glint in the air. More screams, more men down, I'm sure you can imagine. And yes, Mr. Silver, maybe I did see something then, in those moments. Some . . . wisp of something, between the trees, there and gone. Gray figures, like ghosts, or just—smoke." Hardy shrugged. "And then, suddenly, it was just the sergeant and myself shooting. Man was bawling at me: *We need to fall back, sir, we must fall back.* He was right, of course."

"That he was."

"We got Lamb up between us, dragged him away. Got out of the woods and back to post. By then, of course, they'd started finding dead Germans all over the place, with the arrow wounds on them. Not many shafts, though."

"No. They'll melt fully into the wound if you give them the chance." Duncan watched Hardy's face. "That's not the end of this story, though, is it."

"Not quite, no."

"I assume Lamb died?"

Hardy met his gaze, almost unwillingly, and Duncan saw a shard of old anger in his eyes that made him like the Guardsman just a fraction more.

"He didn't just die." Voice tightening like a tourniquet. "That boy . . . suffered. He was running a fever, almost from the moment we got him back to the command post. Never seen anything like it. It seemed to burn the flesh from him. You could almost see it happening. In and out of delirium, screaming nightmares. They moved him out to a field hospital the following day. And he died there, two days later, I'm told."

Duncan heard the way Hardy's voice trailed off. "But?"

"But I already knew."

"Knew he was going to die?"

Hardy set down his teacup, got up, and went to stand at the window, hands crossed behind his back and gripped together. He stared down into the street. His voice, when it came, was still tight with the anger he'd buried that day.

"You ask me, Mr. Silver—did I see what killed my men? And, truthfully, I did not. But the night we escaped, I found I couldn't sleep, and so I went back to check on Lamb. He'd stopped screaming you see, and I wondered . . . Well, you know what I wondered. They had him in a dugout down the line—alone, because of the screams, you see. It must have been about two in the morning when he stopped. Clear night, good moon. I walked down the line, and when I was about twenty yards away, someone pushed back the flap on the dugout and came out."

He jarred to a halt. Took a breath and started again.

"No. That's not accurate. Some *thing* came out of that dugout, Mr. Silver. It looked like . . ." Turning to face Duncan now, hands open in front of him, like a potter trying to mold something in clay from his memories. "I don't know what it looked like. A gargoyle, perhaps? A figment from an Arthur Machen tale? It was pale, like something sculpted from marble. It seemed . . . hunched? Crouched. It stood like nothing human, despite its form. There was something around it that smudged my vision, like a heat haze, or fog, or—" He shook his head. "It stopped me dead in my tracks. It froze me, despite all the training I have ever had. And while I stood there, locked in place, it turned and looked at me."

Hardy drew a deep breath, came back to his chair, and sat down.

"I will never forget those eyes so long as I live," he said. "The emptiness in them."

Duncan said nothing. Hardy summoned his tight smile once

more. "And then, of course, it was gone. Up and over the lip of the trench, scuttling, faster than my eyes could track it. I swear it bared its teeth at me before it fled—like some predator, warning other animals away from its prey. And I knew, in that moment, there was nothing we would be able to do for Lamb."

He crossed one leg over the other, brushed at something invisible he seemed to see on the fabric of his trousers.

"There is, as I'm sure you're aware, a fashionable theory that the war is what brought about this . . . change we are living through. That the millions who died, the horrors they endured, the—how do the Theosophicals put it—the *psychic scream* all that combined suffering unleashed, that this somehow tore a hole in the fabric of our universe and let the Huldu in.

"But I know that to be a lie."

Duncan wasn't going to argue. There were a dozen different theories for why the Forests had returned and the Huldu with them. None of it made much sense. As far as he could see, none of it mattered that much either.

"It's a lie, Mr. Silver, because I know that in August 1914 in the retreat after Mons, only weeks into the conflict, they were already here among us."

Some response seemed to be required. Duncan shifted in his seat.

"Perhaps they could sense what was coming," he offered. "I'm told by people who know that it takes very little blood in the water to attract sharks. They come in anticipation of a feast, apparently, even if it hasn't yet begun."

"Is that what you believe?"

"I don't need to *believe* anything, Colonel. I deal with the Huldu as and when I find them. I have tools that work, some insight into their behavior, an appreciation of the risks." Duncan shrugged. "It's enough to get by."

"Indeed. Enough to do rather better than just *getting by,* if my sources are to be believed."

Duncan felt his hackles rise. "Sources?"

"Oh, we canvassed extensively among the woodsman community and other associated . . . practitioners. You have quite the reputation, it seems."

"Well, it isn't a difficult community to excel in."

"No?"

"No. What you said earlier—smoke and mirrors and cheap conjuring. And a lot of charlatans out there making money from desperate people. Men who wouldn't know how to bring a lost child out of the Forest if the Huldu served it up on a silver platter with a bow on top. It isn't hard to do better than that."

"I suppose not. Though your success rate is quite remarkable, apparently. Uncanny, even."

"Look—"

"Mr. Silver, tell me something." A new urgency rising in the other man's voice. "What if there were a way not to retrieve these children, painstakingly, one by one, from the Forest, but to put a stop to their abduction altogether? Once and for all, forever. What if I could offer you the chance not to *get by* fighting these creatures, but to drive them out entirely?"

"You believe that's possible?"

"Certain people do." Hardy snapped to his feet again—something in the memories he'd shared had clearly agitated him out of his ex-Guardsman sangfroid. He went to his desk, began lifting and moving papers, shuffling them together. "We have a number of top men working on the situation in Cambridge and in London. Level heads, not the usual Blavatsky hysteria brigade. We are mapping the Forest, trying to understand it. We are excavating the European myth base, sorting the fanciful from the potentially useful. In time, we hope to evolve weapons and tactics far beyond the crude tricks with iron we rely on now."

He finished his paperwork, held up a loose sheaf of typed foolscap sheets.

"For now, I would need you in London."

Duncan blinked.

"Come again?"

"London." Hardy brought the sheaf of papers over to him. "We'd really need you to get the train down this week. I've had your contract backdated to the beginning of the month; it'll come with a small advance to cover any relocation costs you might incur. And of course, for now, we'll arrange your accommodation. It is a matter of some urgency, you see."

"You're offering me . . . a job?"

"Did I not make that clear to your secretary yesterday?"

"Not entirely. I assumed that this was the work I usually do. That somebody was lost in the Forest."

"What's lost in the Forest currently is our future as a nation and an empire, Mr. Silver. We're hiring you to get it back. For the duration. It's all here." He dropped the papers on the table in front of Duncan. "I think you'll find the starting terms agreeable."

Duncan glanced through the documentation. Agreeable was right—*twenty-five fucking shillings a day*! He'd finished the war a major and had been on a lot less. Paid tickets to London, accommodation covered, work he could likely do standing on his head . . .

For a moment, the soft comfort of it all beckoned—like the too-good-to-be-true promise of a four-day rest order, dropped on you while you were still in the fire trench—some fuck-up with scheduling back at HQ, you wouldn't even have to do your close reserve stint first. All the way back, lads, all the way back right now. Warm baths, decent cooked food, a bed with sheets on it, maybe even so far back from the front line you wouldn't hear it anymore. All there, just waiting for you. Grab your kit and scramble.

Your daughter is in the Forest.

Irene Rush and her pleading eyes.

He set the paperwork carefully down on the table again.

"Very generous. But I'm afraid this week isn't going to be convenient."

Hardy did the thing with his eyebrow again. "I . . . beg your pardon?"

"I'm currently under contract. It'll take me a few days to clear, maybe longer. So there's no way I can be in London this week."

"You're . . . turning down this appointment?"

"No. But I'm going to have to revisit it when I have discharged my existing obligations." In the general ache and blur of his hangover, his words seemed to be coming out of someone else's—some other profligate idiot's—mouth. "I'm sure that's something you'll be able to understand."

"And your obligation to your *country*?" A snap in Hardy's voice now, the peeling of the officer veneer off harsher layers beneath. "Where does *that* weigh in your considerations?"

Duncan heard the screams at Messines again, the howl and *crash-boom* of the sky torn open. The busy natter of the machine guns to each other, the pleading of men caught up on the wire.

He got unhurriedly to his feet.

"I answered my country's call to arms nine years ago, Colonel. And I saw my country spend men's lives like toilet paper to wipe the arses of leaders and generals too fucking stupid or lazy to understand that the world they lived in had changed. This time around, my country will have to wait its turn."

Hardy went white. "How *dare* you!"

It got very quiet in the sun-soaked room. They faced each other at not much more than touching distance. Hardy's pale combat face, his right fist balled at his side. Drift of dust motes in the angled rays of light. Steam from the tea in the china cups. Duncan waited, faint smile floating to his lips, dreaming all the damage he might do.

The moment passed.

"You really think, Mr. Silver," Hardy, biting the words off, "that you're the only man who suffered, that had to live through those four years of hell?"

"No. But I sometimes think I was one of the few paying attention along the way."

A thin sneer. "What are you, then? Some of kind of Communist?"

"Well, they make some interesting arguments, don't they. But no, I'm not any kind of Communist. What I am is a man of my word. If that's unacceptable to you, or to His Majesty's government, then perhaps we're wasting each other's time."

"His Majesty's Gov—" Hardy visibly held down his temper. "There is a large difference, Mr. Silver, between affairs of state, and the tribulations of cooks and seamstresses and C3 bookkeepers who should have kept better watch over their children in the first place."

"Not to me there isn't," Duncan said evenly. "Thanks for the tea, though. I'll see myself out."

FIVE

BACK OUT IN THE STREET, HE DRIFTED AIMLESSLY FOR A WHILE, nobody at the helm. Tightening grip of the hangover, mild adrenaline drop from how much money he'd just walked away from and the barely averted fistfight with Hardy—the cocktail mix of it all left him listless and cold despite the sun.

. . . the tribulations of cooks and seamstresses and C3 bookkeepers who should have kept better watch over their children . . .

Fucking prick.

He wasn't looking forward to telling Niamh what he'd just done. But the look on Hardy's face had been worth it.

It dawned on him where his feet were taking him just before he arrived. As he turned the corner onto Morton Street, the smell of frying bacon hit him in the face and did not, contrary to expectation, turn his stomach. Apparently, he'd regained his appetite and his feet already knew it. He duly followed his nose across the street and into the steamy interior of Grimaldi's.

It was dim and peaceful inside, dark wood floor and fixtures, limited strands of sunlight sluicing in from the high, blinded windows. Background rattle of plates and cutlery, the murmur of conversation between customers, the *crackle/flap* of a newspaper being tugged open or turned page to broadsheet page. Grimaldi senior was behind the counter, lean and grizzled and bristly of chin, wiping a glass with a rag. He spotted Duncan as he came in, bustled out to greet him in an accent from sunnier climes that twenty years in Erlsley had still not quite managed to kill.

"Eh, Silver. You wanna coffee." It was an observation, not a question.

"Why I'm here. Give me the breakfast works, too, while you're at it."

"Is coming up. You been inna Forest?"

"Not recently. Why?"

"Eh." Grimaldi gestured at his own face, like putting a mask on and off. "You look like it. You look tired like that."

"Thanks. How's Eduardo doing these days?"

"Good." The brief stir of old terrors in the man's eyes, thrust firmly down. "He don't remember nothing now, I think. Happy boy, getting good at his sums in school."

"Glad to hear that."

Grimaldi headed back behind the counter, ducked through into the kitchen to shout instructions at Luisa. Privately, Duncan thought he was being overly optimistic about Eduardo. Recall of time with the Huldu wouldn't disappear the way other early childhood memories would. Instead, it seemed to retreat behind the same wall that kept your dreams apart from your worldly experience. Then it sat there intact, ready to erupt whenever something less worldly—strange noises at night, fog under trees at dawn, scenes from some cheap pulp tale—stirred it back to life.

The food came—eggs, bacon, black pudding, sausage, beans, and a hunk of rye bread. Pungent black coffee in a mug, a small jug of cream. With the promised end of wartime rationing repeatedly pushed back, vast tracts of grazing land lost to the Forest, and good meat in short supply, it was a feast fit for royalty.

"Onna house," warned Grimaldi as he unloaded it all from the tray, in case Duncan made the mistake, once again, of trying to act like a paying customer.

"You know, if you let me pay for things, I'd eat here a lot more often," Duncan told him, not for the first time.

Grimaldi snorted. "You eat here a lot more often, maybe Luisa gonna start makin' you pay. But I wouldn't count on it."

So look, Niamh—I may have flushed twenty-five shillings a day down the crapper, but I can always take you out to dinner for nothing at this Italian greasy spoon I know.

He dug in, appetite kindling like dry moss in sunlight bent through a lens. The bacon first, smoky on his tongue. A forkful of beans. Bread torn off—he broke a yolk with it and dipped in, chewed it down. He dosed his coffee with the cream, stirred it in. Drank half the mug down in one.

Better. His brain grumbled to life.

Force of habit, he was carrying his notebook. He fished it out, flipped through sketches and maps from the Forest, found a blank page. He penciled a list:

- CRUMLEY & KEGG. SHELLS ETC.; (& PAY BILL!)
- COLLECT BOOTS
- WITCH
- BANK IRENE RUSH'S CHEQUE
- CHOCOLATES FOR NIAMH
- CALL GARNER

He stared at the list for a bit, then wrote carefully underneath:

- CHEMIST'S

Which was code for *See if Crammond's holding.* Getting Mimi Rush back from the Huldu looked like being a protracted affair. A good long stint in the Forest, which meant he'd likely need to do without sleep for a while. There were ways to handle that with a glamour, but they were complicated, required irritating levels of discipline, and risked giving you away to any Huldu nearby. Far better just to lean on the old cocaine for a few days. Crammond was one of only five men in Erlsley—there was one woman, too—whose supply you could trust. He'd either sell you some very good snow, or would be able to point you to someone else who could.

Of course, a couple of years ago Duncan would have just gone ahead and written *Crammond for Cocaine* on his list. But that was back in the halcyon days before the Dangerous Drugs Act came and fucked everything up. Wartime panic over cocaine *sapping the moral fiber of our beloved troops* had seeped through into mainstream public life back home, restrictive provisions in the Defense of the Realm Act got carried over into general law, and next thing you knew, you wanted cocaine, morphine, heroin, even bloody opium, you had to see a doctor, get a prescription, jump through hoops, and pay through the nose. Overnight, the business of nonprescription supply got nasty and secretive and risky, and one thing you *never* did anymore was commit anyone's name to paper.

Duncan finished up his breakfast, drained the last of his coffee. Grimaldi came over to clear the table.

"Feeling better now, eh?"

"Aye. Tell Luisa thanks for me." Duncan produced a shilling from his pocket. "Here, that's for Eduardo. For doing well at his sums."

He slipped back out into the street, set off the half mile to Crumley & Kegg's feeling newly energized, as if just thinking about Crammond's happy dust had been enough to bring on its best effect. *As if by magic,* he thought sourly, and then grinned to himself at the thought. He quickened his pace. Perhaps the postadrenal soak from his near fight with Hardy, perhaps just Grimaldi's coffee and the ebbing of his hangover. Whatever it was, he felt an armor-plated good mood coming on.

Even the belated realization he was being tailed didn't do much to dent it.

WHOEVER IT WAS, THEY WERE pretty good. Duncan's time in the Forest had sharpened his senses to levels most humans would never attain, but even with that edge, it was a couple of city blocks before those senses triggered. Awareness crept in slowly—a skulking figure, there a little too often in the dark mirror surfaces of shop windows he passed, nagging at the corner of his eye. Duncan gave no sign he'd spotted the other man, but he shifted his route so he'd pass the Woolworths on Exchange Street, and as he crossed the street toward the big store frontage, he got his first clear look at his new friend.

Pale coat wrapped tight, flat cap pulled low. Short and wiry, the energetic gait of a young man. What Duncan could see of the face looked pockmarked and painfully clean shaven. When he stopped in front of Woolworths as if to browse what was in the window, his tail breezed past, reached the next corner, then drew some kind of map or gazetteer from his coat and affected to check street names.

Nice touch.

Right.

Duncan closed the gap between them in a dozen rapid strides. The other man saw him coming, didn't register it for the assault it was until far too late. His eyes widened, he dithered left and right, and then Duncan was on him. He froze. No fight reflex—whoever Hardy was hiring, it wasn't ex-Guardsmen. Duncan shelved a brutal gut punch he'd been readying, spun his tail from the shoulder instead, and put him face-first into the wall. He got in close, crowded the man out of options to react.

"Better if you don't move," he advised bleakly.

He patted the man down for weapons, found none. Took him by the shoulder and spun him again so they were face-to-face.

"Wait," gabbled the man. "I don't—"

Duncan backhanded him hard, loaded up from the shoulder. The blow staggered the man, bloodied him at the mouth, took his cap off. Without the wall behind him, he'd have fallen. Duncan hit him again, openhanded, from the other side; leaned in.

"I'll save you some trouble, shall I?" he growled. "I'm headed up to Crumley & Kegg's on Deansgate. After that I have to see a witch, then pick up some boots from a cobbler on the Shambles, and later

I'm going to the bank; that's the Barclays on West Cavendish Street. Then I'm going home. How about you put that in your report to Hardy and file it. And file this, too—*I don't like being followed.* I've been tracked by elf hounds, *foh-mhorai,* and night shamblers, and it didn't end well for any of them. I catch you behind me again, *I'll put you in the fucking hospital.* You got that?"

The man flinched, fingers touching his bloodied mouth. His lower lip trembled. It made him look suddenly very young. Duncan became aware of stares from passersby, and shocked faces. He realized he'd been shouting.

He drew a hard, steadying breath.

"Now," he said evenly. "Pick up your cap, and your map, and fuck off."

He stood there and watched as the man bent to do as he was told. A well-dressed couple paused to gawp. The woman's face was flushed, eyes angry on Duncan.

"Shame on you," she snapped before her partner could usher her hastily away.

"A soldier, I'd wager," Duncan heard him saying to her as they went. "Combat stress reaction, you know. There's a lot more of it than the doctors realize."

Certainly fucking is.

He walked the rest of the way to Crumley & Kegg's at an irritable forced pace, trying to recapture his prior mood. Caught up with it, more or less, as he shouldered open the venerable oak frame door of the emporium and breathed in the familiar blend of scents it held. Leather, tweed, shoe polish, cordite, and solder—some skewed sense of homecoming to it all.

Reuben Kegg saw him come in, put aside a pair of walking boots he'd been buffing, came out from behind the wooden counter with a grin. He was a big, untidy man, stiff grizzled beard out of some Viking tale, barrel chest above a proud publican's belly and a rumbling Yorkshire baritone to round it all off. Larger than life, unflappable, impossible to dislike.

"Hoy, Crumb!" he called back to the inner sanctum of the shop. "Look what the cat dragged in!"

Crumley's voice came back, indistinct. Kegg nodded.

"He's working on t' new loads. We're trying this mix of extra-small grape with fowling shot. What our American cousins like to call buck and bird. Interested?"

Duncan shook his head.

"Gives you a right good spread," Kegg persisted. "Good for mobs. A lot of the woodsmen are carrying it now."

"Then a lot of woodsmen are going to end up not coming home. Birdshot's good for driving off tree pixies, maybe. But warrior-caste Huldu?" Duncan shrugged. "They'll just charge right through it. Live with the damage, gut you before it even starts to sting. No, thanks."

"Just in for half a gross of standard small grape, then, is it?"

"Came to settle up, actually. But sure, add another half gross to the total while you're at it. I'm getting low."

Kegg brightened. "Well, now. Business must be looking up. Hoy, Crumb, get up here! Man says he's in to settle the account."

Feet on the short run of stairs that led down to the workshop at the back. Shane Crumley came through, wiping his hands on a rag. He stood next to Kegg like the other half of a music hall double act—lanky and gaunt, neatly clean shaven, a pair of bifocals pinched onto his long, thin nose. If Reuben Kegg was a walking hangover from the days of Jorvik and the Danelaw, then what Crumley most resembled was some overindulged comedy lord's disapproving tailor.

"Silver," he said carefully. "How's that standard load working out for you?"

"Good as ever."

"He means he'll not be wanting any of our newfangled buck and bird," said Kegg. "I already tried."

Crumley pulled a face. "A lot of the other woodsmen like it."

"So I hear."

"And I suppose I still can't interest you in a bayonet? Got some Vickers stock in, very nice blade work."

Duncan shook his head again. "Told you before—got no use for the length. Forest undergrowth will tangle that blade up the first tight turn I have to make. And the Huldu know that; it's how they fight. They'll get a wisp or a bog siren to lure you in, and then jump you as soon as the brush thickens up. There's a *reason* I had you cut down the barrel on the McCulloch. How tight you can turn and fire is life and death in there."

"Could still come down to knife work, though, am I right? You seen that trench knife our American cousins brought out just before Armistice?"

Duncan skinned a grin. "Already got a knife, Crumb."

"Talking about that *sgian dubh* of yours?" Crumley snorted. "That's barely four inches of steel, man. What's a woodsman going to do with that in a tight spot?"

"Pray you never have to find out. But at least it doesn't have a triangular blade that'll snap as soon as you look at it. Fucking trench knives, they can't be used to slash worth a damn either."

Crumley snapped his fingers, stabbed a triumphant index at Duncan. "Hah! And there you go! Not talking about the old M1918. This is something else, and you're going to fall in love with it just like you did the McCulloch. Come on down, have a gander."

Duncan looked from one man to the other. Kegg twinkled at him. He sighed.

"Aye, all right then," he said. "Let's see what you've got."

THE WORKSHOP AT THE BACK of the emporium was long and low, furnished with a single row of workbenches under a pitched roof of glass panels designed to let the maximal amount of daylight in from above. It also boasted a pricey set of patent Claude Neon Company tube lights, suspended one over each bench for when work ran late. Crumley and Kegg were nothing if not enthusiastic where any new technology was concerned.

It was to one of the workbenches that Crumley now led Duncan.

"Take a look at that," he said proudly.

Laid out on the scarred wooden surface was a black trench knife with a double-edged blade six or seven inches long and a grip featuring a knuckle-duster wrap. It looked a lot like weapons he'd seen French soldiers carrying toward the end of the war. But when he picked the weapon up and examined it, he saw the legend US 1918 stamped into the grip.

"American, you say?" Elaborately casual.

Crumley grinned like a shark. He knew when he had a customer hooked. "That's right. Modeled on the French Vengeur 1916. Yanks made about a million of them, and then the war ended and they never got issued. Got these off a Yank quartermaster at a show down in Birmingham last year. Practically giving them away, he was."

"Good. I guess that'll reflect in the price you give me." Duncan held the knife up to the light. "This isn't tarnish, right? Tell me that much."

"Tarnish?" Crumley's grin broadened. "You're going to stand there and insult me in my own shop? That, my friend, is a black oxide finish on the blade to stop it glimmering in moonlight. And chemical blackening on the grip to match. Grip's bronze, I'm afraid. But bronze or not, you punch one of your Forest playmates with that, they won't be getting up again in a hurry."

Duncan slipped his fingers into the guard loops, hefted the weapon. It wasn't especially well balanced, but there was no denying the weight. Each knuckle bow came with a blunt spike cast into the bronze, and there was a brutal-looking six-sided conical nut screwed to the end of the hilt, which presumably held the blade in place. This, at least, seemed to be steel.

"Bronze grip, though," he said. "I mean . . ."

"We'll do you a good price," said Kegg hurriedly. "Could always put it on your tab."

"The tab I'm just about to clear, you mean."

"Exactly!" Crumley, beaming. "We know you're good for it. Come on, that's a six-point-eight-inch blade there. Go right through a greatcoat and still have more than half left over."

"Huldu don't wear greatcoats. They don't wear much of anything at all."

"You know what I mean! We're not talking about a bloody sgian dubh here. This is a *killing knife,* man. Built as such. Combat science in action, right there. It's the shape of things to come."

Duncan grimaced. "If you say so."

But all three of them knew by now he was going to take the trench knife, so why pretend? He sighed and slipped his hand back out of the grip, put the weapon down.

"All right, then," he said.

Crumley clapped his hands. "Good man. Oh, and while you're down here, speaking of combat science, see what you think about this. Something else we've been playing around with."

He gestured at the last bench in the row. On one side were the buck and bird cartridges he'd been loading, with all the associated mess of powder, balls, and crimping tools. But on the side opposite stood a row of what looked at first glance like big onions with the skin off and just starting to sprout. Wonky, irregular, squashed looking, more like something grown in a garden than a weapon machined in a workshop.

"We're calling them Fae-fuckers." Kegg, proud as a new mother of twins. "What'd you reckon?"

Duncan crouched and peered at the packages curiously. "I reckon if you're applying for a patent, you're going to need another name."

"You don't say," drawled Crumley. "Call it the Kegg bomb if you like—it was his idea."

Kegg made modest huffing noises, but you could see he was pleased. He picked up one of the devices, held it out to Duncan. "Here, take a look—triple-wrapped muslin, iron filing load, all wrapped around a low-yield powder charge with a sprung pin and detonator. Tight grip here—or you can use your teeth, it's leather—

pull out the cord, hard, you got six seconds to chuck it and make sure your eyes are closed."

Duncan took the device, weighed it in the palm of his hand. It was a hefty, pleasing fit.

"Like the Mills bomb," he said.

"Where we got the idea," agreed Crumley. "Same basic principle, but there's not enough force in the charge to harm anything human. Just throws a thick cloud. Like I said, you need to watch your eyes, but apart from that—shouldn't hurt any worse than sand on a windy beach. Your Forest pals, on the other hand . . ."

"Aye."

HE ORDERED A CRATE OF twenty-five.

A little premature, as it turned out. Crumley had only built eighteen Fae-fuckers—or Kegg bombs—so far, including the ones on the workbench. And they used one of those in the yard out back, for a demonstration Duncan pretty much insisted on before he signed the order.

It wasn't that he didn't trust the two armorers—their small grape load had saved his life in the Forest more times than he liked to look back and count. But both men were inveterate tinkerers at heart, overloaded on the kind of forward-leaping faith that abounds in both scientists and entrepreneurs, and the fact they believed in one of their inventions 100 percent was no kind of guarantee it would actually work, come the crunch. And *ho-hum back to the drawing board* isn't much of a consolation when you're knee deep in the suck of a Forest swamp, hemmed in on all sides by creeper and brush in the dark, and the rustling, sharp-fanged Bright Folk are drawing near . . .

Anyway, the Kegg bomb worked admirably, at least under test conditions, so Duncan took the leap, added his order to the cost of the trench knife and the fresh half gross of shells plus delivery of everything first thing tomorrow morning without fail. He paid off his outstanding account, then left the emporium approximately as indebted to Crumley and Kegg as he had been when he walked in the door. Some things never seemed to change.

Right.

Time to see the witch.

SIX

NO ONE WAS VERY SURE WHY THE WITCHES OF ERLSLEY HAD chosen to congregate their shopfronts and offices at the top of the steep, clambering curve of Victorian tenement architecture known as Crawgate, out on the northern edge of town. There was a theory going around that the street name had once been pronounced Crowgate, referencing, back in some period or other of medieval gloom, the hordes of querulous black birds that would gather to pick at the rotting bodies of criminals left on gibbets at the top of the rise and so, y'know . . .

There was another, less lurid theory. That it was a bloody long walk down Crawgate to the cross with Heath Street at the bottom for any halfway decent shops and the nearest tram stop into the center, and so the rents were dirt cheap.

"Couldn't possibly comment either way," Wolfbane Sally Bethune had told him when, newly arrived in the city, he'd asked her about it. "Wise women are the *keepers* of secrets, young man. We don't go just spilling them to any Tom, Dick, or Harry who shows up looking all earnest and edible."

She hooted out loud with laughter, leaned in with a lecherous gleam in her eye and a toothy grin. Slapped one long-nailed hand lingeringly on his thigh and treated him to a view of her crinkly but still quite remarkable cleavage. Like a lot of witches he'd met, she carried around with her an air of ribald arousal that her messy, gray-threaded dark hair and corpulent, middle-aged frame did nothing much to dispel. She made him stand her another double brandy to add to the one already on her breath, over and above the cost of the spell he was supposed to be buying from her in the first place, rambled on about her exploits as a woodswoman and spell-spinner and friend to pixies, and eventually took him upstairs to fuck his brains out. He woke the next morning to a screaming head, a stained and empty bed, and the cost of the room added to his tab.

That was four years ago. He'd been going to her for spell-work ever since.

"Enchantment, you see," she was known to chortle whenever the story came up. "Once you've had a taste of weird sister, there's no going back. You're forever bound."

Though, curiously, she'd never once attempted to lay a hand on him again.

In contrast to her unkempt and witchy looks, Sal kept an austere set of rooms on Crawgate at Number 37, above a shop of potions, remedies, and occult jewelry run by one of her less serious-minded colleagues and titled above its windows in peeling copperplate ZIROONDEREL'S CAULDRON—WAKEN TO THE NEW AGE. Duncan supposed it was about as good an exhortation for the times as any he'd seen anywhere else. He paused by the display window to get his breath back from the climb, gazed in for a moment at the assortment of talismans and incense candles and polished crystals that wakening to the new age apparently required. He pushed the electric buzzer on the entrance to thirty-seven next door. Heard it ring somewhere deeper in the building.

The door creaked stealthily open.

No visible human agency he could detect. That was new—whether just for effect, or some sign of Sally's burgeoning powers, he had no clue. He shrugged it off, took the poorly illuminated flight of stairs upward. On the middle of the first flight, a lean black cat arched its back at his approach, made no attempt to get out of his way, and pinned him with its slit jade gaze as he went past. He affected not to notice. On the half landing turn to the next flight, something small and bat winged dropped right out of the heights of the stairwell, brushed his face in the gloom, and flitted away.

Fucking witches.

He found Wolfbane Sally waiting on the landing above, in a spill of light from the open doorway of her apartment. She was still in her dressing gown.

"Going to tell me how you did that?" he asked.

"Did what?" Grinning. The gown notwithstanding, she had her face on. Shadowy eyes, carnal red mouth—a stray fleck of lippy on one upper canine, like a spot of gore.

"With the door. How did you open it from up here?"

"I'm a witch, darling. Come on, get in here. I've just made some tea. Tell me all about this next little poppet you're out to save."

"How did you kn—"

This time, she just rolled her eyes, went back inside, and left the door ajar for him. He stood on the landing for a few moments gathering himself, then followed.

"I'm not here just for that," he said, closing the door behind him.

"No," she agreed, voice close and tickling intimate in his ear. "You want to know if there's anything I can do about little Ellie Furlough."

He turned about sharply, found himself alone in the shadowy entry hall, at least as far as his eyes could tell. Tiny spike of cold on the nape of his neck at the realization. Then he heard her again, voice pitched louder this time, more emphatic, coming from the brightness at the end of the hall.

"And, of course, we both already know the answer to that one, don't we?"

He followed the sound down the hall and into the light—Sally's reception room, where she sat on the threadbare sofa in front of a low table, slopping tea from a curious pot-bellied iron teapot into two enamel mugs that looked as if they'd seen use on the Somme.

"Do you have to do that?" he snapped.

"Do what?" she asked mildly. "Leave my voice in the hall, or tell you uncomfortable truths you don't want to hear? Sit down, for Hecate's sake, Duncan! You look like a virgin in a knocking shop, stood there like that. You don't want milk or sugar in this, do you?"

He shook his head, took the proffered mug, and sank into the armchair opposite. Stared into the teak-colored depths of the tea, the cauldron rise of steam off the surface.

"I am sorry," she said.

"You can't know!"

"Yes, I can. It's what I do for a living. And unless you're keeping back some important details, I have a very clear picture indeed of what happened to both you and Ellie."

She paused, looked keenly at him—he wasn't sure if it was deliberate. He'd never told her about the vision of his home that had triggered the fight at Kettley Cross, and he wondered if she could somehow detect that reticence in him. But he'd come clean on everything else.

"Darling, you crossed Huldu nobility. Put a Forest scion within inches of death in front of his peers, maybe actually killed him for all we know. It's a heart's blood curse, and it's all over you. I can still smell it from here. Damn thing's like a bee sting, it's real suicide magic, Duncan. Little Ellie copped the weight of it, but you were the target, the crux, and you still are. Until your heart stops beating, she's stuck with it."

"What about if *his* fucking heart stopped?"

She sighed—maybe at the violence in his voice, maybe for something altogether broader and more general in the state of the world. The compassion in her eyes hurt to look at.

He looked away instead.

"His heart may well already have stopped," the witch said gently. "You certainly seem to have put enough iron into him. In which case, it would merely be a matter of scouring the whole Forest for his corpse, finding it, de-warding it, digging it up, then cutting out the heart and eating a portion of it. Which would doubtless kill you anyway, given the way they steep and ooze in death. Even a *live* Faerie heart would be pretty hard to choke down for a human. They say Arthur Pendragon managed it once—but then again he's a myth, and so is that story. And anyway, if you believe the legends, he was Faerie kin in the first place. What I'm saying, Duncan—*there is no path to this.* What's done is done."

"Could you not at least go to see her?"

"Would I be welcomed there if I did? From what you told me, these are respectable people." Light irony on the last two words. "Not sure they want to see a weird sister show up on the doorstep asking after their precious daughter."

It was fair comment. Witches weren't much better regarded these days than they ever had been. They still inhabited much the same gray area they'd been left in a couple of centuries back, when the Witchcraft Act passed into law under Walpole. For the best part of two hundred years, you weren't allowed to hunt, persecute, or harm anyone on the basis that they were a witch, but nor were you allowed to claim that you were one, much less offer services as one, on pain of prosecution for fraud. Witches were simply not supposed to exist.

Then again, nor were forest-dwelling Faeries, or millennial oaks that erupted fully formed from the ground overnight. Fresh legislation was apparently under review, but the legacy of two hundred years' genteel disbelief had Parliament paralyzed, endlessly consulting supposed experts—none of them actual witches—and dragging its heels for all it was worth. In the meantime, in the absence of clear legal guidance, a rattled society fell back on tried-and-tested responses. Like the suffragettes, like the upstart women entering universities in the closing decades of the last century, witches were tolerated . . . just about. They practiced their craft, were not prosecuted for it, but they also weathered the standard blanket of distaste, mistrust, harassment, easy contempt covering for real fear, and occasional outbursts of actual violent abuse thrown in. Numerous practitioners had been assaulted, almost all had been threatened more than once, and one or two, famously, had been murdered.

Duncan looked at her again. "Sal, please. As a favor to me. Will you go?"

"Oh, Duncan. That's adorable."

"I'll pay you, whatever you ask. I'll write to Ellie's mother, get her written permission for the visit. I'll go with you, keep you from harm."

Wolfbane Sally snorted. "Keep myself from harm, thank you very much. Ellie Furlough's daddy gets handsy with me, he's going to find his fucking cock drops off."

"So you'll go?"

"Ohhhhhhh, Duncan!"

Shuddering with the force of her sigh. Whether intended or not, it set his own cock to stiffening. She gave him a look, an arched brow, and sipped demurely at her tea.

"Look. Here's what I'll do for you, darling. And I'm listening to my instincts here—for which I really need my head examined, should *really* know better at my age, but anyway—here's what I'll do: you go and retrieve your latest poppet from the woods, bring her safely home, and we'll revisit this conversation when you get back. We'll talk about a price."

Hot burst of joy through him. He swallowed. "Thank you. You know I'm good for it, Sal."

"Oh yes." Slyly. "I know you're good for all sorts, Duncan. Now—shall we talk about your needs for the present?"

IN THE END, IT DIDN'T amount to much. A couple of luck spells, the sort of thing that might make the Huldu less likely to spot him in a thicket—and might not. He was agnostic about a lot of what witches claimed they could do, especially where the Fae were concerned—a renewal of potency for the sleeping glamour he'd used for Ellie Furlough, and a new iron talisman that he strongly suspected was out of discounted stock from the shop below. *You're sure about all this*? he said without much force, and was impatiently shushed. It was a matter of the Sight, apparently, and what it dictated. *All good stuff for a barnyard squabble,* she declared cryptically. *Can't hurt to have, I'd say. Now just hold still for me.*

How the Sight was different from the instincts Sal was supposedly getting too old to trust, Duncan couldn't see, but neither could he be bothered to argue. He'd come mostly for Ellie Furlough in any case, and counted himself more or less served. The rest was window dressing, could do no harm. Wolfbane Sally drew the curtains in the living room, lit some candles, marked Duncan up with fingertip dabs of some oriental-smelling oil to his brow and throat, backs of hands. Then she blew some scented smoke over him and went around the room widdershins, muttering under her breath.

He sat it out and drank his tea.

She saw him to the door afterward, took his money, and gave him a maternal peck on the cheek. Something in her eyes, there and gone too fast for him to fully register it. He hesitated. She waved him away, still mock maternal, but it was enough to make him turn back after a couple of steps—

And for just a moment, he thought he caught a glimpse of something standing at her back in the shadowed hallway, something dark and hunched and grinning sardonically at him over her shoulder . . .

Then she closed the door.

Duncan clattered hurriedly down the stairs, glad to get back out in the sun. He trudged down the slope to Heath Street, got lucky with his connections—were Sally's enchantments at work already, he wondered, not quite ironically—and picked up a tram to the center a couple of minutes after he reached the stop.

Back in town, he stopped to bank Irene Rush's cheque, got the chocolates for Niamh, and completely forgot to collect his boots. Couldn't be bothered to retrace his steps. He got into the office a little after four in the afternoon. Niamh was already there, taking a call. She nodded at him as he came in, handed him a scribbled address on a torn-out notepad page, and gestured at the rank outside. He dutifully went out and gave the address to the first cab in the line—another Beardmore, he noted with an odd little twinge of Scottish pride; they really were pushing out the Unics these days. The cabbie grinned when he saw where he was going for pickup—presumably it was a tony address. He fired up the engine and rattled off with a cheery klaxon blast. Duncan went back inside.

"So," Niamh wanted to know. "What did Mr. Martin Tea-at-Three Hardy have to say for himself? Is it work?"

"Might be," Duncan said evasively. "Down the line a bit, you know."

Niamh looked at him. "You fucked it up, then."

"Not at all. Just some scheduling issues. Did you sort out some accommodation in Dowgreave yet?"

It earned him no rebate from the hard banshee stare. "I did not. Because you told me not to until you'd spoken to your man Garner. Done that yet, have you?"

"Next on the list, going up there to do it right now. Hold off line two for the next little while, would you?"

"Aren't you forgetting something?"

He blinked. "I am?"

She nodded down at the little bow-wrapped parcel in his hand.

"Aye, so I am." He held the chocolates out. "For you! Some more of Mr. Cadbury's finest, in appreciation of all the hard—"

"Knock it off, Duncan. I'm not just off the fuckin' boat. I only get these when you've done something you reckon'll piss me off. Losing a big contract with a government department, say. Suppose you'll be inviting me out for dinner at Grimaldi's next?"

"Funny you should—"

The phone rang.

Jangling insistent. They both looked at it. Duncan made an expectant better-get-that gesture, put the chocolate box on the desk and patted it.

"Talk about this later," he mouthed as Niamh lifted the receiver, and then beat a hasty retreat upstairs.

SEVEN

"GARNER. WHAT IS IT?"

The same gruff Lancastrian voice, roughened over long seasons of cheap whisky and cigarettes and rain, and not very interested in hearing whatever the person on the other end of the line had to say. Duncan grinned at the sound, crimped the phone against his ear with one shoulder while he rummaged in a drawer for more aspirin.

"Garner, you old bastard. It's Duncan. How you keeping?"

"I'm a year older than when we last spoke and no better for it. Aching joints and scars and the same bad back. What do tha want, lad?"

"Maybe some advice. Might be across in your neck of the woods soon, thought I could pick your brains before I do that."

Long pause. Duncan found his aspirin and sat up straighter in his chair.

"Something wrong with that idea?" he asked softly.

"If you mean neck of the woods literally, then aye, lad, there's summat wrong with that idea. Happen it'll get thee killed."

"More than it usually might, you mean?"

"Aye, more than it usually might, Mr. Pulp Hero." Garner's trademark sarcasm coming over oddly restrained this time. "The Huldu are reet stirred up over here at the minute. We're three woodsmen down in the last month alone. A couple of them I knew, and they were canny lads. Years in the business. Not the sort to make stupid mistakes."

Duncan frowned. "When you say *down*? You mean declared missing, or—"

"I mean impaled alive on conjured fire-thorn right in the tree line, left there to scream and bleed out so folk come running to find them. Took more than a whole day and night in one case, no way to get the poor bastard free. Someone had to put a .303 in his head in the end, he were begging for it. That's messages sent, lad—messages to stay out. Does that paint a clear enough picture for thee?"

He supposed Garner was angry and trying to unload some of it, to shake him by forcing a shared revulsion. A small part of him even wished it would work. But he'd heard men out in No Man's Land die as slow, more often than he could easily now recall, and a few times in the deep Forest he'd stumbled on men and sometimes women to whom far, far worse had been done. Garner was just going to have to shop his tales of Huldu horror to a queasier audience somewhere else.

He popped the aspirin tin, crunched a couple of tablets down. "Any of them say anything before they died? About why it happened, I mean?"

"I wasn't there taking bloody notes," Garner growled.

"All right. Here's something else, then. You want to do me a favor? A paid favor, that is. Usual rate."

"Could do that, aye."

"Need you to look up a clerical worker called Irene Rush. She worked for"—he checked the notes he'd made—"Caulders Stationery and Office Supplies. They're on Chestergate."

"I know the place. Been past it a couple of times."

"Aye, well, she was there until about six months ago. Renting rooms out in Dowgreave with her infant daughter, Mimi, and a maid called Susan. Number 17, Tegg's Road. No husband; he died in the war. Job at Caulders dried up, so she moved to Erlsley. Ask around, see what you can find out. How long you reckon you need?"

Garner considered. "It's late, won't get much done at this hour. I can make a couple of calls, maybe swing by the house if it's occupied. But I'll need the morning tomorrow, some of the afternoon, too. Tha want it all posting out?"

"No, I'll take the train over and collect. Can you be done by five, say? Meet me at the station in Macclesfield?"

"Don't see why not."

"Good. Oh, and listen, would you book me somewhere to stay? There, in the village. That place we had drinks last time I was over, maybe? White Horse, was it?"

"The White Mare. Maggie Worrart's place."

"If you say so. Get me a decent room, if she can spare it. I'll buy you dinner there after we get done."

"On expenses, then? Big contract?" Something very like jealousy in the Lancastrian's voice. "Is it the girl? The daughter?"

Duncan hesitated, then realized his silence had already answered for him. "Aye, it is."

"And tha think she were taken here? Before they moved?"

"It's not impossible."

This time it was Garner who went quiet.

"There, or Erlsley," Duncan prodded him. "Trying to rule one or the other out."

"Aye." Still oddly hesitant. "Then I'll tell thee what, lad. Tha'd better pray to whatever gods tha still have that it were Erlsley, not here."

ANOTHER KIND OF WAR. HARDY's words of that morning, floating back through his still faintly hungover skull. *With new enemies and rules we have yet to learn.*

Garner thought the excruciated woodsmen were a warning to stay out, and maybe he was right. He'd been a sharp enough woodsman himself before the accident, he still had good instincts. But there was no way to be sure. The murdered men could just as easily have fallen foul of some whimsical Huldu hunting band new to the region. It was a tumultuous part of the Forest among the Fae, no well-established eternal figures the way there were down south or up in Scotland. A lot of young males, vying for legend, a lot of churn among the clans, hard to predict. It *might* be a warning off, right enough. It might equally be some form of challenge or other ritualistic display. It might even represent—and here Duncan had to admit he was reaching a bit—some sacrificial rite in honor of deeds or deities long past, some ancient anniversary no human calendar had ever marked. Huldu had long, tangled memories, reaching back centuries, in some cases thousands of years into the premodern dark. No telling what you could dredge up out of that morass.

Duncan sat at his desk long after he'd hung up the phone, drenched in memories of his own, none of them good. Eventually, he fetched a glass and poured himself a judicious, medicinal hair-of-the-dog measure of Port Ellen.

Beyond the office window, autumn tipped the afternoon over into early evening with what seemed like ungracious haste. The sunstruck blue sky grew a little more solid, a little less blue. Its high, bright chime faded out, tarnishing toward indigo and the night to come.

The mansion crashes into his mind—blond sandstone Victorian grandeur, wooded rise of the Munro behind, torn and tarnished silver evening sky, light on in the window of his third-floor room . . .

Like a storm wind howling through his head . . .

Knees soaked through from the cold, wet grass, blood on his clenched fists, a trembling through his limbs like fever . . .

He blinked. Aye, well. Enough of that.

He took a chunk off the Port Ellen. Grimaced as it went down.

Sunlight marching away golden red across the rooftops of the city outside. Shadows lengthening across the room, puddling in corners . . .

Knocking at the door.

He frowned, swiveled his chair about.

"It's open," he called.

She cracked the door and slipped into the room, stood with hands laced together behind her back, modeling her bust for him. She gave him the heart-stopping lopsided grin.

"Gordon just got in. He'll be holding the fort until midnight."

Duncan raised his arm, ostentatiously checked the Mappin & Webb on his wrist. "Well, now, that is a lot of time for an innocent Irish lass to be alone in a strange man's rooms, is it not?"

Niamh pushed the door gently closed. "Strange is about right. You after some company, strange man?"

"Aye, I could be."

She sashayed toward him across the room, reaching back to the nape of her neck for the top buttons at the back of her white lace blouse. The movement lifted her breasts under the material. Unaccountably, his thoughts flashed back to Wolfbane Sally in her dressing gown, her shuddering sigh with his name on her lips. He hastily banished the thought as Niamh reached him. He breathed in, caught the green herb scent of soap and a recent bath.

"A little help, sir?" Feigning a demure maid's voice, fumbling behind her neck, jiggling the material of the blouse. "I fear my buttons might be caught."

He reached round, gathered her in to him as he worked at the fastenings. Buried his face in the soft yield of her breasts through the lace. No corsetry or brassiere beneath, and Niamh was a woman who bucked the new flapper trend for boy-like figures with outrageous, voluptuous disregard. Her bust drew looks in the street at twenty yards. Duncan felt himself hardening in the trousers he wore. Niamh made soft, encouraging noises, put her hands either side of his skull, pulled him tighter to her, pressed her lips down hard on the top of his head . . .

Not the first time it had come to this, not even the first couple of times, but it was fresh and unaccustomed enough each time that they were still learning each other. They got the blouse awkwardly off between them, his hands moved to cup her breasts, tongue seeking a nipple, but she scotched the move—grabbed him forcefully by the wrist, put one foot abruptly up on the chair and dragged his hand under the lifted folds of her skirt. This was new. She pressed his hand up between her legs, he found her naked there, wet and eager and open, and they both gasped with the hot, lewd shock of it. His cock throbbed suddenly tighter, hard as the pump-action slide on the McCulloch, aching with the new rush of blood. Niamh moaning now, *oh-like-that-oh-yes* as his fingers moved in her, and she was reaching down, fumbling impatiently with his belt. He helped with his spare hand as best he could, got his trousers opened. His cock wagged out and she grabbed it, squeezed it viciously around the shaft with one long fingered hand. He worked his own fingers faster, deeper. Her moaning notched up, became a guttural, rhythmic grunting, gathering pace. He got her breast in his mouth, sucked up the nipple, breathed in her scent. She let go his cock as if it were suddenly burning hot, threw back her head. Gripped his wrist tightly with both hands under her skirt, pressing, pushing, urging him on, until, abruptly, violently, shuddering, she came.

Last time had been hot and rushed and frantic, but this—this was more raw and abandoned still, fresh vertiginous depths opening up under them. Niamh collapsed over him in the chair, head still tilted back, a loose wide grin spilled across her face like dribbled wine. He held her up as best he could, only vaguely aware of the throbbing demand in his abandoned cock. She looked down at him, wiped tear-trace out of her eyes with the back of her hand.

"Was it the chocolates?" he asked her, grinning.

She laughed, involuntary, unguarded. Felt his cock wagging against her breasts and clutched it again. She let herself slide artfully down into a disarrayed heap at his feet, eyes never leaving his face. Got elbows up on the chair edge, looked up at him through tousled, oil-black locks. Her 'do had come loose in the festivities, and then some.

"C'mere, strange man," she said throatily.

Then she took his aching cock in both hands, plunged her soft, warm lips down over the glans.

And when—*very* shortly after that—he exploded in her mouth, she gripped him hard in her pumping fist and sucked, until her cheeks pulled concave and he thrashed and arched in the chair and, eventually, begged her to stop.

LATER, LYING AWAKE AMID THE tangled sheets and blankets of his cramped bed in his cramped bedroom, listening to Niamh sleep at his side, he sifted the storming intensity of the encounter for sense.

As much as anything, he supposed, it was the times. The war, the Forest, the Huldu—all the old certainties were in their graves, the old promises defunct. Faith and flag and patriotic song had failed, catastrophically, rammed the iceberg, were sinking fast. The old order was on its arse. Like some dissolute aristo clan, the House of the West had spent wildly in the coin of noble causes, duty and honor, until all that remained was a debt-ridden, derelict ancestral seat; faded structural glory, stacked with mildewed old masters and chipped Greek bric-a-brac; dripping water ingress from a roof that could no longer be patched and paid for with promissory notes. Now, the flappers and the Jack the Lads were chopping up furniture to make a bonfire in the great hall, jittery syncopated music echoed off the walls in time with the leaping shadows cast by the flames, and faced with the frenzy of it all, most just shrugged assent and joined the dance.

Life was something you snatched off the tray as it went by, and when you drank, you drank deep. Because who knew how long this party would last.

Against that backdrop, two lonely people who didn't really know each other all that well had collided in the drafty, high-ceilinged empty spaces of their lives, known a good thing when they saw it, and so clung to the warmth it gave.

But it wasn't just that.

Not this time around, not with what he'd just felt go shuddering between them.

Niamh mumbled in her sleep, twisted in the mess of the sheets. He gathered her in, spooned her, murmured reassurances in her ear.

Was she hot to the touch?

He put a hand on her brow. Couldn't tell. Her skin always felt warmer than his anyway.

From her lungs, the soft, edge-of-hearing crackle and wheeze, like a radio being tuned a thousand miles away.

She'd finally seen a doctor in the summer. Had still not shared with Duncan what she'd been told. And he carefully hadn't asked. But he saw how a haunted stillness crept in on her at times, how her bright and brash colleen humor could suddenly corrode into something with a more ragged edge.

He looked at her sleeping face and, as if she felt the weight of his gaze, she stirred. Blinked awake, stretched.

"Mhmm. Midnight already?"

"No. We've got a while."

"That a hint, then?"

He forced a smile. "Go back to sleep, succubus. You've had all the fun you're going to get out of me tonight."

"Drained you dry, did I?" She licked her lips, vampish parody of Greta Schröder in Murnau's *Carmilla*—they'd caught it a couple of weeks ago at the Scala. Under the sheets, she grabbed his shrunken cock. "All that sweet, *sweet* woodsman's elixir?"

He forced a laugh to go with his forced smile. But for just a moment, he wondered.

Because a whole lot of shite was talked, wasn't it, about what miraculous cures and balms could be found deep in the Forest, if you only had the nerve to go; what lurid properties those who spent time there might come out imbued with, which they might then bestow in turn. The Americans he'd met in the trenches had a sharply apt name for the con—*snake oil.* He'd known woodsmen who exploited the new superstitions unmercifully, got themselves taken care of time and again in back rooms and brothels and some of the more bohemian salons up and down the country.

One or two witches and wise women he'd heard of pulled the trick, too, though the favors they extracted were rarely known to be as blunt.

Maybe she saw some of this in his face. She poked him in the ribs. "I'm fuckin' kiddin' you, Duncan. We're just passing the time here, all right? Now for Christ's sake, wipe that look off your face and give me a fuckin' kiss."

She puckered up and he leaned over her to do it.

"Go back to sleep," he said with an attempt at lightness. "You've got lots of time."

But he felt how she winced with the words, and he cursed himself, too late.

EIGHT

He let himself lie in late the next day, dozed gradually awake with the increasingly insistent light through the blinds and the noises from the street below. Niamh had not come back when her shift downstairs ended. She'd doubtless gone home to sleep it off, and he was alone in the sheets. He grabbed his Mappin & Webb off the nightstand, checked the time. It was after nine. There were things he could be doing, but nothing that wouldn't keep until he came back from Dowgreave, so he sprawled idly in the bed awhile longer, revisiting the lurid memories of the night before. Niamh's breasts, Niamh's hot, supple mouth, Niamh sitting on his chest, pushing her sex hard into his face . . .

He masturbated briskly, wiped himself off, and got up. Drew a bath, soaked for a bit, then dressed and went downstairs.

"Mornin', Mr. Silver!" Gordon, wincingly bright and cheerful at the front desk. He was a nice lad, fresh-faced, hardworking and loyal, young enough to have missed the war, and as a result sometimes overly innocent for his nineteen years. "Did you get through those accounts with Mistress Connelly all right last night?"

"Aye, that we did. Lot of hard work, but we got it done."

Gordon nodded sagely. "She looked right tired when I came in this morning. Went straight home to bed. She said to tell you she'll see you when you're back from Macclesfield. Are you going out? Do you want a car?"

"No, you're all right. Want to stretch my legs."

A paid shave and a late breakfast at the corner greasy spoon on Skoldergate—food Grimaldi would no doubt have curled his lip at—then out to pick up his forgotten boots. It dawned on him he'd forgotten the cocaine, too, but Crammond wasn't out with the chestnut stand yet, and he didn't fancy calling over to Mitchell Street to get him out of bed and likely face the wrath of May into the bargain. He'd just have to go powderless, at least for now. Probably wouldn't need it quite yet anyway.

By the time he got back to Erlsley Bird, the delivery from Crumley and Kegg was waiting in the office. He carted it all upstairs, laid it out, and assembled his gear, which, with all the new toys, made for more luggage than he'd originally intended. He took a cab from the rank, made Erlsley Central just after one, bought a ticket on the 14:05 express service for Manchester Piccadilly. It was one of the new armored trains, pride of the L&YR, iron spike defense railings along the sides of the carriages and an open top turret with a mounted Lewis gun on every second roof. Waiting amid a thin crowd on the platform, Duncan recognized a face among the guard crew as they went to board. He scrabbled after recall, a name or context. Got it—one of Crammond's pals, once a low-level runner for the backstreet snow crew.

"Dusty?" he called out. "Dusty Ferguson?"

Ferguson pitched about, spotted him, and his face split in a huge grin. "Duncan! You for Manchester?"

"Aye. Macclesfield after."

"Want to ride on top with me?"

"Sounds good. Let me just stash my kit."

Duncan put his backpack and holdall in the carriage, got a sour look from the crew chief as he came back out, then followed Ferguson up the ladder to the roof—not proper procedure at all! But he gave the man an amiable warning smile and nothing was said. He and

Ferguson trotted along the carriage roof and squeezed inside the iron confines of the turret.

"Going to get kippered up here," Duncan said, nodding ahead toward the locomotive.

"Nah, they raised the stack. It's not too bad. And the pay's pretty good. You still doing the waif and strays thing, still going to the Forest?"

"Whenever they pay me."

"Mad way to make a living if you ask me." Ferguson lifted one of the Lewis gun's distinctive pan magazines from a box on the floor, checked the load, and fitted it onto the weapon. "Standing behind this thing is about as close as I like to get."

Down at the locomotive end, someone blew the whistle. On the platform, people moved back and the train jolted arthritically to life. Duncan steadied himself with a hand on the turret rim. Another jolt. The engine stirred awake, treacle-slow thump-cadence from the pistons, but building up as they began to move in earnest. He tilted his head back, watched the big, arched roof girders and glass panels sliding slowly by overhead, and then gone, as they came out under a pale gray autumn sky. Another blast on the whistle, the scuff and thud of the engine, buildings sliding by on both sides now with increasing speed, into the long shallow curve the rails made away through the city west-southwest; smoky wind and a fistful of halfhearted rain in his face, and abruptly he realized he was enjoying himself.

"Good, eh?" Ferguson, grinning at him again. He had to pitch his voice above the scuffling wind along the roof.

"It's not bad, aye," Duncan shouted back.

"Could probably get you on, if you wanted. Put in a word. Service manager's a retired captain, invalided out after Passchendaele. I was his runner. Cool under fire's pretty much all he's looking for in a man. You'd be ideal."

"I'll bear it in mind. Thanks."

"No bother."

They hit the outskirts of Erlsley, the thinning out of habitation, soon after saw the loom of the Forest ahead. Broad, natural cleft in the trees, where the iron rails ran. The same path carved through the slain piles of deadwood from the failed Re-clearance. They rattled into a curve on approach.

"Always makes me twitchy, this bit," Ferguson yelled. "Once we're in, I'm fine. But this—"

He gestured, wordless, as the tree line rushed them.

At Messines, he'd apparently stormed a German machine gun post single-handed when the rest of his squad got pinned down. And, according to Crammond, he'd proven pretty handy in a couple of tussles over supply with Erlsley's east end gangs as well. But now, as the train rushed in under the first of the nodding canopies and the path ahead became a gloomed fairy-tale tunnel, roofed in with overarching branches, Duncan saw how the fear rose in Ferguson's eyes, how he grew taut at his post and patted the Lewis gun now and then, as if reassuring a favorite dog.

Duncan leaned on the turret rim at his side, watched the tree wall go by a scant five yards from his nose. He tried to be companionable.

"They been burning this back?" he shouted.

"Yeah. Flamethrower units on a short train couple of months back. Doing the same thing everywhere, they tell me. Part of the Railways Act directives; it's one of the reasons we're amalgamating with LNWR and the others. Lot of extra costs now."

Another kind of war. With new enemies and rules we have yet to learn.

Just as the Forest had seemed to find natural boundaries well back from any large human settlements—and had also spared a surprising amount of fenced farmland in the south and east—so the trees had stayed back from the railway lines wherever they ran. No one knew why. Duncan had always assumed it was the iron that did it. He'd certainly worked off the assumption enough times. But such premises, he knew, were rooted in very shallow soil. What had held true for the last five years might all change, literally overnight.

Because it already had once before.

He could almost summon sympathy for Martin Hardy, beleaguered officer on the poop deck of a floundering once-proud ship of the line, whose timbered certainties were now coming apart under storm and cannonade. A long century of imperious Victorian mastery and the inheritance it left—dazzling conquests on the borders of science and engineering, proven dominance over the natural world, progress and prowess and pride in both, piled up like the loot of some daring imperial campaign in theoretical realms . . .

And now it was gone, tumbled to makeshift barricades, and the old terrors of night and the unknown returned.

The train barreled hastily through a couple of abandoned stations, serving small villages the Forest had swallowed—eerie places where the tree growth had punched through walls and roofs like the coils of some gargantuan squid. Some form of low undergrowth was already sprouting on the fallen mulch of leaves across platforms and what little they could see of the spaces beyond. Once, Duncan thought he spotted furtive movement behind a window in one of the station buildings, but they passed too rapidly for him to be sure.

The train made no whistle to mark transit in these places—perhaps the crew was afraid of what they might wake. But eventually the whistle did blow and they began to slow as the first of their express stops at Huddersfield came in sight ahead. They coasted in at the platform and the train came to a slow, screeching halt. Ferguson's relief was palpable.

"Don't like to think what happened to the people in those villages," he muttered.

Duncan said nothing. He'd come across enough examples to have some idea, and Ferguson didn't deserve the nightmares.

THEY PULLED OUT OF HUDDERSFIELD on time, made Manchester Piccadilly a couple of minutes ahead of schedule. Duncan thanked Ferguson, begged off going for a jar with the crew, and got his bags from the carriage below. Hefting them felt awkward—his hands as much as his face were chilled almost numb from the journey in the turret. He checked for his connection to Macclesfield, ran and missed it, had to sit and wait an hour for the next service. Garner met him at the other end with the horse and buggy.

"Still not joining us here in the twentieth century, then?" Duncan ribbed him as he swung his bags aboard.

"Prices they're charging for a motor taxi ride around here?" Garner curled his lip. "No, thanks. They can keep their bloody internal combustion engines. For all I care, they can keep their bloody twentieth century, too."

He was a big, untidy man with a scarred and weathered face, shrewd blue eyes, and a short temper covering for deeper sorrows, thickening in the waist and jowls now as he moved steadily into his sixties. He'd shaved his head to preempt baldness a few years back, wore a grubby woolen cap over the resulting sheen. In his youth, he'd been a fell runner and a pugilist of some local note. When the Forest came and took his farm, he worked in re-clearance for a while, made a name for himself by slaughtering a Huldu scout with his bare hands. Steady work as a woodsman followed, some successes that only added to his reputation, and it probably would have gone on that way if he hadn't broken a leg in a deadfall somewhere beyond Tegg's Nose. Famously, Garner had dragged himself back alone, hand over hand, to civilization. It took him two days, and the fracture was far from a clean break to begin with. Now he walked with a heavy limp and took what work he could find—sometimes as a contract inquiry agent, sometimes as an adviser on local Forest conditions. Duncan had heard he was writing a book.

"You know they're going to start banning horses in town sooner or later, don't you? Already got letters to the editor in the *Erlsley Evening News,* bitching about dung in the streets. Just a matter of time, really."

"Aye, well, until that happens, Mabel and I do well enough."

"Sounds like you're married to her. Is he married to you, Mabel?" Sidling up to the big brown mare, rubbing along the hard bony flat of her forehead. "Is he *married* to you, is he?"

"Stop that, tha clown!"

Mabel, to be fair, seemed to feel the same. She rolled her eyes and nickered nervously. Horses in general weren't at their best around Duncan—perhaps they sensed something of the same thing Crammond's girl did with her tinker's sight. Perhaps the stink of the Forest and the Huldu was on him, and no amount of time or bathing would wash it off.

Or maybe it was just that every horse he came near kicked his mind violently back to the shelled-out roads and churned mud at the Somme, the screaming of the pack and wagon horses as they lay shattered and dying, or thrashed about and tried to rise in the tangle of the traces and their own blown-out intestines. He'd been on detail putting them out of their misery more than once. It remained one of the most gut-wrenching things he'd ever had to do in uniform. So perhaps Mabel, with some animal sense long ago blunted in humans, could feel the memories rise in him, and somehow make connection back to the death and pain of hundreds of thousands of her own kind.

He climbed aboard the buggy and let Garner cluck Mabel into motion. They tugged forward, rattled away from the station and into the streets of the town.

"Lot of luggage tha've got there," Garner commented. "Planning on staying long?"

"Depends. You find out anything useful yet?"

"Not sure tha'd call it useful. But there's summat strange about thy lass Irene Rush. First of all, that job she had didn't *dry up* like tha said. Folk at Caulders were very happy with her, everyone I spoke to anyroad. Makes sense; Grade C3 clerical workers don't exactly grow on trees in these parts, and it seems she came highly recommended. Lovely girl, delighted to have her, fitted right in—so on, so forth. But when tha push any of them for detail, there's nowt. For a lass that made such a good impression, they don't remember a whole lot about her."

Duncan frowned. It didn't sound like the Irene Rush he'd met two days ago. She'd made quite an impression then.

"Paperwork?" he asked.

"Nowt I could get to see. Tha want to go back and grease a few palms, we might get further ahead. But I wouldn't count thy chickens."

"What about the house?"

"Seen it from the outside. It's closed up right now, couldn't find the landlord."

"Talk to the neighbors?"

"No. By the time I got across to Dowgreave, it were late. Near dark. Villages round here, nobody likes to be out at that hour, and they mostly won't answer the door either."

"Welcome to Indian Country," said Duncan sourly. "Christ, they got streetlamps around here, don't they?"

"Aye, and the Forest less than a quarter mile away in most directions. Not sure if tha've noticed, lad, but we're not in the big city anymore."

"Seems not."

Though, in fairness, attitudes to the hours of darkness weren't much different in Erlsley, not least as you got toward the outskirts. Duncan was being an arse, and he knew it. Thorns snagged in his head—Ellie Furlough's sleeping bouts, Niamh's breathing, the whole wide fucking tortured world beyond. He wanted to kill something with his bare hands.

"I guess we'd better go over there right away," he said, attempting a softer tone. "Before it gets dark all over again."

"Hold thy horses. Let's get thee installed at the Mare first. And tha can stand me a pint on account."

The White Mare Inn was much as he remembered it from the year before—low ceilings beamed in oak, rough plastered walls and small, heavy framed windows, the pervasive but not unpleasant smell of recently spilled ale. The landlady, a gaunt war widow whose name Duncan had managed to forget all over again, was building a fire in the lounge bar as they arrived. She had her eldest son run Duncan's bags up to his room, then went behind the bar to get their drinks. True to his word, Garner ordered a pint of some obscure local brew. Duncan settled for Whyte & Mackay and water. They took a table in the comfy gloom of a corner, clinked glasses, and drank. Garner sank a good opening portion of his ale in one swallow, came up for air with a sigh of satisfaction that somehow made Duncan envy him.

They sat in silence for a while.

"Tha like this one, then," Garner rumbled finally.

"Sorry?"

"The widow Rush. She's got thee, eh?"

Duncan gave him a hard stare. "She's paid me."

"Aye, I'm sure that's it."

"You think I'd go to the Forest for what, for fun? To impress a woman?"

Garner sank a little deeper into his chair. He sipped at his ale, squinted at Duncan, as if seeing him clearly in the gloom of the bar was hard. "Never have been very sure why tha go, lad, truth be told. Most men in this trade, I can read. Not thee."

Duncan shrugged. "It's a living. It's no worse than the war."

"Well, I'll have to take thy word for that." Even when the draft rolled around in '16, Garner's farm exempted him from service. He never saw combat, never put on a uniform. "But there's something burning in thee, lad. I smell it plain as day, but I'm damned if I know what it is."

"You're telling me there's nothing burning in you? Christ, man, they took your farm. They take our fucking children." Duncan saw the flinch in the other man's eyes, jumped hurriedly on. "Garner, you were doing this stuff even before the Forest came. Before anyone else believed in it."

"Oh, plenty of us believed. Plenty of us always have. It weren't all steam trains and iron bridges and Royal Societies back then, despite what they prattle. Brunel and Darwin and Davy and the like, the great, grand leap of British science and engineering, propelling the empire into the modern age. That's a Crystal Palace fairy tale Kipling and his ilk liked to write poems about. It's pure propaganda, lad. Outside the cities? We've always known the Huldu were there."

"Aye—and you went to war with them."

Garner snorted. "War? I went into Macclesfield Forest twice—once to get my own son back, and once again nearly ten years later for a friend. Hardly call that going to war."

"Maybe you should have. Maybe if you'd taken the fight to them more often, they'd have thought twice about bringing it to us."

"They did think twice." Leaning in, earnest. "Lad, back then the Fae were careful, they were penned up in the last few bits of woodland we'd left them, hiding from all our iron, shrunk to myths and old wives' tales. This changeling thing didn't happen all the time like it does now. It were occasional then, once or twice every ten or twelve year. We'd no need to *go to war with them,* as tha put it. We went to war with each other instead, and look what we did. We touched off a horror that's shattered our whole grip on the world. The Huldu didn't do this to us—we did it to ourselves."

Duncan studied the depths of his whisky. "I know a Guards colonel who'd give you an argument about that."

"The powers that be will always lie to thee, lad. Never forget that. They lied to get everyone into uniform and slaughtered under German guns. Tha think they won't lie again to get our young men charging into t' Forest by divisions and dying there, or coming out screaming insane? *Dulce et decorum est,* same as it bloody ever was."

It was a fair analysis, and to be sure, Garner had reason enough for his bitterness. But, as always, cries of injustice from men who weren't actually there tended to sour Duncan's blood a little.

He knocked back his drink, gestured at Garner with the empty glass. "Come on, finish that up. Let's go see this house."

NINE

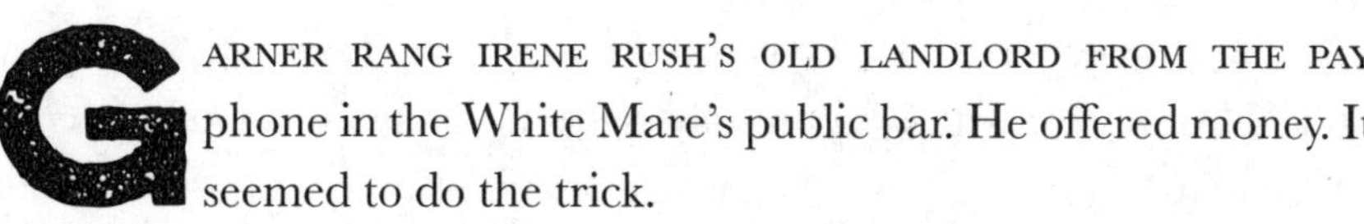

GARNER RANG IRENE RUSH'S OLD LANDLORD FROM THE PAY phone in the White Mare's public bar. He offered money. It seemed to do the trick.

"An hour," he told Duncan. "He'll send someone to let us in. It's close; we can walk it from here in a quarter of that."

"You say why we wanted to see it?"

Garner stared at him. "Don't be daft."

An hour later, past sundown but with plenty of residual light in the sky, they stood waiting outside Number 17 Tegg's Road. It was part of a modest Victorian terraced row in red brick, set back a little from the road behind waist-high iron railings and gates for the short paths up to each door. Tall sash windows looked out over the road from the first floor, gave views into fairly spacious front rooms at ground level. Soft curl of smoke from chimney pots, homely odor of it on the evening air. Duncan saw fires in fireplaces, lamps already lit against the promise of evening, cozy rooms. In one, a well-dressed middle-aged man sat and dozed over a book. In another, a young mother played with two toddlers on the rug. In sharp contrast, the windows of Number 17 were shuttered, nothing to see behind the glass but white-painted wood panels locked across.

"Odd they haven't rented it since," Duncan mused.

"Not necessarily. Lot of lost jobs around here the last year or so.

Money's tight, and they say it's going to get a lot worse before it gets better."

"Aye, might be that."

Garner caught his tone. "Tha think different?"

"I don't think anything yet. Oh, look—here we go."

A taxi had come puttering to a halt just ahead of them in the smoky, early evening light. The rear door opened and a small, gray-whiskered man in a suit bustled out clutching a satchel. He introduced himself as Simon Wilkins, agent for the owner, opened the gate to seventeen and led the way up the path. At the door, he wrestled a large key ring out of his satchel and worked his way round it until he found the right key.

"Most irregular, this," he insisted in a slightly high-pitched voice, which, combined with his painfully unfashionable mutton chops, put Duncan in mind of comic characters out of Dickens. "We really would expect to see references before . . ."

"Got thy references for thee right here," said Garner impassively, handing over one of Duncan's ten-shilling notes. "I was told that'd be acceptable."

"Oh, yes," Wilkins sniffed. "Mr. Carruthers made himself very clear on the amount."

He made a show of unfolding and turning the note over, though the green and brown print was visible at a glance, marking it out pretty clearly as 1918 issue and perfectly legal tender. Duncan cleared his throat, shifted impatiently. Wilkins looked his way, flinched as their gazes met. He stuffed the note away and got on with opening the front door.

Inside, the house offered a short no-nonsense hallway, staircase straight up on the right, doors off ahead and to the left.

"As you can see, it's spacious living over two floors," Wilkins exaggerated and threw the switch by the door. A feeble bulb glowed to life inside a small stained glass lampshade over their heads "Fully electrified. Comes fully furnished, too, though I believe there's space in one of the bedrooms for—"

Duncan shouldered past him and up the stairs. Sudden gooseflesh along the inside of his arms. Whisper of something unquiet, up there waiting for him.

"I *say* . . ."

Garner slid in behind Duncan, turned to block Wilkins on the threshold. Duncan heard him talking in uncharacteristically plummy tones.

"My client's in the way of being a bit peculiar about these things, Mr. Wilkins. He'd rather form his own impressions alone, if that's all reet with thee. It's a habit of his. Perhaps tha could wait for us down here while he gets a feel for the property."

Wilkins coughing, muttering, "Irregular, *highly* irregular," but by then, Duncan was up on the short landing, looking at another set of closed doors, listening to the stillness in the dark and dusty air. He found a light switch, flicked it, and watched more feeble light spring up in lamps along the wall. He felt the trace again. It wasn't much—if it was four or five months old, he was honestly surprised it was there at all—but he could feel the slight rise in his pulse as he cast about and—

This room.

He opened the door. Stepped into a darkened bedchamber.

Soft loom of furniture under dust sheets, the faintest filter of light through cracks in and around the shutters closed across the window. Bare boards underfoot, a threadbare Persian-style rug laid across the center of the floor, most of it under what looked, under its sheet, like a brass-frame double bed. The small fire grate in the far wall was dead and cold.

By the shuttered window, a basketweave rocking chair, uncovered. He looked at it and felt every hair on his nape stand up.

Something was sat there, grinning at him—

Ah, there you are, Duncan, so glad you came. We've been waiting for you . . .

Death and the Forest, right there, woven together in some nightmare embrace of bones and pale dead tree limbs, spilled and lolling in the embrace of the chair. A worm-eaten grayish skull crowned and grown through with ivy and thorns, a mossy rib cage hung with more of the same. Skeletal fingers gripped the arms of the chair, as if the thing was poised to rise and greet him in some parody of manners it had been told must be honored—*What a pleasure to have you here finally!*—and the twig-dry grip of those fingers around his own. The eager grin of the skull. *So much to talk about, so many,* many *things to show you . . .*

A Huldu claim spell—marking territory, the way a wolf might raise its hind leg and piss on a tree. A vortex of disturbance in the order of things, chaos peeping through. Magic laid down like a proclamation nailed to a forest oak. *I was here. I did this. Witness, if you dare.*

High-pitched Faerie voices calling him from beyond—*Duncan, Duncan, come to us, Duncan . . .*

Something behind him.

It reached out and touched him lightly on the shoulder blade. He whipped around in the darkened room, fists clenched.

"Duncan!" Garner, backing rapidly off, hands raised. "Come back, lad! Get a grip!"

He swallowed, grunted. Nodded jerkily. Garner lowered his hands, but not all the way. Duncan stood aside a little, gestured at the rocking chair.

"Can you see that?" he asked tightly.

"Not clearly, no." Garner grim faced, hands still partway to the instinctive guard. "But I know it's there. I can feel that much."

The thing in the chair seemed to shrug. It rustled, it grinned. The shadowed empty eye sockets in the skull dragged at Duncan's gaze. He felt like someone off the *Titanic,* flailing desperately against the suck of icy waters as the big ship plunged into the depths and tried to bring him with it . . .

Duncan, Duncan, come to us, Duncan . . .

"Are tha all reet, lad?"

Garner's voice, too faint, coming from too far away. He clung to it like a piece of driftwood, drew a deep breath and shut out the vision in the rocking chair.

It's just a fucking chair, Duncan. All right?

As if huffily disappointed, the thing seemed to shrug again, fold in on itself in whispers and wavering resolution he had to blink to focus on, a cold wind moaning, a hole in something through which the core of the apparition flowed, and then nothing much at all but a musty green odor that hung in the air and a kind of floating dust that sparkled briefly and then went out.

It's just a fucking chair.

It is now.

But he knew that a little over four or five months ago, some Huldu of rank had sat in that same chair with unhuman immortal patience, watching Irene Rush and her daughter sleep together in the big brass frame bed, perhaps night after night, for who could tell how long. And then, at some point—maybe that night, maybe a few nights later—that same Huldu had risen unhurriedly, cast a casual glamour, taken the sleeping child from its mother, left a changeling in its place, and slipped away with its prize into the Forest.

Duncan knew these things with the same conviction he knew that the men he'd killed in France and Flanders were still dead.

And with the knowledge came the same icy, murderous rage he'd used to kill those men, the same rage he carried unslaked into the Forest with him, as ever, time and again, to unleash there in the woody gloom like some savage chemical flare.

"THA'RE SURE ABOUT THIS, LAD?"

"A trace that strong?" Duncan unrolled the oilskin gun wrap on the bed in his low-ceilinged room under the eaves at the inn. The McCulloch gleamed up at him in the low light. "A trace still hanging around like that, better than four months after the fact? You got any idea what it takes to leave that kind of imprint in our world? Had to be high-caste Huldu. No one else gives off magic like that. This fucker's a thousand years old, at least."

"One for the trophy hall, eh?"

Duncan took the trench gun from its retaining loops. "That isn't what I meant."

"Is it not?"

"I'm not being paid to kill Huldu. Not unless they get in my way." He opened the ammo pouch on the wrap, scooped out a handful of Crumley & Kegg's small grape cartridges. Fed them one by one into the McCulloch's loading port. "What they pay me to do is bring back the weans. For that I need a trail. And a high-caste Huldu passing through the Forest with a human child in tow is going to leave a lot of trace. Local Fae will talk about it, the Haunts will talk about it, Christ, even the fucking trees will talk about it."

"And tha think they'll talk to thee?"

The McCulloch went one better than the American combat shotgun models it'd been copied from. It was built for a seven-shell load. Duncan fed in the final cartridge and laid the gun back down. He looked at Garner.

"The Fae? It's not like I'm going to give them a choice. You ever see what iron filings will do to a Huldu's eyes?"

The other man broke gaze, looked away, as if Duncan was suddenly somehow too bright to stare at directly. Duncan snorted.

"Oh, come off it, Garner! Don't get prissy on me. You choked one of these fuckers to death with your bare hands not so long ago. I bet they still stand you drinks on that story."

"That was him or me, lad. I took no pleasure in it, then or now."

"You think I take pleasure in these things?"

Garner said nothing.

Duncan sighed. "Look, it probably won't come to that anyway. I can get the trees to talk to me most of the time. The Haunts are trickier; they like to play games, but you can usually work around that, too. It's not like torturing Huldu is my preferred option. It's just . . . it might come to that, is all. And if it does?" Duncan shrugged. "Well, I'm not squeamish about it."

"Aye, I've heard that."

Silence stretched in the cramped bedchamber. Garner would not look away. Duncan nodded. Started to lay out Crumley & Kegg's Fae-fucker bombs on the oilskin.

"Tell you a story," he said quietly as he worked. "Back in the summer of '16, I went out as part of a reconnaissance party at Delville Wood. We got pinned down there in a bombed-out sap, and we were still there when the German counteroffensive kicked off. We were low on ammo already, ran through what was left pretty fucking fast, and they just kept coming, so it was down to bayonets and whatever else you could grab. Fucking mud everywhere from days of rain and the artillery, men slipping and sliding in it as they fought. Screaming, bloody chaos—"

"I don't need to hear thy bloody war stories, lad." Something abruptly broken off in Garner's voice. Duncan raised a pacifying hand.

"This won't take a minute. I'm not trying to bore you."

They'd never talked about Garner's loss, and he didn't want to start now. What it must have done to the other man, to take his son back from the Huldu, to bring him home safe, bundled up in his arms, and then to lose him sixteen years later to a poster of a mustachioed fuckwit in a field marshal's cap over the mawkish plea *Your Country Needs You.*

Duncan held down the old rage. He drew a long breath.

"So like I said—bayonets and whatever else you could grab. What I could grab was a signal pistol, and when this big fucking Fritz came over the top and down at me bayonet first, I shot him in the belly with it, pretty much point blank."

Garner grunted. "Guess that stopped him well enough."

"Aye, worked a treat. Flare went right into his guts, buried itself there. Killed him." Duncan's face twitched with the memory. "Eventually."

Silence again in the small, homely room. Beyond the attic window, above the Forest skyline, a fading glow as the last light of evening drained down to amber dregs.

"You want to know what that sounds like?" Duncan asked. "A grown man screaming for his life as a flare burns his insides out? Slithering around in the mud and rain, tearing at the wound with both hands, trying to dig it out with his fingers as they scorch? You want to know what it *smells* like?"

Garner shook his head, wordless.

"That's right, you don't." Duncan finished laying out the Kegg bombs, stared down at them for a long moment. "And you know the thing about that Fritz? He was a total stranger, probably a husband and father, a man who never did anything to me."

"Apart from come at thee with a bayonet."

"You know what I mean. He was just a man, slapped with a uniform that said he had to kill me, or I him. Seven years later, I close my eyes and I can still smell him burning to death. I can still hear and smell what I did to that man." Duncan swung his gaze on Garner. "So if you think it should bother me in some way, working my way through a handful of these Fae fucks one scream at a time to get Mimi Rush back to her mother, well, that ship has sailed. Now, I'm going to the Forest. You're welcome to sit this one out. Not sure I could afford to pay you enough to come along anyway."

Garner nodded at the window. "It's getting dark out there."

"Aye, but it's a good moon. Clear skies, still mild. Come on, it's as perfect a woodsman's night as you'll get this time of year."

"Daylight would be better."

"Not for me, it wouldn't."

Garner gave him a *come-off-it* look. "Forest is a quieter place during the day. A safer place, and tha know it."

"Aye. Which makes getting the answers I want a harder, slower slog." Duncan found his rings in another pouch on the oilskin wrap, dug them out. "That's no use to me, Garner. The evidence says Mimi Rush has been gone at least four months. If I don't act fast, the trail is going to be cold. Look, you don't have to come. I'll understand if you don't. But I'm not wasting any more time."

Garner stood for a moment, watching him slip on the rings in silence. Duncan finished, flexed his fingers a little, and glanced at the other man. Garner nodded.

"I've a short-barrel Woodward's over-and-under in the cart," he said gruffly. "I'll get it."

TEN

THEY HIT THE FRINGES OF THE FOREST ALMOST IMMEDIATELY. The White Mare was a little way out of the center of Dowgreave, and Garner hadn't been exaggerating when he said the new growth came within a quarter mile of the village. They went across the downslope of a wildflower meadow at the back of the inn, climbed a stile, and found themselves within a stone's throw of the tree line. Here, there'd been no real attempt to cut back during Re-clearance, so the deadwood border was thin—a sparse handful of felled trunks up and down the line, long since stripped clean of their usable branches by locals either brave or desperate enough for firewood to get that close. In the early evening moonlight, the remnants looked like the scattered gray bones of some colossal beast out of myth, slaughtered long ago and left to rot there in the long grass.

Beyond, the Forest bulked dark and fronded and, if you looked carefully, stirring faintly in the breeze, as if they'd woken it from sleep.

"There's a mere about a half mile in from this side," Garner had told him. "Might be a good place to start. Black water, unquiet. It were only a bent bulge in a stream back before the Growth, but it always had the waft of magic about it. Folk said an elf queen were drowned there, and if tha threw offerings in and they sank, it'd mean good fortune for thee and thy family."

Duncan grunted. "And if they floated?"

"Then she were angry and tha were cursed."

"Right."

In under the trees, and the low moon started to fail them almost immediately. Here and there, a small dappled pocket showed up, metallic on leaves of ivy in the undergrowth, or painting a certain trunk partway down, as if to signal buried Faerie gold. For now, it would serve. They'd brought storm lanterns and big electric torches with them, but Duncan preferred to keep them stowed in the packs until they were absolutely necessary. His eyes were pretty good in low-light conditions anyway, and he just had to hope Garner's more aged vision would manage, too. They found a well-worn, winding path between the trees and pushed deeper in. Somewhere ahead, an owl hooted.

Duncan hoped it wasn't warning someone that they were coming.

The Forest closed around him, familiar odors of green and rot, the somber bulk and rise of the trees in the gloom. He felt the old, shivery mix of homecoming and horror, the blend of terrors known and unknown, kept just beneath the skin of conscious concern, where they prickled in his belly and whispered into his ear, but were balanced out by the sensation that here he *belonged*, here was where he could make meaning at levels the rest of his life had denied him, here was the place to deliver on the promise made long ago . . .

"Hold up, lad." Garner shouldering past him on the path, the over-and-under held across his body. "Listen."

They stood beneath an exuberant elm whose principal branches went up into the canopy like the arms of an Olympic champion raised and fisted in triumph. Moonlight through its leaves hatched the ground around them, silver and black. The path dribbled off to the right, but—

The faint chuckle and rush of flowing water, off and down to the left.

"Here, look." Garner held back a swath of brush with one arm.

Behind it was a leftward fork off the main track, winding down a slight incline, broken to view by the encroaching undergrowth. "All changed a bit since I was here last."

Duncan peered dubiously down the revealed track. "And when was that?"

"Couple of years ago, maybe a bit more." Garner slapped his left leg. "Before this, anyway. Used to come through regular, like. Lot of grieving folk back then, lost someone in the war, wanting word from beyond. They'd come to throw things in the water, hope for something back. I got paid to bring them in and out."

Duncan nodded. It was a common enough trend.

The Forest was mystery, magic, the unmapped uncanny in the corner of the human eye. It was the promise of something more, something that might nourish more deeply than the hard iron contours of a relentlessly mapped and measured world and the brutality of the truths that world contained. It didn't always take a blackwater mere. Sometimes it was a thousand-year oak or a lone standing stone that commanded the pilgrimages. But the story was always the same—venture in, find the place, the shrine, the core of mystery, and your bleak unimportance in the scheme of things would be salved, your needs addressed, if not actually met, your longing at least acknowledged. You would be seen, by things older and wiser than you. You would be seen, by things that held court in the universe instead of merely existing there, by things of power that could listen and judge and respond. You would be *seen*.

And the woodsmen made money from the unspoken pact—as guides, as escorts, and, when in the gloom of the Forest it all went wrong, as desperate skirmishers or retrievers of the remains.

He wondered fleetingly if Garner had ever come on his own account, too, mourning his son, wanting word, any word at all.

"Come on, then." Garner, now on the revealed path and looking expectantly back. "No time for wool gathering, lad. Let's get on with it."

He shook himself loose of his thoughts, followed Garner down the path, skirting the bushy encroachments of undergrowth, twitchy to any sound they heard or thought they heard from the foliage or the moon-glinting trees overhead. The older man was moving slow and careful—his over-and-under was shorter barreled than the norm for a farmer's gun, but nowhere near as chopped as the McCulloch. It snagged on brambles in the dark more than a couple of times.

Below them, the muttering of the stream gained force. They moved into a shuffling side step as the incline grew steeper, mindful of the weight of their packs and the risk of toppling. Duncan thought he caught the sounds of some more major disturbance in the water, flop and splash of something, somewhere ahead. They forged awkwardly through waist-high banks of nettles and thorn, ducked the branches of a twisted-up and oddly leaning alder tree, and came out abruptly on a ragged rock promontory five feet above the ink-black surface of the mere.

Ripples still crossed the moonlit stretch from whatever movement they'd heard on approach. Duncan knelt and watched them damp out, looking for a likely point of origin.

"Something heard us coming," he murmured.

"Aye. Something shy."

"Well, then. Let's not make too much noise."

They moved carefully along the promontory's edge, found a way down at the far side to where the mere was fringed with more leaning alders, some of them almost prostrate to the water and branches spread out more like tentacles along the ground than anything you'd expect from a normal tree. There was a soft earth overhang along most of the shore, but here and there it had been eaten out by the flow of water over time, and small dirt beaches a few feet or yards across went down to the water instead. Near the far end of the mere, there was a beach broad enough to set up camp, and from the scattered traces, it looked as if someone had done exactly that not too long ago. Stones had been used to form a rough fire circle, scorched black ground and the ashy remnants of a fire within. A few half-charred fragments of deadwood were scattered about in the near vicinity, and the stones themselves had been disturbed at some point, too. Duncan met Garner's eyes. Almost imperceptibly, the older man nodded.

"Right, then," Duncan said briskly. "This'll do."

THEY UNSHIPPED THEIR PACKS, PUSHED the fire circle back into shape, gathered deadwood from up and down the surrounding bank. They started a small campfire of their own. Then, while Garner nursed the infant flames, Duncan scouted around, senses peeled for anything left behind.

Up by the earth overhang at the back of the tiny beach, where the roots of an undermined alder had been exposed by winter spate action from the stream that fed the mere, he found shreds of fabric caught on the spike of a snapped root end. It looked, at a guess, like fragments from a woolen shirt. And as he turned back toward the mere, as if it had been waiting for him to look, the moonlight slipped in and made something glint down near the water's edge. He squinted, walked a little closer to be sure. Recognized the soft brass gleam of a single discharged shotgun cartridge, half buried in the moist dirt. He toed the brass thoughtfully with his boot, dug it loose, then scuffed it away into the water. Tiny plop as it sank.

"Good a place to sleep as any," he called across to Garner. "You need a blanket?"

Garner shook his head, poking the fire. "Coat'll do me, lad. It's not that cold."

They turned in without further real conversation, Garner huddled up in his coat against the earth bank near the struggling alder, Duncan wrapped in blankets between the fire and the water's edge. Drowsy quiet crept in. Soft crackle of the flames, softer rush of water from the stream at either end of the mere, softest of all the hush of the wind in the trees overhead. Duncan stared up at the sky above them, a seeming inverted pool of stars fringed by tree canopies, fit to fall into . . .

He let his eyes slide closed, let conscious thought unknot itself in preparation for dream. Pleasing images of Niamh, demure smile feigning on her lips as she walked toward him, hands lifting to the buttons at the back of her neck. Her wet heat over his fingers, her mouth over his cock, soft, impatient longing and thrust and . . .

And there!

Under the whisper of the trees and the stream, the sulky argumentative snap and hiss of the low burning fire, another sound came, the one he'd been waiting for—water shifting silkily, as something surfaced and moved in toward the shore.

He held the dream state, prevented conscious response with a further cascade of remembered images from the lovemaking of the previous night. At one point in the narrow bed, she'd mounted and rode him reversed, head thrown back, lost in herself, long hair tangled down her back . . .

Furtive *drip-drip* of water off to his right, as something came stealthily ashore . . .

One lower corner of his top blanket, lifted as if by a stray breeze . . .

Duncan, decently versed in second sight when it got this close, felt the grab at his ankle an instant before it happened. He shifted, fast.

Sudden, damp grip on his right leg. He had already tilted on his side. His eyes snapped open, saw the grinning, dripping thing that crouched over him, the piranha fangs. He swung one booted foot in a short arc. Felt the kick connect with skull bone. His attacker yelped and shook itself, tried to drag him back toward the water's edge. Duncan kicked again, this time a hard stomp direct into the fangs and snout. The thing shrilled, but hung on, still not willing to forgo its prey. Duncan let it drag him, went with the motion, squirmed in close. Narrowed yellow-glowing eyes, a cadaverous face almost human, lank black hair straggling back off the head, fanged mouth agape, aye, right, here we fucking go . . .

He punched hard, right cross, into the toothy lantern jaw. The skull ring, the ankh ring and the Iron Cross ring he'd hacked off a Prussian machine gunner's corpse at Passchendaele. Sally had blessed each one for him, called them all auspicious.

More important, they were all forged hard in iron.

Greenish-white flash, a splatter like the sound of an electrical circuit shorting out. This time, the apparition shrieked in earnest and let go his leg. Smoke ribboned off its face, a low stench of burning flesh filled the air. Duncan was up now, snagged one flailing arm at the elbow—more smoke coiling out as the rings on his left hand burned into the arm. Nothing from Garner, and no time to shout or wonder why. He punched again, repeatedly, into the thing's face. He was snarling himself now, a noise not much more human than those the creature made. Splattering, splintering, flickering green-white flash—three blows, and then suddenly Garner was there, stomping on the thing's broad, filigree-finned back, crushing it into the dirt of the beach. It thrashed and nearly got free. Garner dropped a hard knee on its spine, showed it the business end of his over-and-under.

"Want to settle down, pond scum?" he roared. "Or should I spill thy bloody brains?"

The tone, at least, got through. The creature went abruptly still. It slumped there in the gloom like something dumped from a trawl net—long, pallid tapering legs half again the length of a human's, finned and fronded near the ankle of powerful clawed feet, swell at hip and thigh, the broad, muscular trunk and shoulders, twinned rows of teats, arms like a Greek wrestler, and powerful hands tipped with talons the hue of pond weed. Call it nixie, call it grindylow, call it *vatnalfr*—or simply, as some of the gothic writers had it, the Mudbank Horror. Names are for the waking world. This nightmare would not care as it dragged you down.

Duncan reeled to his feet, panting. "You fucking fell *asleep*?"

Garner shot him an apologetic look.

"Great!" Duncan, still panting, walking a small circle in the beach dirt, working at bringing his breathing under control. "Guess you old folk need your fucking rest."

He flexed his right fist open and closed a couple of times, came to a halt. He stood over the quiescent grindylow, grinning fiercely with the comedown after the fight. The old trench hand-to-hand tremors. He composed himself with an effort. Switched to Skogurtal.

"Well, well," he managed, still between breaths. "Jenny fucking Greenteeth. You really were hungry, weren't you. Brood season, is it?"

The creature's eyes bulged a bit as it heard the language. It squirmed under Garner's dropped knee, twisted its head, tried to get a better look at Duncan.

"Not what you were expecting?" Duncan crouched closer, still unable to lose his comedown grin. "Tougher to get than the last chunk of man-flesh that wandered in here, was I?"

"You aren't—you don't . . ." The mere dweller husked in Skogurtal so badly accented Duncan struggled to follow the syllables. "You dream *different.* Awake, like them! You scent of men, but—"

"Aye. Sorry to disappoint."

"I—you—" The grindylow averted its gaze pettishly. "Look, I have no quarrel with the Bright Folk, nor their thralls. I did not realize, I did not know you. Tell Svalenkari and Mebhuranon it was an honest mistake."

The names detonated behind Duncan's eyes. He covered for it, masked himself in tones of stony contempt. Had to hope that Jenny Greenteeth here would not spot the sudden new jump in pulse, the renewed uptick and thump of his just-now-calming heart.

"Honest or not," he said impassively, "this must be paid out in blood. Will I order these waters purged? Must I bring the tangle iron and sink it here?"

"But I meant no disrespect!" The fang-distorted sibilant voice grew urgent, almost hoarse. "Please. They are but weeks old. Helpless pups."

"Helpless or not, they must learn respect. The edicts are clear."

Panic in the yellowish, unhuman eyes now. Duncan glanced at Garner, switched back to English. "What do you reckon?"

"Reckon to what?" Garner sour and snappish in response. "Didn't get the half of whatever tha're nattering about! Tha know I conner follow their gibberish the way tha do."

Maybe it was lasting embarrassment at his sleeping lapse; maybe his heart was still pounding, too. Or maybe it was just a flat-out case of green eye. Like most woodsmen, Garner would have a limited smattering of Skogurtal, words and phrases gleaned and handed down locally over generations, along with the rest of the myth base and a mishmash of Forest lore. He wouldn't be the first to envy Duncan's gift with the Huldu tongue.

Right now, sour and snappish would do, was in fact ideal for Duncan's purposes. He saw the way the grindylow already quailed at the tone.

"I'm asking if we let Jenny here off with a caution. She thinks we're changeling thralls to the Huldu, scared we're going to dump iron junk in the mere and poison her young. It gives us leverage. I could offer to let her slide if she answers a couple of questions for us."

"Do what tha bloody like, lad. I'm not the one she tried to eat."

Still jittery, Duncan chuckled. He couldn't help it. "There is that."

The grindylow looked from one to the other of them. They were not especially intelligent creatures, but they were cunning, and would know cunning or trickery in return. Duncan marshaled his words carefully, playing the role the creature had imagined him into, leaning into the ornateness that Skogurtal tended toward anyway.

"In truth," he said, "I would not wish to bother my lord Svalenkari nor the Fae queen with something so trivial as this. And tangle iron is heavy to haul. But my bondsman here is not so forgiving, and he is my elder. He'll need persuading. What can you offer us, vatnalfr?"

The grindylow gaped at him, hope and horror oscillating in its gaze. "Offer? To mortal men? I have no Faerie gold. I do not—"

"Tales," Duncan interjected helpfully. "My bondsman here has a great love of Forest gossip. If you could tell us something? Some morsel of knowledge we do not have, perhaps? Some local news or rumor of it? Anything concerning other thralls such as ourselves?"

It was the perfect note to strike. Cunning crept back into the yellow eyes. The creature sneered. "Afraid your mistress will find sweeter favor, are you? Is it the child you fear?"

"The child?" Duncan, elaborately casual, hoping to Christ and High Heaven that, once again, the grindylow was too rattled to notice the uptick in his pulse. "What child is this?"

"You will leave? You will not bring the tangle iron?"

Duncan nodded at Garner, who lightly touched the business end of the sawed-off Woodward to the nape of the grindylow's neck. Sizzling and fishy waft of scorched flesh. The creature shrilled and thrashed under Garner's knee. Another nod, and Garner lifted the gun away. Duncan crouched closer to the vatnalfr's pain-wracked face.

"We are not negotiating here, nixie. You are trying to earn back your life. Now *tell me what you know.*"

"Yes, yes!" Almost a scream. "The child. The chosen child. Mebhuranon brought her out from the lands of men a hostage."

"Hostage?" Duncan frowned. "Hostage for what?"

"I know not." The grindylow saw the way Duncan glanced toward Garner and screamed. "No, it is the truth! I do not know! Only that she is no plaything, no simple thrall. In the Forest, they say that among the mortals, she is of noble blood. That she has high value beyond simple self."

"Noble blood?" Duncan grabbed the grindylow's hair—oily wet, coarser than human—redoubled his grip and yanked the face upward close to his own. "Are you lying to me? Are you spinning me some fucking yarn to save your miserable hide?"

"It is no lie. The whole Forest knows it."

"What's this child's name?"

The grindylow gaped at him. "Name? I do not *name* mortals. How should I know?"

This last had the gritty rub of truth. The Fae grasp on detail in human affairs was muddy at the best of times, even among those who didn't actually eat them. A creature at this level would be as incurious as the next pike in a pond.

"Then Mebhuranon?" Keep the pressure on. He held his fist in the grindylow's face. Iron rings a searing inch away. "You tell me why a southern range Bright Folk queen would come to poach mortal children all the way up here? Has she returned south with the girl?"

"I know not—no! No! The child abides!" He lowered his fist. The grindylow sobbed. "Mebhuranon, too. As came Svalenkari in all his glory, so came she. Some grand purpose, they say. But I know not why they stay." Down to mumbles and grizzling now. "I know not. It is all I know. I swear. I swear on my brood. It is all I know . . ."

He let go the creature's dripping hair, shook his hand to snap the oily residue off. Stood back up, nodded at Garner. The other man got out of his crouch, a lot more creakily. He still held the over-and-under trained on the grindylow's skull. The yellowish eyes flitted between the two of them, trapped, unsure.

"Hear this," Duncan told it slowly. "If I ever meet you on dry land again, I will send you back to the Gray. And if you speak of this, to the Bright Folk or anyone else, I will sink tangle iron into these waters sufficient to poison your brood for a hundred years to come. Now, while my favor lasts, get yourself gone."

He kicked the creature hard in the ribs by way of emphasis. It snarled and recoiled, thrashed coiling limbs in the dirt of the beach, bared fangs at them both, and then, like some conjuror's sleight of hand, was abruptly gone back into the mere. The darkened waters barely rippled to mark its passing, no trace left of what now swam in its depths.

Yes, Duncan, and a less-seasoned woodsman would have been down there, too, coiled around and bitten apart by now, and fed piecemeal to the pups.

Perhaps, he brooded, he should have killed the fucking thing after all.

"Get what tha wanted?" Garner asked.

Duncan stared somberly at the fading ripples. "I got enough for now."

ELEVEN

"NOBLE BLOOD?"

"That's what it said." Duncan slashed irritably at the underbrush ahead with a switch he'd cut from the struggling alder when they left the beach. "Apparently the whole fucking Forest knows about it, too. I don't know what that bitch Mebhuranon's up to, but it's not just another changeling wheeze for thralls or giggles."

"Aye, thought I heard that name when tha were jabbering back and forth with Jenny."

"You heard right."

"Old Queen Meb herself." Garner looking uneasily around in the moon-hatched gloom, as if just naming the Huldu might summon her up. "Tha do like to get thisel mixed in right to thy neck, lad."

"I take the jobs I'm offered."

"Well, tha waint have to feel guilty about taking their money on this one."

"Nobles aren't always wealthy," Duncan said absently. Most of him was brooding on Irene Rush, picking apart his recall for clues he'd evidently sleepwalked past while fixed on her gown-clad curves. "Families I've known, some of them have been broke since the Georges. You're better off working for industrialists."

"If tha say so, lad. I bow to thy superior experience in exalted circles."

That cut a little close for comfort. Change the subject. "Told you, though, didn't I? This one was a thousand years old, at least."

"At least," echoed Garner. "More like four or five thousand. They don't call her Old Meb for nowt."

They called her, in fact, any number of things, dating back as far as human record reached. Meb, Mab, Mara, Maeve, Morrigan, and that was just the M's. Elsewhere, she was Skjalf, Tuonetar, Valfreyja . . . so forth . . .

Pointless to track.

Even among her own kind, Mebhuranon was a legend. They said of her that she was already old when men first came to cut and burn the great forests of Britain, with only stone and wood and cured hide for tools. She was, to all intents and purposes, a god.

"Thought I heard another name, too," Garner said quietly. "Svalenkari, was it? Him, I don't know."

Duncan grunted, elaborately noncommittal.

Skogurtal, with its antique structure and ornateness in expression, insisted not just on gender inflection, but on an honorific particle before proper nouns. Even if you didn't speak the tongue especially well, names were easy to spot. Even names you'd never heard before.

"Tha seemed to recognize him, though," Garner probed

"Aye, it's a name I've heard. One of the northern clans, I think."

"Perhaps it's a Gathering, then. Meb's outside her range up here as well—last I heard she was down around Dartmoor." Ordinarily taciturn, Garner seemed to have discovered a sudden urge toward gossip. "They say it's where she was born, like. It's all oak and beech regrowth down there now; must feel like some kind of homecoming for her. Like stepping back in time to her youth or summat."

Duncan let him talk. If it helped bury the discomfort of his lapse into sleep at the mere, or calm his obviously rattled and out-of-practice woodsman nerves in the night forest, so be it. It didn't hurt that the conversation slipped further and further from things he didn't want to talk about, things he carefully hadn't even *thought* about in—

Recall, marching across his skin, raising hairs. The night around him leaned in, interested. He breathed deep, summoned from out of the remembered terrors a steady, burning rage. He breathed it in, tried it on for size, imagined some of the things he could do with it.

He quickened his pace into the rising slope ahead of them.

"Want to tell me," Garner, huffing a bit with the incline, "where we're going?

"Top of this rise. See if we can find an adoption cairn."

"Tha think . . . someone like Mebhuranon . . . would bother to do that? This . . . far from home? I can see . . . some young buck . . . wanting to make . . . his mark. But a . . . five-thousand-year-old clan queen?"

"You're missing the point."

"Which . . . is what?"

Duncan took pity on the older man. He stopped on the sloping path, turned about to face him. Let Garner catch his breath.

"Look, Mebhuranon is old school. Living ancestor stock. That's something special these days. The younger Huldu like marking their abductions, because they've lived their lives driven to the margins and they think this is a glorious return to the days of yore. They're doing what they're told their ancestors did, aping the forms. But really, it's just cheap posturing and vengeance for all those years cooped up in tiny forest plots and woodlands, hiding from the iron. Every changeling, every cairn, is them pissing in our faces and telling the Forest all about it. There's no *class* to any of it, no resonances, no—"

Garner was looking at him curiously. Duncan shook his head.

"Doesn't matter. The point is, Mebhuranon's seen the Forest come and go and now come back again. She's been dealing with humans since a time when they treated her as a god. Then, when the cross-god came, she was suddenly a soulless demon succubus, then just a haunt in the trees to scare children to bed, then a harmless woodland sprite dancing on toadstools in nursery rhymes and bedtime tales. She's seen it all, she's watched the eras turn, and here she is again, a Faerie queen. She's forgotten more grudges against humans than most younger Huldu have ever held. So—she'll build a cairn, not for vengeance, not for pride; she'll build it because *it is the done thing.* Nothing more. And if it's true Mimi Rush is some kind of nobility, and the Forest knows that, then that ritual is going to be even more important, more resonant of the changing times." Duncan jabbed a thumb over his shoulder at the rising path. "I'm telling you, there's a cairn up there. And it's got Mebhuranon's name on it. I'd stake the cost of a brand-new Beardmore on that."

"What's a Beardmore?"

Duncan rolled his eyes. "Motorcar. One of the new ones."

"Bet me something else. Told thee I've no use for those contraptions."

"Aye, you told me. You got your breath back yet, old man?"

"Ready when tha are, lad. Tha're the one who bloody stopped."

Duncan nodded, turned away to hide his grin.

Moon scatter on foliage. Small rustling through the shadowed undergrowth. Somewhere in a tree not far off, a song thrush ran through its repertoire, as if warming up for some more major performance.

They slogged on up the rise.

IF DUNCAN HAD BEEN LOOKING for a suitably dramatic vindication, the gods of the Forest seemed eager to provide.

The rise topped out on a balding sandstone ridge running roughly north–south with a steeper drop-off on the far side and views out across the Cheshire plain. Down below, beyond the reach of the Forest, the lights of Macclesfield and its outlying villages glimmered like a fleet of fishing vessels at anchor on the dark. Farther north and west, Manchester announced itself with an unhealthy yellowish glow that lay against the sky like a stain. It seemed a long way off. The trees had thinned out as the two men crested the summit, but the open ground gave no sense of relief. Instead, it was as if the foliage were drawing aside, like curtains pulled back off a stage set for some bleak drama to begin. A buffeting autumn wind came out of the west, in across the plain, hit them in the face.

Bulking against the view, hunched in silhouette like some pantomime witch in hat and cloak, was a cairn nearly five feet tall.

From the uneven stonework, Huldu runes gleamed soft blue in the moonlight. They seemed, somehow, to sing in the gloom.

Duncan gestured, still a little out of breath himself from the climb. "There you go. You owe me a motorcar."

Garner nodded. He stepped closer, touched one of the runes.

"Mark of Mebhuranon, right enough. Can tha read the rest of this stuff?"

Duncan prowled about the structure, lips moving silently. The glyphs were largely formula—honorific references, clarion calls to ancient names, only some of which he knew. They clumped in short phrases, occasionally stood out alone where the rune was sufficiently inflected and complex. The juxtapositions between each piece of engraving followed a geometry he was familiar enough with to avoid concentrating on too much. That way headaches lay, twinges of sudden vertigo, disturbed sleep, nightmare, and eventually, the witch had warned him, madness.

"It's about what you'd expect," he said. "The Huldu Star rises once again. Those who had Faith are Nourished, Those who Doubted are . . . ehm, Confounded. The Crowned Queen returns, uhm, treads the Old Forest Ways. The Old Ways are Made Anew. Rejoice."

"That mean she's still around?"

Duncan scowled at the glyphs. "It's more likely figurative. But you never know."

"So what now?"

"We leave a message of our own." Searching around in his coat pockets. "You'll want to stand back for this bit. Shield your eyes, too."

"My eyes?"

"That's what I said."

He produced one of Crumley & Kegg's Fae-fuckers, scanned the cairn for a suitable blast point, finally pressed it into a narrow gap between two glyph-marked stones at about chest height. In contrast to any cairn built by human hands, the stones here were smoothly joined, flowing into each other as if cemented. He checked to make sure the bomb was well seated, then braced a hand on it and tugged out the fuse. It went with a soft crunch that he felt through his palm, like a tooth being pulled. Six seconds, Crumley had promised. Duncan skated rapidly backward from the cairn, shut his eyes, and put up a shielding arm for good measure.

The bomb blew with an oddly mild crump.

No flash, or at least none his eyes could detect through their closed lids. True to Crumley's word, Duncan felt the iron filings lash at his raised hand and his brow, no worse than wind-driven sand. Strangled involuntary curse out of Garner, though. And strange seething sounds from the cairn. He gave it a couple of seconds, lowered his arm, and opened his eyes.

Unless you knew what to look for, the effect had been undramatic. But where the stones of the cairn were once smoothly cemented together, now deep cracks ran between them, radiating out from the place Duncan set his bomb. The glowing runes were in trouble, too, bleeding a thin bluish sleet through their edges, seeming to stain the surrounding stone like a luminous verdigris. The seething sound, seeming to emanate from the cairn's core, grew more insistent.

"And what the hell was that?" Garner wanted to know.

Duncan dug out another Fae-fucker and held it up for the other man. "Kegg bomb. As in Crumley and Kegg's. Combat science. Shape of things to come, apparently."

Garner snorted. "Those two lunatics! Toys they make, tha wanner to be careful tha donner blow thy own hand off."

Duncan put the bomb away again. Nodded at the cairn. "Seems to have worked, though, doesn't it."

"It's poisoned the binding glamour, for sure. Happy with that?"

"Nope. Here, give me a hand." Duncan set his shoulder to the cairn, waited for Garner to join him. Fitful bluish light from the damaged runes speckled the older man's face in the dark. "Right. Hard as you can, on three. One, two, *three*!"

They strained, leaned into it. The cairn shifted, gave with a reluctant grating, subsided a little, slowly at first—

"Harder! Come on!"

Then, with a long, grinding rumble, and a yell of triumph from Duncan, the whole structure collapsed sideways to the ground, individual rocks tumbling and bouncing away, some of them right over the drop-off and into the treetops below.

The two men stood, bent over and panting.

"Right . . . then," Garner huffed. "Tha happy . . . now?"

Duncan straightened up. "Couple of finishing touches yet."

He surveyed the tumbled field of rubble they'd made, the rough stump of stonework that remained where the cairn had stood. The stubborn dying glimmer of a few glyphs in the mess. He cast a glance around at the nearby trees.

Then he opened his fly and pissed carefully over the stone stump in a gentle back-and-forth figure eight loop. Steam rising off the urine in the autumnal gloom, hiss and patter as it fell. Garner, breath still not fully caught, gaped at him in silence.

Duncan finished, buttoned himself up, then unshipped his pack and dug out a screw-top steel canister of iron filings. He tipped the contents slowly and steadily over the humbled cairn in the same figure eight loop. Where it touched them, the dying glyphs went out like blown candles. Duncan examined his work with the care of a joiner checking a finished table, then he resealed the canister and stowed it again. He gave Garner a small, preoccupied smile.

The older man shook his head. "Please tell me we're done."

"Almost." Duncan drew the McCulloch from its sheath on the pack, racked a round, and pointed the weapon at one of the nearer trees.

"Lad, what—"

Door-slam bang from the gun. The tree's foliage rustled, something yelped and fell out. Duncan, face gone suddenly harsh, stepped forward, racked the gun again, pointed it downward. Whatever the thing he'd flushed out was, it scrabbled rapidly to its feet in a crouch—glinting eyes, clawed feet and hands, pallid gleaming flesh. It hissed and bared its teeth at the two men, then fled into the undergrowth with a noisy crash. Duncan watched it go.

"We're killing tree pixies now?" Garner asked mildly.

"If I'd wanted it dead, it would be. We're trying to send a message. I just want to make sure the message gets carried."

"So what now?"

Duncan shrugged. "Now we head back."

"That's it? We piss on Meb's adoption cairn and then just go home?"

"We've done enough for now."

"I thought this were about information?"

"It is. But I don't think anyone else is going to talk to us tonight." Duncan gestured at the tumbled cairn. "Not after this. What it *will* do is stir up—"

He stopped. Cocked his head, oddly lupine, stared away into the gloom under the trees.

"Stir up what?" Garner, brusquely impatient. "Stop thy bloody woolgathering, lad. Stir up *what*?"

Duncan snapped out of it, turned and peered over the edge of the drop-off instead. "Forget it. You reckon you could navigate us back to Dowgreave from down there?"

Garner came and stood beside him. "Don't see why not. There's Macclesfield"—sighting down his arm, swinging it to point nearer in, gauging—"Wizard's Oak about . . . there. The old Haughton place just north of that. It's ruined now, but the farm track takes thee right out into the fields on the south side of St. Edith's. Easy enough—once tha make it down in one piece."

"Good."

"I said *once tha make it down in one piece.*" Eyeing the drop-off mistrustfully. "But we're not, lad, we're up here. That's a long drop. Steep, and not much to hang on to on the way down. Happen we'd scrape our arses raw, if we donner just get in a bloody tumble and break a leg. Tha have some good reason we conner just go back the way we came?"

Faintly, through the gloom under the trees behind them—a low, moaning howl. It froze both men in place. It lifted the hairs on the nape of Duncan's neck.

It didn't sound that far off.

Duncan gestured.

"That a good enough reason for you?"

THEY RAN A HASTY CHECK along the edge of the drop-off, found a couple of promising gullies—long, thin earthen scoops in the sandstone cliff wall making a scant few degrees better than vertical, fringed with squat deformed trees and bushes whose branches reached obstinately across the gap. In the patchy moonlight, it was hard to see what might be waiting for them farther down. Duncan picked the broader of the two channels, dragged his pack off, and seated himself on the lip.

"This gets my vote," he said.

Garner glared down the gully. "I conner see a bloody thing down there!"

"Aye, well—like the man says, if you knows of a better 'ole, then go to it."

"Oh, now tha're a bloody humorist?"

Another long, drawn-out hunting howl from the Forest behind them. This time, they heard it answered.

"It's fight here or run, old man." Duncan got his pack situated between his legs, protecting his groin. "I know which I prefer."

"Tha knew this was going to happen, then?"

"Aye, well—thought we'd have a little longer than this. Days or hours. Not minutes, anyway. Can't be helped."

Strangled, wordless growl from the other man. But you could hear that he was done arguing. Duncan nodded.

"Keep an arm up to shield your face. Lot of brush down there. I'll see you at the bottom!"

And he shoved himself off the lip.

TWELVE

IT WASN'T FALLING. NOT QUITE.

Gut swoop of gathering speed—repeated smash of branches across his face in the dark—eyes narrowed to slits. He kept his arm up as best he could. Still, he felt a sharp sting in one eye as some thin twig or leaf edge got through. With the other hand, he held his pack in place between his legs and under his arse. Boots dug in for brakes, bleeding what momentum they could from the ragged, accelerating toboggan plunge of his body down the slope. The pack juddered under his hold. Boots tearing up dirt that slipped in under his coat, his shirt, rubbing with gritty intimacy up across the skin of his back.

It was all he could do not to whoop as he barreled down the gully toward the ground.

Making enough fucking noise as it is.

Above, he heard Garner coming down fast behind him, yelling curses and crashing noisily through the same branches and brush and darkness.

The bottom came up and hit him—his boots went ankle deep into scree. The sudden arrest snatched him almost fully upright. The pack went flying. He tumbled sideways, clouted his ribs on a boulder, bounced off. Landed in a winded heap facing back the way he'd come. He was just in time to see Garner arrive in much the same messy fashion.

They both lay still for a moment, looking at each other.

Then, reluctantly, Garner began to laugh.

It started as a chuckle, lifted an answering grin from Duncan's lips, and then suddenly he was chuckling, too. Garner laughed louder, then winced and stopped. He propped himself up on one elbow, pressed tentatively on the left side of his chest with his other hand. Winced again.

"You all right, old man?"

"Cracked a bloody rib by the feel of it. Got any more bright ideas tha want us to try before we call it a night?"

"Aye. How about we don't lie here moaning and get on the move instead? We bought ourselves some time with this, but it's nothing you could stretch. Warrior-caste Huldu could jump that whole drop in a couple of bounds and come up grinning."

"Warrior caste?" Garner looked back up the cliff wall. "Tha think that's what's coming?"

"I think I'd rather not find out. Can you walk all right?"

"Just bloody watch me."

They picked themselves groggily up, went about retrieving their gear. It took longer than Duncan would have liked. His pack had burst open on landing, spilled across the forest floor around them, and it was darker under the drop-off than it had been up above.

No time for torches. He grabbed up what he could easily see, gave up the rest as lost. Luckily, the Kegg bombs shone pale in the low light, and hadn't scattered far. He found and counted off fourteen of the sixteen he should still have, was not prepared to beat the bushes for the remaining two. He fastened and shouldered the pack. Looked expectantly at Garner.

"Haughton place, you said?"

Garner nodded, pointed with the Woodward. "That way. About half an hour, if we get lucky with the undergrowth."

Duncan racked another shell in his own gun, fed two replacement cartridges into the receiver. Harsh, metallic sounds in the mulch-odored gloom.

"Come on, then, Hawkeye." He grinned. "After you."

Grumbling, the older man led off, away from the scree pile they'd landed in, down a faint, shelving incline beyond. The going was easy enough, soft and springy underfoot, without too many roots to trip on. Duncan let Garner pick their way, most of him listening back behind them for signs of pursuit.

He had no intention of showing it, but beneath the outer calm he affected, the speed of the Huldu response had shaken him. The Forest breathed gossip and rumor and news like a single huge nervous system. Everything was known somewhere by something, everything was *felt*, and if for some reason the trees themselves would not carry the word, then you could rely on something that lived among them to do it instead. The *bladande*, the tree pixies, were particularly swift and garrulous, but no one took them especially seriously, least of all the haughty, insouciant Bright Folk. This was unlooked for. By rights, he and Garner should have been back at the White Mare in front of a blazing hearth, drinking away the eldritch Forest shivers before any Huldu took note of what had been done to the cairn.

Instead, in his confidence and easy rage, he'd stormed right through some kind of trip wire he still didn't understand, set instant alarms ringing far and wide.

Run, Duncan, said the chiming voices in his head. *Run, run, run.*

He looked at Garner's hesitant gait, the way he pressed his arm against his side every couple of steps. Run—aye, chance would be a fine thing!

"Can we pick up the pace a wee bit?" he asked, straining to sound amiable.

"If tha wanna to go flat on thy fat face over an oak root every ten yards, be my guest." Garner, irritable, didn't stop or even turn. His gaze never came up from the ground they walked. "If, on t' other hand, tha don't like that idea, then we're going as fast as we can. Now stop bothering me, lad. Hard enough to see in this bloody light as it is."

Duncan grimaced. They walked on in silence. Owl hoot from

somewhere off to their left. Twitchy sounds and motions in the undergrowth, as living things scuttled away from the human scent and noise they were tracking through the woods. The trees stood sentinel stiff around them. The minutes crawled by. Duncan sent his senses out, stretched as gossamer thin and far and wide as he knew how. The Forest shifted around him, somehow darker and more luminous at one and the same time. Intimations of doom nipped at his heels, put up the hairs on the nape of his neck. A cold, creeping knowledge was in him, and no way to convey it to Garner at levels the other man would understand.

Something is coming.

It wasn't the howls they'd heard in the darkness under the trees, it wasn't the names the nixie had given him. Those were just the flicker-flash of lightning on the fringes of a storm whose looming shape and size he could still not grasp.

He thought briefly of Martin Hardy again, the colonel's somber declaration.

Another kind of war. With new enemies and rules we have yet to learn.

Enemies who now, apparently, wanted a word.

Should have taken that train to London, Duncan.

About two hundred yards farther along, they came across a mossy drystone wall drowned beneath the trees, waist high and running what Duncan estimated was due north. Garner grunted in satisfaction. He stopped and breathed deep, winced. Patted the top of the wall.

"Look at that. Craftsmanship. Old Arthur Haughton's grandfather built these back when we were both still weans. Man was a dry-stack master."

"Was he, aye?" Duncan, trying hard to keep a tight, ballooning impatience from his voice. "So will we cross here?"

"No, we can follow it awhile yet. We'll move faster that way. Cross farther up, once we're close to the farm. We're nearly there."

"Right, then. Want me to take lead for a while?"

Garner shot him a look. Led off again, faster, forcing the pace, but with sharp, hard breaths, and that arm pressed tight against his side. Duncan sighed, cast a mistrustful glance back the way they'd come, then fell in behind the older man. He ran a hand along the moss-grown march of stonework at his side. It looked longer abandoned than you'd expect.

"What state's the Haughton place in these days?" he wondered aloud. "The farm buildings, I mean."

"How would I bloody know? Haven't set foot in there for years."

In the edge on the other man's voice, Duncan thought he detected mourning. The Garner family farm wasn't a lot of miles from here, and was presumably in a similar state of neglect. Like the wall they walked alongside, most man-made structures under the Forest canopy seemed to decay at an accelerated rate, almost as if the new growth carried some kind of attendant rot, a miasma intensely corrosive to anything built by human hands.

It had to be hard, seeing something like that happen to the place you were born and raised, the place your memories were rooted in, the place you once called home.

You'd avoid going back there, or even thinking about it much, if you could.

And—since the man was already on his mind—Duncan had to wonder if there was some similar sense of loss in Martin Hardy's thinly buried rage at anyone who would disparage the country and empire he served. You came back with the indelible stench and desolation of the trenches on you, saw—or thought you saw—a similar rot setting in at home. Cracked glass and stone, bulwarks and battlements thrown down, Victoriana bereft. You saw things fall apart, begin to slide, brought low by forces the previous century had taught you were yours to dominate and direct . . .

Aye, that might be hard to take.

And then the tiny shock—up through the earth under his feet midstep, the way you'd sometimes feel the impact of distant artillery much farther down the line. The tremor of incoming, so faint he believed, *wanted* to believe for one desperate, willful moment, it might be the onset of a cramp in the sole of his foot.

But it wasn't.

It was something hitting the ground back at the base of the drop-off, and landing in a crouch. Something alive. Something that hissed and snarled, and rose back up to stand tall in the moonlight like a demon summoned. And scent the breeze for trace.

They were out of time.

"How much longer?" he asked Garner sharply.

"The Haughton place? Five minutes, I'd say, maybe ten."

"I'd say we've got about two."

Garner jerked around to stare at him. Ashen faced.

Duncan nodded. "Aye. Can you run?"

"Bloody have to, won't I!"

"If we can get to the farmhouse, defend it, we have a chance. They catch us on the run, we're dead or worse."

"Better stop standing about flapping our gums, then!"

"Aye. Quick as you can manage it. I'll watch our arse." Because that way he wouldn't have to set a pace and then clip it so Garner could keep up. "Can we stick with the wall, or do we have to cross?"

"Stick with it for now." Garner settled his cap more firmly on his head. "I'll tell thee when."

"Go!"

Garner loped off along the wall line. Duncan let him get ahead a dozen paces, brought up the rear at a brisk pace that wouldn't force the other man beyond his limits.

The first howl of pursuit through the trees at their back.

An answering call, almost playful.

Run, Duncan! Run!

Duncan snarled a grin.

Aye, come ahead then, you Fae fucks! You're not chasing a wean now!

Along the crumbled line of the drystack at the loping run. Twice, he had to dial back his pace so as not to overtake Garner, who by now was showing signs of distress. They passed a place where a young oak tree had sprouted under the stonework, broken the line of the wall, tumbled fragments wide on either side. Duncan caught one with his foot, tripped, nearly went flying headlong . . .

More howls, back and forth in the trees behind them. The sounds were coming quicker now, excited—joyous with the hunt!

And suddenly, Garner jammed to a halt, leaning on the wall. Duncan almost ran into the back of him, had to slam on the brakes hard and jigger to a stumbling stop. For a moment, he thought the other man was done—bent over, breath whistling out between gritted teeth. He slapped him on the shoulder.

"What's got you?" he asked. "Need to stop for a piss."

Gritted laugh. Garner's hanging head shook back and forth. He threw out an arm, stabbed fingers mutely across the wall. Duncan peered, saw trees and little else.

"Farmhouse!" Garner panted. "Hundred yards. Look there . . ."

Duncan narrowed his eyes, peered again. Caught the dim ghost of angular architectural lines through the trees. By the look of it, closer even than the hundred yards Garner had called it at. He'd covered similar ground on retreat at Messines, harried by machine gun fire and mortar shelling—if Garner could make it too, this was a walk in the park.

"Right! Let's get over this fucking wall, then."

Garner nodded, breathless. Hauled himself on top of the stones, swung-fell off the other side as the weight of his pack tugged him down. Duncan shifted grip on the McCulloch, held it one-handed halfway down the barrel. He braced with his other hand on the wall, settled for an ungainly vault, tottered a bit on landing, but—

Shrieking, leaping, out of the cool night gloom, the first of the Huldu came at him like some deranged hybrid of man and stooping bird of prey. He saw a falling flash of pale flesh, iridescent cloak-like wings, then the creature pounced and knocked him to the ground. The McCulloch went flying. He rolled desperately, saw a long-armed set of talons lash at him as he moved. Thought they missed. He braced hard with one hand, tried to rise, the pack a dragging weight at his shoulders. The Huldu cannoned into him before he made it halfway.

"Duncan Silver!" the fanged mouth spat out the name like a curse. "We come for *you*!"

He rammed a forearm up at the Huldu's throat, punched hard into its ribs with his other fist. The iron rings did their magic, the greenish-white flash, and the Huldu snarled in pain, but it didn't give up its grip. That was bad. Fucking hard bastard here. The fangs dipped in. Duncan did the only thing possible, hunched and headbutted into the attack. He felt a canine tear his scalp. He bridged up hard with his whole body, tried to tip his attacker off—

Boom of Garner's over-and-under, like thunder right in his ear.

Blinding magnesium flash-flare, a scream, and abruptly, the Huldu's grip was gone. It thrashed briefly atop him, like some massive pallid fish in a net, then keeled over. Duncan got a knee up and in, shoved the dead weight of the body off.

Saw Garner's face hovering over him.

"Sorry," the older man gasped. "Had to get in close, didn't want to pepper thee. Here."

He put out a hand, hauled Duncan up with a surprisingly solid grip. Broke the Woodward and ejected both shells, reloaded with shaky haste. Duncan caught his breath, stared wildly around, cast out his senses into the darkness.

Nothing.

Nothing yet . . .

"Don't stand there bloody gawping!" Garner huffed at him. He closed up the breech of the over-and-under with trembling fingers. "Go get thy gun."

"Hold your horses, old man. We've got some time yet."

Garner glared at him. "How's that?"

"This is an outrider you shot. The rest are still a good ways back."

The dying Huldu twitched at their feet, bled black into the Forest soil. In decent light, the blood would be a rich crimson shading into blue, and you could watch it give off a faint tinseled fuming, like the tiny stars you saw if you got hit too hard in the head. If you got close, it smelled like cardamom and summer rain. Duncan caught a whiff, from sheer quantity alone; Garner looked to have rammed the Woodward into the creature's side just above the hip and given it both barrels. Massive damage, faint blue-green fire still burning around the wound, eating into the flesh. No Fae, not even warrior caste, was coming back from that.

The gleaming cloak lay tangled off to one side like a comet trail from the Huldu's neck, or a strangling cloth in shattered rainbow colors. The kaleidoscope glimmer was already dulling out in sympathetic echo of the congealing light in the creature's eyes.

"Outrider?" Garner repeated, like he didn't dare believe it.

Duncan nodded, prodded the smoldering body with his boot. "Advance scout, looks like. They sent this one out to force our pace. Wind us. Maybe take us down, if it thought it could."

"Well, I guess it thought it could." Garner gestured at him. "Tha're bleeding, by the way."

Alerted, he felt the warm wet strip of blood down the temple from his scalp, where the Huldu's canine had gashed him. He found the wound—it stung a little—pressed it and found it shallow. He wiped the blood off his brow.

"It's nothing," he said, and went to pick up the McCulloch. He racked out an unfired shell to check the action, then fed it back into the receiver. He'd never had the trench gun jam on him before, no matter the bangs it took, but it wouldn't do to get complacent now.

"Right then," he said. "You bought us a couple of minutes. Let's get in the fucking house!"

THIRTEEN

THE HAUGHTON PLACE.

They reached it on the run, panting again—farmhouse, outbuildings, big, high-roofed barn, all sunk in under-ocean silence and gloom, crosshatched pale and black in what little moonlight there was. Scattered silver birch trunks in the surrounding woodland, caught in the corner of the eye, gave the unnerving impression of a pallid siege army, watching and waiting. The two men circled warily in through the trees, scanned the dark, abandoned structures for threat or signs of life.

Creeper and climbing plants had long since swarmed the farmhouse walls, grown like cataract across the windows that still held glass, thrust eagerly in through the frames that did not, then gripped and tangled on upward toward a sagging roof with problems of its own. Less than a sense of siege, it gave the two-story structure a softened look in the moonlight and murk, as if it was melting slowly into the Forest floor. The clearing the farm stood in was thick with grass and saplings, rising higher in some places than the low drystack walling that delineated the yard. A gateless gateway gave access. They found the farmhouse door, moss-grown, cracked and rotted, flat in the middle of the yard like a murdered body. At some point, something had torn it off its hinges and tossed it contemptuously away.

Adjacent to the farmyard, the long, low outbuilding had been shattered by the eruption of a massive yew tree through one end. What roofing had not been smashed aside by the emergence of the tree had later collapsed inward, dumped its tiles and joists across the interior, and taken some of the supporting walls down with it. The resulting space was ragged and exposed, far too open for two men to hold against numbers. Taller, more intact, the barn stood a little farther off, but much of the roof looked to have fallen in there as well, and the doors were gone, leaving a wide-open gape too broad and high to usefully defend.

The house itself, then.

Duncan moved cautiously up to the empty doorway, peered inside. Saw a derelict kitchen space within, an earthen tile floor, cracked and cratered as if by repeated violent blows. Up through the cracks, the Forest was already sprouting its early assaults in sprigs of green and flowering yellow. Over in one corner near a slumped and shattered porcelain sink, a decent-sized bristling of bushes had gotten a hold. Elsewhere, wooden kitchen furniture—table and chairs, Welsh dresser, sideboard—was scattered about, tumbled or upended, yielding to moss and rot just like the door in the yard. A single window over the fallen sink still had glass, was overgrown with vines. Hard to come through in a hurry, and the casements looked to be iron. On the other side of the room, doors ajar led off into other rooms, two of them, where the gloom descended into near total darkness. Duncan grimaced. Not ideal, but—

Long, floating howl from out among the trees. It sounded close.

He wondered if they'd found their fallen comrade.

"Right, this'll have to do." Stepping fully into the kitchen, scoping it with a fire trench commander's eye. "That dresser. Quick! Help me get it across the door here."

They dumped off their packs, dragged the massy chunk of carpentry screeching over the cracked tile floor, rammed it side-on across the doorway. It formed a fairly serviceable parapet. Duncan knelt behind it experimentally, glanced up and saw the upper hinge of the kitchen door was still in place, hanging like a stiffened iron pennant from the frame. He grinned and worked the rusted hinges until it jabbed slightly outward into the night air. Might dissuade any overly enthusiastic warrior caste from trying to leap the dresser top.

They checked the interior doors. One led into a low-beamed sitting room, overfilled with heavy dark wood furniture, hosting a broad brick chimney breast, a fireplace you could stand in, and a staircase to the upper level. The other door opened onto some kind of larder, shelves long denuded of all but a few forlorn rows of canned goods, no window beyond a tight iron grate set high up in the wall.

"This one we don't need to close," Duncan decided. "Let's get that table jammed against the other door, pile the chairs on top and behind."

"This going to be enough to keep them out?" wheezed Garner as they hauled the table. "What if they try to ram it open from the other side?"

"Then we tickle them through the door with small grape until they fucking stop. I can hold the main doorway alone while you do that, if it comes to it."

They rammed the table the last couple of hard inches in under the handle, pinned the door closed. They went about gathering the chairs, piled them on the tabletop to add weight. Then they stood back and looked at the resulting blockade in silence. Duncan grunted in satisfaction.

"Ought to hold up well enough. Short of smashing through from the floor above, which I don't think they'll come equipped to do, their only way in now is the kitchen door there. And that's fifty feet of open ground we can turn into a killing field." He clapped Garner on the shoulder. "You know what—a bit of luck and a following wind, we might live out the night."

FOR A WHILE, IT GOT very quiet in the darkened kitchen.

Garner leaned against the edge of the table with the Woodward over-and-under grounded butt-down between his spread feet, hands clasped on the barrel. With his head bowed in the gloom, he looked like some somber memorial statue of a sentry on eternal guard. Duncan sat on the floor across the room from him, back to the wall, knees up. He rested the McCulloch sideways across his lap. The cracked tiles were hard on his arse, but he'd learned long ago that you take your ease as and when you can; no telling when and for how long you'll be back up and on your feet for the fight.

The silence hung between the two of them like an early morning mist waiting on the sunrise. Duncan let his eyes defocus, ran the preparations they'd made in his head, just in case they'd missed something. A soft sigh eased out of him. His mind bounced around in a state of mild arousal: Niamh in the sheets of his no longer lonely bed; movie-star looker Irene Rush mourning in her flimsy nightgown by the window; Wolfbane Sal Bethune and her raucous, unapologetic aura of sex. Damp moss for a bed and the eldritch, twiggy fingered weave of the tree spirit as she descended upon him . . .

Jesus, Duncan! Give it a rest! Not like you didn't get laid yesterday, is it—

"That Fae I killed in the woods back there." Garner's voice came mild enough, but Duncan felt the other man's gaze on him. "It called thee by name."

"You heard that?" Trying not to sound evasive.

"And . . . it said *we're coming for you*? Something like that?"

Duncan sighed. "Close enough, aye."

"So, lad. Tha've been making friends in t' Forest tha dinner tell me about? Want to tell me what we've got ourselves into here? Tha knew this was going to happen all along?"

"You keep saying that," Duncan snapped. "What am I, a fucking witch? You think I have the Sight? You really think I would have walked us both slap into this barnyard bollocks if I . . ."

Voice suddenly robbed of all force, fading out as he said the words . . .

Wolfbane Sally, her scented oils and candles and spells. Her widdershins walk. *All good stuff for a barnyard squabble.*

Somehow, she'd seen this—*and prepped him for it.*

Garner picked up the broken thread of the conversation, voice still low. "All as I'm saying is, tha don't seem very shocked by any of this."

"Shock won't help." He said it automatically, an old truth from the trenches. "Shock'll just get you killed."

"Is that right?"

"From my exp—"

Somewhere overhead in the abandoned house, timbers creaked.

Garner's head tilted up a fraction. "Hear that?"

Duncan nodded. They listened, eyes raised to the ceiling above. The sound was not repeated. Garner swallowed audibly.

"Old beams," he whispered. "This place has—"

He saw Duncan's eyes widen. Jammed to a halt.

Duncan lifted one hand, pointed in utter silence. Garner looked behind him.

The handle to the door they'd blocked with the table. Turning stealthily, left, then right . . .

It was all the warning they were going to get.

Duncan, up on his feet, stabbing with his finger, nodding, a snatching fist gesture—Garner spinning to point the Woodward's barrels at the door, close by the handle—

The over-and-under bellowed—wood splintered apart, leapt from the cheap paneling in bits. Beyond the door, something shrilled in shock and pain.

Duncan grinned at the sound—was already turning away to the dresser barricade—

Two Huldu, swarming over the dresser, fangs bared, awful, blank black-pupil stares . . .

The noises they made as they saw him . . .

He swung the trench gun up, grin still gripping his face—

The canny Glaswegian engineers at McCulloch & Ross were, on their own admission, great admirers of Winchester and Remington, and had digested all the two American firms had to offer on the subject of wartime weaponry. As with the shotguns that carried those two names, the McCulloch Trench Tactical gave you the option to simply hold down the trigger and pump until the gun ran dry.

The Americans called it slamfire.

Duncan clamped the trigger, slamfired three shells, the old accustomed rhythm, point-blank range. The reports blended almost into one.

The two Huldu fell back off the barricade in shrieking ruin.

Bang and splinter of Garner's second barrel, fired again into the door. Another howl. Something hit the floor on the other side with a thump. Duncan spared a side glance across to cover the other man if he needed it. Saw Garner break the Woodward, handily hook out the spent shells with farm-calloused fingertips, drop them smoking to the floor—fresh load slammed in, the gun snapped up closed, a curt nod. Duncan nodded back, went back to watching the barricade. He thought he heard one of the Huldu he'd hit crawling about in the dirt outside, moaning weakly. No words, in Skogurtal or any other tongue he knew; he guessed the owner of the voice was bleeding out.

"How many'd tha get?" Garner hissed, into smoldering quiet.

Duncan held up two fingers.

The other man nodded at the blocked-up door behind him. "And mine's down for sure. Three. That's a bloody good start."

"It's a bloody nose, at least." Almost absently, Duncan fed three new shells into the McCulloch—actions automatic now, all one with the odor of cordite around him, his thudding combat pulse. "Now we find out how upset they really are about their cair—"

Faint scrabble of talons overhead, rustle of foliage. The two men stared at each other.

"They're on't bloody roof," snapped Garner.

"Get ready! This is it!"

Duncan raised up to peer over the parapet they'd made with the dresser. The two dead Huldu crumpled in the dirt, one still twitching. And across the space beyond, over the drystone wall and into the yard came the next wave; he counted at least six as they leapt the wall. He grabbed a Kegg bomb from where he'd set them out in a little pile. Yanked the cord with his teeth—sudden, soft swooping, pale bodies through the air from above—he'd already tossed the bomb . . .

Two more Huldu, almost in the doorway—they'd hung and dropped from the roof—landed at touching distance. The Kegg bomb bounced off one of them, fell back into the room.

"Shit!"

No time to grab it again. He settled for a desperate sweeping kick, sent it flying, right across the room to the larder door. "Loose bomb! Cover!"

He just had time to see Garner huddle by the table, one hand up to shield his face. Then a long-taloned arm lashed inward over the dresser, grabbed him awkwardly at the shoulder—he guessed the Huldu had been aiming for his throat. He felt the claws go down through his coat, shirt, the skin beneath, sudden searing pain in furrows—

The Kegg bomb blew.

Sludgy *thump/bang*, like furniture being moved badly. Sandy blast of the iron filings across the room. His ears picked up the shockwave; it wasn't too bad. He'd already slitted his eyes shut, got no worse than surface sting. But even through his closed lids, he saw the pinprick flare as filings hit Huldu flesh. The Fae shrieked, let go his shoulder.

Duncan swung away, skittered back on the broken tile floor on his arse, dusty smolder in the air, pointed the McCulloch not quite blind, and fired. The Huldu who'd had him reeled back, fell from view. He lurched to his feet, pumped the action, made out a second figure, fired again. He hit something that screamed.

"Garner!" Pumping in a third shell, ears still ringing.

"I'm alreet, lad!" The deep bellow of the Woodward—another shriek from outside. "Get up here!"

Duncan scooped up another Kegg bomb left-handed, tore the stalk out with his teeth, hurled the bomb out into the night on not much more than instinct. He leaned into the barricade beside Garner, saw the advancing phalanx of Huldu freeze and turn as the bomb hit the yard in their midst. One of them even reached out—

At distance and out in the open air, the crump as the Fae-fucker exploded was mild and unwarlike. Nothing like the hard metallic *whang!* you'd get from a Mills bomb.

But the impact on the Huldu was something to see.

Those closest to the bomb as it detonated were wrapped in instantaneous bluish-green flame that seemed to stick to them as it burned. They staggered, screaming, clawing at their own eyes, limbs, torsos, wherever the iron filing scourge had hit. Those farther out yelped and beat at the smaller patches of flame where they'd been touched. The one or two who'd escaped harm froze a fatal moment, staring at their comrades. Garner's over-and-under boomed again and one of them jerked backward, fell scrabbling at its own guts.

Snap/clunk of Garner breaking his gun.

"Reloading, lad!" he yelled superfluously.

Duncan was already firing—spaced shots, aimed as calmly as he could. The shorter barrel on the McCulloch meant he had less range than Garner, but in the killing field they'd created it made little difference. He put down three more Huldu in five shots.

The rest scattered and fled. Or slumped over and collapsed in the farmyard, shrilling weakly as the blue-green fire ate them to death. Garner, reloaded, chased the few survivors with a final, booming shot from the Woodward. Duncan, slamming fresh shells into his own gun, stared out at the mess they'd made, realized suddenly that he was laughing out loud, harsh and hard as some shell-shocked maniac in the aftermath of German guns . . .

"Two fucking lunatics, was it?" Burbling wildly, waving a hand at the still-burning bodies of the Fae, grin like a razor slash across his face. "Crumley and Kegg? *Hah!* Toys, was it? Fucking *toys*? Look at that, Garner! Just *look at it*!" Grabbing the other man by the shoulder, shaking him. "Know what that is? Combat science! You're looking at *the fucking future there, old man*!"

Something in his own voice, the tone, like the creaking of an overloaded cable about to give way.

As abruptly as he'd realized he was laughing, he snapped his jaw shut. He let go of Garner's shoulder. Cleared his throat.

"I mean." Blinking back sudden tears—rage, joy, something else, he couldn't tell. He coughed, made a noise, midway between a stifled snigger and a sob. "I'd say the Kegg bomb lived up to its name, wouldn't you?"

Garner was still staring at him, as if he was speaking in a foreign tongue, as if nothing he said made any sense.

Ah. He realized he hadn't told the other man Kegg's original name for the new weapon.

He chuckled again, more dryly now. Cleared his throat again. "See, Kegg's first idea for a—"

"Duncan. Duncan, listen to me. Snap out of it!" Garner, pressing a hand urgently on *his* shoulder this time. "Tha're not well, lad. Tha're in shock—"

"Oh, shock won't help. Shock'll just get you—"

"Killed. Aye, tha said that already."

"Never a truer word." Duncan felt a slow, graveled sliding off in his good humor, the beginnings of the postcombat drop. He drew a deep breath, held it for a moment. Let it slowly go. For the first time since it happened, he registered the sting and throb in his shoulder, where the Huldu had clawed him.

"Aye, sorry." Wiping at his eyes with the cuff of his coat. "Got a wee bit carried away there. Won't happen again."

"Duncan—"

"I'm not in shock. God's honest truth. I'm just . . ."

He looked out at the still smoldering corpses, the few faint remains of life and motion in the bodies. Impossible to explain to the other man. He lied instead.

"Look, Garner, you live through summer on the Somme, there's not much left that shocks you. This?" He gestured around—the cordite-reeking kitchen, the smoldering dead, the whole rotting farmstead and the Forest that had drowned it. "This is manageable."

"Hoy, Treefuckahhh!"

It came out of the night like a lone artillery shell falling, a cry driven hoarse, a weight of rage and longing that dripped off every syllable as it smashed into the shadowed room. Even Garner, with no reason to recognize the voice, flinched visibly at the sound. For Duncan, it hit deeper than the shock he'd just told the other man he was numb to.

Instantly, he was back in the spring evening cool of Kettley Cross.

The same voice, the same amiable menace, now tightened and ratcheted into something worse. He saw the Huldu noble amble toward him again, fanged mouth grinning, one taloned hand reaching . . .

I don't think you realize who I am.

"Do you *hear* me, Duncan? Did you think we were *done*?"

"This another friend of yours?" Garner glancing at him in the gloom. "Lad, are there any Fae in this forest tha're *not* on first-name terms with?"

"Aye, very fucking funny. Keep your head down, let me handle this. Let's just hope he didn't bring archers."

Duncan edged up to the dresser, risked a quick glance over and out into the farmyard. No movement there but the smoke off the bodies. The trunks of trees beyond loomed in the darkness like some massed audience gathered for a blood rite.

"Do you *hear* me, Duncan?"

"It'd be hard not to, you Fae fuck," he yelled back, straining the ornate strictures of Skogurtal for the most vulgar registers it could manage. "You want to stop screeching the Forest down like a tree creep and get on with it? Send some more of your useless tongue-to-arse sycophants to die with the iron while you cower to the rear and fondle yourself and watch? Happy to help out with that!"

The silence that followed was like a bomb in its own right. The

Forest seemed to stagger with it, like some pub tough hit with an unexpected left jab.

"You . . ." The same rage, but reaching now, knocked back. *"You are in our world now!"*

Involuntarily, Duncan's upper lip peeled back off his teeth.

"Yes, and here we've already handed you your own guts!" he called. "What will we do to you next, you tree skulkers, you fucking *pixies*? Tell me—can the gathered host of Faerie do *anything* except sneak and steal children too small to fight back? Can you meet on an even field of battle with even *one* of us—"

Voice draining abruptly out on the last syllable he uttered . . .

The sudden idea—the understanding of what he was about to do, what he might earn, what it might cost—leaping fully formed into his head like a vision.

He stood up at the barricade, all fear of archers fled in the drain-swirl force of his realization that *this* was what the witch had seen, *this* what she had prepped him for, *this* the answer to his pleas, *this* the path. Faint, numb delight through his whole body, a kind of taking leave. It was as if a small, cold voice dictated the words into his ear, and all he need do was spit them out, assume the role.

"Face me, you Waste of Blood and Root and Age! *Face me!*"

It was an antique insult to honor, deeply formalized, one from the Huldu annals, taking in denigration of family, lineage, rank, and prowess. Duncan raised his voice again, paced and pitched his words for the whole Forest to hear, roared out the challenge.

"Blades and bodies, if you dare! You think I need the speaking iron to take *you* down? *Blades and bodies! Come on out to play, you nameless fuck!*"

FOURTEEN

GARNER GAPING AT HIM FROM THE SIDE—DUNCAN WAS ONLY vaguely aware of the man's presence now. His gaze and whole focus was hooked on the tree line beyond the drystone wall. His pulse, once ebbing from its combat high, built back once again to a slow, steady pounding . . .

And out of the trees they came.

From the formality of it, he knew the fight was on. Two Huldu, emerging from the darkness like wan candle flames in still air, taking up flanking station at the gaping gateway to the farmyard. Farther back, he saw more figures gathering, perhaps a dozen, a dozen and a half, hard to tell. Some could have been the trunks of the silver birches they'd passed among on their approach to the farm.

A crowd, however you looked at it. An audience. Witnesses to the challenge.

"Here we fucking go," he heard himself mutter.

"What the bloody hell are tha doing, lad?"

He drew a deep breath in over teeth set tight. "Getting somewhere, looks like. You stay in here, Garner. You need to sit this one out."

"Tha conner mean to—"

"You'll be fine." Getting fully to his feet now, showing himself above the dresser barricade, fears fading out to make way for something more insistent. "That's a noble-blood Huldu I just called out. I'm going to set terms for this. Safe passage for you, whatever happens. They won't touch you."

"That's not what I meant!"

He turned to look at the other man. Aware he was grinning now, in a way that probably just confirmed to Garner that he'd gone barking mad. He tried for calm, could not suppress a bubbling black hilarity beneath it all.

"It's fine, old man. It's destiny. A witch saw this coming."

Into the space between the first two Huldu, he saw a third figure step out. Bigger, taller than the others, richly cloaked, but something not quite upright or symmetrical in the way he moved. Duncan felt his grin tighten into something more feral as he saw it. Hot leap of joy in the pit of his stomach. The small grape's iron had done its work, left lasting harm. The Huldu had healed badly. The fight was already tilted, however infinitesimally, Duncan's way.

"Stay put," he told Garner one more time, eyes fixed on his opponent.

Then he took the McCulloch one-handed by the barrel, swung his legs over the barricade, and dropped both booted feet to the ground on the other side. He slung the trench gun casually in the crook of his arm and walked out to meet the Fae.

They saw him coming. He saw them bare their fangs. Felt his own lips peel back from his teeth in response.

He stopped, about ten yards off. The Huldu noble tilted his head, wolflike, as if listening to some sound beyond the range of human ears. His eyeballs were featureless pitch, not enough light to put even a gleam on their surface. Duncan made himself meet the blank stare. As if he were facing no more than the next flat-capped Erlsley street thug.

The fanged mouth opened. The longing, musical voice floated on the night air. "Oh, Duncannnnnn. You should rejoice. Your dishonor ends tonight. Your return to the Gray is at hand."

"At *your* hand?" Duncan forced a chuckle, licked the lips of his grin. "It'll take more than a nameless tree pixie like you to put me in the ground."

He saw the pitch-black eyes narrow, saw the outraged pride. Stomped on any response before the Huldu could utter it.

"Terms," he said, slipping into the ornate utterances of the challenge. "I am Duncan of Stac Dubh, I bring blade and body only to the glade. Before the eyes of the Forest, the roots of life, I offer myself. But my companion walks free."

"He has until sunrise," snapped the Huldu. "This is the word of Stordalen, line of Drasundva, ordained of the Final Isles. Lay down the speaking iron, face me, and it will be honored."

For just a beat, Duncan felt the slither in his gut, the shock and jolt of a missed step.

I don't think you realize who I am.

It had always been a safe bet the Huldu was noble born. Duncan knew it in his bones at the time. Wolfbane Sal had confirmed it when he told her the tale.

But the Final Isles . . .

He masked his sudden disquiet. There was opportunity here as well.

"That's not all," he said.

"Not. All?" The Huldu showed the tips of his fangs in a smile that was almost friendly. "You mistake yourself, ingrate. Do you think your mud-puddle human rank, your pitiful, limping line of cattle-rustling ancestors camped out in a pile of hacked stone less than a hundred years old, entitles you to face *me* as an equal? *Did you not hear who I am?*"

Duncan let it sit for a moment. Saw the Fae faces on either side of Stordalen grow avid with anticipation.

"This is not the Final Isles," he said evenly. "And I claim no rank here, human or otherwise. I did not need rank to cripple you this spring past; I will not need it now to send you back to the Gray. And if I do this, these are my terms—I best you here, your word and bond will release to me the human child Miriam, taken by Mebhuranon."

As if the whole Forest abruptly held its breath.

They stared at each other, human and Fae. Duncan tried to staunch the sensation that he was falling into the Huldu's eyes, the effervescing panic that came with it.

"That is not within my gift." Stordalen, matching him for even tone, for all that it visibly cost him to keep his cool. "Mebhuranon . . . walks her own path."

"Really? You came quick enough when her cairn was defiled."

"That—you—it was a *desecration*!" Fanged mouth biting down on the word.

Duncan grinned. "It was a message. I want the child back. If you don't want the Forest on fire from here to the Final Isles, you'll give her to me."

Stordalen, hissing now. "I *said*, it is not within my *gift*!"

"Then what are you good for?" Feeling the antique rhythms and depth in the Skogurtal phrasing, the way it piled cadence on cadence like the incantations it so often served to enable. He had, he remembered, spoken it insanely well for a human. "What are you, Stordalen of the line of Drasundva? Some useless misadventure by-blow of vatnalfr dalliances? Some swamp-end bastard? The word of the Final Isles is the law. So say the stones at Dun Ringil and at Dartmoor, at Estelanon and Erl. Will Mebhuranon not obey the law?"

And then he heard it—the rustling whisper of commentary among the Fae at Stordalen's back. The curious, bright speculative word let loose.

Stordalen heard it, too.

"You do not command us, ingrate!" he snapped. "You will not speak to a scion of the Final Isles this way!"

Duncan shrugged. Shifted his hold on the McCulloch. "Then I go back into the house there, and we see how many of your kind the speaking iron will converse with tonight. You can watch from the rear."

He made as if to turn and go, saw Stordalen's mouth open, the bite reflex triggered. Held in check. He waited.

"Your terms are irrelevant!" the Huldu snarled. "You will die by my hand, here, tonight!"

"Then you'll have nothing to lose by granting the price."

Another long pause. The Fae were silent, but Duncan saw the glances run between them, like the scurry of rats through undergrowth. He smiled at Stordalen. They both knew.

"Bring me the *saemdil* blade," Stordalen said softly. "This ingrate mortal has breathed Forest air too long."

THE SAEMDIL BLADE. THE DUEL-FOR-HONOR knife.

He'd seen one maybe a dozen times in his life; seen it in action twice. The Huldu had little use for bladed weapons when their own physical strength and shape-shifting capabilities provided all the close combat tools they were ever likely to need. Observing humans over the millennia, they had, of course, seen innovation in armament as in all other things, could probably have copied much of it if they chose. Instead, save for the arrows, they shunned the changes it implied. To the immortal mind, the timescales human invention happened on looked headlong, reckless, probably best avoided. Fae society was intensely clannish, self-referential, hierarchy bound. Tradition was honor, change disruptive, the deep-rooted Forest all. When rising human technology turned on the trees, burned them back, chopped them down, turned them into objects of deadwood at the thousand-fold level, existing misgivings were only reinforced. This could not be the way. A deep melancholy seeped into the Faerie consciousness—a possessive, defensive, seeping rage. But nothing much else changed.

Or so he'd been told.

A young Huldu male brought the weapon forward, held reverently on both palms like an offering. Over a foot long from its jeweled pommel to the point, the blade glinted bluish in the low light. Its surface was puddled and uneven, as if it had once been subjected to great heat and melted a little. More than any metal, it resembled some kind of smoky glass. Thin white runes were scratched in it along both sides of the runnel, in no script Duncan had ever learned how to read.

Stordalen took the weapon by the hilt, lifted it, hefted it handily back and forth a few times in the quiet gloom. It made a subdued whoop on each stroke, seemed to leave bluish lines in its wake, as if somehow slicing into the air itself.

"Your terms are met," he said, distantly now, eyes seemingly fascinated by the puddled glimmer of the blade. "Set down the speaking iron, show us your weapons. Prepare yourself, ingrate, for the death you earned long years ago."

For the flicker of an instant, the last words put a ripple on Duncan's pulse-pounding calm, a faint shiver of doubt. *Long years ago?*

He shook it off. Skinned the Huldu noble a grin, laid the McCulloch on the ground. He shouldered his way out of his coat, laid that beside the gun; it was only going to slow him down. Caress of cool night air through the loose shirt he wore beneath. The trench knife was shoved unsheathed into his belt, the Slaven family sgian dubh thrust into the top of his right boot. He knelt and pulled the ancestral weapon, took it in a blade-down grip. For one poignant breath, he remembered the moment his father handed it to him, the day he left for the Channel and a troop transport across to the front. He thrust the memory down, no time for that now, slipped the fingers of his left hand into the guard loops of the trench knife, and pulled the weapon free. He faced Stordalen, poignard and rapier style, like some musketeer hero out of a Dumas tale.

He jerked his chin at the Fae. "Come ahead! Let's see what you've got, *pixie*!"

Stordalen drew in breath, an eerie moan. At its peak, abruptly, he leapt forward, fangs bared, screaming, slashing right to left with the saemdil blade.

"For the Final Isles!"

Duncan flinched back. He knew better than to try and match the Huldu's speed this early in the duel. The Fae were mercurial, quick to anger, cobra swift. No weakness there at all.

But—

They were instinctively flamboyant, too. The blade came flailing back, blue glint, the slash reversed. Predictable. Flinch back again, then dodge the reach of the blade again and *there*—Stordalen, frustrated, off balance, raising the knife now on high—Duncan kicked out, hard. Stomped full force, into the Huldu's left thigh.

His opponent staggered, snarling, lost the stroke. Came straight back in, but clumsy this time, the saemdil knife chopping downward. Duncan threw up his left arm to block, met the Huldu's arm with a force that stung his own forearm, drove back the blow. In close, he hooked with the sgian dubh, tried for the eyes. Stordalen threw a lightning block of his own, snagged Duncan's right hand at the wrist, twisted the blow away. They locked up—trial of strength the human had no way to win. Duncan leaned harder into the clinch for a beat, then yanked his arm abruptly back, the way Stordalen wanted it to go. The Huldu stumbled with the sudden give, side of the face offered. Duncan set his neck, headbutted Stordalen full force in the temple and cheek.

Stordalen yelped, flung the human bodily away from him. Duncan flew back with the force of it, barely stayed on his feet.

Stordalen swayed a moment, shook his head groggily.

"Had enough?" Duncan spat. "Not up to much, these Fae from the Final Isles, are you?"

The taunt was calculated, tribal, in front of witnesses. It could not go unanswered. Snake-strike swift, Stordalen rushed him.

Far too fast for another kick—Duncan blocked low with his arm, was slow. The saemdil blade got partway past, licked his ribs. Hot line of fire, sudden seep of blood. Aye, well, fucking live with it—the sgian dubh hooked in again, gouged a thin line across Stordalen's chest. Where the steel touched flesh, it smoked and flared like a lit fuse. The Huldu howled, twisted away—Duncan came up from the block with the trench knife, sliced his opponent across the right arm with a jubilant yell. More dazzling fuse-burn flare, more smoke and smolder. Stordalen screamed and whipped his arm free, was turned almost side-on now. Duncan yelled again, stomped for the nearest knee.

He felt it connect, heard Stordalen grunt with the pain. On a human, the joint would likely have popped, but the Fae were simply better built. Stordalen staggered, did not go down—

Fuck!

—lashed clumsily sideways at the human instead. This time, getting out of the way was easy. Duncan kicked out again as Stordalen went stumbling past, put a boot into the Huldu's arse, knocked him forward almost to falling. Not much force to it, there wasn't time, but the ignominy must have burned deeper than the iron cuts Duncan had already inflicted.

Stordalen swung about, face distorted with fury, involuntary scraps of shape-shift, bone deep transformative instincts boiling up, urge to remold features, fangs, the mouth gaping wider, teeth sharpening, lengthening past anything that could ever pretend to be human—

Duncan rallied, panting. Raised both arms to guard.

"Come on!" he screamed.

The Huldu lunged—as fast as anything Stordalen had so far done, but it was wild with rage, erratic, prone to ill luck and maybe, just maybe, a certain ribald witch's thumb in the balance . . .

Duncan flinched into the block, slipped sideways, chest into the move, solid body blow. Slam down with his arm, keep the blade at bay. He felt the tip of the saemdil knife skip across his ribs again—

Ignored it again—

Hook slashed again with the sgian dubh, this time head height.

The blow landed lucky, opened a wide, coruscating wound across the Huldu's forehead, spilled fragrant blood in a curtain down Stordalen's face. Blinded him. But Duncan was not done. His elbow scythed in behind the knife, hard into Stordalen's temple. Some shit still going on with that saemdil blade—all artifice and elegance lost, the enraged Huldu shrilling, trying to batter the weapon up through Duncan's block with gravity against him . . .

And Duncan went to work with the sgian dubh.

Into neck, and throat, and throat, and chest, and belly, and belly, and chest—a savage, indiscriminate volley of blows, machine gun speed, each stab and twist a detonation of greenish fire and roiling smoke and fresh shrieks from the Fae as it hit. It was butchery, sheer thuggish desperation given flesh, the hand-to-hand trench savagery of France and Flanders. A tight fury that Stordalen could not, in his languid centuries of life, have known, could not begin to understand.

For the Huldu, the duel was ritual and form, courage and honor, a working demonstration of thousand-year-warrior origins and lineage, a cold, structured mastery of weapons and will before peers and witness.

In the chaotic confines and press of one overrun trench after another at the Somme, Duncan had learned a different warrior's lesson.

Close in, close down, swarm and batter, hurt and damage, until there is no more damage to be done. Field-gray uniformed bodies prone and prostrate at your feet, begging or dead. You don't stop, you don't measure, you don't listen, or feel, or care, you don't *stop.*

You take that trench.

Eye to eye with Stordalen, he tore smoldering ruin into the Fae's flesh with the sgian dubh, felt the Huldu weaken and the saemdil blade fall away. He loosened his blocking arm, smashed upward with the spiked knuckle-duster guard of the trench knife, hit Stordalen under the jaw, sent him crashing to the ground.

Dropped and straddled him.

Slashed his throat open with the trench knife, so deep he felt the edge of the blade catch on the spine.

Threw back his head and howled at the watching trees.

NOT DONE YET, DUNCAN.

The flare from the wound in Stordalen's throat had Duncan part blinded; blotchy patches of green swam across his vision. He tried to blink it out of his eyes, made out horrified Fae faces staring at him from the margins of the arena. His shirt was plastered to his left side—blood seep from the wounds across his ribs. He grimaced, suddenly aware of the damage and the cold night air on his opened flesh. Stealthy trickle, all the way down into his waistband—it didn't feel too bad, but it'd need looked at.

Later.

He pegged the sgian dubh in the dirt at the dead Huldu's shoulder, got stiffly off the body. He swapped the trench knife to his right hand, raised it high, brought it down hard into the rib cage. Flare of fire at the wound, but more muted now in the dying flesh. He sawed downward hard, felt ribs shearing and snapping apart before the blade like the bones on a malnourished chicken.

He reached into the wound he'd made, wrenched the severed ribs upward in the wound with his free hand. Reached deeper inside.

Seized the still-warm heart, dragged it out in his fist.

Pipes and all manner of clinging tissue like bloodied muslin came with it. He sliced it all impatiently away, eyes slitted against the glare it made.

Crammed the heart into his mouth and bit down.

They say Arthur managed it once—

Tough and knotty under slick, he had to dig in his nails to hold it. Warm blood sliding past the chunk in his teeth, down his throat. He tried not to retch, tore a morsel loose . . .

—but then again, he's a myth, and so is that story.

He chewed, over and over, for what seemed like an eternity, while his gorge tried repeatedly to heave itself all the way up his gullet. There was an awful, nameless taste in his mouth, a ringing in his ears. Finally, he swallowed some macerated fragments. Then some more. Gagging a little as muscle strands caught in his throat.

He looked up—saw the Fae still gathered, peering at him like frightened children. A grin plastered itself across his face. He spat out blood and tissue.

"The *fuck* are you looking at?" he roared.

And—in the same instant—felt something *give.*

Intimate, unbalancing—like the crack of a rotten tree root giving underfoot as you step, the little plunge. Like a decayed tooth come finally free of the gum.

And a sudden clearing in his head with the snap, sense of clouds coming loose of the sun behind him and the brightening of everything as they leave . . .

The curse, lifting.

He knew it the same way he knew he had to hold down what he'd consumed. He made a soft noise through gritted teeth, raised the hand with the bitten heart in it.

"Do you see? Do you *see*—what is done?" Words tripping over themselves in their haste to be out of his mouth. "Let the Forest see, come and see, the whole fucking Forest witness this, it's done, tell what's done is done . . ."

The post combat relief, the surge of victory chemicals in his veins, a kind of black hilarity, and whatever the fuck this, the flesh and blood of a Faerie heart, was doing to him—he felt the way he had when they jabbed the morphine into his arm that first time at Delville Wood, as if some arcane warm wind blew right through him, swept his limbs out of existence, the way a brusque sketch artist erases unwanted lines on a parchment page . . .

He grins, beatific, pivoting effortlessly around to take in all their gaping faces in a ring. Somewhere, he thinks he hears Wolfbane Sally's ribald laugh.

"Go!" he bellowed at them. *"Go tell Mebhuranon! I come for the child! I bear the given word of the Final Isles! Who will deny me?"*

One of the taller Huldu peeled lips from fangs, made a half step toward him—

Duncan growled low in his throat, a wolf at bay over its kill. He dropped the mutilated heart to the ground, raised the trench knife like an offer, like a libation. Skinned his teeth in a grin.

The Huldu thought better of it.

"Go!" Surprised at how low his voice was now, how cold and dismissive. "Go and tell what is done!"

He stood over Stordalen's wrecked corpse and stared them down. Watched as, one by one, they turned and walked away, fading into the Forest gloom like lamp flames turned slowly down. He realized he'd been holding his breath, huffed and blew, working to cope. Heard whispers through the trees, looked down at the blood on his hands . . .

A hard hand, grabbing him by the shoulder—

He whipped around, trench knife rising to guard.

Saw Garner gaping at him, not much less horrified than the departed Fae. One hand out, warding. "Whoa, lad! It's me! It's *me*! Put that down!"

Duncan swallowed. Tasted the blood in his mouth. Blinked. He lowered the knife. He'd forgotten Garner was there—forgotten, if he was honest, that Garner even existed. He swayed a little, looked at the trench knife and thought vaguely he'd probably better clean his blades sometime soon. And look at his wounds. And—

He drew a deep breath.

"Listen to me, Garner. There's not much time."

"Lad, tha're bleeding—"

"It doesn't matter. Just listen. You get out of here. Get home. They won't touch you tonight. This dead fuck"—jerking a thumb at the gashed and smoldering ruins of Stordalen—"gave his word, and it's good till dawn. Tomorrow morning, you take the first train to Erlsley—"

"Bloody *Erlsley*?"

"Just fucking *listen,* will you? Erlsley, yes. You go to the Forestry Commission on Albion place. Albion place. There's an ex-Guards colonel there, Martin Hardy. You tell him from me he's right about the new war, and if he wants to strike an early blow, he needs to get some men to Maltby Ferry for midnight tomorrow night. Tell him I'm bringing out a high-value hostage, and I'll likely have half of fucking Fairyland on my heels when I do!"

Garner gaped. "A high-value hostage? Miriam Rush? She's a four-year-old wean! Have you been at the bloody pipe? Tha're talking like a—"

"Garner!" The snap in his voice brought the other man up short. "I don't have the fucking time! Just do it. I'll see you paid, or Niamh will, if I don't make it out."

"It's not the bloody money!" Garner lunged across the small gap between them, grabbed him by both shoulders with bone-crushing force. "It's thee, Duncan. Take a look at thisel, lad! Tha're a bloody mess! Tha'll not bring Miriam Rush home like this. Tha're in no fit state to bring a pork chop home from market. Tha conner go up against Old Meb! She'll eat thee alive!"

Echoes off the shout, departing among the trees.

Garner, perhaps only now aware that he'd actually grabbed Duncan, let go as if the other man was hot. Duncan, wanting only to cackle like a lunatic and lash out, worked up a small, measured smile instead. He looked at the ground.

"Don't worry about me, old man," he said gently. "Just get yourself home safe, and carry that message tomorrow. That's all I ask. I'm not going up against Mcbhuranon. That's not what this is anymore. Whole set of relationships in this fucking Forest just . . . changed. There's not a Huldu in England going to deny me what I want right now."

Garner took a step back from him, perhaps to turn more easily and go for his gear, perhaps . . . not. Something had shifted in his face. It took a moment for Duncan to peg the expression for what it was.

Fear.

Garner went back to the farmhouse, clambered awkwardly over the dresser barricade to get his pack and the Woodward. Duncan looked down at his own gun where it lay on the ground with his coat. For long moments, it seemed to him like an artifact dug up out of the ruins of some other time and civilization, a tool whose use you'd have to guess at. The trees hushed around him, and he felt, distantly, dizzyingly, the wheel of the stars in a sky he mostly couldn't see, high above the canopies that hemmed him in. He teetered a little, almost had to catch himself from falling . . .

"Lad?"

He blinked again. Garner was back, rough and blunt as any human in the whisper and lull of the Forest. Duncan summoned the small smile again.

"Told you, I'm fine. Now get moving. Remember what I said."

"No, lad—listen. Before I go. Tell me the God's honest truth, and tell me right now. Who the bloody blue blazes *are* tha, Duncan? Really."

Duncan stared away past him, into the gloom beneath the trees. Vaguely aware that the small smile was still on his face.

"Who am I?" he said quietly. "I'm the biggest fucking mistake they ever made."

FIFTEEN

He's cold and he doesn't know where he is, and he feels a bit sick because his body's moving too fast for his feet in the dark, and he keeps stumbling over tree roots he can't see properly and the others won't slow down, and more than anything now he just wants to go home.

He knows better by now than to show any of *that.*

"Come *on,*" snaps Drasvinad, shoving him in the back, and so of course he stumbles and falls. "Fucking foot-drag tree-thief little *bitch*! Oh, *now look*! Isnorvi, he's fallen over *again*!"

Face in the leaf-mold dirt, Duncan feels a fresh stab of fear. Drasvinad's horrible to him most of the time, unless she's just ignoring him; he's a tree-thief child after all. But it's Isnorvi he goes in real fear of—Isnorvi of the quick hands and feet and fists, the sudden shifts from amiable contempt to violent fury, like the rains the Forest gets in autumn, from nothing to ominous leaf patter to sudden, drenching downpour in a matter of seconds. Isnorvi, who'll tell Duncan he's his friend, honest, he really likes him, well, as much as you *can* like a tree thief—and in the beginning Duncan used to feel pathetically grateful for that—and then, out of nowhere, Isnorvi will punch him in the stomach, watch him collapse trying to breathe, and laugh in the high, musical tones of the Bright Folk that Duncan tries as hard as he can to copy but somehow never gets right . . .

In the beginning, he cried bitterly each time it happened.

But his tears just seemed to open some kind of door inside Isnorvi to even deeper cruelties, and the rain of blows and kicks would intensify until he was left sobbing and curled around himself at the base of some protective tree until Isnorvi lost interest and wandered off laughing with the others.

And that, truth to tell, hurt even more than the blows.

In the end, he learned not to cry.

"Did you push him, Dras?" Isnorvi has been a good few paces ahead. Duncan hears him coming back. He tenses—it's hard to tell sometimes what's in Isnorvi's voice. "I told you not to do that. You know he can't see in the dark like us."

"Course he can't!" Festinal, joining in with a cackle. He's tagged along, Duncan knows, in hopes of just this kind of pile-on. "He's a fucking tree thief, isn't he? They can't see for shit once they get out of the sun. Don't know why you bother."

That's not *true,* Duncan wants to shout. It's just nighttime when it's hard. It's not his *fault.*

But he stays down, dirt on his face, earthen scent of tree mulch in his nose, palms stinging where he skinned them as he fell.

"Shut up, Festi. You're being unkind." Isnorvi crouches at Duncan's side. "You all right, Dunc? Did Dras push you?"

The softness in his voice almost achieves what the blows no longer can. Duncan feels tears welling up. He sniffs them back, sits up, tries to swipe the dirt off his face.

"I tripped," he says stoically.

Back a long while ago, so faded now in memory he doesn't often think about it anymore, he sought protection and comfort among the adult Huldu. But he got short shrift. The Fae are a dreamy folk, distant in their own schemes, brooding and scary and almost as quick to anger as their offspring when provoked, disinterested anyway, partial always to their own children and not much bothered what happens to a child of tree thieves, however well behaved and desperately eager to please. Even Svalenkari, the one Duncan has been taught he must call Father, turns away his pleas for help.

Without us, you would not have lived, he has told Duncan, often and sternly. *I rescued you as a baby, I gave you all this*—gesturing around at the trees, the rainbow-colored spiderwebbing his people conjured amid branches for shelter—*but you are no baby now. The Forest is your home and you must earn your place in it. You must* belong. *That means you must atone for your ancestors, for what the tree thieves have done, to our Forest and to us.*

I know that, Father. So desperate for approval it ached in him at some root too deeply buried for him to fully understand. *And I will carry the iron for you, like the thralls do, just ask me. I am not afraid. But the others—*

Svalenkari cut him off with an impatient gesture. *The others do as they must. And so must you. Now go. Enough of these endless childish wants and whines, do you think I have nothing else to concern myself with?*

Turning away, leaving, and Duncan stood there with trembling lip and tear-fringed eyes and limbs that felt like wood.

Then—

Listen, Duncan—the sudden, hot upsurge of hope in Duncan's tiny chest as Svalenkari paused, looked back at him, not unkindly. *Here's something. A path you might take. Be grateful. Be thankful the Bright Folk took you in when we did. And think every day how you can pay us back.*

He's been trying ever since.

Despite the way that hot leap of hope turned instantly cold and leaden in his chest as Svalenkari spoke. Still, he clings to the way the Huldu noble looked back at him just that once, and he tries to earn that returning regard every day.

"You tripped?" Drasvinad repeats scornfully. "About all he's good for. Tripping and blundering and breaking things. It's no wonder your people burned the Forest. It was probably an accident the first time they did it! Probably burned themselves as well, they were so clumsy and stupid. Running around on fire screaming, *Oh no, oh no, the flames, they hurt!*"

The others—Festinal and Corri and Stam—fall about laughing, tinkling chimes amid the trees that still, after all these years, raise the hairs on the back of Duncan's neck.

But not Isnorvi. He's not laughing at all.

"That's enough," he snaps, and offers Duncan his hand. "Come on, Dunc. Get up. Not far now. It's your birthday. You're seven today! I promised you a birthday surprise, and I'm not going to let these idiots spoil it."

Looks slip and slither among *these idiots.* Duncan thinks, as he takes Isnorvi's offered hand and is pulled effortlessly back to his feet, that there's still the old Fae cruelty in those looks. But it's mixed with something else, something he can't work out.

And they're not laughing anymore.

"We go on," Isnorvi says crisply. "We have ground to cover. And no more pushing Duncan, or you'll answer to me."

They pick up the trail again, perhaps a little slower now, but still faster than Duncan likes. He hurries along as best he can on his clumsy tree-thief legs. He doesn't want to fall again and risk spoiling Isnorvi's mood. Behind him, muttering and sniggering between the Huldu children, but none of them shove him again. And soon the moon starts to break through the trees overhead, making it easier to see where he's going. He starts to feel a little better.

The moonlight strengthens, from patchy to an almost uninterrupted silvery glow across the ground. Duncan looks around him and realizes the trees are thinning out. They're coming to the fringes of the Forest, and he feels suddenly nervous again.

The Forest is your home. And he's been warned enough times to stay in it, to never risk exposure to whatever lies outside.

They come to a halt on a small knoll with a view down into open meadows below. Beyond the open ground, set against a steep, jagged hill, a big stone house. Duncan looks at it and a sudden, unexplained lump forms in his throat. His nervousness washes back through him, doubled.

"Down there?" he whispers. "We're going down there?"

"You'll be fine." Isnorvi stands at his side. He claps him on the shoulder. "Promise. Just follow me."

They thread their way single file down into the glen, clinging to the copses and short runs of woodland that still stand, crossing open ground in a quivering ecstasy of thrill and terror, crouching low, sprinting flat out. They come on a small herd of dozing cattle with long matted auburn coats of hair and broad-forking, dangerous-looking horns. Isnorvi throws out an arm, makes a ward, and the cattle seem not to notice them as they pass. Only with Duncan's footfalls—he's slipped to the rear again in one of the meadow sprints—one of the larger animals turns its head to face him. The long matted hair falls across its face, makes it seem blind and monstrous, but—

A spasm of memory goes through him like a thorn. Startling, warming. Someone holding him up near the cow's head. He sees his own chubby fist, reaching to grasp the matted hair, he feels—

Happy?

Safe?

Warm sensations he has no reference for, except—

He knows the cows will not harm him.

As if he's rubbed something out of his eyes and sees them clearly now for the first time. The blank fall of shaggy hair across the face no longer monstrous, just comical, patient and kind . . .

He makes a soft, surprised noise in his throat. He chuckles. Surprises himself with the unfamiliar sound.

"Tree thief!" Someone hissing at him.

He blinks, sees Drasvinad gesturing impatiently.

"Move, Duncan! Don't get left behind!"

On through the damp grass, to the next stand of trees, where the others are already waiting. They huddle there in the shadows together, all five of them pressed close under the shelter of the canopies, and for just a moment Duncan has that fleeting sense of belonging Svalenkari has told him to seek.

Then, Isnorvi grabs him by the arm.

"Come on, birthday boy. Let's go!"

He pulls Duncan out onto the meadow, leads him toward a low stone wall. Beyond the wall, the big stone house they saw from the hillside looms like a crag. Isnorvi vaults onto the top of the wall, helps Duncan up after him. Between the house and the wall, there's a broad expanse of the shortest grass Duncan has ever seen in his—

not *ever* . . .

—life. It looks nothing less than magical, like the soft, warm carpets of greenery the Huldu sometimes conjure in clearings for their orgies and ceremonies. But it goes on and on, up to the tall darkened battlements of the house itself, the sparse scattering of lit windows across the stonework. Isnorvi makes a noise that's almost girlish, almost like a giggle. He tugs Duncan down off the wall and onto the grassy expanse.

"Want to see some *humans,* Duncan?"

Humans? Not *really*—

But before he can voice it, Isnorvi is off again, haring across the glamoured grass in zigzags like some demented squirrel, dragging Duncan with him. Duncan struggles to keep up—as much with the idea that *seeing some humans* could be worth all this fuss as with Isnorvi's manic burst of speed. He feels a slow-seeping sense of disappointment, excitement fading, that all his birthday surprise is going to be is peering in at a bunch of clumsy, mucky mortals like the thralls you see shambling about camp . . .

And then they're up to the house, up to one of the lit windows and peering in at the cozy scene on the other side of the glass, at things he'll only later understand. He sees a fireplace as tall as he is, wider than he can hold out his arms, a leaping, dancing fire on heaped-up logs within. High ceiling, a glistening candelabra, soft light from lamps on tables around the room, chairs and sofa colored like the back of nettle leaves . . .

On the sofa, a young woman, cleaner than any thrall he's ever seen, smiling a way no thrall he's ever known has smiled, long dark hair gathered artfully up on her head. She wears a gown that wraps her neck to ankles in deep, voluminous green. He sees her face and her smile, and it's like someone stabbing him in the belly with a saemdil blade. Big, brightly colored book open on her knee. And cuddled up with her, looking with her at the turning pages . . .

A boy.

A boy about his age . . .

—and the boy turns, as if sensing by glamour their presence in the dark beyond the glass—

A boy *exactly* his age—

A boy *with his face*—

Duncan gapes—mouth open to cry out with the shock—

A cool Fae hand, slapped across his mouth, irresistible force, muffling, killing his cry. Isnorvi, dragging him back from the glass and the glow. Isnorvi, laughing delightedly in his ear.

"Know who *that* is, Duncan? That's your mama! The mama we took you from, the mama who *never knew you were gone.* The mama you can *never, ever go back to now,* because the changeling has her heart, *now and forevermore*!

"Happy birthday, Duncan, you tree-thief fuck! Happy fucking birthday!"

And they drag him, kicking and weeping and thrashing, away again into the Forest.

DUNCAN GRIMACED. THIN PAIN AS he dripped iodine along the gashes across his ribs, the claw furrows in his shoulder, finally the fang gash in his scalp. As wounds went, they were nothing much—in the trenches, he'd dressed far worse on himself and others, over and over again—but the iodine stung nonetheless. It always did.

Ideally, he'd get the damage stitched, if he made it home. For now . . .

Stripped to the waist, he murmured a quick and dirty healing charm Sal had gifted him a couple of years ago, hand pressed onto each affected area as she'd taught. The trees whispered around him in the gloom, shook their canopies, as if in recognition of the spell. He took scissors and bandaging gauze from his pack, bound himself up. He tested the dressing, thought it would do, stowed his gear back in his pack. He dressed himself again.

In the quiet beneath the trees, he knelt by Stordalen's mutilated corpse, stared into the dead black pupil-less eyes for what seemed like quite a while.

Who the bloody blue blazes are tha, Duncan? Really.

Garner's parting question, dinging in his head. The old man had left with the cryptic answer Duncan gave him and not another word, turning and slipping away between the sparser trees downslope from the farm, heading for open fields and home. But the look he darted backward as he walked away was filled with the same fear he'd shown when he asked. Whatever he'd seen when he looked at Duncan before tonight, it was irreversibly changed—a portrait on canvas slashed through and torn, a man seen in a mirror that had cracked.

Well, at least he's not here to see this bit.

Duncan took a fistful of Stordalen's luxuriant dark hair in his left hand, took up the trench knife in his right.

Proceeded to hack the Huldu's head loose from its body.

It wasn't easy work, even with the iron blade. The talismanic effect of iron on dead Fae flesh was far less dramatic than its impact on the living. No flash-flare burn, no searing dissolution. Perhaps the tissue gave way somewhat more easily than its mortal equivalent would have, but a spine is still a spine, and it took some sweaty, determined sawing to get through it. It was a while before Duncan could slice away the last retaining flaps of flesh and hold Stordalen's head aloft.

Oddly, he felt no triumph now at all.

Who the bloody blue blazes are tha, Duncan?

He grimaced again.

I'm the biggest fucking mistake they ever made.

Biggest fucking mistake Isnorvi ever made, at least. The wrath of Svalenkari fell on him almost the instant they got back. Duncan was not there to see it—the others had left him curled up and sobbing inconsolably between the roots of an ancient yew tree in the outer encampment—but the beating Isnorvi took lived in legend among the children for years after. The Fae healed fast from everyday injuries; they could sustain burns and bruises and be whole again within hours. Even broken bones, properly set, would generally heal in a few days. Isnorvi walked wincing and limping for weeks. It would be months before he dared be caught even standing close to Duncan, and though he stared broodingly across encamped clearings at the human boy sometimes, he never laid hands on him again.

The others were similarly evasive. Duncan never found out if they, too, were beaten for their part in Isnorvi's scheme—if they were, it happened separately, and was done with a more judicious hand than Svalenkari's. All he knew was that the bullying pretty much stopped. Drasvinad might sometimes mock him for the mortal clumsiness he showed around camp—high, cruel laughter tinkling like tiny silver bells across a clearing as he stumbled. And from time to time, there'd be the odd shove from one of the others, but these incidents were few and far between.

But, of course, by then the real damage was already done.

So near as Duncan could work out, piecing it together as an adult, the Fae had taken him from Stac Dubh at not much more than three years old. Young enough to quickly lose all memory of a mother's face and warmth, save for, perhaps in the beginning, some tiny, hopeful expectation that someone—some big person, not a child—might offer comfort when he cried, but even that dwindling away in recall as life among the Fae became all his young mind retained. He might have lived out his whole life with nothing left but that vague, faded inkling of loss, grown to manhood, become a thankful thrall, carried iron for his Huldu masters, died finally in the Forest without ever remembering what he had been. It might all have sunk safely without trace, but for his birthday surprise . . .

Aye, Isnorvi had fucked up there, right enough.

The memories wakened, the mother's face recalled, scarred-over wounds of loss ripped open, right down to the quick.

Presumably, it was what Isnorvi, in his feral young-Fae innocence, had wanted. One exquisite extra measure of cruelty to overflow the glass, to bring the tears spilling out once more. He'd apparently seen no further than that. All adult Fae had the Sight to some degree, but it took them decades of growing up to attain it. Isnorvi, evidently, had some ways to go.

Duncan wondered idly how much of what was to come Svalenkari had, in his fury, foreseen. His mastery of the Sight was a legend across the Forest. Had he seen what would become of Duncan, where the renewed grief and loss would eventually drive him? Or was he simply enough of a seasoned changeling maker, a good enough student of humans, to understand the damage to his future thrall that Isnorvi had risked for sheer malicious whimsy and spite? Was it vision or merely the wisdom of years that drove his rage?

Or some muddied, half-clairvoyant grasp of things in-between?

Duncan looked up into the tree canopies above. He thought the sky beyond might be starting to tinge lighter with intimations of dawn.

He held Stordalen's severed head high, for whoever and whatever might be watching.

See this, do you?

See how the mortal child returns with gifts for the Forest and all within?

The head swung from the grip he had on its hair. Spare gore dripped. Spotted his cheek.

He wiped it, smeared it in broad lines.

Lowered the severed head, held it pensive for a moment or two.

Then he turned it upside down pressed his bloodied fingers deep into the ragged stump of the neck. Smeared the gore he dug out on his other cheek, to match what was already there, then across his forehead as well.

Daubed with it, he raised his head to the trees and the brightening eastern sky.

Now do you fucking see?

SIXTEEN

DAYBREAK HIT THE FOREST IN SHEAVES AND LANCES OF PROBING light. Autumn was already thinning out the leaves in the canopies overhead—it let in the sun's early morning rays with abundant largesse. It turned low-crawling mists incandescent between trunks, stitched dew-diamonds across spiderwebs, chased out the somber gray chill of the predawn. Birdsong drenched the air. Woodpeckers went to work, like the stutter-stretch of a ship's mooring ropes as the vessel shifts on the swell. Somewhere, through the gaps between the trees, the creaking-hinge call of a deer, seeking its kind.

Nothing bad, you thought, could happen here.

Duncan, moving rapidly northeast over scraggy ground, was not fooled. Some of the most savage killing he'd been a part of had happened under radiant blue skies, in snowscapes out of some serene Christmas greetings postcard. Death was not picky in these things, and nor were the nape-of-neck horrors the Forest owned. The Huldu came out at night from preference, their powers were ascendant in moonlight—they would shun the sun's brightness if they possibly could—but driven to it, the most seasoned warriors among them would not let it stop them from much.

He carried the McCulloch, briefcase style in his left hand, fully loaded, just in case.

Meanwhile, Stordalen's severed head swung weightily from his pack, tied on by its hair. He'd aligned it as close to centrally as he could, but still it unbalanced him as he loped across the few patches of open ground he could use to put on speed. From time to time it got tangled in underbrush as he forced his way through thickets, tugging him insistently back. It was far from ideal.

And now he was in a hurry.

He checked his Mappin & Webb at regular intervals. He checked the sun when he could get a clear view of it through the trees. Like it or not, he was racing against the day. The sleeplessness of the night before piled up behind him, another night on his feet ahead.

He could have used some of Crammond's cocaine.

Whatever jittery shit he'd ingested with Stordalen's heart would have to serve instead.

IT CAME AND WENT, WHATEVER it was, surging and stuttering in his veins, disrupting his pulse. With it came visions, distortions, stuff he could well have done without.

They say Arthur managed it once, but then again—

In any given moment, the Forest might present as normal, natural—or, without warning, it might not. He saw berry patterns shift across bushes in changing light, as if the berries abruptly became some species of ladybird, cracked their wing casings and swarmed determinedly to left or right. He saw elegant ash and silver birch come to life—turn haughtily away from him, like tall women draped in evening wear with high, shawled shoulders, offended by his shabby human manners. Or they'd turn his way instead, with hungry grins and long, slim segments of thigh exposed for his delectation. He saw things emerge from the openings of burrows and badger sets to look him over—things that were not badgers nor rabbits nor anything else you'd expect to see in British woodland outside of nightmare. Some of them seemed to know, or at least to recognize, him.

Once, a wolf spider not much smaller than an actual wolf came scuttling across his field of vision in pursuit of a squirrel, but suddenly froze, scooted awkwardly sideways to look at him out of eight unblinking eyes like polished jet beads. His blood iced up in his veins, he went to raise the McCulloch. The spider raised its forelimbs in some weird kind of obeisance—*look, all right, you got me*—then swiveled and swarmed up the nearest tree after the squirrel, which had long ago made its escape. The dog-sized scurrying spider body blurred, merged with the abstract patterns of the bark, and then was gone. Foliage twitched. Duncan's heart remembered to pound. The stuff in his veins surged anew, hot over cold, and he felt abruptly light in the head, dizzy on his feet.

Once, he stepped on the gnarled horizontal branch of a great yew where it grazed the ground in a long, low loop, twice as wide around as his leg, and the bark changed underfoot where his boot landed to the mottled reticular skin of some huge serpent. The tree limb flexed and jolted him violently so he lost his footing, fell stumbling forward, and nearly ended up flat on his face. But when he recovered and looked back, the branch was once more immobile, nothing but a branch.

Once, he saw dead autumn leaves and other detritus whirled up off the Forest floor in a tornado of toylike proportions that grew to the height of a man, then twisted artfully into roughly humanoid form. The swirling conglomerate appeared to fold its arms and stare at him across the ground between them, then raise its hands at him in a gesture similar to that which the spider had given him earlier. For some reason, it recalled the jocular dark presence he thought he'd seen standing behind Wolfbane Sally as she bid him farewell.

He stared back as best he could and the apparition blew away in wisps between the trees.

On the plus side of the ledger, the pain from his various wounds seemed to be easing a lot faster than you'd expect from some run-of-the-mill witch's glamour.

Sometime after noon, he came across a stooped and ancient oak, whose bole topped out with a space between the spread of branches low and broad enough to clamber up into and sit. He dragged his pack up after him, dug out some provisions, and made a selection—cured sausage and cheese, biscuits, a tin of stewed peaches. In truth, he wasn't very hungry—the shreds of Faerie heart in his stomach weren't digesting well, and the steady march of hallucinations in his head had left him queasy—but he knew well enough he'd need the fuel before nightfall. He dutifully unwrapped the cheese and sausage, used the sgian dubh to cut slices. Set to chewing the food.

On a macabre impulse, he untied Stordalen's severed head from where it hung on the pack. He set it on one of the branches opposite for company.

"See that spider back there?" he mused through a mouthful of cheese. "Some beastie, aye?"

He swallowed, took a swig from his canteen. Wiped his mouth.

"Gotta wonder whether you folk see stuff like that all the fucking time."

The dead, black-eyed gaze, resting on him as empty now as it had been in life. Duncan bit into a biscuit. Nodded at the severed head.

"So. The Final Isles. They say it's nice." He stared off into space for a moment. "Well, truth is that was mostly Isnorvi, boasting about going there with his clan when he was younger, but he always was a lying little fuck, so who knows. Supposed to be hard to get to, all glamoured up; only those with the Sight can pass or some such shite. Dreaming in mythic isolation, calling all the shots, handing down the law. I used to think it was the Hebrides, or maybe Ireland, but no one ever talked about taking a boat, crossing the sea, anything like that. Like it's someplace not on human maps. That about right?"

He finished his biscuit.

"And if you're some kind of big man back in the Final Isles like you seemed to think you were, then what the fuck are you doing in these parts? Meb comes up from the south to steal Mimi Rush and build her cairn, the vatnalfr said Svalenkari's down from Scotland, too. And the Final Isles sent you. What's going on, pal? What's this gathering for?"

He waited, pensive, but the Huldu prince had no answers for him, and after another slice of cured meat, he gave up the pretense that he was hungry, that he wasn't alone. He left the canned peaches unopened, stowed them with the rest of his provisions, and tied Stordalen back in place on his pack. He dropped lightly back to the Forest floor, took a bearing on the declining sun, and started walking. His hallucinations—or whatever they were—came back, shadowed him on and off, as they had before. But they showed up less often, seemed less intense, and less inclined to get close. He found he could largely ignore them. He picked up his pace.

He came, finally, a little ragged at the edges, to Miller's Frith.

He didn't see the village at first—it was a couple of years since he'd been here, and even then he'd been approaching from the east. A lot of time for the Forest to cover and consume and change. He was past the first cottages before he even realized they were there. No dramatic eruptions of tree growth to shatter homes here, just thickets of brush and small trees that had sprung up around each building, breaking up the outlines of walls and windows, and cobbled streets long lost beneath carpets of mulch and low-level brush. His first intimation that he'd arrived came from the corner of his eye, rays of late afternoon sun striking egg-yolk-orange off the glass edges in a broken windowpane. He stopped and pivoted about, spotted the slumped roof of one of the camouflaged cottages—oddly not the nearest one to him—then, abruptly, the others. He stood for a moment, worked to get his bearings. Made out the rise of a two-story house, then the modest railway station roof beyond. Up the rise, the church tower beyond that. A sense of qualified relief soaked through him.

He'd made it well ahead of nightfall; he had some time.

The station building was about as desolate as he remembered. Most of the glass in the windows gone, the main doors jammed partway open, detritus on the floor inside and out. Dead leaves scampered and scraped about his feet as he walked in. Three wood-paneled phone booths on the far wall, one with the door torn off and lying on the floor, a second with it hanging drunkenly from the top hinge, the third sealed shut. The waiting room off to the right. On the left, one big difference from last time—there was a skeleton in a station master's uniform pressed forward through the broken glass of the ticket booth window, lying on the counter. Twin bullet holes punched through the brow of the graying skull.

Last time he'd been here, the station master was still alive.

Twined about and penetrated with creeper and ivy, pinned in place at the booth by explosions of bushy growth that had burst from the wall behind him, tendrils spiraled through his eyes, into his ears, cramming his mouth so full his jaw was dislocated. But somehow, through some filthy woodland glamour—still alive. It looked as if he'd smashed the booth glass himself, tried to drag himself through and out, but whatever had erupted inside the booth had dragged him back to have its way with him at leisure. As Duncan stood there and watched, what was left of the man kept trying to drag his throat down onto the jagged edges of the broken booth window, presumably to saw it open. But the creeper gave only teasing fractions before wrenching him back up.

He'd seemed to sense Duncan's approach. Twisted around, tried to bring his tendril-infested eyes to bear. Impossible to know what choked, rustling plea came gagging out between the dislocated jaws, the stuffing of creeper and leaf. Duncan took a guess and honored it.

He put a .445 round from his Webley service revolver into the man's head.

Then another.

Short, thuggish reports in the stillness of the deserted station, flat echoes off the walls. Inside the booth, something seemed to thrash and wail. The remaining fragments of glass blew out on a vicious gust of wind that smelled of green and rot. The station master sagged until his head touched the counter woodwork and lay there at rest.

Duncan stood frozen in recall for a moment, then crossed the room, shoved open the far door, and went out onto the westbound platform. More dead leaves, twitching and shifting on the concrete, as if dying to rush up and meet him. A forlorn ribbed steamer trunk, abandoned and rotting halfway down the platform's length. A porter's trolley, lying on its back. Sundry smaller items of luggage scattered around—handbags, suitcases, a hatbox, a slim instrument case that looked like it might contain a trumpet or trombone. Like sparse markers in some avant-garde cemetery for unimaginable times, each one a memento for a soul now gone. Farther along to the left, the tailing slope as the platform ended, then the rise of the railway cutting and eventual tunnel, where gnarled oak and yew had erupted from the embankments at crazy angles and clogged the way.

Looming in the channel, rusted now to the rails, the shrine to human ingenuity he'd come to beg favors at—the long, black iron hulk of L&YR Thunder Child, her tender and carriages.

He didn't know the locomotive—the name was detailed in time-dulled bronze lettering arched over the L&YR crest—but from the size of the thing, it must have once been the pride of the Lancashire and Yorkshire line. He wondered, as he had the last time he was here, looking at the stalled train, the abandoned luggage on the platform, how it had been when the Forest stormed Miller's Frith. Had the erupting trees across the cutting been enough to panic passengers and crew? Had they already come through something worse to the east and dared not reverse course?

Or had something else come out of the darkness of the tunnel and scattered them screaming from the station in madness and despair?

Duncan moved cautiously up to the quiescent bulk of the locomotive, stepped across the short gap from platform to footplate, ducked into the driver's cab. Broad loom of the boiler backhead with its firehole hatch, cracked glass in the forward ports, a festooning of gauges and pipes and levers everywhere—he had not the faintest idea what most of it did. It was a taller, more comfortable space than you'd think. But there was no fast way into it that didn't involve touching iron in some shape or form.

He was safe.

He unshipped his pack, stowed it with the McCulloch in a corner between the fireman's bench and the fire-hole hatch. As the weight came off his shoulders, all the breath seemed to come out of him at once. Relief, this time absolute. His cheeks puffed out with the force of his sigh. He slumped boneless on the driver's bench. Spiteful stitching of pain across his ribs from the knife wounds, but the furrows in his shoulder, the fang gash in his scalp, these were down to no worse than a dull ache. It dawned on him that this was the first moment he hadn't been wound tight and combat tense since he entered the Forest last night with Garner at his side—he checked his watch—the best part of twenty-four hours ago.

He fed himself with provisions from the pack—only realizing then how hungry he was—and then he sat there blank for a while. He let go of his pains and thoughts, as if soaking in a hot bath—strung-out nerves slowly easing, tensions dissipating, all thought washed away . . .

Easy, lad. It might almost have been Garner's voice in his ear. *We're not out of the woods yet.*

Awareness crept back in behind the admonition. Shadow stripes across the cab. He rolled his head to look up at the driver-side forward port. Reddish evening light caught there in the cracks. The day was almost done.

Reluctantly, he sat forward, gathered his thoughts. Brooded on Stordalen's blood-daubed head where it dangled to the floor of the cab, staring away at an angle, as if offended. Duncan thought there might still be a fractional amount of smolder where the dead Fae's cheek touched the iron floor. Couldn't be sure. Finally, he got up and unfastened the hair, hefted the head between his cupped hands, held it before him like a football. The dead black eyes stared up at him.

"Time to make thisel useful, lad." Managing a passable imitation of Garner's Lancastrian twang. "Let's go see the vicar."

He collected the McCulloch from where he'd leaned it. Checked the load, put the gun across his shoulder, picked up Stordalen by his hair, and stepped back out onto the platform. Cooling evening air, overpowering scent of greenery and mulch. He sniffed at it, grimaced, then pushed through the station building again and out into the streets of the village. Nape of neck prickles—the station master's skull, watching him go.

On up to the church.

Duncan supposed that even in its medieval heyday, St. Oswald's at Miller's Frith had only ever been a fairly homely place of worship—part timbered, part sandstone, a huddled, truncated nave and a stubby square tower, trading as much on its elevated position as anything architectural to assert itself over the hamlet it served. From the station, you reached the lych-gate up a short rising curve, a street now overwhelmed with waist-high brush and wild grass. The growth had washed right up to the front doors of the modest two-story Georgian houses that lined the street, drowning low garden walls and gates in the process, making the thoroughfare seem much wider than it actually was. Duncan picked his way carefully through the grass, around the thickest of the shrub growth, trench gun leveled, ready to drop Stordalen's head at a moment's notice and fight. The houses stood mute on either side, like witnesses to some awful crime. The empty gaze of top-floor windows bore down on him all the way—gave him sniper's itch, a constant urge to look up, stare back, be ready.

He held it down. He reached the top of the rise.

You came across abandoned churches all over the Forest, in varying states of rot and disrepair. Some had been smashed apart by the returning trees, some had simply been swarmed with moss and creeper over time and left to decay, mute testimony like the unloved moss-grown marker stones in their graveyards. These places were not, in the grand scheme of things, much different from any other ruin. Duncan had heard tales of more outlandish remains, glamoured sites, but St. Oswald's was the only one he'd seen for himself. The church was neither smashed nor decayed. Instead, it seemed to have come to some kind of otherworldly life.

Wherever the building was timbered—the upper levels of the

tower, the broad door porch, ornately carved beams under the huddled roof—planks had sprouted fresh twigs and tendrils as if in memory of the living wood they had once been. Not to be outdone, the stonework elsewhere was veined with the same soft blue light as the cairn Duncan had desecrated the night before. The whole structure appeared to breathe gustily to itself—hard to tell if this was some glamour-induced illusion, but the cracked and crumpled earth around the church's walls seemed to suggest not.

The gate under the lych-roof was jammed permanently ajar. He slipped through the gap. Tracked through the long, damp grass around the gravestones. Up on a corner of the tower, a fanged gargoyle twisted to watch his approach. It winked at him. He made the porch, set amidships along the body of the church. The great oak door, like the gate, was ajar. The same soft blue glow, spilling out through the gap, brighter here in the gloom under the porch.

Shadows, shifting across the spill. Scuffle-scrape of something large moving within.

Duncan grimaced.

He booted the big oak door wider open. Edged cautiously inside. Cleared the nave, left and right, with the McCulloch. No obvious threats. Just pews sunk in soft blue gloom, visibly dust coated but otherwise neatly arranged. Pervasive smell of damp—there were cracks in the cream plastered walls, blue light spilling out. Here and there, chunks of plaster had fallen away. Detritus crunched under his feet as he moved up the aisle toward the base of the tower. There, things like bell ropes hung down twitching, as if in a fitful draft.

But there was no draft.

The church seemed to sigh and suck in upon itself. The bell ropes twisted gropingly about, tentacular, finally, in eerie unison, raised and pointed their ends toward him. Jet, unblinking eyes like the spider's at each rope end—did he really see that? Or was it the Fae heart's blood he'd ingested, surging and suggesting, still in his veins?

Higher up in the tower space, something bulky rasped and moved about. Duncan eased to a wary halt.

Close enough, lad.

"I've come to toll the bell," he called out.

Long silence. Duncan grimaced again. He shouldered the McCulloch for a moment, hefted Stordalen's head carefully to get the weight, then heaved it down the aisle. It made a low arc into the tower space, hit the floor there with a dull thump. The bell rope appendages recoiled upward. Wet, throaty whispers and scraping echoed in the tower.

Duncan cleared his throat, pitched his voice louder, quelling fear and doubt, driving them out the way he had in the duel last night.

"Do you *hear* me? I have come to sound farewell to Stordalen of the Final Isles! That's his fucking head, by the way. Stordalen of the Final Isles, cut down by mortal hands. By *my* hands! Let the bell toll for him, and let the whole fucking Forest hear it!"

For a long moment, he was afraid it wouldn't work, that the whispered tales among the woodsmen had gotten it wrong, or at least left out some vital detail. Some piece of intricate spell-craft, some ritual step. But then, the bell-rope appendages drooped down once more, lowering themselves, lengthening themselves, like threads of drool from some immense predator's jaw. They touched the severed head tentatively, as if it might be hot. They walked their tentacle ends over it, prodded and pushed it, finally took it and turned it over like some interesting pebble picked up off the beach. The rasping sounds grew more definite, louder. Something immense sagged down into view. Duncan stared, tried to make sense, finally just gagged and backed up one instinctive step before he could stop himself. A gibbering litany dinned in his head, none of it right.

—drowned, swallowed, shrouded, sunken, BURIED . . .

In the trenches, he'd seen whole bodies immured. Artillery hurled and buried its victims with the coarse, good-humored abandon of a school bully stuffing heads down a latrine. They ended up everywhere, might crop up anywhere and—as a drawling American medic he'd met put it—any which way up. Then, shoring up a captured trench, extending, digging in after a successful advance—these things had to be done in haste and without regard to niceties like disposal of the incidental dead. The results were like horrors from some overly imaginative alcoholic's DT dream—disembodied arms and legs protruding stiffly out of trench walls, getting in the way, sunken, skullish faces emerging from the dirt like revenants, a general stink that soldiers masked with cigarette and pipe smoke as best they could.

You got used to these things. The sights and stenches grew mundane. One sweltering summer morning after a dawn assault, Duncan watched one of his corporals, a noted company wit, hang up his water canteen on the booted foot of a corpse sticking out of the recently rebuilt revetment. He'd laughed, and so had most of his men.

—not like this . . .

Whatever lived in the tower was mostly amorphous, had the wet gleam of internal tissue all over, punctured here and there with what might have been protruding bone, and there were human limbs and faces embedded in it, *and they were alive.* Mouths worked, eyes implored. Expressions of anguish, yearning out from the mass of tissue, embedded, pressed, crushed together. A congregation, praying unanswered down the years since the Forest came. Fingers flexed and gestured, muscles stood proud like ropes. Arms twitched, reached fitfully out. Begging, perhaps, for the same end as the station master.

The thing, the congregation, lowered itself to within a couple of feet of the stone floor. It swung there, massive, the way that corporal's canteen had swung from the dead man's foot. It confronted Duncan like the enormity of every single day of slaughter he'd ever lived through made flesh. The thing's nearest arms took hold of a back row pew, grasped and worked the wood until it creaked with the force of their grip. The pew shifted, grating, on the stone floor. Higher up, on the knobbed and crusted top of the main mass, thick, tentacular limbs—brutally muscular versions of their underslung bell-rope cousins—webbed back up the tower beyond view, held the creature suspended.

It made a soft, lowing, hooting sound that stung tears into Duncan's eyes. It held up Stordalen's head in its tentacles like a question it seemed to think he could answer.

Shaken, shaking, Duncan stood his ground. He lifted the McCulloch in warning.

"Just ring the fucking bell," he snarled.

And fled.

SEVENTEEN

THE BELL TOLLED, HIGH CRYSTALLINE CHIMES THAT SEEMED TO splinter in his ears, put a shivery dinning on the inside of his head.

It went on and on, a manic repetition.

It followed him down the hill.

In the station, a flimsy wooden door with long-ago shattered glass panels led into the waiting room beyond. With cold, methodical savagery, Duncan kicked it loose of its hinges—booted blow after blow after *blow,* until the whole door toppled, took half the frame with it, and crashed to the glass-strewn floor. Blinking back tears, couldn't seem to get rid of them. The sound of the tower dweller's multi-throated hooting stuck in his head like some catchy tune you'd hear a soldier whistle down-trench and not be able to forget. He dragged the door across to one of the waiting room benches, leaned one end of it up on the edge, and with the same measured savagery, stomped it to splintered fragments and kindling.

He stood for a few moments, getting his wind back.

The bell had finally stopped its chiming.

He gathered the larger fragments of wood, carried them out to the platform, and built a small fire next to Thunder Child's footplate. He put his back to the locomotive and sat cross-legged before the flames. He lay the McCulloch across his knees and waited.

Darkness creeping in, thickening in the streets of Miller's Frith, drowning the tree-shrouded, abandoned houses, the station, the paralyzed train. The fire began to paint capering black shadows across the platform and up the station house wall. The sun was long gone now, down over the shoulder of the hill, the waxing moon still tangled low in branches to the east. Above the trees, it looked like the same clear skies as the previous night, stars starting to pinprick through. But for the first time that Duncan could recall that year, there was a raw autumn edge on the air.

The station door to the platform blew open, banged shut.

Duncan's gaze shuttled rightward to the sound, watched the door repeat the trick twice more, then stop as if embarrassed. Whispers blew in on a faint, chilly wind, worried at the fire.

When he looked back to the flames again, Mebhuranon sat opposite him.

"Hello, Duncannn . . ."

Low carnivore purr in her voice, the effortless sensuality he remembered. Her achingly perfect lupine features wavered and twitched in the heated air above the flames, perhaps a little more than the refracted light could strictly explain. The curtains of unruly dark and silver hair streamed back off her forehead and cheekbones as if blown that way by a fierce wind he couldn't feel. Over twenty years since he'd seen her outside of dreams. He tried not to show the jolt it put through him.

"Meb," he managed. "Didn't take you long to get here."

"It's the Final Isles, Duncan. You've made quite the splash this time. What did you expect?"

"Something like this, I suppose. Did you bring the girl?"

"Did I have a choice? Where is Stordalen's head?"

"Left it up at the bell tower."

"Ah." She tilted an elegant glance away from the fire, up in the direction of the church. "And how did you find the bell keeper this fine evening? Is the poor thing keeping well? Still talking to itself?"

He held down the gooseflesh shiver of recall.

"You did that to them?" he asked.

"The Forest did that to them. In misunderstood answer to some prayer they offered up, perhaps. Or in punishment. Who can tell? It listens, Duncan—I did tell you that once. But it's a fickle god at best, and not much given to tolerating younger rivals. Perhaps it was offended."

"And did the Forest enchant the bell as well? Because that's not the story I heard."

"Oh no, we did that. Not me personally, I wasn't up here at the time. One of the local clan-masters. I understand it was by way of a joke."

"Aye. Anyone could see the funny side of that."

She smiled. Sharp ivory teeth. "Do you presume to judge us, Duncan?"

"No. I presume to take Miriam Rush from you and leave. Where is she?"

"All in good time."

Rustle and crunch of autumn leaves disturbed, somewhere down the platform. Shadows leaning in. Duncan smiled thinly, curled his right hand on the butt of the McCulloch.

"Tell them to back off," he said. "Unless they want to join Stordalen in the Gray."

Mebhuranon shuttled her liquid black eyes to the side. The shadows retreated from the corner of his vision. "They don't intend to attack you, Duncan. I think they just want to see you for themselves. It's not every day a mortal kills a Final Isles noble and eats his heart."

"I didn't eat all of it."

She tilted her head, preternaturally lupine once more. "No. But you ate enough, I think. As always, Duncan, you teeter on the brink of things. What are we to do with you?"

Oh, Duncan, what are we to do with you?

The words, striking through, dragging back, as she must know they would, the memory of the last time he saw her, the aftermath of the revels . . .

Picking her way, tall and svelte and utterly naked, out of the clearing in the hollow where the sated bodies of the other guests carpet the moss-soft ground. Their body fluids gleam on her like snail track, across breasts and belly and thighs, smear from her lips, cling sticky in her tangled hair. She trails her rainbow cloak along the ground behind her with one languid hand. Faerie music still piping faintly in the stunned quiet between the trees at her back. Shimmer and shiver of glamours expiring . . .

And Duncan—crouched watching from behind a beech bole where the giggling tree sprites have led and left him, paralyzed by what he's seen. His most recent bruises forgotten, numbed away by the spectacle of the Faerie queen in her abandon. Through the thin, ragged cloth of the shorts that Svalenkari has had stolen for him, he holds on to his throbbing penis as if it's the handle on the door to a room he's trying desperately to escape.

He's maybe eleven years old.

Helloooo, Duncannnn. Switching suddenly round the bole of the beech tree, finding him there—aha!—as if they've been playing hide-and-seek all along. Have you been watching me?

Terror, shock. Shame. His mouth moves, but no sounds come out.

She looks down at him for a moment, empty black stare. Then—something the Bright Folk almost never do—she makes almost human pupils of her eyes, squeezes the black out to the corners, leaves a violet residual core. She folds herself elegantly down to sit beside him.

There's a scent to her naked body that he'll never forget as long as he lives.

Oh, Duncan, what are we to do with you? You keep running away. Don't you like the Forest? She leans in closer, all violet eyes and scent. Don't you like us?

Some instinctive impulse—he lets go of his penis. Puts his palms flat on the mossy ground, pushes himself backward away from her, into the hard bark of the beech trunk.

I want to go home, he says.

Yes, but you can't. Voice reasonable and kind, soft as the moss under his palms. She reaches delicately out, touches a bruise on his grubby shoulder with one cool hand. Is Svalenkari not making that sufficiently clear to you?

I want my mother!

Do you? Her hand falls from his shoulder, fingertips tracing down his arm, touches his thigh. Stays there. She leans close. Her scent, her violet eyes. Is that what you want? Your mother? Really, Duncan?

He's trembling, a churn of feelings new and old, an upending of the steady yearnings he's held on to for the years since Isnorvi's birthday surprise. He feels dizzy with the shift. He—it's sudden, the realization—wants her to move her hand. He wants those cool fingers to spider up his thigh to take his penis between them, he wants her to . . . to do . . . do the things he watched her do among her kind down in the hollow and the revel . . .

The violet eyes, watching him close.

And suddenly, in the core of this new storm, he finds something new to hold on to.

A new uncovering, like the revealed violet pupils in the eyes that watch him so closely now—the sudden understanding that this creature, in fact, wants something from him, *and it is his submission to her will and to the will of Svalenkari . . .*

And he can deny it.

For the first time, he can stop them taking something they want.

I want my mother! Through gritted teeth now, a new, tightly focused form of the resistance he's lived with for so long. He swats the Faerie queen's hand from his leg. Breathing hard. Lets his voice out, rising to a shout. You stole her from me and I want her back! I'll never love you! I'll never love the Forest! I want to go home!

And Mebhuranon flinches.

It's tiny. But it's there.

The dawn quiet flows back in around his words. But they hang there in the air anyway, like the after-smoke from one of the glamoured lightning-bolt flashes Svalenkari sometimes likes to conjure when he's angry.

Well, she says softly.

Dense inky black flooding back in across her eyes—it swamps the violet pupils, renders her gaze blank and pitiless and elf-like once more. He sees himself reflected back in each eye, small, grubby, at bay between the root sinews of the beech. She tilts her head at him, like a wolf.

You disappoint me, Duncan. Voice no longer soft now, something harsh and imperious and ancient rising in it instead. For now I must own to Svalenkari that he knows better than I do, knows you *better, at any rate, and so I will hand you back.*

She prods at his bruised shoulder again, no delicacy in it now. Maybe you actually enjoy these . . . caresses he rewards your rebellion with. You humans are, when all is said and done, a brutish lot. My *caresses, at least, you will never know.*

She gathers up her crumpled rainbow robe, draws it about her shoulders, shrouding the body beneath. Some new, raw part of him feels it as loss. A fresh, hard-to-decode hurting, to add to the well-stocked winter store he already has. Mebhuranon rises, as elegant as when she arrived, turns to leave—

Oh, and Duncan. Looking back over her shoulder. Be wary of what you say about the Forest. What feelings you vent about it. It listens, you know.

And it never forgets.

She wanders away between the trees, singing to herself now, low, limping cadence, antique, ornate words even his eleven-year-old grasp of Skogurtal can only paw at. Maybe it's a spell, he thinks.

And years later, he thinks instead that it had the tone of a lament—though what for, he could not say . . .

Anyway.

He loses sight of her.

Loses the sound of her voice.

Loses whatever might have been.

Only this hot, new ache remains.

He looked impassively back at her across the flames. "We're wasting time, Meb."

"Speak for yourself, mortal. I have all the time there is."

There is no response to this worth making, no truth he can wield to defeat hers. He feels the cool granite chill of eternity blowing off her. For just a moment, he feels as small and grubby and alone as he did that day. He breathes hard on the embers of his rage, draws them to him.

"Nice for you," he said. "In the meantime, Miriam Rush, her mother, and I are all in a hurry living and dying like the mortals we are. So how about you stop fucking around and bring the girl out, and we can all go home."

She looked at him in silence for a beat.

"It won't help," she said.

"What won't?"

"Little Mimi. Little Ellie. Little Eduardo. All the others. It doesn't matter how many children you bring out of the Forest, Duncan. The one you could not save will always be here. The one you cannot go back and find and comfort, the past you cannot unwind. You will not heal this way."

Duncan nodded. "Who told you I wanted to heal?"

"Then perhaps you can tell me what you do want." An odd urgency in her tone now, something he might have read in a mortal woman as desire. He stifled his memories of the body beneath the cloak as best he could. "You need only ask, Duncan. Look around you. The world is made anew. And it belongs to us now."

"I wouldn't jump to any early conclusions on that if I were you, Meb."

"Early?" She smiled, more gently, no teeth now. Her voice was low and musing. "I was here when men first came to burn these forests. I saw them lay waste and take away our domain, acre by acre, hill and dale. I heard the trees scream. I saw empty pastures and rutted mud fields replace my world. In time, I saw even that razed and raped abomination of the land clotted over in turn with brick and black smoke and ruin. And I waited, Duncan, because it was always foretold that the cycle would turn, and our time come round again. I waited, and counted centuries, and waited again. You think this is early? I have waited six thousand years for your race to exhaust their dream and give in once more to ours."

Duncan thought about Martin Hardy, ex of the Coldstream Guards. The offices on Albion place, the sober, subdued bustle in the corridors there. *Another kind of war.*

"I don't think we'll go under without a fight," he said.

She shook her head. "You are already drowned. You are emptied out, all of you. You are hollow men. You drained yourselves fighting each other to a standstill in a pit of mud, and for what? Your fires and iron are become your funeral pyre. Your gods are tumbled, their promises broken. You have plumbed this dream of mastery you once had and found it a shallow, malnourishing lie. You cannot master the living world; you cannot even master yourselves. You have nothing left to resist us with."

"Tell that to Stordalen."

A muscle in her cheek twitched. It was the only indication she gave that his barb had gone home. She rolled out the carnivorous grin again.

"Stordalen was a fop. A swaggering youth who mistook rank for prowess, ancestry for wisdom. He was barely two hundred years old. Do not mistake him for the best of us, or the most powerful. That is not the fight you are facing."

"Is that right? What is the fight I'm facing, Meb? Is it that fuck Svalenkari, maybe? Because he's welcome to step up. Just name a time and place. Oh—or is it you?"

Her smile deepened. "Oh, Duncan—all that rage, and still you cannot see? Still you do not hear? Listen to your poets! To your learned men! The fight is within, it always was, and you have already lost—all of you. We do not come as warriors, to conquer you with blades and flame and arrow shafts. We come bearing gifts, Duncan! We bring you the roots of being, the ancient swooping rise and fall, the gut deep depths of dark joy and abandon, the cravings you could never feed with all your dreams of measuring and mastery and mind."

She leaned in. Her eyes threw back twinned flames on black. Her lips drew back off her gleaming teeth. Her face became a Greek theater mask, harshly lit and shadowed, as her lips mouthed.

"Know this, as I have known it for millennia—you will embrace the gifts we bring, just as you did before, because the call to them is as strong and urgent in you as it ever was! We smell it on you, now as we did then. We hear you calling, crying out for dark simplicity and savor and release, and we have answered you, as we did in the time before.

"Now look into your heart, Duncan, look into that truth, and tell me what you really want."

He sat very still, let himself feel the languid ooze and thrust of her power, the glamours flickering around her words. He'd expected this.

He knew how to withstand it, knew where to look inside himself for the strength. He'd known at eleven years old, with nothing on his side but childlike hate and loss. Now, France and Flanders lived in his head, a hammered-iron certainty of self that Mebhuranon's conjurings broke against like waves on a granite headland.

In a way, he was almost disappointed.

"All right," he said mildly. "Tell you what. Bring me Svalenkari's head on a spike. Then we can talk."

He locked gazes with her, let his senses sift outward for any sense of ambush up and down the platform. He watched the grin ebb slowly from her face. The sharp white teeth covered, the last ghost of her smile glimmering out.

"Very well," she said. "I tried."

"Aye, you did. Didn't work any better than last time, did it?"

She looked aside, a sudden shrugging motion, as if she were finally offended beyond recourse. Something seemed to go rippling down the platform in the direction she looked. He sensed movement in response, vague shadowed comings and goings at the fringes of his vision.

Then, from out of the shift of shadow, a diminutive pale figure. It stood for a moment, then made hesitant steps along the platform toward the fire. Duncan felt his pulse pick up.

"Just her," he said. "Everyone else stays back."

"Of course." Mebhuranon stirred impatiently where she sat. "If it had been our aim to contest the girl here, you would not even have sight of her. Come, Mimi. Come to me."

The little figure tripped meekly closer, stood at Mebhuranon's side like a summoned maid. Dark uncombed hair, stunned pale face, smudges of weary blue under the eyes. They'd wrapped her in a simple robe of some sort, not the rainbow glories they wore themselves, but still—it was cleaner and more cared for than the rags Duncan had made do with during his time in the Forest. It covered her, shoulders to toes, had tailored sleeves her pale hands peeped their fingers out of.

It had a sheen, a bluish tinge that seemed to slip about on the fabric with the flicker of the firelight.

In one hand she clutched a grubby little rag doll that had seen better days.

Duncan made a smile. Made his voice gentle. "Hello, Mimi."

Nothing. The girl stared back at him numbly.

"Mimi, your mother sent me. I've come to bring you home."

Still nothing. But he saw a flicker in her eyes. The vivid liquid fill of tears.

"Would you like that? To go home and see your mother?"

Her throat moved as she swallowed. A tear tripped the holding wall of her eyelashes, striped down her cheek. She made a tiny noise. Bobbed her head.

"Well, good. Come and stand by me, then."

He saw how Mebhuranon twitched with the effort of restraint, of letting the child walk away from her. He made his face stone, stared intently across the fire into the candles of her eyes. Let the rage boil up in his blood so she'd feel it, so she'd know.

Miriam Rush reached his side of the fire. She clutched the rag doll in both tiny fists, tight under her chin, so its mud-streaked face brushed her lips. Duncan lifted his right hand from the McCulloch, offered it to her, but she just stared back at him, hollow-eyed. He dropped his hand again. Under his coat, his left tightened on the trench knife, clenched in anger.

Perhaps Mebhuranon saw.

"We won't try to stop you, Duncan. Not right now." Her voice hardened. "But you should be aware that what you have done will strain even the bonded word of the Final Isles. You have woken older forces than you know. Sooner or later, there will be a reckoning even I am powerless to stop."

Stir of old terrors—Duncan forced them down, ignored Mebhuranon's gleaming lit-wick gaze, twisted instead to look into Miriam's four-year-old face. He made himself smile again.

"Don't worry, Mimi. It's all right. Here, take my hand."

"Are you a knight?" she whispered, big eyed.

He grabbed on to his smile, just stopped it sliding into a startled cackle. "Something like that," he said as seriously as he could. He cleared his throat. "I'm a soldier, like your daddy was. I'm working for your mother."

"But I'm a princess." Blurted out, darting a fearful glance back at Mebhuranon. "She says I am, she says I can be. But I have to stay. Then I can be a princess and Mummy won't cry anymore because she doesn't have enough money for my shoes, and my feet won't hurt."

"She said that, did she?" Duncan turned a withering stare on the Huldu queen. Got nothing back but the blank musing smile. "Well, see, princess, the problem is—Mummy's been crying every night since you've been gone anyway. She misses you so much."

Miriam looked stricken. She looked at the rag doll in her hands. Her fingers worked at it. Her lip trembled.

"But she has another me to care for. Like a doll. They told me that."

Fresh pulse of rage in his guts. "They lied, Mimi. She's on her own. She wants you back. It's why she sent me."

The tears already clotted along Mimi's lower lashes spilled over in earnest now, ran down her cheeks. Duncan reached up and cupped her face with his hand, wiped the tears with his thumb. It left a grubby smear, not unlike the dried streaks of Stordalen's blood he'd put across his own cheekbones the night before.

"Don't cry, Mimi," he said softly. "You don't have to stay here. You can come home."

"But . . . shoes," she wailed.

"Get you a brand-new pair as soon as we're back. That's a promise." He chucked her under the chin. "All right?"

Tearful nod. She gulped. Duncan breathed deep.

"All right, then." He jerked a thumb over his shoulder. "See this big train? How'd you like to sit on the driver's seat, look out the window, and maybe hoot the whistle, like a real driver?"

A tiny brightening in her at this, as if the hurricane lamp at her core had just had the flame turned up half an inch. She sniffed and wiped forlornly at her tears, but when she nodded this time it was firmer. Duncan built her another smile.

"Go on, get in there and have a look. I'm just going to talk to the lady here for a moment, and then we're done."

She went, one hesitant step at a time. Duncan heard her feet on the steel plate, gave his full attention back to Mebhuranon.

"Fucking princess, aye? That's new."

The Fae queen shrugged. "As I have told you—the world *is* made anew."

"Should have told me I was a prince. Maybe I'd have stayed."

"That sounds like regret, Duncan." Her mouth split in a fresh predator grin. "Is it? Do you wish you had stayed with me when you had the chance?"

Quiet. Soft crackle of the fire. The question hung between them in the twisted air.

"Would you have fucked me?" he asked harshly.

"Oh, yes. Sucked and fucked and brought you into manhood, yes. It would have won my bet with Svalenkari. It would have held you in place where he could not. And you were so . . . fresh, Duncan. So *untasted*." Her tongue flickered briefly, touched her upper teeth. "You would have had attention from others soon enough, I'm sure—there's a reason mortals choose to dwell among us, after all, and it's not because of our singing. But yes, I would have been your first."

"You talk of choosing. I had no choice."

"But you did. There and then, Duncan—you made your choice. You ran from me, you ran from the Forest and all its smoldering joys. Am I to blame if now your curdled remorse seeps into the confines of the drab mortal life you chose over us?"

The fire popped and murmured to itself, stories it knew, as old as time. A stray gust of wind grabbed at the flames, dragged dead leaves rasping along the darkened platform.

"Well, then, I guess we're done," Duncan said into the quiet.

Mebhuranon inclined her head. "For now, yes. But we will be watching, Duncan. Wherever you go with the girl, whatever you try to do, our eye is on you now."

"Funny. That's exactly what Stordalen said to me, back in the spring. See how that worked out? You'll not want to follow his example."

"I have already said I will not contest this, Duncan. The word of the Final Isles is my bond, as it will be for all who honor the old paths. But I cannot speak for younger hearts than mine, nor those steeped in hate."

"Not much of a queen, then, are you?"

"This is not my range, Duncan. I am of the south. You will remember that much, at least. I hold ceremonial title here, but little more. I offer counsel, I advise. But my word, even the word of the Final Isles—these usages belong to older times than now. The world is made anew and there is a storm coming. I cannot command it, nor see how it will end."

He stared at her. "You send any of your young hotheads after me, I can see exactly how it'll end. I'll leave them for you in screaming pieces right across the Forest floor."

He levered himself up from the fire, stiffened wounds protesting a little. Cold joints, aching muscles. Mebhuranon had not aged a day since he'd seen her last. But *he* had, and in that instant all those days seemed to hang off him like weights from a butcher's scales. He straightened his back against the combined pull of the years, the time gone away, and he held the McCulloch across his body like a ward.

"You warn them, Meb," he said evenly. "You clear a fucking path. The word of the Final Isles can hold fast or crumble and rot, I don't care. But Miriam Rush is going home."

EIGHTEEN

THEY ALMOST MADE IT.

Almost home dry, Duncan almost daring to believe his hastily cobbled-together strategy had held up, when instead it all fell apart.

Shotgun blasts and hoots and screams and frantic plowing through unforgiving undergrowth, dragging a terrified four-year-old by the arm.

Everything he'd wanted to avoid.

Looking back on the whole thing with a cold, postcombat eye, Duncan would have to allow that Mebhuranon probably did her best to honor Stordalen's word, and that things just got out of hand.

Hard to explain the mess it all became, otherwise.

HE GAVE MEB A WHILE to clear her band out of the village, stood on the footplate of Thunder Child's cab, watching intently for any sign that any of them had stayed, with or without her command. The station door did its *bang*-open, *bang*-shut trick a couple of times, like the bark of bitter laughter down the platform, but after that everything grew silent and still. The platform, the station building, the just-visible loom of the church tower up the hill beyond. The moon untangled itself from the trees, put a frosted light on everything. Even the breeze seemed to have made itself scarce.

"Are we going now?" Miriam asked him, playing with her rag doll, walking it carefully along one of the myriad pipes that crossed the boiler backplate.

"In a little while," he said. Still not quite able to believe they were going to get away with this.

"In a little while," she repeated to the doll, barely above a whisper. "We're going in a little while. Mummy's waiting for us."

She must have felt his stare on her. She huddled the doll up closer to her face, peeped timidly sideways at him. He looked away.

"Not long now," he said gruffly.

He gave it another half hour by the Mappin & Webb. Impatience was the enemy, the itch that moved you too early, too fast, got you a sniper's bullet in the brain. He'd stepped over too many tumbled bodies in the trenches, privates and officers alike, not to learn the lesson. He waited and watched the platform outside. The little girl went on playing. From time to time, he caught her sneaking glances at him, then whispering very low to the rag doll in her hand.

"All right," he said finally. "Come over here, Mimi. Listen to me carefully."

She stopped playing on the instant, turned her face dutifully toward him. He crouched in front of her, put hands on her shoulders, went very slow.

"We have to walk out of here now, Mimi. We're going to go down the platform, follow the carriages back, and then walk between the rails until we get where we're going. You can do that, can't you?"

Timid nod.

"That's good, Now, there are two things I want you to remember, because they're very important. First of all, whatever happens, I want you to always stay between the rails. They're made of iron, and the faeries don't like iron, so they won't want to come close as long as we walk in the middle. It's like if they had to jump over lava. Understand?"

He got the nod again, more emphatic this time.

"Right, now the second thing—this is a long walk and you're probably going to feel tired before the end. But it's very important you keep up with me. I'll go as slowly as I can for you. If you can't keep up, if you need the toilet, if you need anything at all, you tug at my coat—like this, look—and you tell me what's wrong. But quietly, all right? We have to be quiet."

"I can be quiet," she whispered.

"That's good, then. We—"

"When Mummy's tired, I walk like a faerie not to wake her. Susan says I'm light as a feather when I . . ."

Tears welled up in her eyes, some sudden flood of memory buried for months. Her lower lip quivered and he saw abruptly how chapped both lips were. How dry. He cursed himself silently for not spotting it sooner. The Fae were slipshod hosts at the best of times, but here he was, woodsman and savior, doing no better. He dug his canteen hurriedly out of the pack.

"Here—would you like a drink of water before we go?"

She wiped at her eyes. Voice a scratchy husk. "Yes, please."

He unscrewed the cap, passed the canteen over. She put down her doll, drank deep, up-tilted bottle overlarge and awkward in her tiny hands, throat working with the effort of trying to quench her thirst. He steadied it for her. She choked a little, and he tilted the canteen back down—*easy, wean, easy*—and she wiped her mouth and made a satisfied *ahhhhh* sound that had him wanting to laugh. He wondered who she'd copied it from, because it didn't fit with the image he'd had of her mother at all.

"And are you hungry?" he asked.

The answer in her face was pretty clear. But she hesitated.

"Is it . . . usual food? It's not . . ." She swallowed hard. "Not breathing?"

Duncan held back a harsh laugh. Fae food, he knew, could take some getting used to in its more exotic forms. He dug out the can of stewed peaches.

"No, it's not breathing," he said gently.

He opened the peaches and fed the girl some slices, tried her with the cured sausage and cheese as well. She fell on the food like a starved dog, stopped only once to wipe peach juice from her chin and to look suspiciously at him, as if this, all this, might yet be some trick, some dream she'd wake from, back into the nightmare of the Forest . . .

When she was done, Duncan gave her more water, sipped sparingly from the canteen himself, recapped and stowed it. He made the pack ready, stuffed his various pockets with Kegg bombs—still an even dozen left after the fight at the Haughton place. More than enough—he fervently hoped—to see off any mutinous young Huldu males who might get the wrong idea. He checked the load on the McCulloch.

"Time to go," he announced.

Mutely, she held out the rag doll. "Will you carry Siggy for me? I don't want to lose her."

"Sure. We'll put Siggy right here in the pack, look? Nice and safe and warm."

"Will they come after us? The . . . the faeries?"

She almost managed to keep the quaver out of it. But he could see the terror in her eyes. Could see she'd been holding down the question this whole time.

"Shouldn't think so," he said breezily. "They're scared of me."

"Of you?" She seemed dubious about it.

"Well." He gave her a crooked grin, put a cheery confidence into his voice that he was a long way from feeling. He hefted the McCulloch. "Of me and this, anyway."

"That's a gun," she said solemnly.

"Aye, it is. And you know what it shoots, Mimi—it shoots big bits of iron. That's like lava for the faeries, remember. They won't want me shooting that at them, will they."

She shook her head with comical ferocity.

"Well, if they come anywhere near you—that's exactly what I'll do."

Abruptly, she cannoned into him. He rocked back on his heels with the force of it, tried to make sense—realized that she was trying to hug him. Her arms went across him as tight as she could manage, her fingers dug into the fabric of his coat. She made a tiny sniffling noise against his chest.

He leaned back into the fireman's bench behind him, set the McCulloch aside, and hugged Miriam Rush back, gingerly, as if she were made of finest Edinburgh Crystal and might shatter easily in his arms.

This one, he promised with savage intensity. *This one comes home safe and sound.*

THE PLATFORM WAS MOON DUSTED and silent as they stepped out. Duncan looked warily up and down its length, then took Mimi's hand and led her back past the long black iron tender and silent line of carriages beyond. The sound of their own footsteps on the concrete seemed to follow them down the line. They went down the slope at the end of the platform, picked their way along the weed-grown hardcore as the track began to curve away. The carriages loomed over them now, darkened windows peering down. He imagined decayed passengers lolling in the seats on the other side of the glass, desiccated, skullish faces, withered skeletal arms protruding from dusty sleeves. Imagined the stir and rustle as they felt the soft warmth of the two bodies pacing past outside, and crowded to the windows to peer out.

From the look on Mimi Rush's face, she was working through something similar.

He cleared his throat. "It's a shame we can't use this train, isn't it."

"Is everybody dead in it?"

"Oh no," he invented rapidly. "The people all left, because it was broken. They walked home, just like we are."

"Did the faeries break it?"

"Aye, they did." *And everything else with it.*

"Why do they break things like that?" Then, in a sudden, vehement rush. "Why are they so *mean*?"

He glanced at her. "Were they mean to you? I thought they said you were a princess."

"Yes, but . . ."

They walked in silence for a few moments, and he thought she wouldn't speak again. She at least seemed to have forgotten about the brooding carriage windows.

"They looked at me," she said in a small voice. "They had mean eyes. They looked at me like . . . like they wanted to eat me."

"Aye." Duncan groped for a way to explain it to four-year-old ears—the possessive hunger that mortal children seemed to trigger in the Fae. Miriam Rush might go another decade before a mortal man looked at her that way, and likely several more years before she was able to digest it for what it was, find some way to face it with equanimity. After a couple of fruitless seconds, he gave up, said weakly: "They do that, don't they."

They passed the last of the carriages, left the train behind. The rails curved on beyond, into the Forest gloom. Duncan crossed them over the first set of rails, took station in the center. Two thin lines of steel on either side, not much of an advantage, but it would have to do. Grass and weeds grew up everywhere from the hardcore between the rails, between the sleepers, reaching close to his knees and to Mimi's waist. Faint bitter green fragrance, rising as they pressed on through. The girl's nose wiggled with it. Overarching trees, long uncut, made the path ahead a tunnel, endless, bending away to some emergence they could not see.

"Right, then," Duncan said.

Miller's Frith station shrank behind them, was eventually lost to view round the curve. Duncan checked once or twice, just to see they weren't being shadowed. The girl didn't look round at all. She clung close at his side, lips moving in silent recitation of something, some nursery rhyme or prayer or other fragment. The trees crowded in, leaned over, snagged the moon and held it there. The hushed Forest became their entire world, only the dull glint of the rails on either side to suggest the human race had ever existed at all.

For all that, they made surprisingly good time, once Mimi discovered that jumping from sleeper to sleeper could be a fun game. She would bound ahead of him like an untrained puppy, had to be called back a couple of times, but soon worked out how long the elastic was that he'd allow her. From then on, she turned back with unerring timing, just as an admonishment rose to his lips. He stowed the words, gave her a smile instead, and after a while she began to smile back. What fears she'd had back at the station seemed to evaporate with the game. He picked up his own pace a little to match her enthusiasm.

He checked the Mappin & Webb from time to time, guessed rough distances remaining, listened intently for noises beyond the normal from the foliage on either side. Rustle of small mammals in the undergrowth, once or twice the call of an owl.

If there were other eyes watching them, he could not feel it.

On, then, through the tunneled gloom of the path the tracks laid down.

There was one choke point he'd anticipated, a place he knew from previous trips where a storm had smashed down some ancient, giant oak, tangled its branches with those of the trees on the opposite side, and left the trunk sloping angled across the lines like a bone in the throat. You could just about duck under it on the higher side to the right—Mimi would get under just bowing her head—or scramble over on the low end to the left, but either way you were going blind to the far side. If Meb—or anyone else so inclined—was going to set an ambush, this would be the place.

Duncan, in no mood for pissing about, got Mimi and himself tucked in tight to the fallen trunk, tugged the stalk on one of Crumley & Kegg's Fae-fucker grenades, and tossed it lightly over the tree to the other side.

"Going to make a bang," he told the girl, and a sudden look of delight lit up her face.

The bomb blew with its signature crump. No screams, no contact flash. Duncan counted two, then grabbed Mimi by the wrist and ducked under the trunk, pulled her with him. The iron filing dust was still settling. It lent the air a hazy, glamorous sheen, like a searchlight beam cutting fog. Duncan quartered about, McCulloch leveled, found nothing worth shooting anywhere in view.

"It wasn't very loud." Mimi, trying with all her four-year-old diplomacy not to sound too disappointed. "Can we make more bangs?"

Duncan shot her a look. "We'll see. You want some more water?"

She did. He passed her the canteen, watched her glug thirstily from it, got it back and capped it. Noted, as he stowed it again, how little water was left.

"Come on, then," he said. "Let's see how many sleepers you can jump this time."

They pushed on, still no signs of pursuit or shadowing, came eventually to a new station stop. It was another good place for an ambush—blunt, derelict rise of the concrete platforms on either side of the lines, tightly hemmed by trees. A warrior-caste Huldu might clear the foliage, cross the platform, and leap in less time than it takes to blink twice. The first you'd know of it would be the whooping battle cry as it dropped on you. Duncan slowed his pace, shuttled his gaze, left and right, kept the McCulloch raised. The girl noticed, came to him and clung to his coat.

"Are we stopping here?"

Dread etching her tone, the suddenly unsmiling set of her grubby pixie features. He thought absently that he really should have cleaned her face, wiped it with a damp cloth or something. It was the kind of thing a mother would do; it might have comforted her.

"No," he said. "We're just walking through. Got a little farther to go before we're home. This is just a . . . a place we have to pass."

"What place?" she quavered.

From memory and the regional maps he kept in his pack, Duncan thought it might be Lower Gortham, Hortham, something like that. But there was no quick and easy way to tell. No platform signs; they'd long ago rotted and tumbled, or been torn down, and almost all trace of the village they'd named was long gone, too. Whatever human homes had stood here once, the Forest had swallowed them whole.

Only the cracked wooden facade and window frames of a modest station building peered out amid thickets of brush and young trees, like a prisoner at the bars of a cell. Impossible to see if anything of the structure behind remained, or if the facade only stood courtesy of the jostling trees and bushes that held it up.

"It's called Lower Hortham," Duncan said breezily. "Little village, like the one we've just come from."

"But it's *gone,*" she said aghast. "What happened to the houses?"

"Well, uh, the people left." Approximation yawing increasingly away from any accurate truth. "And then the Forest came, and it grew over the houses."

"Why?"

Good question. As ever, there seemed no rhyme nor reason to it. Some places, the Forest ate entire, others, like Miller's Frith, went slowly, stealthily colonized with growth. Still others somehow survived untouched, even when the inhabitants were gone. There were theorics, Duncan knew, among the woodsmen and witches, in smoke-filled rooms of thinkers in Whitehall and Oxford and Cambridge alike. Maybe it was churches, consecrated places, that kept the Forest at bay—in view of what lived in the bell tower back at Miller's Frith, Duncan had to doubt that one—or maybe it was something geographical, geological even, some resonance of subterranean crystal or rock. Maybe even something to do with blood spilled in the ground, either mortal over the slaughterhouse centuries of human history, or Fae at some prehistoric juncture recorded history did not recall . . .

Truth was, no one had any answers. And nor did he.

"It's just what happens when people leave," he said. "You have to look after places if you want the Forest to stay out."

She looked up at him in silence. He saw tear sheen in her eyes, saw how very tired she was. He cupped her face with one hand.

"Come on. Not far now. We're nearly home, I promise. Stay at my side."

He dialed back his more obvious wariness, but strained his ears and kept the McCulloch up until they'd cleared the far end of the platforms and left the station behind. After that, he encouraged Mimi to skip from sleeper to sleeper again, as she had been. She went with the suggestion, as gamely as she could, but you could see her heart wasn't in it anymore. The twinned jut of the platforms fell behind, like paired reefs at low tide, in the wake of a ship steering well clear. Presently, the whole place faded into the gloom.

They trudged on.

MIDNIGHT CAME AND WENT. THE land around them began to tilt, rising to the right, increasingly steep, like an incoming wave, falling away more mildly to the left, so the roots of the trees and the ground itself on that side were hidden from view. L&YR's engineers had put in a modest sandstone embankment to support the looming slope on the right-hand side, blocks now heavily mossed, cracked, and crumbling in places. A similar wall below on the left shored up the line, made a terrace of it above the sloping lie of the land. A little farther along, Duncan caught the first, faint sounds he'd been waiting for—the rinse and chatter of a stream coming down fast through the trees on their right. He spotted it soon after, the glinting, broken rush of water over rocks as it tumbled to meet them, reached the line, and then disappeared under a small purpose-built gap in the embankment's stonework. You could hear the stream gurgle underneath, then emerge from the far side and carry on in cheery splash and hurry down the hill, though thickets of undergrowth and then the trees themselves hid it from view.

Farther down, he knew, this stream would find and empty into the River Ashop as it flowed southeast into ever deepening valleyed stretches to join the Derwent. But before that, the Ashop passed the bustling village and ferry station of Maltby, which, for reasons still unexplained, had not been engulfed by the Forests when they came. And where—he checked the Mappin & Webb—ex-of-the-Guards Colonel Martin Hardy should by now be installed and waiting with his men.

They were all but home and dry.

The curve on the rails tightened left, as the line bent northward, seeking Maltby and the station it had once served there. He'd probably—

Fast motion, corner of his eye, up in the trees to their right.

It was all the warning he got.

NINETEEN

PALE FLICKER FLASH, BETWEEN THE NARROW TRUNKS OF TREES.

Then another.

"Duncan . . ."

The girl, tugging at his coat—

He just had time to say, "I know."

Frenzied, bone-chilling screech across the cool night air. The first of the Huldu came hurtling from the wooded bank, leapt like an Olympian, hit the ground on Duncan's flank. Fucker gauged it to perfection, too—missed the rails, all of them, landed spring-heeled and poised and *in too fucking close* for Duncan to bring the McCulloch about . . .

Mimi shrieked—piercing, higher even than the Fae's war cry.

Duncan hooked round. Stared into a face out of a nightmare. Rage driven, the Fae had shape-shifted way beyond humanoid norms—face a grotesque elongation of fangs and tusks, long hands spun out like taffy, winter tree branch stark and stabbing. Black talons slashed. Duncan took the scant space he had, slammed the McCulloch crossways into the thing's face. Not much of the barrel made contact, but enough to burn. The Huldu reeled back, batting at the smolder. Duncan dropped the muzzle of the trench gun, blew off the creature's leg at the knee. The Fae went down screaming, collapsed across the closest rail, shrieked and thrashed away . . .

He spun back. Saw more crouched and spindled figures break onto the line ahead . . .

He grabbed Mimi Rush around the waist, lifted her, ran at the left side of the tracks and the drop-off to the slope below. It wasn't a long way down, but—

"Hold on!" he yelled. Heard her yelp in fear as they went over.

It wasn't elegant. They hit, he tripped, went staggering. Through some miracle—or witch's luck—he stayed on his feet. Stumbled again, still unbalanced, turning protectively to shield the child as best he could, crashed into the nearest tree trunk with his shoulder. It smashed a grunt out of him, tore something in the healing furrows of his shoulder, left him momentarily spin-headed.

No fucking time for that, Duncan!

He let Mimi go, braced himself fully upright with his back to the trunk, faced upslope. Up beyond the mossed and cracked embankment stonework, the Huldu he'd shot was still screaming. He pumped the McCulloch's slide, jacked in a fresh round.

"Mimi?" he rasped. "You all right?"

A whimper. "I hurt my hand."

"Aye, we'll fix that." Fumbling left-handed in his coat for another Kegg bomb. "Now get behind this tree and stay there till I call you!"

She scuttled to do it. The first of the Fae came hissing and snarling to the top of the embankment; he counted four, five, maybe more. They saw him below, sent up eerie, triumphant howls. He tugged the stalk on the bomb, lobbed it hard to the base of the stonework. The Huldu spilled off the ledge, landed a couple of seconds later than the Kegg. Duncan threw up a shielding arm and the Fae-fucker blew. He felt the rough sandpapering lash of the iron filings across his hand, brow, jaw, got some in his mouth . . .

But the Fae . . .

He dropped his arm, stared in awe at the harm he'd done. It was like watching the *flammenwerfer* assault at Hooge all over again. Staggering figures, screaming, blinded, beating at the flames that consumed them. The ones nearest the blast were already down, twitching spastic in the last throes of the death he'd brought them. Elsewhere, he saw one Huldu writhe through a full shape-shift, trying mindlessly to escape the fire that ate its flesh—down into some animal crouch, then a withering, a shedding, one poorly formed eagle span wing thrown skyward, but pulled back down again, eaten by the fire, crumpling to nothing . . .

Only one member of the hunting party remained on its feet, swaying, seared everywhere, still smoldering, but apparently still in the fight. It sensed him—whether with what remained of its vision or scent or some other sense he would never know—found direction, came at him in a limping rage of fangs and claws. Duncan levered himself off the tree. Leveled the McCulloch.

"Should have kept your fucking queen's word," he said, and pulled the trigger.

The shell tore a hole right through the Huldu's rib cage and out the back—he saw through the hole it made. The Huldu made a hissing, sighing sound, crumpled undramatically to the Forest floor.

He'd already pumped in the next round. He hung like cranked cable, scanned the line of the embankment. No movement. Thinning trees on both sides around him, no sign of further pursuit. He blew out a long, relieved breath.

Easy, lad. We're not out of the woods yet.

He listened—caught a howl, farther upslope, beyond the railway lines. Then another. More, answering. He grimaced. Looked like the revolt against Meb had spread wide. No telling how many angry young males were coming down the hill now. They might even bring archers . . .

He looked at the carnage around him, hoped they'd find it, hoped it might give them pause.

But it wasn't much of a hope and he didn't waste time clinging to it. He dug in his pockets, found two fresh rounds, and fed them into the McCulloch's receiver.

"Mimi?"

"I'm here," she quavered. Peeping around the trunk of the tree at him, eyes and nose, tiny hands braced on the bark. He put together a smile for her.

"Right, let's have a look at that hand of yours. Which one is it?"

Solemnly, she held out her left hand. He knelt, took it gently in both of his. Bent it a little, this way and that—*does that hurt? that?*—until she yelped. Looked like a sprain. They'd gotten off lightly.

"You'll be all right," he said. "We can put a bandage on it when we get there. You want me to kiss it better?"

She looked a bit uncertain about that, uptight Englishness too ingrained, or maybe it was just the years of hardship on the run with her mother had—

On the run?

Where'd *that* come from?

"You're hurt, too," the girl said, and pointed. "You've got blood."

"Have I?" He touched his face, found his fingers wet. Traced up to the slow seep of blood from his scalp—the fang gash from the night before had torn open again in the excitement; must have hit the tree with his head as well. He wiped the blood away, manufactured a grin.

"Looks like we've both been in the wars, doesn't it? Listen, Mimi, we have to hurry now. Down this hill, fast as we can go. There's a river at the bottom and people waiting for us there. Soldiers, policemen. They'll protect you."

Duncan took her by the uninjured right hand, started them down the slope. It wasn't great ground to cover at speed—plenty of roots to trip over in the gloom, humps and tuffets and hidden sink spots, now starting to cover over with the first autumn layer of leaves. He'd hoped to follow the railway right out of the tree line and into the meadows before they cut across and down the slope to the ferry crossing, but that was botched now, no chance of going back up. Downslope direct would have to do, and just hope they made the tree line ahead of their pursuers.

Howls upslope, not so distant now. He tried not to look back.

"See if you can see lights down there," he told the girl. "It's not far."

True enough—he could see the trees thinning out around them, more space and moonlight everywhere. It was all he could do not to pick up the pace and drag Mimi along behind him like the rag doll he'd packed away for her. He kept the pace steady, wove their path a little to favor the more open ground. Once, the girl tripped, but he dragged her upright so she didn't fall.

"Oops." Bright and breezy as he could manage. "Don't worry, I got you."

Some creeping sense in his gut, he glanced sideways to the right. Caught the flash of motion, something leaping, plunging downhill to pace them.

"There! There!" The girl's high, piping cry. For a moment, he thought she'd seen the same thing he had. "I can see lights!"

His heart slammed in his chest. "Where?"

"There! Right *there*!" Tiny arm raised, pointing. He followed the line it tracked, spotted the gleaming through the foliage ahead. Aye, a whole fucking cluster of lights and—he strained his senses—yes, faintly, voices. Human voices, raised in alarm. Someone had heard the shotgun blasts.

They were close. Five hundred yards at worst.

Movement on their left flank. He snapped about, saw the pallid, leaping shape, coming in fast . . .

"Run, Mimi!" he yelled. "Run for the lights!"

And swung about to meet the new threat. The Huldu charged in, all fangs and talons and staring blank black eyes. He snapped the shot, hit it in the shoulder, saw it spin about with the impact and go down. Not a killing shot, he knew. No time to make it good, no time. Pump, fall back. Out of the corner of his eye, he saw the diminutive figure of the girl running full pelt down the slope. He went after her, turning constantly about, scanning the trees on all sides. Saw movement, off on his flank, snapped another shot, no idea if it found its target or not. Pumped the slide.

"Keep running, Mimi!" he bawled.

Wailed assent.

He saw the Huldu now, two or three of them at least, skulking between trees, trying to flank him. He dug out a Kegg bomb, pulled the stalk with his teeth, spat it out. Tossed the bomb and fell back as rapidly as he could. Grabbed another bomb—tug—toss. The first one blew, must have caught somebody, he heard a yowl. He fell back again, McCulloch weaving for targets, none found. The Kegg bombs were giving them pause. Or maybe some stopped for injured comrades, aye, you could fucking hope . . .

Fall back, fall back.

Down this fucking slope backward.

But over his head, the gap between the crowns of trees stretched, spread out, let in a sky shoveled with the broken glass of stars, thick and twinkling, they must be—

Mimi wailed. A different note in it, sharp with pain. She'd gone over, fallen.

Duncan snapped around, saw her sprawled full length over a root. So did one of their pursuers—he felt more than saw the Huldu leap past him a solid yard over head height. Yank up the barrel of the McCulloch—he felt a tug in his wounded shoulder with the speed of the move—gunned the Fae out of the air, no idea where he hit it, saw it go tumbling and screaming down the slope. He ran to catch it, pumped the slide as he moved. Reached the Huldu as it struggled to rise, stomped down hard on its neck, put another shot between its shoulder blades—

The second attacker cannoned into him from the rear. He felt talons slash across his side, dig in deep. He screamed as the old wounds from the night before tore open anew. Swing and face this fucker—the Huldu's rage-distorted fangs snapped inches from his face. He uppercut left-handed, into the elongated jaw—weak shot, in close, but the iron rings in the punch did their job. Magnesium splutter and flare, the Fae reeled back, Duncan followed with the McCulloch in both hands, slammed the barrel hard in at eye level. Second flash-flare, broader this time. Blinded, the Huldu lashed out again wildly, caught him in the shoulder, he felt fresh furrows torn deep, yelled pure rage at the pain, slamfired the McCulloch and took off his attacker's head. The Fae's body stood strong for an insane second, fountain of coruscating blood out of the neck, then dropped like a puppet with its strings slashed through. Duncan, swaying on his feet . . .

The girl.

And howls through the trees around him.

Stand, sir! Stand up! Shredded memory, some bluff Aberdonian NCO at Ypres, Duncan's first bombardment, and thrown flat in the trench, sprawling stunned in a hail of muddy clods and body parts from the same shell that knocked him flat. *Stay in the fight, sir! The men need to see you! Sir! Just—fuckssake, sir—stand!*

Aye, c'mon, Duncan, ya big sook. Stay in the fucking fight.

He jacked a fresh shell into the McCulloch, staggered to Mimi, crouched at her side, and rolled her. She was crying, deep, desperate sobs, tear-ribboned face, blood from a nasty scrape down one cheek, mouth a down-drawn oval emitting the cries. Gut-punch relief that she hadn't winded herself or broken anything. He grabbed her upright, steadied her, put one hand on her bloodied cheek.

"You're not hurt!" he yelled at her. "You're not hurt!"

Wide-eyed, trembling. But she seemed to nod. He turned her bodily to face downhill. Saw the spread of lights down at the river's edge. Torches, hurricane lamps, at least one campfire. Activity on both sides, and it looked like they had at least one ferry boat up and running. Two score men, at least. Not more than two hundred yards now. The final fringes of the Forest clung around them, lone trees and copses pushing out the line, but the last 150 yards to the water was pasture, open ground, a killing field for Hardy, if he'd brought the right hardware.

"There!" he said hoarsely. "Look, the soldiers! Your mother's waiting! You run for your mother! Run for the lights!"

"You!" she wailed, clutching at him. "You!"

"I'm right behind you, wean! Don't you worry about me. Now, *go*!"

She went. Tottered unsteadily away down the slope, like some ill-used mechanical toy. Howls behind them, on both sides now. Mimi heard and cried out, speeded up.

He dug his pockets for shells, fed them to the McCulloch with desperate, fumbling speed. He was five down, dangerously low. Blood running copiously down the inside of his shirt. Fresh, searing pain across his ribs and down from his shoulder.

Stand up!

Duncan felt his lips draw back from his teeth. Flogged back to his feet.

"Come on, then," he snarled.

As if in answer, the howls. He faced the sound, thought he caught flickered movement in the copse off to his left. He racked the McCulloch, winced at what the action did to his shoulder, began a slow retreat, out of the trees.

Something snapped and hissed in the copse, came at him crouched. He fired from the hip, never knew if he hit—the Huldu dived away, back into the trees, seemed disinclined to show itself again. Duncan grinned, found another Kegg bomb and tugged the fuse. On general principles, he tossed it where the undergrowth and foliage were thickest, walked steadily backward as he waited for the blast . . .

And into the open of the meadow.

It took him seconds to realize he'd done it. Suddenly, open ground. Stars, an uninterrupted glimmering display now everywhere over his head, the moon beaming from low on the horizon to his right. Oddly, the darkness felt suddenly deeper, more complete. Long damp grass to his knees. He looked cautiously over his shoulder, saw torch beams jump and wag in the darkness, figures running out from the river's edge to meet Mimi in the meadow as she tottered toward them. They knelt to her height, someone swept her up and carried her. He puffed out a long sigh of relief, felt himself sag.

Stand, sir!

He caught himself, cast about for one more check along the tree line. Swung back to the men below in the meadow, hand raised to wave—

Wink of light from over the river—was that—?

Something slammed him hard across the side of the head.

Meadow grass and stars went spinning around him crazily, like painted sheets in a pantomime backdrop grabbed and flapped by some improbable, gyring wind. Distant thunder. He hit something hard with his whole body. Realized it was the ground.

Scrabbling for coherent thought—that couldn't be right, that was—

Something massive snatched the thought away, crushed him apart from it.

Sucked him down, away.

Into fresh-smelling, earthen dark.

TWENTY

DUNCAN DREAMS HE LIES IN WET GRASS, LIMBS PINNED DOWN, clothing soaked through, heavy with the moisture. Gray fleece of a dawn sky stretched overhead, faint whisper of rain, down into the meadow and onto his face, splashing in his eyes, blurring his vision.

Blinking it away seems an impossible task.

His body, beneath the drenched clothes, is a catalog of damage, rips and gashes, stiffened with the cold and the damp, crusted blood—

Movement, close by. Someone—or something—is coming to sniff him over. He twitches, but really cannot move. Roaring in his ears, icy panic along his veins.

Stand, sir! Stand up!

No dice, Sergeant. Sorry about that. Just going to lie here, if that's all right with you.

Duncan!

Mimi Rush, crouched over him, staring.

But she's supposed to be gone, safe, not still here—

Now he'll fucking move. He'll move, if it takes him . . .

Nope.

And—awful, creeping dread in his bones the longer he stares at her—there's something *wrong* with Mimi, with the side of her face, something terrible has been done to her . . .

The rain, filling up his eye sockets, drowning his sight. Time running out like sand. He strains to tip his head sideways, to spill the pooling water out. He blinks hard, looks again at Mimi.

She doesn't look well, that's for sure, pallid and worn and—

You've got my doll, she hisses at him.

HE KNOWS, BEFORE HE EVEN makes the first ridge and the pale smudge of dawn that hangs above it, that it's going to be Isnorvi.

Isnorvi, who's been shadowing him around camp the last few days, sneering and trying to provoke him with ribald comments about Mebhuranon's attentions. Isnorvi who seems, with terrifying Fae clairvoyance, to know that he's planning to try again. Isnorvi, with strength and sight and fleetness of foot beyond the mortal, who stalks him now, farther down the slope, hanging back, biding his time, waiting for his moment.

And all Duncan can do is play the game.

He pushes himself as hard as he can for the ridge. There'll be time later to conserve strength, to pace himself through the long run ahead, but for now he must get out of any possible line of sight back to the camp. If his early failures taught him nothing else, it was this. *The Fae see far, see fast, catch splintered glimpses no mortal eye can match. Distance and daylight alone will not serve to save you. You must break your pursuers' gaze with the rise and fall of mother earth herself.*

Or so says the pretty tree sprite who took his hand and showed him where to dig . . .

He flounders up the last few yards to the top, gasping for breath, grabbing at slim birch trunks to lever himself onward. It's not yet morning, but enough light seeps in from the east to put faint color on everything around him—the leaves over his head begin to be green again, the stones in the Huldu cairns shade from darkened silhouette to stony texture and tone as he passes among them. Moss shows on the stone in soft, velvety green clumps, lichen in patches speckled mustard yellow and gray. And the faint blue glow of their glyphs is fading, retreating deeper into the engraving, gone altogether in some eastward-looking places . . .

"Duncan!"

Deep tremor through him as Isnorvi spits out his name. He stops dead.

"Where you think you're going, you sniveling tree-thief waste?"

Trembling, he makes himself turn. Isnorvi stands twenty feet off, grinning hard, apparently not even out of breath.

"I'm going home," Duncan manages, through teeth gritted against his fear.

"No you're not."

Bored contempt dripping from the words—how many times has Duncan run and then been run down? How many times dragged back, bruised and weeping, and flung at Svalenkari's feet for punishment?

Why would this be any different?

Duncan reaches into the rags he wears, clutches the thing he dug up. Hunches over it for comfort. Some tiny flame licks up inside him.

"I won't let you take me back," he yells shakily.

It comes out a lot less loud than he wanted.

Isnorvi's grin broadens, lengthens, his fangs come out—long and wolfish with shape-shift effect. He'll have grown them that way as he followed Duncan up through the thinning darkness. All the Huldu young are doing it now, growing into their powers, testing them on each other, sprouting sudden, distorted faces full of bestial teeth and tusks, armored brow ridges and jaws. They snap and snarl at each other, scare the thralls into dropping their loads, groveling at their feet.

Fun and games.

Isnorvi rushes him.

Three long strides, Fae elegance in motion, it looks almost like gliding. Maybe two more steps to reach Duncan and flatten him on the spot.

But Duncan isn't waiting.

Tears squirting in his eyes, shaking like he's come down with a fever, yelling wordless, Duncan comes running to meet Isnorvi in a head-down charge.

It throws the Huldu completely.

Isnorvi's taloned hands are reaching, but they're reaching wrong. His timing is off. The mortal boy just isn't where he should be. He flinches a little, trying to correct. Duncan screams, pulls the thing he found, swings it savagely at Isnorvi's face.

Made by the road builders, the sword and spear men, the eagle worshippers, the ones who came from the sun, the tree sprite giggled, pointing shyly at the thing once he's unearthed it. *The Bright Folk can't touch it, but you can. You can fight with it!*

Many years later, looking back hard through the memory of his time in the Forest, trying to separate truth from nightmare and hindsight myth, Duncan will understand that what he dug up was a Roman nail, eight or ten inches of ragged iron, maybe more. Lost there maybe two thousand years in the dirt, corroded rough and crooked, but still weighty, still strong, still apt for puncture and harm.

He gouges the rough edge of the nail right into Isnorvi's face as he dodges past. It raises a flaring fire in its path, greenish bright. Smoke billows, a weird, acrid stink on the air. Isnorvi shrieks and spins away, clutching the wound with one hand. He recoils from Duncan, fending off weakly with the other hand, *and somehow that's enough.* That's the trigger. Something happens to the trembling in Duncan's limbs, some deep-rooted human alchemy switches the shaking over from weakness to thrumming force. Fear vaporizes, is gone, yields instead to a towering, incandescent fury, years and years of terror and hate and need let loose.

Duncan closes with his prey.

He advances, slashing hard, overarm, full force, back and forth, and every strike rips fresh lines of fire, fresh shrieks from the Huldu boy. Isnorvi staggers backward, both hands up now warding, and Duncan carves lines of fire across them, too. Isnorvi stumbles, goes over, falls on his side between the cairns. He tries dizzily to ward off his attacker one more time, but Duncan stomps down the arm, is on him, on top of him, punching down everywhere with the nail. Fire blooms across Isnorvi's pale ivory neck and shoulders and flanks, like fistfuls of crocus across some chilly snow-touched clearing at dawn. The shrieks are a punctuated howl, then a sustained wailing, finally a mewling. Isnorvi twists and cringes, tries feebly to crawl away, and Duncan can't seem to stop, he's still punching down, over and over and over, wet, blood-choked rupturing sounds from the Fae boy. The nail has snapped under the force of the blows, lost nearly half its length, but still he rains the blows down, hissing at Isnorvi to *shut up! shut up! shut up!!!*

And, finally, Isnorvi does.

DUNCAN LIES BROKEN UNDER THE soughing canopy of a wind-whipped elm. Night sky above, the day has come and gone, it seems. Pattering of rain through the leaves above, occasional speck on his face. His head is banging, it feels gritty and hot along one side. The sensation is familiar enough, paradoxically, to let him relax. Sluggish dream panic ebbing away, a sour, customary resignation taking over. It's almost like seeing an old acquaintance's face, not one you liked very much, but one from whom you knew pretty much what to expect.

He's been shot.

And this, he's starting to realize, is no fucking dream.

THEY COME AFTER HIM, OF course. The others, Svalenkari's hunters, roused now with his absence from camp, sent to find him, finding Isnorvi's mutilated corpse instead.

He hears them, shrilling outrage to each other across the wooded glens, sounds a normal human might write off as overly loud and querulous buzzard cry. Each time he hears it, his heart climbs up and jams into his throat and his trembling returns in force. Because this time, he knows, there can be no return. No beating, no matter how severe, would be sufficient punishment now. The law of the Forest is clear. No mortal may ever do harm to a Huldu, no matter what the provocation. He's seen thralls, some of them barely more than children still, executed for daring even to draw Fae blood in a quarrel. He's seen examples made.

They will kill him for what he's done to Isnorvi. Svalenkari will do it with his bare hands.

It's easy now.

Get home. Or die.

Something about the iron simplicity of it kills his fear, puts fresh strength in his stride, a grim new determination. And—he will realize many years later—by now the odds have tipped in his favor. Winter is in retreat, early spring chopping back the nights, bringing in longer, brighter days, light that will dazzle his pursuers as they look for him, perhaps even drive them back. The forests of Argyll are not yet what they will become again after the Unbinding. Man's mark is still upon them. Across Scotland, the burn-back and logging, the careless husbandry of millennia has long since left open ground everywhere you look—peat bogs and bleak moors, patchwork planted river valleys, drystone-walled small holdings, whole sweeping estates of fenced pasture and fallow ground. *Seek the wide open,* the tree sprite whispered with ticklish intimacy. *Shun the shadows we cast, look for the burning ball, look for renewal, for it is the season, and you are young and juicy.*

And she giggled and stuck her green tongue in his ear, giddy with the rising sap of spring.

But it isn't that easy.

For as long as he can remember, the Forest has been his home, and where it runs out, a creeping sensation of . . . *exposure* touches with icy fingers at his nape. He hovers on the fringes at first, held back with ingrained fear of stepping out from under the sheltering canopies into unbroken sunlight and space. But the balancing terror of Svalenkari's wrath drives him out. Forces him to dart forward into this meadow or that, whenever he hears, or thinks he hears, signs of pursuit. He mingles with herds of sheep or cattle, skulks along fence lines and drystone walls, shelters once shivering and afraid in an abandoned shepherd's hide until the bark of an approaching dog chases him out and on.

At midday, he drinks from a rusted iron trough he finds in the corner of a field.

Once or twice, across the fields, he sees actual humans in the distance, hears the barking of other dogs, but he dares not approach.

As the day tips over into afternoon and the quality of the light begins to fail, he grows desperate. Estimating as best he can, he tracks the edges of the woodlands he remembers, dips back into the forest to take his bearings, ears pricked for any sound of his Fae hunters, then ducks back out and trudges on, backtracking the path they dragged him weeping away on, the night of Isnorvi's birthday surprise . . .

It's almost full dark when he finally reaches Stac Dubh.

Unused to seeing structures of its sort, he spots the geometric yellow glow of one or two lit windows in the gloom before the mansion itself. But as the house emerges in somber, crenelated bulk, as he creeps through the surrounding farmed fields and onto the magical lawns, the seared memories of the last time he was here take over. Everything seems a little smaller than he recalls—later, he'll understand it's because he's older, grown larger—but beyond that, the deep realization *that he's made it,* that he's here at last, hits him like one of Isnorvi's punches to the gut.

He stands breathless before the stone edifice and its cheery yellow cutouts as if before an altar to some power he still cannot name.

From the uppermost cutout, a sudden, wooden creak and bang, as the sash window lifts.

A darkened silhouette of head and shoulders against the yellow light, hunching outward, peering down.

THIS—IS NO FUCKING DREAM . . .

Right.

He lies with his head in the fork between two tree roots, skull pressed back gently against the bole. The rain seems to have stopped. The pain in his head is still there, but softened, receding. Odd stickiness across the site of the previous heat.

Shot, he pieces groggily together once more. He sees the glint from over the river again, from among Hardy's assembled men. The distant roll of thunder. *They fucking shot me!*

Well, they did their mortal best, trills someone gaily over his head. *But what avail crude lead and mortal's schemes against witch's luck and Fae heart's blood and now my own small sticky contribution. What avail against the potency seeded in you now? Oh, all across the Domain shall know* this *tale!*

Only one possible source for that voice—no one else talks that way. He tilts his head back and up, sees narrow green-glowing eyes peering down, set in a nut-brown pixie face. Confirmation, and with it understanding dawns—what he'd taken for the fork between two tree roots is no such thing. His head is cradled between the spread thighs of the tree sprite, soft, peeling texture against his cheeks like the bark of young aspen trunks. Green tendril fingers grip his face and jaw—one slips, playful and squirming, into the corner of his mouth—and they turn his skull gently, side to side.

What small contribution? he mumbles indistinctly, and tries to push out the tendril finger with his tongue.

The skogsra's features crease in delight beneath her mop of tangled, spriggy hair. Silver birch gleam of teeth in the grin. She squeezes her thighs tight around his face a moment, quivers, loosens them again. She smells of fresh loam and mulch and rain, shot through at moments as she moves with the sharp whiff of crushed blackberries and mint.

Here, she breathes, and reaches back past his head to the juncture of her thighs, brings back fingers thick with sap, smears the fresh secretion along the line of his wound. *This heals all. But my sisters will have taught you this already, many, many times, on your visits to them, is it not so?*

Word gets around, I see.

The tree sprite giggles, reaches back inside herself again, moves to smear the furrow along his skull one more time. He raises a hand to stop her, to touch the wound.

Wait, that's fine. That's enou—

Instantly, she locks fingers around his wrist, stops him touching, tendril grip abruptly hardened to polished wood, immovable as a buried root, as if her grasp grew around him over decades while he was plunged into some glamoured sleep. He knows better than to fight this. He makes himself relax.

All right, all right. But tell me what happened, at least.

You shall be told, for it is a tale. But take my balm, it has already sealed the gashes elsewhere on you, even this one, and will do more with time. Your wound was not deep, for you turned as they loosed upon you, the lead they hurled barely kissed you on its way past and into the Domain, where it buried itself, and lies buried still, in sturdy bark.

Right. It makes some sense. Glint across the river, the muzzle flash, but—memory sharpens, details return—aye, he *was* turning, *had* turned, once already, to sweep the tree line for pursuit, then turned back again . . .

Aye. Fucking nightmare for any sniper working at that distance.

Was it your *sturdy bark they hit, then?*

The tree sprite giggles, puts her other hand up to her lips, then lets the tendril fingers trail down onto her softly peeling pale breast. *Oh, not* mine, she says archly. *My bark is smooth and unblemished wherever you may touch it.*

Not for the first time, Duncan gets a sudden flash of memory from the war—this flinty blue-eyed French granny in an inn he was billeted at with the Americans in Saint-Nazaire. The woman had to be well into her seventies—though spry with it, immaculately turned out and helping her daughter out around the place with seemingly boundless energy—but when she dealt with the billeted men, there was a sudden sparkle in her eye and step, an outrageously flirtatious girlishness to her manner that you couldn't help responding to. It was as if there *was* somehow still a young French sexpot dreaming just beneath the rough and lived in seventy-year-old skin, as if, at a moment's notice, she might split her aged carapace to shriveling fragments and climb on out, lithe and smooth and ready to back up her flirting to the hilt.

He knows the skogsra, once contained within the bark of their chosen tree, live on a timescale in which human affairs blink by like cocaine moments out on the town. Stepping out of their deep dreaming and into that speeded-up whirl is clearly a dizzying business for them, a release they seem to relish, but also handle with, for such rooted, serene beings, an alarming lack of gravitas or reflection. They present as flirty, flighty, here for the party and not much else.

Duncan frowns, makes an effort. *They didn't hit you, so what brought you out looking for me?*

Oh, we did not look for you, I or any of my sisters. The skogsra released his hand, gestured with her sap-dripping fingers across the clearing. *It was* she *that dragged you to us.*

He props himself up an inch or two to look. Sees Mimi Rush seated in the darkness against the bole of another tree.

Except, of course, it isn't Mimi at all.

THE CHANGELING SEES HIM INSTANTLY, across the dark and distance from window to lawn. Gleam of teeth and eyes in the silhouette of its face.

Perhaps it could already sense his approach, with whatever remained of the magic used to bring it into being. Or perhaps its misgivings were more general, tossing it from uneasy sleep, sending it to the window to look. In either case—

Duncan froze when the window went up. Now—sudden intimations down his spine of what's about to happen—he snaps into motion, jumps forward on the lawn, desperate to reach the door and hammer at it to be let in. But the changeling is faster. With unhuman speed and flexibility, it grabs the window frame, hinges itself bodily out onto the facade of the house, falls casually ten feet upside down, then grabs hold of some detail in the stonework. Duncan's mouth drops open. The changeling swings one-handed, grabs with the other hand and both feet, spiders downward over the stone with no more effort than a squirrel coming down a tree. Duncan's running full tilt by now, breath sobbing in his throat, he's close . . .

The changeling lets go again, leaps, does a high, flopping somersault in midair. It lands cat footed, naked, in Duncan's path across the lawn. Duncan slams to a halt, staring at his own face in the gloom. He thought he'd be prepared for this; he isn't. The changeling lifts arms like something bat winged wanting to take flight, blocking Duncan from the house and everything in it. It bares its teeth at him.

"No! Mine!" it snarls.

The words are in English—it takes moments for rusty wires in Duncan's head to cross and spark, firing up recollection of the other language, just barely learned before the Skogurtal came to crush it away. In that gap, that moment of memory and hesitation, the changeling flies at him, tooth and nail.

Perhaps if Duncan had not come with Isnorvi's blood already on his hands, he would have gone down under those flailing blows. Perhaps, exhausted at journey's end, wanting only warmth and comfort and relief, he would have fallen at this, the last hurdle.

Instead, he meets the changeling with a scream of his own and the broken stub of the Roman nail in his clenched right fist. A hand grabs his throat, digs in. But it has no talons, not even nails a decent length, and the skin of the fingers is soft. A kind of fierce joy rises in him. He tears the hand loose without thinking, uses a Huldu wrestling trick to dump the changeling over his hip and onto the lawn on its back. It lands hard, breath exploded from its lungs, and he scrambles to straddle it. A wild, looping punch lands in his eye; he barely feels it. He shakes it off. He raises the ragged iron remnant in his hand, hammers down.

There's no flash fire, no smoke or smolder, but the nail rips down through the changeling's cheek and blood jumps across the chilly night air. Sprinkles hot on Duncan's face. The changeling makes a noise like a furious cat, lashes out. Duncan shrugs off the blow, punches down again and again with the nail. He feels it skid on teeth or maybe exposed bone. Soft hands flail at him, paw at his chest. He gets an eye. The pawing hands fall away, go to covering against the rain of blows. Hoarse cries from the changeling now, half submerged, repeated words coming through, and once again Duncan's rusted English is slow to catch it . . .

"Father! Mother! Mother! *Mama!*"

It detonates a whole new level of fury in him he would have thought impossible. The iron remnant of the nail in his hand has broken again, barely protrudes from his clenched fist at all. He goes to work with his fists instead, pounding, pounding, into the face the changeling wears, obliterating the mirror of his features, blood splattering on his hands, up beyond his wrists now . . .

"Mummy, Mummy," bubbles the changeling, and then stops.

Something leaves it like a sigh, like a sudden, fierce gust of wind through trees, rustling, tearing at leaves, and then gone.

Duncan sits astride the ruin of his twin, cocked fists suddenly frozen, panting, tears streaming down his face. He sees the damage he's done, and his mouth moves, wordless, making the forms he saw on the changeling's lips only moments before.

Mummy, Mummy.

As if in response, the body under him shifts and moves, seems to crack open and collapse inward across the chest. An odor of swamp and rotted wood billows up, makes him gag.

Behind him, lights spring up everywhere in the house.

PART II

AFFAIRS OF MEN

It is not a very fragrant world, but it is the world you live in.

—Raymond Chandler

TWENTY-ONE

LATER, THE CHANGELING CAME AND FOUND HIM.

He'd clambered up into the bole of a massive, ancient beech, just back from the tree line. It was high enough above the surrounding canopies to offer damp, tranquil views across the meadows, the river, and the village of Maltby beyond. Tiled roofs huddled on the rising ground, gathered around the inevitable church spire. Smoke wisped up prettily here and there from cottage chimneys and the stack of the little flatbed ferry as it made the crossing. Whatever presence Hardy had established there two nights ago was long gone, dismantled, packed up, driven away. If you looked hard in the autumn sunlight, you could see one or two ammunition crates, abandoned and presumably empty, on the boards of the wooden jetty where the ferry made landfall on the meadow side. The grass close by had been trampled, churned up in places, but beyond these signs, you could have been forgiven for thinking none of it had ever happened.

Duncan touched the scoring left by the sniper's bullet along the side of his skull. It was still faintly sticky with the tree sprite's secretions, but there was no longer any pain.

Fucking happened, right enough.

But why?

He closed his eyes, pressed finger and thumb against his eyelids, and tried once again to extract sense from the reversal. The ambush, the rendezvous, the sniper. Shuffle the face cards, deal them out faceup—Mimi Rush, Garner, Hardy. Did Garner garble the message? Did the Huldu attack spook Hardy's men? Did Mimi herself say something they took the wrong way?

He could make no better hand of it now than in his previous dozen attempts.

Stealthy rustle of leaves.

He blinked, looked round. Saw Mimi Rush's changeling seated there on a nearby branch across from him. It really was looking the worse for wear—face sagging on one side, one eyelid drooping, mouth pulled down at the corner. Hair in grimy ropes. Skin pallid gray and stretched seeming under clothes now grubby, ragged and torn, the same clothes it had been dressed in when he'd taken it from the Rush household only days ago. Below the muddied cuffs, the hands had turned clawlike and were sprouting outcrops of something that looked like tiny beige mushrooms across the backs and knuckles.

For all that, it sat in the tree with an elegance and ease that no human child could have managed. It looked solemnly at him out of its lopsided face. Said nothing at all.

"Why?" he asked it finally.

It shifted daintily on the branch, held out one hand, for all the world like a debutante examining her manicure. Stared at the fungal growth across the back.

"*It's not your fault.*" The imitation of his voice was so good Duncan almost touched his own lips to check he hadn't been the one to speak. "*No hard feelings. Get yourself under cover.*"

The murdered tree line outside Erlsley, days ago. His own words. The sickened feeling as his long-held hatreds curdled, puddled away into something even less bearable.

Pointing at the forest like it was some kind of solution.

He sighed. "All right."

"Why did they shoot you? Why kill you?"

The changeling's own voice still held a faint trace of the real Mimi, but the sibilance had crept in more in the days since Erlsley, and there was another, rusted tone beneath, like broken gears grinding, like dead autumn leaves crunched underfoot.

"I don't know why." He looked bleakly out at Maltby Ferry, the chimney smoke from the hearth fires of men. "But someone out there does. And sooner or later I'm going to find them and make them tell me."

"You will go back?"

"Oh, aye. I'm going back right enough."

"It will be dangerous?"

He grinned unpleasantly. "Not so much. No one's going to be looking for a dead man."

The changeling hesitated. Bit its lip. One canine went right through and it winced. Pale gray fluid leaked from the puncture. It licked at the wound, frowning.

"Will you give me the doll?" it asked.

Startled, Duncan looked down into the clearing, where his pack stood against an elm trunk. It was still neatly fastened shut, just the way he'd packed it back in Miller's Frith. "How did you know it was in there?"

"I . . . smell it. I smell her, I smell . . . Mother."

"But you didn't take it? You could have taken it. While I was—" He gestured at his own head. "The skogsra would not have cared."

"Dolls are . . . giften." The changeling frowned, clearly trying to formulate something in its head, maybe hold on to some fast-fading memory from before. "Gifts. Gifted. Mother-given . . ."

It blinked rapidly, looked away.

"Will you gift it to me?"

"Aye," he said gently. "I'll gift it to you. Seems like the least I can do."

BELOW, IN THE CLEARING, HE unfastened the pack and dug out the doll. In the filtering late afternoon light through the trees, it looked even smaller and grubbier than he remembered. The changeling stood at his side, trembling a little. He was already crouched to its level; he could hear the tiny scraping wheeze of its breath. He hunkered awkwardly around, held out the doll. Cleared his throat.

"Here. It's yours. Take it."

The changeling took the doll in one clawed hand, barely looked at it, clutched it to its chest. Duncan hung there, felt himself unaccountably reach out a hand and press it briefly to the changeling's sagging cheek.

"It's yours," he repeated.

"You . . . have your mother?" the changeling husked.

"Had." He swallowed. "Gone now. I don't see her."

"Your mother . . . gifted you?"

"Aye." He held down the bitter memories with an effort. "As best she could. She tried."

. . . saying there's something wrong *with him, Archie. He's not right, you know he's not. Something* happened *that night. He's not been the same since . . .*

Hissing, desperate voices from behind the paneled door, his mother's pleading tone. They think he's in bed, they think he cannot hear.

His father, pleading, too, in his own way.

. . . just sleepwalking. He's been doing it nearly since he could walk. How many times, Julia, how many times has he been out of his bed at all hours and wandering about, half the time outside? Remember when—he was what, three or four—we found him in the paddock with the cows? Or when Craig found him almost in the woods that time, just standing there, staring at the trees . . .

And the blood on his hands? On his fists, *Archie?*

Julia—

Like some . . . drunken gillie after a square go with his pals at the ceilidh? How do you explain that *away, Archie?*

Finlay found a carcass on the lawn the next morning. Not much left of it, he reckoned foxes or polecats had been at it. Maybe—

Maybe he'd been punching *it? Punching a bloody carcass in his sleep, until his knuckles were raw? Do you hear yourself?*

Tight silence. Duncan's Forest-attuned hearing brings him the clink of Edinburgh Crystal, decanter neck on tumbler. His father sighing, taking the first whisky sip of the evening. Duncan imagines the man's sunken eyes, glowering across the room over the rim of the glass.

Then what?

I—I don't—

Then what, woman? What?

I don't know! Voice rising to a shout. *All I know is that child sleeping upstairs is not my Duncan!*

Silence, shuttering down behind the shouted syllables of his name. When his father finally speaks into the resulting quiet, there's a dangerous, even calm in his tone that Duncan, newly arrived at Stac Dubh, has not yet heard.

But it reminds him of Svalenkari.

Julia, we are not going through this nonsense again. You are an educated woman. I won't have this . . . this descent *into belowstairs superstition and bloody delirium. The Huldu are tales, told to frighten small children and ignorant peasants, and you, my dear, are neither. No one has swapped your child, stolen it out from under your nose—not seven years ago, and not now either!*

That was different!

Not at the time, it wasn't! Don't you remember how you wept? How you swore he was looking at you in some way that wasn't right in a bairn? How he scared you?

I—Archie, I was tired then, it was different, I didn't realize what being a mother . . . This is not the same, this is real. *I can't believe you don't see it, too! His voice is different, his expressions, the way he looks at me, his whole body, his hands—have you looked at his hands? They're rough, calloused—*

Oh for Christ's sake, Julia! The boy is growing up. Of course he's not your soft little bairn anymore! You just haven't bloody noticed till now is all.

Growing up? Is that why he barely speaks to us above single-syllable words and grunts now? Is that why he suddenly doesn't understand English properly when his tutors have him? Why he can't write it anymore?

He's just being difficult. Boys of an age—

Boys of an age! A choked laugh, rinsed clean of all humor. *Last night he climbed up with me on the chaise longue, tried to snuggle up to me, and asked me to read him a story! At his age! Archie, it made my skin crawl!*

Crouching, Fae-still and poised to bolt from his listening post on the staircase, Duncan feels his eyes tear up again, the way they did that day on the chaise longue.

Well, I'm afraid that does you no credit at all, my dear. Duncan knows he's going away to board this year after the summer. He's likely feeling soft and daft, that's all.

Going away? The hard laugh again, clearer now. *You mean Cadogan's? Archie, they aren't going to bloody take him at Cadogan's in this state.*

They bloody well will! Real anger now. *With what I contribute to the Old Boys' fund, they have no choice. If they're not getting rained on in chapel right now, it's down to me. They should be calling it the Slaven kirk, the amount of money I put in. They bloody well will have my boy, and they will do right by him.*

Duncan's mother makes a small, hopeless noise. He thinks he hears footfalls across the room. He hears his father's voice soften, can hope he's gone to her, put a kind hand on her shoulder or held her cheek . . .

Julia, listen. It's only a few months until he's gone. And you'll weep from lack of him then, you know you will. Make the effort, woman. If you want back on the laudanum, I'll allow it, provided Elsie keeps a check on dosage with you every day—

She sniffs. *I don't need laudanum.*

But it helped last time, did it not?

Did it? Something despairing in her voice now, something broken. He hears her keening, down at the lower limits of his hearing. *He's gone. My bonnie lad, he's gone again.*

She tries, though. All through that spring and summer until the school year at Cadogan's begins and Finlay takes him in the trap to the train, she does her best. But her embraces are conditional, braced and wary, her voice will often falter when she talks to him, and a shadow crosses her face as often as not whenever he enters a room.

Cadogan's, when he gets there, for all its casual, boyish brutalities and dour, cold-water discipline, comes as a relief. A relief he can feel in every fiber of his being.

It's an arena he knows only too well how to fight in.

DUNCAN GAVE IT UNTIL SUNSET before he set out.

In part, it was simple prudence. Faces are harder to see in the gloom, harder still to recall. And Maltby Ferry was his easiest way home—at best, there'd be a late bus back to Erlsley; at worst he could get a bed for the night in the village. The ferry itself could be hailed from the Forest side until eight o'clock, he knew, but he preferred not to take the last crossing, where he'd likely be either the solitary passenger or one among a very nervous few—in either case noticed, maybe conversed with, certainly remembered. If he timed it right, though, he'd get to the river at dusk, just in time for the press of passengers hurrying home before real darkness fell. He might even be able to surreptitiously squeeze them for some details on what happened the night he was shot.

That was part of it.

But alongside the bare logistics, some other part of him simply wanted to stay in the clearing, camp there in the Forest, build a fire and stare into the flames and the warmth, let the stars wheel up in the sky overhead, the tree canopies sough and shift in the wind, the mortal world beyond bustle and scurry without him as it wished . . .

Well.

Fading aura from the skogsra, most likely. Tree sprites were known to trail a musk about with them when they stepped into mortal time, a heady mix of glamour and resonance that might haunt a clearing or a grove—*or a man*—for some time after they departed.

He shook it off.

He dug a knitted cap out of his pack and put it on to cover his wound. Refastened and shouldered the pack, thrust the McCulloch into its sheath across his back. He took one last look around the clearing in the failing light, then set his back to it and headed out.

The tree sprite hadn't shown up to say farewell. Either she was watching, mischievous, from afar, or she'd gone once more beyond the veil, stepped sated off the frenetic cocaine-rush conveyor belt of human timescales, bedded instead back into the glacial flow of Forest time, dozily dreaming an early spring.

The changeling tagged along at his side until the tree line. It held the rag doll pinched up under its arm for safekeeping. Duncan paused a few steps into the meadow, turned back to face the diminutive form.

"Mebhuranon," he said, for what it was worth. "The one who made you. Her name is Mebhuranon. She is . . . ancient. Very wise."

"Mebhuranon."

"That's right. Maybe . . ." He gestured vaguely. "Maybe she can do something for you."

The changeling looked unblinkingly back at him across the gloaming. He hunched against the weight of the pack, a kind of shrug.

"Aye, well. Just a thought."

He turned to go, but its voice stopped him. His voice. The perfect copy again, from the day they rode the tram together, and he ran it out of Erlsley to the tree line. The day he held on to it, saved it from burning itself on the metal trim of the seats.

"*Just watch yourself.*" It nodded out at the meadow, the open sky overhead, the ferry and the human settlement beyond. "*You can get hurt.*"

Wordless, he nodded.

Turned and walked on into the open fields.

When he looked back from halfway down to the ferry crossing, the changeling had already faded into the gathering dark.

HE CROSSED THE RIVER IN the company of a half dozen taciturn smoke-smelling men whose business on the Forest side looked to be either game or maybe mushroom gathering and herbs. Braces of rabbit slung around necks, a decent-sized roe on a burly shoulder, canvas bags and army-issue packs. One father-and-son team had a small wooden barrow, piled high with carcasses. Every man there was armed with either shotgun or rifle, or both. Most wore obvious iron talismans around their necks, and some wore crude mail vests. Outside of nods and clipped pleasantries, none of them had anything much to say to each other as they waited.

The ferry puttered in. The motorman drove the vessel neatly against the landing stage, held it there with casual skill over tiller and engine, while his partner urged the passengers to hurry and get aboard. Both men glanced nervously up toward the tree line, over and over again, throughout the clambering, and as soon as the last passenger was on, the motorman let his boat drift out into the flow again with evident relief. He let the prow come about, gunned the engine, and sent them forging back toward the lights on the other side.

The last man aboard, still not seated, stumbled and nearly fell against Duncan with the turn. The rabbits slung around his neck swung with the motion. A shotgun hacked down to flintlock pistol dimensions slipped out of his belt, clunked on the bilge timbers at his feet. He cursed and braced himself on Duncan's shoulder.

"Sorry, mate," he muttered. "Bloody water babies still not got their nerve back from the other night."

"Last night?" Duncan shrouded his accent, pushed it eastward, went cut-glass English City. He showed as little interest as he thought he could reasonably get away with. "What happened last night?"

"Nah, not last night." The man stooped to retrieve his hand cannon, got himself seated on the bench in front of Duncan. "Couple of nights ago, would have been, let's see, Thursday. *Three* nights ago. Lot of bother, there was. Something to do with the Hidden Folk. Had the army out and everything."

Duncan grimaced. So it was Sunday. Somewhere with the skogsra, he'd lost three days.

"What—was there shooting?" he asked casually. "Did you see it?"

"Heard it, right enough." Stuffing the hacked-down shotgun back into his belt. "Everyone in the bloody village did. And we all saw them swing into the square that evening. Three army lorries and a closed tourer. Special maneuvers, they said. Then we heard the shooting, later that night."

"Anyone hurt?"

The man shrugged. "Dunno. If they were, the army cleared 'em away after. Tell you what, though. Bloke I know who loads barrels up at the Turk's Head swears blind he saw them taking away a little girl, had her in the back of one of the lorries. Says she couldn't have been more than five or six."

Duncan held down his reaction, not sure whether to feel relief or rage.

"Wasn't drunk, was he?"

The other man chuckled. "Well, wouldn't rule it out. So—you not from these parts?"

"Edinburgh. John Craigart." Duncan offered his hand. "Craigart and Sons—purveyors of fine herbal remedies and *tisanes.* We're on North Bank Street, if you ever get up that way."

"Not likely, the way things are these days." The other man shook his hand. "Sammy Hodges. Used to be a poacher, back when that was something you didn't talk about. Now I'm a—let's see—*game procurement agent.*" He beamed. "All of a sudden everybody loves me. Not a pub this end of the Pennines where they'll let me buy me own drinks."

Duncan nodded. It was a common reversal. The Forest took vast swaths of livestock pasture in the Unbinding—haphazardly, but in large volume. It forced the extension of wartime rationing even further, and the unspoken assumption was that, any day now, even more grazing land might go the same way.

You had to get your meat from somewhere.

"Got a girl here in Maltby, too. Real looker. Bed for the night anytime." Hodges winked at him. "You know how it is."

Duncan pulled a rueful face. "Not really. Herbs and roots don't bring out the same passion as meat, I'm afraid. Just hoping I make the last bus to Erlsley. I've a hotel booking there."

The ferry swung out broadside as they drew in toward the other bank. Someone hailed them from the landing stage. Hodges settled his belt and hand cannon more securely, preparing to disembark with evident relish.

"Last bus for Erlsley?" He grinned. "You'll be lucky. Left an hour ago, mate. Sunday service. You won't be getting back tonight—not unless you've the money for a bloody long taxi ride."

"Any chance this Turk's Head has rooms, then?"

Hodges shrugged, still grinning. "Don't ask me, never checked. Never needed to, know what I mean?"

THE TURK'S HEAD DID, IN fact, have rooms to spare. Cramped and somehow drafty, despite having only one window, and that the size of a pocket handkerchief. Duncan got settled, then went out into the street to a call box he'd seen on the corner. He checked his Mappin & Webb, dialed the operator, got put through to Erlsley Bird Cabs.

The phone rang and rang. No reply.

Duncan grimaced, hung up. Thought about it. Niamh's tiny under-eaves flat up on Spender Street had no phone, and he knew of no other way to contact her.

Trying to ignore the gathering leaden weight in the pit of his stomach, he dug out his notebook. Found Garner's number in Macclesfield and asked the operator to connect him there instead.

The phone rang and rang. And rang.

Like some tiny, tinny rendering of the doomed, manic church bell in Miller's Frith—but this time tolling only for him. He felt himself toppling ponderously into the endless sound . . .

"Sir, there doesn't seem to be anyone there to answer." The operator, diplomatic and quite chirpy for the time of night. It snapped him back to awareness. "Can I help you with another number?"

He felt his grip tighten with bruising force on the black Bakelite of the receiver at his ear.

"No, thank you," he said evenly. "It's something I'll have to handle myself."

He hung up the receiver as if it were mined to explode.

TWENTY-TWO

THE LIGHTS WERE OUT AT ERLSLEY BIRD CABS.

Duncan hung grim-faced at the mouth of an alley a dozen doors down on the other side of Skoldergate, taking in the scene. For all that he wasn't surprised, seeing it for himself was a blow. The frontage windows were all darkened; there were no cabs in the rank. Two tall-helmeted, caped figures stood out front, stamping their feet against the cold.

There was a thin, early evening crowd trudging up Skoldergate toward the cross with East Cavendish Street. Duncan drifted from the alley, joined them as casually as he could. He tugged the woolen cap he wore lower on his forehead, kept his head down. People were spilling off the pavement on the Erlsley Bird side, crossing the street to avoid the apparent crime scene, so he was well covered. He made his way slowly past among them, glancing across a couple of times at the police like everyone else, then moved on with the crowd to where Crammond's chestnut stand was doing its usual roaring trade. He stood behind a portly woman with a crocodile of small children who was buying chestnuts for them all. He waited until she was gone, slid up to the head of the queue.

"Got anything for an old soldier?" he asked softly.

Crammond, to his credit, never missed a beat. He stared into Duncan's face a bare second with his one good eye, then went back to raking the chestnuts over with his prosthetic arm. With his other hand, he took a ready bagged packet from the warmer plate on the side of the cart, handed it over to Duncan. Leaned close.

"Bricklayer's Arms, Ivy Street," he murmured. "Ask fir Angie, tell her the Big Man says tae show ye the facilities."

Duncan nodded and slipped away. Heard Crammond giving the next customer a casual line of chat, for all the world as if nothing at all had happened. He made his way across town to Ivy Street, found the cheery corner glow of the pub soon enough. He cracked the door and slid inside, was wrapped instantly in a bright, cozy fug of smoke and noise and cooking smells. He went to the bar, asked for Angie, and was presented with an ample, amiable blond barmaid who could have passed for Reuben Kegg's younger sister. She took in Crammond's message and nodded, led Duncan back through cramped corridors, down a tight stair and into a cold basement room stacked with crates, where she switched on the lights—cheap, dim bulbs strung on hanging wires from the ceiling—and gestured at a well-worn wooden table and chairs in one corner.

"Take a seat. He might be a while. I'll see if I can scare you up summat to eat. If you need to piss, there's a sink over there. Don't worry, it's seen worse."

She locked the door behind her as she left.

Duncan sat under the dim bulbs and ate the chestnuts, slowly, one by one. Angie never did come back with better food, but about an hour later, Crammond showed up instead, followed by a different barmaid bearing a tray.

"Pirate coffees," she announced brightly. "Bit of snap. Cheese and ham butties, all right?"

Crammond waited in silence while she laid out the two steaming mugs, a nearly full bottle of Lamb's navy rum, and a plate of sandwiches cut doorstep thick. He saw her to the door, closed it after her. Gestured at the food.

"Dig in, pal. Looks like ye could use it."

Duncan caught the whiff of smoked ham and pickles, realized suddenly how hungry he was. The chestnuts aside, his last meal was breakfast, a crack-of-dawn bread-and-sausage platter in the Turk's Head fourteen hours gone. He'd been too wary to risk eating anywhere in public once he got back into town, too tense even to dig provisions out of his pack while he waited in shadowed, abandoned places he knew, for night to come, so he could approach Skoldergate and Erlsley Bird Cabs under cover of darkness.

He took one of the doorstep sandwiches and bit deep into it, felt his hunger really stir. Rush of saliva into his mouth, light kick in the stomach. He closed his eyes and chewed in something approaching ecstasy.

"Sorry aboot the wait," Crammond said. "Had tae haud oaff closin' up the stand till it looked right. They fuckin' busies wiz there, the whole time. One o' them even came over, bought a bag."

Duncan swallowed his current mouthful, washed it down with the pirate coffee. Warm bite on his tongue—the rum slug had been generous. He put down his mug, harder than he'd intended. "Where's Niamh?"

"Whir dae ye think? Fuckin' polis took her."

"When?"

"Friday night. Woulda been aboot seven. Big fuckin' production, too, whole vanful o' they bastards. Plainclothes in charge. Took three of they cabbies, too, an' that young lad?"

"Gordon?"

"Aye, if ye say so. Musta let they drivers go pretty sharpish, mind you. They all came back, drove the cabs away before Ah packed up fir the night. Nae sign o' the lad, though, or yir lassie."

"She's not my—" Drop it. "This was four nights ago, aye? Anything in the papers yet?"

"No' that Ah saw." Crammond's eye-patched face grew somber. "Ye know whit that means, Ah suppose?"

Duncan nodded, jaw set. "Fucking Special Branch."

"Aye. They'll have took her for a Fenian. That's indefinite fuckin' detention wi'oot trial. Defense o' the Realm Act; they can haud her as long as it fuckin' suits them."

"I remember when DORA was going to be a temporary fucking thing, just for the war. Remember that?"

Crammond shook his head. "That much power an' regulation? They're never gaunnae give it up. Fuckin' temperance wifeys are aww creamin' their knickers over the restricted licensin' hours, all the shite they kept on fir the Dangerous Drugs Act. An' the polis love it, right enough. They fuckin' IRA idiots shooting Wilson dead last year in London didnae help either. Ah mean, that's a British field marshal murdered oan his own fuckin' doorstep. Nae chance Churchill's sittin' still for that. And the way things are goin' over there now? Nae cunt buys this Irish Free State shite, it's all gaunnae fall apart."

"You reckon?"

"Already happenin'. Don't ye read the papers?"

"Not if I can help it."

"Aye, well—this, all this, is wi'oot even considerin' the fuckin' Forest. Got some heid cases Ah know back in the toon used tae say Collins an' De Valera are in league with the Huldu, the whole Unbindin' is a Fenian plot tae bring doon the empire."

"Seriously?"

Crammond gestured. "Aye, they're fuckin' Orangemen, whit dae ye expect? But the point stands. The way things are the noo, Special Branch can disappear yir lassie fir as long as they fuckin' like, just fir bein' Irish. That's aww it takes."

"I don't think this is Special Branch, Billy. Or at least—it's someone else using them."

Above the eye patch, a cocked Glaswegian eyebrow. "Ye have good reasons tae believe that?"

"Aye."

"Awright." Crammond sat for a moment, then leaned in and took a sandwich. Took a gargantuan bite out of it, chewed, and went on talking through a filled mouth and a spray of crumbs. "Ah'm listenin'. Whit the fuck have ye got yisael tangled up in?"

DUNCAN GAVE HIM THE TRIMMED version. The meeting with Irene Rush, the invitation from Hardy and the Forestry Commission, his trip with Garner. Combat with Stordalen, the sworn word of the Final Isles. Bringing Mimi Rush home. The betrayal—or whatever it was—by sniper at Maltby Ferry, the changeling and the sprite, his healing in the Forest. He took off his cap, showed Crammond the long, pale scorch line through his hair where the bullet had gone.

He left out the matter of Stordalen's heart, the complications of his past with Mebhuranon and Svalenkari. No point in fogging further what was already a tangled-enough mess.

Crammond sat through it all in almost complete silence.

"So whit noo?" he asked when Duncan was done.

"Now?" Duncan stared off into the corner of the basement. Big porcelain trough sink, slow drip from the tap that overhung it. "Now I'm going to get Niamh back from the fucks that took her, and I'm going to kill anybody who objects."

"Includin' this Hardy?"

"Especially fucking Hardy."

Crammond grunted. Poured from the Lamb's bottle into their empty mugs—they'd finished the pirate coffees a while back, gone onto straight rum refills. "Ye realize it may no' be Hardy behind this. Ever think maybe he wiz relieved o' command? Disnae make a lot o' sense, him wantin' ye oan salary down in London, then three days later havin' someone put a bullet through yir brainpan."

"Aye, but it does." Duncan knocked back a chunk of the rum, grinned through the harsh burn it left in his gullet. He'd had time to think this through—lying faceup beneath tightly tucked bedclothes, sleepless with tension in his drafty room at the Turk's Head, he'd turned it this way and that, worried at it like a dog with a rabbit's corpse. He drifted off to sleep, finally, in the early hours, snapped instantly awake a moment later with the missing piece of the puzzle right there in his head. "See, I don't think Hardy wanted me down in London at all. I think he just wanted me well away from Irene Rush and her daughter. Job offer was just the bait."

"An' if ye'd accepted?"

"Oh, I daresay the ticket was there, at least. They have the funds, that's very clear. I imagine they would have run me down to the big city, put me up there for a few days, hotel or something, however long they needed, then made some excuses and sent me home again. Or maybe not." Duncan mimed a pistol with his fingers. "Maybe they would have just taken me off the train, put two in the back of my head, and dumped me in the Thames."

"Wi' fuckin' Special Branch, that wouldnae surprise me. They cunts shoat an uncle o' mine dead oan Gallowgate in broad fuckin' daylight back in '08. He'd done business with some Fenian publican up in Rutherglen, see. Said he wiz armed and dangerous, but nae cunt even looked into it. Nae investigation, nae arrests. Fuckin' law untae theysaels."

Duncan nodded. It wasn't the first story of the sort he'd heard.

"Question Ah have for ye, though." Crammond frowning now. "Ye say Hardy wanted tae keep ye away from Irene Rush. How would he know about her in the first place?"

"Haven't worked that out yet. But he did. See, when I turned him down, Hardy was furious. He lost his rag, made some comment about affairs of state being more important than the troubles of cooks, seamstresses, *and C3 bookkeepers* who should have kept better watch over their children."

"Charmin'."

"Aye, he's an officer-grade cunt. But what's interesting is the C3 bookkeeper line. That's a very specific government-administered grading system. Only came in just before the war. Now, I had Garner make inquiries about Irene Rush over in Macclesfield, and one of the details he turned up was exactly that—she was a C3 qualified bookkeeper."

"An' cooks an' seamstresses? Whit did he mean by that?"

"Ellie Furlough's mother works part-time as a seamstress. And the cook might be Luisa Grimaldi. Hardy had to have been looking into my client list." Duncan gestured with his mug. "That's maybe to be expected. Thing is, in Irene Rush's case, he knew something about her that I didn't. Before I spoke to Garner, I had no idea. *She* didn't tell me. But somehow, Hardy knew."

"Been keepin' tabs oan her before ye showed up, aye. And didnae want ye involved."

"Looks that way."

"And noo he has Mimi. Ye think he's put her back wi' her mam?"

Duncan grimaced. "I'd like to think so. But if he was happy to see that happen, why try to stop me working the job in the first place?"

"And why put a hole in ye when ye delivered? Aye, he's likely no' got the lassie's best interests at heart. Ye want me tae have someone check round oan the mother?"

"No, that I can do myself. I'll head over there tomorrow, see what's what. What I want you to do is find out where they're holding Niamh. That's first order of business right now."

Crammond nodded soberly. "Awright. Ah'll put the word oot. Goat a few inside men oan the force, paid tae look the other way when we need it. Mostly beat boabbies, but we've a couple o' ears inside the stations, too. Can see if any of them know anything."

"I appreciate that."

"Ye're more than welcome. Anythin' to give the Branch a bloody nose. And look—if we can find Niamh an' get her back, Ah can find ways tae stash her, too. Goes wi'oot sayin'."

"Not to me, it doesn't. I'll cover your costs for that. You have my word."

"No ye fuckin' won't, 'cause Ah'll no' let ye." Crammond lifted his eye patch for a moment, ground the heel of his palm into the scar tissue knotted beneath. "Fuckin' itchin' again, man." He put the patch back. "Ye dae enough, Duncan. Ye dinnae realize it, but no' one in a hundred men came back fra' that meat grinder over there and still cares the way ye dae, still acts the way ye dae, like things still actually fuckin' matter."

Duncan chuckled. "C'mon, man. The Lamb's is getting to you."

"Ah mean it, Duncan." Awkward, rising emotion in the other man's tone. "Ah see it every fuckin' day in ma line o' work. Broken men, worn-oot men, twisted-tae-fuck evil men, men old afir their time, men wha've given up anythin' but clingin' tae life day tae fuckin' day, coz that's aww they had fir four years, and now, in this land fit fir fuckin' heroes we apparently live in, they cannae even find a job tae keep a roof over they heads. These are faithless times, man. Times o' betrayal."

Duncan tapped the long score mark in his head. "Tell me about it."

"Aye, meant tae say—that disnae look too pretty." Crammond sipped his rum, visibly thankful they were headed back onto safer, less emotive ground. "An' ye look like boiled shite, by the way. Ye sure that tree lassie's fanny did the trick?"

Duncan fingered the bullet crease more carefully. It had the faint itch you sometimes got from old scar tissue, but beyond that he'd healed faster and more fully than any mortal had a right to.

"Right as rain," he said.

"Well, if ye plan tae stay that way, we'd best keep ye oaff the streets, at least fir now. Truth is, I'm no' sure hangin' around in Irene Rush's neighborhood durin' daylight hours is the smartest thing ye could dae wi' yir time tomorrow. Still cannae believe ye just waltzed up tae the stand like that the night, large as fuckin' life. And the polis right there across the street."

"They're not looking for me, Billy. I'm a dead man, remember?"

"Aye, well, ye look it right enough." Crammond drained his mug. "C'mon, enough o' this shite. We'd better find ye a safe bed fir the night."

DUNCAN KNEW ALREADY THAT HE wouldn't be bunking at Crammond's place, and, truth be told, he was thankful. Last thing he needed was May following him around the apartment with her tinker's Sight and disapproving scowl. But it was a few minutes before he cottoned on to where they were actually going.

"Oh, c'mon man," he said as the taxi turned onto Salter's Row. "I got to listen to other people fucking all night long?"

Crammond laughed. "It's an undereaves room. No' much but storage goin' oan up there midweek. Ye'll be fine."

"And if they get raided?"

"No' gaunnae happen, pal. Belle pays good money tae see that it disnae. Whole point of puttin' ye up there in the first place."

"You tell her who I am?"

"Ah have not. And she disnae need tae know. That's what *Ah* pay *her* for."

The taxi pulled to the curb. Duncan climbed out and dragged his pack after him. He looked at the discreetly darkened frontage of the Doorbell Club and sighed. Crammond bustled past him to the door and knocked. The black-painted, paneled wood opened a crack, let a long, sharp tongue of light out into the street. A fright mask face looked out, saw Crammond, approximated a smile with its inhumanly distorted features.

" 'lo, Sergeant."

Crammond nodded. "Arthur. Belle about?"

"She's at the bar," said Arthur, and opened the door wider. Duncan caught more of the face, the shiny doll simplicity of the features, the obvious wig atop it. It was pretty bad, one of the worst he'd seen. From build and stance, he thought Arthur might still be a young man, but the burns damage and the resulting plastic surgery made it impossible to tell. He looked the man in the eye, then affected an interest in the warmly lit hall interior beyond. You didn't stare. It was a given.

"Good man." Crammond banged Arthur on the shoulder with

his prosthesis, led Duncan inside and down the hall. They went past a front-room parlor dimmed and cold with disuse, no fire in the grate. By contrast, the next door on the right let into a larger, longer room kitted out to look like an American speakeasy. Red flock paper on walls and ceiling, some damask weave pattern, wall lamps casting cherry-red light over empty booths on the right. A long mahogany bar down the room on the left, somewhat brighter lighting behind it. No customers there either. A solitary barman stood wiping cocktail glasses at the end. Halfway down, a rake-thin blond woman sat in full flapper regalia in front of her own cocktail and smoked from a long, jade cigarette holder. She raised a languid arm, gestured them over.

"Pirate Billy Crammond!" Greeting him with airy French-style kisses on each cheek. Her voice was throaty, her accent neutral, no local twang, but no attempt at faux French allure either. "So nice to see you after all this time. You come by so rarely these days. How is marital bliss treating you?"

"Ach, stop that, Belle. Ye ken Ah've been busy."

The blond woman pulled back from her embrace with Crammond, looked Duncan brusquely up and down. Her eyes were muddy green, cocaine-blasted pupils enormous. Her hair was fashionably short, stiffly coiffed up off her neck, tangled artfully across her brow. She would have been about forty, he thought, but the intensity of her stare shaved some of that off, gave her a more nubile, seductress air. She sipped at her cigarette holder, plumed smoke directly at him.

"And this will be the friend in need you mentioned. Mr. . . . Campbell, was it?"

She put out the languid arm and Duncan took her hand. Firm, dry grip, faint hint of a tremor from the snow. "I am Belle. Belle D'Or. Welcome to the Doorbell Club. Always happy to help out another of our brave boys."

Perhaps she wanted to see if he'd laugh at the pun. He stayed expressionless.

"Is it that obvious?" he asked.

"That you have been a soldier? Yes, it is, but then I have a great deal of experience. A lot of our clientele here have been through the fire, some"—a brutally pointed glance at Arthur—"more literally than others. But the common stamp is in you all. I find it in the eyes, Mr. Campbell. And you should know that here we do our best to reward men like you for your sacrifices. Inspired by the illustrious Mrs. Meyrick at Dalton's Club, you might say. Providing comfort to troubled young men returned from war, and so forth."

Crammond grunted. "Didnae fly fir Meyrick, that line. Ye seen they closed her doon again. Fined her twenty-five quid intae the bargain this time."

"You worry too much, Billy. We're a little less . . . flamboyant up here than La Meyrick. We've made fewer enemies, too. Now, Mr. Campbell. A few house rules."

"Hands off the girls?"

Belle D'Or sipped smoke, looked at him. "Is certainly one of them, yes. As is confidentiality about anything or anyone you see within these walls. We are a discreet establishment and you will need to play your part in that."

"Fair enough."

"If you should require a . . . companion, of course, that can be—"

"I won't," said Duncan shortly.

The tunneled cocaine stare held him again. "Man of conviction. I like that. Will you have a drink with me, at least?"

Duncan shuttled a glance at Crammond, then back to Belle. "Is that the price of my bed for the night?"

For the first time since he'd met her, Belle D'Or smiled. It wasn't a wholly reassuring look.

"More or less," she said.

TWENTY-THREE

Next morning found him in the commuter press on the Number 4 tram westbound, standing room only, one arm looped through the overhead hanging strap, trying with his free hand to pick one of Belle D'Or's pubic hairs out of the back of his throat. Warm, mingled scents of wool and human bodies, overlaid with cheap perfume and hair pomade. Faint roll of nausea as the carriage rattled and swayed on corners. He was mildly hungover, feeling in his bones the sudden autumn chill that had draped itself across the city like a damp muslin shawl. His wounds ached. It looked like it was going to rain.

Can see why you'd want to be hiding out. Belle D'Or, postcoital, tracing one of the barely healed gashes across his ribs with a restless, pointed little tongue. It sent little electric sparks through his nerve ends as she did it. *You* have *been in the wars. Who did this to you?*

A dead man.

She made an approving sound deep in her throat, like a contented cat. *So you killed him for it. How did you go about that?*

With a knife.

And will I be reading about this dead man in tomorrow's Gazette*?*

Shouldn't think so. Curbing his impatience with an effort. Trying to work out exactly how long he needed to hang around in this silk-draped four-poster to properly cement his status as her impromptu guest. *It's been taken care of.*

Good, and so have I. Eyes rising slyly to meet his. *At least for a little while.*

The sex was hard work—an uncomfortable, episodic, barely satisfying business, flurries of frenetic thrashing punctuated with high-pitched, grunting cries from her and the odd, painful clash of bones padded by far too little flesh for Duncan's liking. He supposed it was down to the cocaine. Between bouts, Belle plied him with gin cocktails she mixed at her dressing table and slopped over him in the carrying with what seemed like deliberate clumsiness, then immediately stooped to lick off him as a prelude to the next encounter. Third time around, he retired limp and unresponsive despite her best efforts, and she let him go. He clutched up his clothes from the floor, let himself quietly out. Left her sprawled prone across the bed, propped on her elbows, eyes closed, coiffed head and narrow arse twitching idly back and forth to some coked-up jazz rhythm evidently still playing for her somewhere he couldn't hear.

He got off at the closest stop to Umber cottages, retraced his steps from memory through the concrete tangle of walkways and tenement facades. There was more light in the sky than last time he was here, but it didn't seem to help. Without the gloom and shadows, the charcoal-daubed runes and sacrifice fire remnants looked, if anything, more desperate than ever.

Thankfully, he saw no bottle toughs. Too early in the day, he supposed.

Number 16 Umber Cottages was easy enough to pick out—someone had kicked in the door, left the jamb splintered and torn loose. Later, someone else had done their best to jam the door shut, but it was a poor fit at best. Duncan went up the concrete steps, knocked. Got no reply. After a moment, he prodded the door back on its hinges and eased inside. He stood in dank hallway gloom and listened.

Someone in the back room.

No noise to give it away, but he knew it nonetheless, with an odd immediacy, a flash flare in the corner of his vision, something like the eerie hallucinations he'd suffered in the Forest. He put his hand to his back for the sgian dubh in its sideways-slanting sheath on his belt. At almost the same moment, another shivery flash swept through him, and he knew he would not need the knife. His fingers, aware of the truth before he was, had already relinquished their hold.

He stepped through the open doorway.

A black-and-white-clad figure sprawled in skirts on the floor at the foot of the armchair by the window, where less than a week ago Irene Rush had sat. For a split second, he thought it was her. Then, as he blocked the doorway and his shadow fell across her, the face lifted and he saw it was Susan, Irene Rush's middle-aged watchdog and maid.

"Ah, it's you," she said dully.

Hair a plundered bird's nest, apron streaked with dirt. She'd been crying, and for some time. Her face was ribboned, streaked with grime where she'd wiped at the tears only to have fresh ones cut tracks down through the dirt her fingers left. She glared at him out of reddened eyes, like some small woodland animal caught in a trap. Her voice was choked, scratchy in her throat.

"If yer after more money, you can fuck off. There ent no more."

Duncan took station against the wall beside the doorway, lowered himself carefully to the floor. He sat with his back to the wall, knees up.

"Where is she?" he asked gently.

"Whereja fink?" Susan scrabbled in her sleeve for a handkerchief, tried to wipe some order into her tear-grimed face. Hard, impatient strokes. "Gone, ent she."

"They took her?"

Susan blew her nose loudly on the cloth, tucked it away again. "Course they bloody did. Big bloody bullies, buncha grown men draggin' 'er aht like that. Was it you—told 'em where we was?"

"No."

She seemed to look properly at him for the first time, where he sat at her level on the floor. She sniffed and levered herself to her feet. "Lot of bloody use you was anyway."

"When did they come?"

"Day after you. In the evenin', when it was dark. Bloody cowards."

After he'd rejected Hardy's offer. It fit. Allow a few hours to put together the swoop. And yes, darkness to cloak the abduction.

"You recognize them?"

She shook her head, turned to stare blindly out of the window, down into the backyards. "Didn't 'ave to. Bloody well know who sent 'em, dun I."

"Who sent them?"

"What's it to you, anyhow?" Her voice came drab, wrung out as an old scrubbing cloth. "Why'd you care?"

"I found Mimi. I brought her out of the Forest."

This, at least, got her attention. She tipped her head away from the window, stared down at him where he sat. "You wot?"

"Aye. And then they fucking shot me." He pushed up the woolen cap, tapped at the scoring in his scalp. "Took the girl. Left me for dead."

Susan goggled at him as if he'd just risen from the grave.

Which, he supposed, he pretty much had.

Once again.

Some might say you're making a habit of this, Duncan.

"I am very interested to know who came and took your mistress, Susan, because I am going to make them pay. And maybe get her back along the way. You want to help me?"

She hesitated, seated herself finally in the chair, leaning tensely forward.

"You really found 'er?" She wanted to believe.

"Aye."

"How was she?"

Duncan reflected. "Strong," he said finally. "She was scared, but she stayed strong. We walked out, some fucking distance, I can tell you, and she never complained once, she never cried. When the time came, she was brave. She made it out because she was brave."

Susan nodded, tearing up all over again. She sniffed, hard. Knuckled at her eyes.

"It's 'im," she said. "That bloody Sir Michael."

Duncan blinked. "Sir Michael . . . ?"

"Sir Michael bloody Endershall. 'er bloody 'usband! That's who dun it."

THEY'D BEEN ON THE RUN for years.

The story came tumbling out of Susan, like unwashed laundry from a cupboard it's been stuffed away in for far too long. Irene Rush, in fact Lady Ada Endershall-Ulver—of the penniless but well-regarded Berkshire Ulvers, apparently—ensconced in the bosom of the Endershall estate, walks the summer lawns at dusk behind a determinedly tottering Mimi and slowly begins to feel the creeping sensation of unseen eyes on them both from the tree line at the edge of the gardens. At first she thinks she's being ridiculous, overprotective, tugged at by the primal tides of early motherhood, and she tells Susan as much. But the feelings persist. She wakes in the night to feed Mimi, feels the same cold creeping fingers of dread right there in the nursery. In the end, she broaches it with her husband. Sir Michael tells her she's being ridiculous, overprotective, giving in to the primal tides of early motherhood.

But there's something in his tone . . .

And her dread redoubles.

Like she jest shrank in on 'erself, Susan told him in the same drab and dusty voice. *Poor mite. Like she was meltin' away wiv the fear.*

Already sleeping poorly and at irregular hours, Irene takes to haunting the corridors of her own home with Mimi gathered to her breast. One night, she chances to pass the door to the library gallery and hears voices, Sir Michael's and others. She creeps in to listen . . .

An' they was talkin' about takin' 'er baby away. Sayin' it's time, the contract's due, and hell to pay if we don't—I couldn't make no sense of it when she told me. But I knew that old bastard was up to somefink. You'd see it in 'is eyes, the way 'e moped about the place, lost 'is temper with 'er, wouldn't even bloody look *at the baby! After that, we didn't 'ave no choice.*

Midnight flit.

Whatever state Ada Endershall-Ulver was in, prone to primal motherhood or not, she seemed to have a cool head under fire, once her mind was made up. Duncan nodding at this—he'd seen the same thing in the trenches often enough, men eaten up with nerves and confinement until the crunch finally came, and then a grim-faced sufficiency seemed to descend. The two women and the baby, spirited away by night on the wings of money Irene had squirreled away out of her husband's view, some meager inheritance from an aunt, some pawned jewelry, so forth. They feinted south, toward the coast and Southampton, laid tracks that seemed to end at a White Star liner shipping migrants to New York. The ship sailed; they were not on it. Instead, they zigzagged across the home counties by train, went to ground in Bristol, where Irene found work. Out of wartime fervor, she'd studied for the newly instituted civil service official clerical qualifications, took the exams, and passed with flying colors, only for the war to end before she could apply her skills. Now, though, she—

"Wait a minute," Duncan objected. "Those papers would have had her real name on them. How did she pass as Irene Rush?"

"Dunno. She jest did. You wanna hear this story or wot?"

He did.

Bristol for the best part of a year. Then, one day in late autumn, Irene comes home from work and thinks a figure is shadowing her in the early evening gloom. She can't describe her shadow, has caught only shaved glimpses, the prickling back-of-neck sensation of being followed, but her fear is gut deep and contagious. They pack up and move. Irene hands in her notice next day, cites family illness. They zigzag across the country again, disappear into the windswept anonymous flats and newly sprouted forest outgrowths of East Anglia. They wind up on the sleepy northern outskirts of Norwich.

This time, they get more than a year. But in the end, once again, the shadow falls.

Oxford follows Norwich.

Coventry, Oxford.

Macclesfield, Coventry.

But everywhere, sooner or later, the shadow follows and finds them, and the old terrors set in once more, and they flee.

"Did *you* ever see these figures?" Duncan asked.

Susan shook her head. "I dunno, maybe once? In Coventry. One night I couldn't sleep. I went an' looked aht the winder, it was snowin' and . . . it was like there was someone on the pavement in the shadders over the road. Not like a man you could see, nuffin' like that. But it looked like somefink was stoppin' the snowflakes, makin' a space they couldn't blow inside." She shook her head again, like someone shown a conjuring trick they can't explain. "Dunno, maybe I jest dreamed it."

"Maybe y—"

Someone in the hall . . .

The same flicker-flash awareness as before. Duncan raised a finger to his lips, shuttled his eyes sideways toward the door.

"Susan," he said casually. "Do you think you could maybe crank that window sash up a wee bit, let some air in?"

She caught on instantly. Rose from her seat. "Yeah, stuffy, innit."

She levered the sash upward with a soft grunt. The wood graunched protest—

Under cover of the sound it made, Duncan was already in motion. Up on his feet, spinning, diving for the doorway and the hall.

Hesitant figure, hovering just inside a front door pushed gently open. Familiar fa—

He saw Duncan, panicked, tried to get back out the half-open door. The splintered jamb caught him at the shoulder. Duncan reached him in two strides, stomped down hard into the back of his knee. The intruder went down hard across the threshold and the raw concrete steps outside, yelped as he hit. Duncan grabbed him at collar and armpit, dragged him back inside. Slammed the door as close to shut as it would go, put his back to it and stared down at what he'd caught.

"You?"

Young, pockmarked face, clean shaven. If the features alone hadn't rung any bells, the big, puffy yellow discoloration around one corner of the mouth would have given Duncan a hefty clue. His incautious tail from the day he met with Hardy, now scrabbling backward away from him on the cheap wooden boarded floor.

"Mr. Silver, I—"

"You don't fucking learn, do you pal?" Duncan hooked the sgian dubh from his back. "You follow me here?"

"No, no! I was watching the house. I mean no harm!"

Duncan crouched closer. The other man's gaze hung hypnotized on the blade in his hand. "That fuck Hardy send you?"

"No!" Grabbing at the name like a drowning man, gabbling. "Not Hardy! I don't work for Hardy!"

It brought Duncan up short. Flicker of movement in the corner of his eye—Susan had come partway out into the hall, stood face half hidden by the jamb, a hand pressed to her mouth, watching. He grew aware that he loomed over his tail in his coat, knife in hand, like some illustration from the cover of a penny dreadful about vampires or spring heel Jack.

He hefted the knife, reversed the blade away from the other man.

"You followed me from Hardy's offices last week. If you're not his, who the fuck do you work for?"

The other man pushed himself semi-upright against the wall. He lifted pleading palms. "Yes—yes, I'll tell you. Show you. Look."

He dug frantically under his collar, tugged out a long gold chain from around his neck. He held out a small pendant on it for Duncan to see. At first glance a crucifix, then, as Duncan peered closer, resolving into a stylized great sword with a radiant golden blister swelling from the crux of its hilt.

Duncan rocked back on his heels. "You're a fucking Orbster?"

"I—that is not—yes." A gulp. "Yes. My name is Jeremy Ewart. I am an aspirant second degree in the Erlsley lodge of the Holy Order of Sword and Orb. Tasked with observing and protecting the life of Lady Ada Ulver and her child."

"Well, you're doing a bang-up job of that."

"Uhm. I—we did not expect such a violent incursion." Ewart fumbled his pendant back under his shirt. "I—I'm not a soldier. It was my part to report back. By the time I did . . ."

Duncan grunted. "Hardy outmaneuvered you. Know the feeling."

He got to his feet, brooding. He had no more time for the Sword and Orbsters than he did the Theosophicals, Rosicrucians, United Church of the Spirit, what have you. Just so many grandiose gilt-laden empty vessels on the stream and flow of the Unbinding.

But they'd crossed his path now. He stared down at Ewart where he lay, sprawled and clearly terrified to move.

"None of this," he said, "explains what you were doing at the Forestry Commission last week, and why you followed me."

"No, I—I followed you *to* the Forestry Commission. You, well, you didn't notice me then."

He remembered his hangover that morning. Truth to tell, he could have been followed through the streets by a ten-foot Christ in effigy and a Welsh male voice choir in song, and he likely wouldn't have noticed either.

"You picked me up here." It dawned on Duncan. "Tracked me all over town until I got home, came back the next day."

The Sword and Orb adept shook his head. He propped himself up a little straighter on the wall. The tremor in his voice had damped out. "My orders were to stay in place. I spotted you when you left with the changeling, and I reported it when I was relieved. One of our telepathists was able to pull your face from my memory, make a sketch of it. They sent me to your offices the next morning with orders to follow you."

"They recognized my face?"

"Oh, yes." Matter-of-factly. "You are quite well known to the Order. Your successes in the Forest are—"

"Never mind that. You were following me. If I hadn't stopped you, what was next?"

Ewart cleared his throat. "I was to make an approach."

"An approach."

"Yes. The arch—uhm, the senior adepts, at the heart of the Order—there are people who would like to speak with you."

"About what?"

"I don't know." Ewart must have seen something in Duncan's eyes. "No, really. I am only a second-degree adept. I am not yet worthy of the greater mysteries."

Duncan hesitated a moment. But under the circumstances . . .

"All right. Get up." He held up the sgian dubh, made a show of stowing it again at his back. He gestured with the cup of his now-empty hand. "C'mon. Get up. I haven't got all day."

Ewart pushed himself up the wall, eyes still warily fixed on Duncan, until he was standing. He did his best to straighten some dignity back into his clothes. He licked dry, bitten lips. Back down the hallway, Susan still hovered.

"Can you get him a glass of water?" Duncan asked her.

She went. Duncan leaned in closer to Ewart.

"You a local boy, Jerry?"

"Yes. I was born in Erlsley—well, Rashford. Just outside. But I've lived in the city all my life."

"You know Crawgate, then."

"Oh. Yes. In—in fact, I—"

"Good." Duncan checked the Mappin & Webb. "These seniors

of yours still want to talk to me, then you meet me outside Number 37 Crawgate at say . . . two o'clock this afternoon. Got that? You can take me to them from there."

"You will . . . ?" Relief flooded the other man's face. He bobbed his head eagerly. "Yes, of course. I can do that. Number 37. I will be there. Of course."

Susan brought the water in a chipped mug. Ewart slurped it down, wiped his mouth. He looked uncertainly at Duncan. Duncan nodded.

"The Orbsters give you money for expenses?"

"Yes, some."

"Good. Give what you've got to Susan here. You can keep tram fare back. The rest—hand it over."

"I—what . . . ?"

"Think of it as an apology. For how badly you've failed these people."

"But—"

"If you have to account for it, tell your seniors it was my price for meeting them."

Ewart hesitated. Duncan looked at him. The other man dug hurriedly in his pockets, came up with a small leather drawstring purse. Duncan plucked it out of his hands. Tugged it open impatiently, spilled coins and a handful of green and brown pellets into his palm—tightly folded ten-shilling notes. He shingled the coins back into the purse, dropped one of the pellets in with them, handed the purse back.

"There you go. Now get out of here. Run that message to your masters."

The Orb adept needed no encouragement. He turned to leave, and as he did Duncan grabbed his arm.

"One last thing. When you come to Crawgate, you come alone. I don't respond well to unexpected company."

Ewart swallowed and nodded. Duncan judged him convinced. He watched him out the door, closed it after him. He came back to Susan and held out the handful of notes.

"Here. Take it. I don't know what's going to happen in the next few days, but you're going to need funds. To fix your door, if nothing else. What I hear, the Gracious Fucking Order of Sword and Orb have money running out of their ears. They can spare some."

Finally, grimacing, she put out her hand and he tipped the pellets into it.

Then he reached into his coat and dug out his own wallet. Crammond had loaned him a fistful of cash to operate on until he could find a way to get into his own funds either at the bank or in his apartment. He took out a loose sheaf of ten-shilling notes, held them out to Susan.

"And that's from me," he said.

She blinked. "But . . . that's yours . . . we—"

"You paid me to bring Mimi back," he said flatly. "Think of it as another apology."

TWENTY-FOUR

There was a famously good pie shop on the corner at the bottom of Crawgate. By the time Duncan got there, the ovens were going full blast. The door was propped strategically wide, leaking warmth and rich gravy odors into the lunchtime street. Trade was brisk, working men ducking in, carrying paper packages out. Duncan walked by, caught a whiff, and his stomach growled. He'd had coffee and a single hastily eaten muffin at the Doorbell Club that morning, nothing else since. He retraced his steps, went inside and ordered. Stood at the counter, still brooding over what he now knew about Mimi Rush's mother, her intersection with Hardy and the Forestry Commission, and, it seemed, the interests of the Order of Sword and Orb.

What the fuck have you gotten yourself into?

Crammond's question last night, near enough.

Duncan still didn't have any good answers.

The Huldu took small children, always had. As future iron thralls, as playthings, as the slaking of some momentary spite or thirst, a possessive passion-on-sight whim that seemed to manifest in mortals only among the truly deranged. (Were the Fae mentally ill? He'd heard it argued, by Russell Maynard Dalton and others, that a species so long-lived could not possibly exist in a mental state humans would recognize as sane.) But there seemed no more method to it than that.

Abductions were local, opportunistic, reversible if you moved fast enough and with enough grit. The Fae mostly lost interest in their acquisitions in short order, or at least didn't often seem prepared to fight very hard to keep them. And like spoiled children with a new puppy, they ended up treating their captives with increasing detachment and cruelty, as the demands of raising a human child made themselves felt. Legend had it they were drawn especially to beauty or precocious intelligence, but as far as Duncan knew, there'd been no attempt, amid the epidemic of abductions since the Unbinding, to see if this was borne out in the statistics. There was, as always, a lot of campfire talk and opinion, and very little hard evidence for anything.

But evidently there was something about Mimi Rush.

Mebhuranon had come hundreds of miles north to take her. And even before that, her own father apparently had her earmarked for some departure or other . . .

Faithless fuck.

He saw the girl's face again—grimy, eyes wide, tear-fringed lashes as she tried so very hard to be brave. He remembered the way she'd cannoned into him in the driver's cab of Thunder Child, tried with all her might to hug him. The delight on her face when he blew the first Kegg bomb at the fallen oak, the disappointment it hadn't made more of a bang. The way she'd walked, hour after hour, along the haunted nighttime tracks without complaint . . .

"Here you go, man." The piemonger took two paper bags, wrapped them up into a single richly reeking paper package, and handed it over the counter to him. "One steak and kidney, one witch's. I marked 'em S and W. You going up the hill with those, eh?"

Duncan gave him an in-no-mood look, paid, and got out. He started up Crawgate at a brisk walk. The odor of the wrapped pies plucked strings in his stomach, grease soaked through the paper at the bottom of the package and coated the hand he held it with. He reached Number 37 in dire need of a cloth. He hit the buzzer and the door did its creepy new open-by-itself trick.

"Come on up," murmured the witch in his ear.

He grimaced and went up the stairs. No cats or bats today, and Wolfbane Sally was waiting on the next-floor landing, leaned indolently on the banister rail in voluminous black silk pajamas, peering down at him as he climbed.

"Oh, you brought lunch! Delightful!"

He handed her the packet as he reached the landing. "Pies," he managed, out of breath. "Got something I can wipe my hands on?"

"Of course." She pecked him on the cheek, pulled back with a grimace. "You might want to wash your face, too, while you're at it. You stink of pussy and cheap perfume."

"Jealous?"

She guffawed. "I've had you, darling. Once was enough for me."

She led him into the apartment, through the lounge and off into the narrow kitchen. She ushered him into a seat at a rickety round table in the corner, tossed him a tea towel for his hands, plated the two pies without taking them from their separate bags. She sat down opposite him with a motherly smile.

"Don't really like their witch's pie," she said, prodding the pencil scrawled W on the bag in front of her. "Too much horseradish and nonsense, not enough meat. Not sure why they do that. You mind if I swap you for the steak and kidney?"

Wordless, Duncan shoved his plate across at her.

"Too kind." Sally tore the greasy paper open and lifted out the pie. She breathed in the odor with evident pleasure. "So what can I do for you this time, Duncan?"

"Look at me," he said.

"I'm looking." She bit daintily into the pie. "Devilishly handsome as ever. What is it I'm supposed to see?"

"I think you know."

She chewed and swallowed, wiped pastry crumbs off her lip with fastidious fingers. "I'm a witch, darling, not a telepath. I'm afraid you're going to have to—"

"I ate his fucking heart, all right?"

The witch sat utterly still. Her eyes widened.

"You told me I would have to eat his heart. To lift the curse, you told me. So I went into the Forest, and I killed him, and I ate his fucking heart, all right? Now—is the curse lifted?"

"Oh . . . ye . . . gods." Setting her pie carefully aside, eyes now fixed on Duncan, as if on a long-lost beloved. She brushed her fingertips briskly together to rid them of grease. "Can I just . . ."

She reached across the table, took his hand in both of hers. Hooked a couple of long-nailed fingers over his wrist to feel for his pulse. She leaned in to peer at his eyes like an oculist. He half expected her to ask him to stick out his tongue.

"You knew, didn't you?"

"Knew what, Duncan?" Absently, still staring intently into his eyes without meeting his gaze. "This? That you'd achieve something only known to have ever happened half a dozen times, and those in legend?"

"You gave me spells and told me they were enough for a barnyard squabble. And that's where I fucking killed Stordalen, in a barnyard. So don't tell me you didn't know!"

"Duncan, I didn't know!"

She let go of his arm. Sat back in her chair, still looking at him, but now with some new dancing thing in her eyes.

"Listen. I won't say it's coincidence. There are"—raising her hand in a curiously helpless gesture—"powers. Processes. Streams and currents in the dark. And we sip at their edges. We are granted glimpses, if we're lucky, echoes of what's coming, hints of what might be downstream. Maybe I . . . I felt something, chose my words on a whim, informed by some intuition I barely—"

"Oh, *come on*!"

"No, this is the truth, Duncan, like it or not." More intense, more *serious* than he'd ever known her to be. "I—I think I can help you with this. I think I can. The curse will be lifted, for sure. Utterly blown out. Ellie will be fine. But this . . . this is untrodden ground. It's the stuff of myths, of actual legend. The once and future king! The master of Lyonesse. Only Arthur ever—Duncan, they say he was able to *command legions of the Fae in battle*!"

Duncan grimaced, flash recollection of the flight to Maltby Ferry in his head. "I think that's out the window, Sal. Number of Huldu I've left in bits these last couple of days, I don't see them lining up to enlist under me."

"Well, not right now, but—"

"Sal." Almost snapping at her. He tried again, more gently. "Honestly, Sal—I don't have time for this. They've taken the child, the mother. And they've taken Niamh."

"They've taken . . . ? What, your little Irish chippy? Who's taken her?"

"The police. The Forestry Com— Look, it's complicated. Forget the fucking once and future king. This is the real world come calling."

HE ATE HIS PIE—SHE was right, far too much horseradish—and laid out the story for her, the same version he'd given Crammond, with the added detail on Stordalen's heart, the reaction of the Huldu, and the hallucinations it seemed to induce. The witch grunted in apparent recognition: *Yes, well, you've crossed over, haven't you, only reasonable you'd see with their eyes now.* She bustled about the kitchen space—*I'm listening, I'm listening*—made tea for them both, poured it out into the same well-worn mugs she'd used last time. Then she sat and let him finish, watching him from over the rim of her mug with an unnerving, beady-eyed intensity, until he finally ran out of words and story to tell.

They sat looking at each other in the slow silence it left. In the walls, Duncan heard pipes gurgle and stammer, a sudden long rush of water pouring somewhere else in the tenement. Mumble of indistinct voices, oddly like chanting, and what sounded like the mewl of an unfeasibly large cat . . .

"So you want me to do what, exactly?" the witch asked him.

"First off, I have to find out where they've taken Niamh." He dug the keepsake from his shirt pocket—an Irish lace handkerchief she'd used, one sweltering August night early in their entanglement, to wipe the sweat from her face and cleavage, then gifted to him with a giggle. "This is hers, it . . ."

Trailing to a halt at the look on Wolfbane Sally's face.

"I'm not a *bloodhound,* Duncan."

"No, but can't you—"

She sighed. "Give it here, then. Let me have a look."

He handed over the little piece of folded cloth. She shook it out, held it up to the light—*oh, look at that, Kenmare needlepoint, very nice, won't have been cheap, this*—buried her nose in it, snuffled at its folds, shook it out again, muttered what he thought might be some kind of incantation, refolded it, stuck out her tongue and tasted a little wadded-up corner of the cloth. More muttering under her breath. He began to wonder if she was laughing at him . . .

"All right," she said. "There are some things I can do. I'll need to keep this. No promises, mind."

"How long?"

"I don't know. Call me tomorrow. Not early."

"And the Sword and Orbsters? You think I can trust this Ewart?"

She shrugged. "He sounds harmless. Most of them are; they don't really grasp the deep magic. Too chaotic for them. They're all about trying to discipline the power. Sword and Orb, Rose and Cross, the Ankh—it's all just cock and cunt for people too stuck up to name the parts. And you ever notice anything about all those symbols?"

Duncan hadn't even noticed the symbolism she'd just named. He shook his head.

"In all those configurations, the prick is never actually in the cunt"—a lewd grin—"where it belongs. No, it's outside, hard and straight and dominant, like some . . . rod, some king's scepter. That's what all those overgrown boys are about in the end. Mastery. Ruling over. And that's why they'll never get it. The ebb and flow, the reach of the storm, the *enveloping.*"

Duncan shifted uncomfortably. "If you say so."

"I do say so. Magic is an ocean, Duncan. You can't bottle and label and limit it—then it's not the ocean anymore. It's just salt water under glass. You have to immerse yourself in an ocean, you have to dive in and swim and drift, give yourself to its power. You have to let it carry you toward your desires, not try to extract your desires from it like lobster potting."

"Any idea why they'd be spying on Irene Rush and her daughter?"

The witch rolled her eyes. "Have you been listening to me at all? They are seeking *power.* And obviously this woman, or her daughter, or both, are powerful. Or symbolic, maybe. Queen Meb clearly thinks the daughter is, at least—she'd hardly have come all the way up from her usual range just to take one more poppet for a thrall. Something's happening, obviously."

And Svalenkari, down from the north.

"You think there's an incursion coming?" he asked.

"No, I do not."

Incursion—the new muttered terror by firelight across the nation. Worse than Zeppelin raids, or a European seaboard under the Prussian boot, or the next and ever more deadly strain of the flu. Bad enough that the Unbinding had brought the Fae back from the brink of myth and extinction, wiped out smaller human settlements, cut off roads and railways. What if the Huldu's ultimate aim was to march on the cities of Britain one night, make them their own, haunt the night streets and alleys the way they now haunted the Forest? What *then*?

"But if Hardy's got the child, and Meb wants her back badly enough?"

"Hardy can surround Mimi Rush with more iron and steel than a Sheffield foundry, and Meb will know that. The Fae know their limits, and they're patient. They'll wait."

"And the Orbsters? What's their angle?"

"For Hecate's sake, Duncan! How would I know? Why don't you ask them yourself? They want to talk to you anyway. It's the perfect opportunity. Oh, and here comes your little pal, right on time."

Duncan blinked at her. "What?"

The doorbell buzzed. He shot a glance at the Mappin & Webb—ten to two.

"How did you . . . ?"

"Oh, Duncan, how many times?"

"Aye. Right. You're a witch." He made a pacifying gesture. Hurriedly drained his tea, reached for the cloth to wipe his pie-stained fingers once more. "I'd better go down."

Sal put a carmine-taloned hand on his arm.

"No. Let him come up. It sets the terms. Fucking phallic orders. I'd like to take a look at him anyway."

THEY WENT OUT ON THE landing to meet Ewart, heard his hesitant steps on the stairs below. He trudged into view with a visible lack of enthusiasm. But when he saw Wolfbane Sal, he took off his hat politely enough.

"Pan's ball sack!" she chortled. "I know *you*!"

Ewart bobbed his head in what Duncan later realized was an awkward obeisance. "Yes, it is I, Mistress Bethune. Jeremy Ewart. May I hope you're keeping well?"

"Well, mustn't grumble. Wouldn't help, anyway. Just wait till I tell Nimble Shanks Annie I saw you."

"Yes," said Ewart tepidly. "Please give her my regards."

"She still speaks fondly of you, you know. Says you showed a lot of promise, before Bainbridge's boys stole you away. So is service to the Orb all you'd hoped it would be?"

"I cannot grumble either, Mistress Bethune. It is taxing, but with each effort I ascend and learn."

"Glad to hear it." Sal moved in, reached out. For a moment, Duncan thought she was going to shake the other man's hand, and maybe he did, too. Instead, she placed a motherly hand on Ewart's shoulder, then cupped the side of his head gently but firmly, and turned it in the light from the landing bulbs. "What happened to your face, though?"

Ewart's hand twitched upward, either to touch his bruised mouth or maybe push the witch's hold away. "A misunderstanding. I . . . did a poor job of explaining myself to Mr. Silver, the first time I attempted contact with him."

They both looked at Duncan.

"You caught me at a bad time," he growled. "I didn't mean to hit you that hard."

Wolfbane Sally pursed her lips. "You should let me put some salve on that, dear. It looks nasty. I've got some in the kitchen."

Jeremy Ewart tried to pull his head politely away. "That won't be necessary, mistress."

"Oh fiddlesticks! Annie would never forgive me if I let a former apprentice of hers walk out of here without so much as a care spell. Look, I'll just . . ." Taking back her hand, deftly licking thumb and forefinger, like some tightly abbreviated sketch of a Catholic crossing herself. She pressed thumb and finger onto the bruised jawline, cupped the side of Ewart's face again, muttered a jumble of hiss-click syllables under her breath. "There! All done! You really must try to be less violent around strangers, Duncan."

"He was following me!"

"Yes, but not with any harmful intent. And, I mean, look at him. He's half your size."

"I already said I was sorry!"

Ewart cleared his throat awkwardly.

"There is a car waiting for us below," he said. "We should go."

Duncan looked at him. "I told you to come alone."

"Uhm, yes, but—Mr. Silver—we must go some distance. A little way out of town. I do not drive. And I would not want to trust to finding a taxi in this, uhm . . . area."

The witch gurgled laughter like a drain. "This, uhm, area? Moving up in the world, are we, Master Ewart? House in the country. Chauffeur driven. No wonder Annie couldn't compete for your affections. Go on, get out of here, before I take back that healing!"

"I did not mean to offend, Mistress Beth—"

"You didn't say anything about out of town," Duncan interrupted. "I'm a busy man, Jerry. I do have other things to do today."

"Oh, we would be very happy to drop you somewhere afterward," said the young acolyte eagerly. "Anywhere you like, really. Our driver would be at your disposal."

Duncan glanced at the witch. She shrugged, nodded.

"All right, then. But just so we're clear—" He pulled the sgian dubh from his back, showed it to the other man. Glint of steel in the low light from the landing bulbs. "I've still got this. You, or any of your Sword and Orb pals, try to put anything over on me, magic or not, I'll make what happened to your face last time look like a playground tiff. I will fucking cut you up."

"Duncan!"

"Are we clear?"

Ewart bobbed his head nervously. "Of course, of course. Quite clear. I would expect no less from you, Mr. Silver. Rest assured, you arc safe with me. With us. We only want to talk."

"They only want to talk, Duncan."

Duncan shot the witch a disbelieving *you-shut-up* look. She ignored it, insisted on kissing them both goodbye on both cheeks, continental style, despite Ewart's fairly clear discomfort.

"Nice to see you, Jerry. I'll pass your best wishes on to Annie, shall I?"

"Please do," said Ewart stiffly. "Now, we really should—"

"Aye."

As Duncan followed the failed apprentice warlock down the stairs, he looked up and saw the witch leaned over the banister, watching them go with a curious smile.

TWENTY-FIVE

THE CAR WAS A CROSSLEY SALOON, THE 1920 LIMOUSINE MODEL, all elegant long-bonnet lines and shiny dark green coachwork, as out of place parked on Crawgate as a debutante drinking at a dogfight. Pricey, aloof, daring you to touch it. It stood facing downslope, as if poised on its wheeled haunches to leap away at the earliest opportunity. A uniformed chauffeur scrambled out from behind the wheel as they appeared, opened the back door for them, and stood at attention. Duncan followed Ewart into a spacious rear seat that smelled of fresh leather, heard the solid, well-made clunk as the door closed behind him.

"Nice ride," he remarked as the chauffeur started up and eased them down the rise. "I'm guessing it's not yours."

"It is an asset of the Order," said Ewart primly. "Ownership is an illusion of the fleshly realm, a temporary state, a distraction."

"If you say so."

They went left at the bottom of the hill. Duncan lounged in his seat, breathed in the scent of leather, worked at not showing his vigilance over the route they took.

"So you were going to be a warlock?" he asked, genuinely curious.

"It pleased Mistress Spence to believe so, yes. But I could not accept the terms."

They turned right off Heath Street, heading southeast, as near as Duncan could tell. "The terms?"

"The feminine principle. The female. In witchery, it is always ascendant."

"And that was too much for you?"

"Only insofar as it is a clear structural mistake." Young Ewart, turning earnestly toward him on the seat, hands framing his argument. "Please understand, I am no brute. I cherish women. But the eternal principles cannot be denied. Female is . . . passive, fecund. A power, yes, but an embedded one. An earthen bedrock strength upon which the world is layered. It cannot be given the ascendant fire and thrust of the male."

Duncan thought about his one delirious night's fucking with Wolfbane Sally, four years past and still oddly luminous in his memory. Passive was not one of the words that came to mind.

"So you chose the Sword and Orb instead."

"Yes. The Order recognizes *both* principles, and accords them each an honored place. Men *and* women, both have their part to play. But for dynamic achievements, dynamic *change,* we must work with the male. We must *direct* these new energies, with vigor and certain aim."

"Sort of thing a sword's useful for, eh?" Left turn, out onto the broad thoroughfare of York Road. Heading east. "Or a penis."

Ewart flushed to the roots of his hair. "Well, uh, the symbology, of course, uhm, is—"

"How far out of town are we going?"

"Oh—really, just the outskirts." Visibly relieved not to be pursuing this line of discussion. "We will be there, uhm, quite soon, in fact."

"Good."

Duncan turned away from the flustered young face, back to the window. It was dawning on him just what a poor fit Jerry would have been for apprenticeship with a witch. He didn't know Nimble Shanks Annie, but with that name, he doubted she'd be any less coarse in her woodswoman's ways than Sal. Ewart would have likely melted into a little puddle of lust and bother at her feet in a matter of months. No wonder he'd withdrawn, sought the firmer ground of Sword and Orb.

The buildings started to thin as they reached the eastern fringes of the town. Terraced frontage gave way to detached Victorian houses, open space around them. The weather was clouding up; rain specked the glass. Duncan shifted in his seat.

"This is it," Ewart blurted, as if he thought Duncan might be about to yank open the door and throw himself bodily out.

The car went sharp left off the York Road, and abruptly they were on a climbing gravel track. Slender young birch trees stood around, screening the view ahead. By the look of their distribution and size, they'd been planted with intent, and not that long ago. A little higher up the slope, track and trees sorted themselves out into a modest avenue, the gravel driveway leveled off and grew straight, the birches assembling in aspirational half-grown lines along each side. At the end stood an equally understated detached house—something of the Victorian vicarage about it, but with the clean, uncomplicated lines of this century rather than the last. There seemed to be more established woodland at its back.

The chauffeur parked the Crossley out front, jumped from the car like some kind of lateral jack-in-the-box, and opened the rear door for them. Duncan stepped down, tilted his head back to take in the architecture. The place had nowhere near the size or grandeur of some other mansions he'd seen—Viscount Savin's family seat, for example, would have been nearly ten times the size; even Stac Dubh was larger and, in keeping with its age, more ornate—but the architecture made its statement nonetheless. There was a businesslike, fresh-scrubbed Edwardian feel to the way the house presented itself, a modern, forward-looking promise, made before the war and the Forest came and smashed it all apart.

"Welcome, Mr. Silver! Welcome to Adept House." It was a voice to match the stonework, brisk and brushed and purposeful. "I'm so glad you could come."

Duncan dropped his gaze, found the imposing front door of the mansion now cracked ajar. Like some piece of cheap stage magic, a tall, slim man in a morning coat stood under the portico, silver-headed cane balanced lightly in one hand. Something familiar about the pose, or maybe the face. For one ludicrous moment, he looked almost like a music hall star about to burst into song.

"Happy to be here," said Duncan slowly. "And you are?"

The man came down the three steps to the gravel, spry and poised, held out his hand. An amber pentangle ring winked on the little finger. "Malcolm Bainbridge, at your service."

A little taken aback, Duncan shook the hand. It was firm and dry, the clasp not trying to prove anything. He supposed Bainbridge didn't have to. He hadn't really thought about which senior acolytes of the Order he might be meeting today. He certainly hadn't reckoned on it being the founder and archmage himself.

"I thought," groping for something halfway intelligent to say, "you'd be in London."

"Well." Bainbridge gave him what seemed like a genuine enough smile. "If I'm honest, we had similar information about you."

In the laugh lines around the other man's eyes, Duncan saw suddenly how old he was. Associate of Blavatsky, Olcott, William F. Barrett, and others in the burgeoning vogue for scientific spiritualism at the turn of the century, founder of his own loosely tributary order in London in the prewar years, scandalous bugbear of British polite society ever since, Bainbridge had to be well into his fifties by now. But you only really spotted it if you were paying attention. Touch of gray at the temples, the creases around eyes and mouth, the faintest of wattling in the flesh of his throat—aside from these things, he looked as trim and athletic as a man half his age. Duncan remembered reading somewhere once that Bainbridge had sold his soul to the devil. Easy to see why it might be believed.

"Perhaps you'd like to come inside." An elegant gesture with the cane toward the open door. "We are still in the process of setting up, but I'm sure I can rustle up some refreshments. Sandwiches and cordial, at the very least."

What Duncan had eaten of the witch's pie sat leaden in the pit of his stomach, memory of the eye-watering amount of horseradish still fresh. Something light and bland couldn't hurt.

"Aye," he said. "That'd be nice."

BAINBRIDGE WASN'T BEING SELF-DEPRECATING ABOUT the early stages of whatever he was doing here. Adept House, for all its fresh stonework, felt like a mausoleum. They went down a cold, dusty hall, grit crunching underfoot, past rooms stocked with the ghost loom of sheet-covered furniture. Only in a rear drawing room—with broad French window views onto a ragged, unkempt lawn and thick woodland beyond—did there seem to be any sign of habitation. A handsome polished-wood table and chairs stood to one side, files and papers and open leather-bound books strewn across its surface. More books, shelved along a wall to the right. There was no carpet to offset the chilly feel, but to the left, a healthy fire burned in the grate of a green-tiled Art Deco fireplace. Set around the fire, two deep armchairs and a low table, to which Bainbridge now applied his trademark elegant gesture with the cane.

"Will you sit?" he asked. "I'll see that food is brought."

Duncan needed no encouragement. The hangover chill was still on his bones; the witch pie dragged at his innards. He sank into one of the chairs, stretched his legs out toward the warmth of the flames. Over the fire, someone had found the time to hang a somber study in oils of Tam o' Shanter reaching the Brig o' Doon astride his mare Meg, with the witch horde in full cry at his back.

Duncan grinned sourly at it.

A sober-looking butler appeared in the doorway, as if summoned by Bainbridge's words. The archmage murmured to the man for a moment, saw him out, then joined Duncan at the fire. He leaned his cane against the fireplace tiles—the heavy silver cap, Duncan noticed, was a leonine head fronded with wings, some representation of a sphinx, he supposed—and folded himself neatly into the chair. He looked benignly at Duncan like something he'd just acquired, not cheaply, at auction.

"Well," he beamed. "You have stirred up quite the hornet's nest, Mr. Silver. I imagine you've realized that by now."

"Who told you I was in London?"

"It was general information I had. Staying well informed is something of an ingrained habit for me, and I feed it with whatever means are to hand."

"You're talking about magic?" Duncan reviewed what little he recalled about the claims of the Sword and Orbsters—clairvoyance and invocation, the third eye's gaze. Sex magic and unity with the numinous, or so it was, somewhat salaciously, claimed. "Scrying?"

"Well, you see." Bainbridge gestured airily. "Magic really is not the riotous carnival carousal that the witches try to sell us, but it does have its uses, when soberly applied. As does money, of course. It took me a very expensive day or two to discover that you had, in fact, turned down Colonel Hardy's offer of employment. But we got there in the end. Remarkable in itself, that refusal, I must say. I understand it was a very generous package. Did you have some . . . misgivings about the colonel?"

"Not as many as I have now. Traitorous cunt tried to kill me."

"Really?"

The archmage's eyes widened, whether at the revelation or Duncan's language, it wasn't clear. Either way, it felt put on—as if neither the news nor the expletive were quite the great shock Bainbridge pretended. Duncan grunted.

"You're not working with him, I take it?"

"Oh, the Godhead forbid!" Chuckling, shaking his head. "No, not at all. Some residual rote Protestantism aside—the rind of his childhood faith, I suppose you might call it—the colonel is a staunch materialist. He'd be loath to have anything to do with the likes of me. Martin Hardy sees the world through a wholly pragmatic lens. He practices what our German cousins are pleased to call realpolitik. You're familiar with the term?"

"Sure. Heard it a lot in the war, usually to justify piles of dead men."

"Well, quite. And of course this realpolitik is why the colonel's endeavors are doomed to fail. Hardy seeks to treat the Forest and its denizens as an enemy no different in principle from Germany or Austria. He eschews the numinous, and the numinous is the entirety of what we are dealing with in these times. Tell me, have you heard the name Niels Bohr?"

"Sounds familiar." Duncan shrugged. "Don't know why. Who is he?"

"They've just given him the Nobel Prize in physics."

"Right." Duncan recalled Bohr now, from a newspaper he'd picked up at Grimaldi's one lazy afternoon—excited headlines, a photo of a haunted-looking young man with fiercely back-combed hair. Some incomprehensible gibberish about atoms. He nodded sagely. "Scientist."

"He has also founded an Institute of Theoretical Physics at the University of Copenhagen," Bainbridge added.

"Good for him. What does this have to do with Martin Hardy?"

"Oh, nothing directly. But bear with me, please. The men at this institute, the work they are doing, concerns something they call *quantum theory.* Now, I can't explain this theory to you, because so far no one has been able to successfully explain it to me. Even the scientist who helped originate it, one Max Planck, apparently doesn't believe it to be an actual truth about the universe, merely a mathematical trick. But others take it far more literally. And what they are saying is that quantum theory demonstrates the laws we thought governed the universe are, in fact, incorrect. They have broken down. The physical world is not as we believe it to be. *There is another world behind it.*"

Duncan pulled a face. Bainbridge saw it, leaned forward. In the closer glow of the firelight, his eyes gleamed. His voice had grown taut and earnest.

"Mr. Silver, believe me, these are not fanciful men. They are hard-headed exponents of modern science, working at the cutting edge of their disciplines. And if men of that caliber say that the eternal laws of physics are now failing, falling away perhaps, to reveal something else—does this not speak to our own experiences since the great forests returned? The world is changing at a fundamental level, Mr. Silver, spilling us out into realms and contemplations hostile to the lives humans have lived until now. Our former outlook cannot cope with what is upon us. And navigating our way through these changes cannot be left to men like Colonel Martin Hardy."

"You'll get no argument from me there. I already told you, he tried to put a bullet in me."

"Of course he did. You intended to bring back the child from Faerie, and that could not be allowed."

"Could not be allowed." Duncan, tasting the words like unfamiliar fruit. "Allowed by who?"

"Why, the powers that be, Mr. Silver!" Speaking as if to a child. "The secret engineers of the world order. Did you think that they would not *react,* when such a cataclysm of change sweeps in to demolish the pillars of their design?"

"Right."

At the end of the war, Duncan had spent an interminable six days at the Thetford Dispersal Unit, billeted in camp and waiting for his demob papers to go through. Officers got better quarters than enlisted men, but he still had to share, for most of the week, with a hectic-faced captain called Pugh, whose entire conversation seemed to consist of bitter rants against Bolsheviks, Prussians, and Jews. The Jews appeared to exercise him particularly. He carried around a grubby pamphlet he called *The Protocols* and was given to pulling it out and quoting darkly from it, over and over, to anyone who'd listen. In the end, Duncan's only enduring memories of Thetford became Pugh's litany of grimly declaimed phrases like *secret world order* and *pil-*

lars of their design, and the dank, industrial waft from the pulpware factory across town.

That Bainbridge talked the same way was not encouraging.

"You don't believe me?" The archmage had evidently worked this out—whether by magical intuition or Duncan's face, who could tell. "You think Mimi Rush is just another abducted plaything of the Hidden Folk?"

"What I don't believe is that there's any world order, secret or otherwise. The men of power I've seen in action couldn't organize losing their own virginity in a fucking brothel."

A discreet knock announced the butler, back with a flourish and a broad silver tray of tea sandwiches balanced on one arm. He was followed in by a maid who brought a second tray bearing a tall glass carafe of what looked like lime cordial and two glasses. Bainbridge said nothing while the refreshments were laid out and the glasses poured full. Duncan wondered if he was feeling offended. The butler and maid withdrew, closed the door soundlessly behind them. Duncan snagged a sliced chicken sandwich and bit it in half, raised his eyebrows at the other man. Bainbridge smiled back thinly.

"Very eloquent, Mr. Silver. Of course, the horrors and the chaos of your time in the trenches will have given you a . . . distinct perspective."

Duncan discovered some appetite, finished his chicken sandwich, and took another. "Take it you weren't there yourself?"

"No, I did not serve in a uniformed capacity. I was . . . invited to spend some time in America instead." Bainbridge drank placidly from his cordial. "Matters I'm still not entirely at liberty to discuss, I'm afraid."

"You at liberty to discuss what's so special about Mimi Rush?"

"Can't you guess?"

Duncan's gaze iced over. "I mentioned to your acolyte out there that I have a busy day. I'm not here to play guessing games with you."

"No, of course." The archmage inclined his head gracefully enough. But not before Duncan had caught the flicker of offended conceit in his eyes. "It is not my intention to waste your time, Mr. Silver. Far from it. To the point, then. Mimi Rush, as far as I can establish, is special because she descends directly from a Huldu clan noblewoman stolen from her people here in Britain more than a thousand years ago. The Huldu therefore consider her one of their own.

"Does that answer your question?"

TWENTY-SIX

DUNCAN SAT RIGID.

Thought and revelation and memory, splintered in jagged pieces around him on the as-yet-uncarpeted floor here at Adept House.

I'm a princess, Mimi Rush had said that the Huldu told her. And he'd ignored it—too wrapped up in his own personal bitterness and rage and the needle match with Mebhuranon to pay close attention where it was needed.

Even the grindylow had heard enough to say the child was *no plaything, no simple thrall,* that she was rumored to be of high worth, of noble blood . . .

"Mr. Silver?" Bainbridge, watching him shrewdly.

Duncan got a grip. "Aye. I'm listening."

"A thousand years, for a species as long lived as the Huldu, really isn't the awful span of time we mortals feel it as. It is almost recent history for them. Of course, I cannot speak to how strongly that Fae blood heritage may still flow in the child's veins, in other words how much of a—what's the term?—a *throwback* to former pedigree she may represent. But you have seen the mother, have you not?"

Flash recall of Irene Rush's fey, filmic good looks. Numbly, Duncan nodded.

"Did she tell you who her husband is?"

"No. She kept that quiet. I only found out this morning."

"Hmm. Susan, the maid, I imagine."

Duncan said nothing. Bainbridge nodded.

"Loyal. And tight-lipped with it. I like that. Well, then. I can't be sure how much Susan—or whoever—told you, or indeed is party to. But I imagine you will also know, or have deduced, that Sir Michael Endershall is very much determined to track down his errant wife and daughter. Has offered quite a reward, in fact."

"And that's where you come in?"

Bainbridge shook his head.

"Wrong again, Mr. Silver. Rest assured, I do not work for Endershall, in that capacity or any other—despite his very best efforts to recruit me."

"But Hardy does?"

"Colonel Hardy and the officers of the Forestry Commission are part of a concerted effort to handle the Unbinding for the greater good of nation and empire, however that may be achieved. Realpolitik, as I believe I mentioned. At times, they believe, this will involve open war with the Huldu. At other junctures, it may require . . . diplomacy. Miriam Rush was to be that diplomacy made flesh. A tentative olive branch, if you will. Emissaries were sent into the Forest, talks offered, and, as far as I can tell, some kind of meeting took place. An attempt to . . . open channels, as it were. Poorly handled, I would think; these are not men versed in magic, after all. Had *I* been there . . ." Bainbridge shrugged. "Well, no matter. I am not privy to exactly what was discussed, what offers or strategic demands were made, but I think we can guess at least one of them."

"Endershall gave up his own fucking daughter for that?"

"Yes, I imagine that must seem brutal to you. Given what I . . . suspect of your past."

Duncan left that one where it lay. "Any man who won't protect his own child deserves a slow death in a ditch."

"Yes, that is one way of looking at the matter, I suppose. However, it's lacking in some distasteful but necessary nuance. You see, in addition to being an esteemed member of our landed gentry, Sir Michael is a career diplomat of some standing, a man who has made it his life's work to serve the realm. He's also an arrogant, hidebound fool, but that's not really the point at issue. He was knighted for services to his country during the run-up to the war. He lost two brothers and his son by a previous marriage during the hostilities, and then his wife by subsequent suicide on the death of the son. In short, he is a man familiar with sacrifice, and quite willing to see such sacrifices through. You will doubtless have met men like this before now."

"Not often. They mostly stayed a long way behind the lines, sacrificing other men."

Another of Bainbridge's thin smiles. Duncan ignored him, still churning through the enormity of the deed.

"It didn't occur to anybody," he said, mostly to himself, "that a mother might value her child above some diplomatic settlement with fucking elves?"

"Oh, I'm sure it did. Which is probably why, as far as I can tell, Sir Michael never troubled to inform his new young wife of these intentions. He is—how shall I put this?—a man cast very much in the Victorian mold. Not a lot of room for the . . . lesser perspectives of women, even less where those might clash with the needs of king and country." Bainbridge seemed to grow aware of his increasingly snide tone. He cleared his throat. "In any case, it seems the mother somehow . . . intuited these dangers ahead of time. Perhaps the strength of throwback in the bloodline did not begin with Mimi. Perhaps the powers of the Huldu are strong in the mother as well."

. . . summat strange about thy lass Irene Rush, Garner had told him in Macclesfield. *Folk at Caulders were very happy with her, everyone I spoke to anyway . . . lovely girl, delighted to have her . . . but when tha push any of them for detail, there's nowt. For a lass that made such a good impression, they don't remember a whole lot about her . . .*

And somehow, according to Susan, no one had ever noticed her real name on the paper qualifications that opened the doors to employment.

The midnight flit. And years in hiding. Charm and beguile and cope, then move, move again, move on, whenever you somehow sense the closing in of the hounds. Draw fogging veils of glamour in your wake, to cloak the path, to cover your retreat. Perhaps you are not even aware you do these things, open up these jewelry boxes of heirloomed power, put on what glitters within, the way you'd turn unconsciously in your sleep, huddle away from a cold draft, creep an arm around the softly sleeping bundle at your side . . .

"How much of this do you know for certain?" Duncan asked.

"Of what has happened here in what we might call the mortal realm, I now know quite a lot. As I told you, Sir Michael, through the Forestry Commission, tried to engage my services, and they briefed me in some detail. That is not to say everything they told me was true, or that they told me the whole truth about any of it. There again, as I also mentioned, I do not care to remain in the dark about much." Bainbridge gestured at the table, the papers and opened books it held. "My research is ongoing. Answers are beginning to accrue. Lady Ada's family, the Ulvers, have what you might call a long association with the otherworldly. Some whisper that it's what has brought such ill fortune upon their house—the illnesses, the losses at war, their financial woes. It is said that a scion of theirs was once sent by royal decree to abduct a Faerie maiden—or perhaps several, the legends vary—and so bring magic into the line of descent of their clan. Sometimes the tale is couched in romance—the young knight wins the heart of his elfin bride—sometimes, it is rather more, shall we say, Roman in tone. In any case, there seems little doubt that the Ulver clan were, for generations, raiders into Fae territory, or at least the borderlands that surrounded it. Decorated for their daring exploits, gifted lands and title, even recruited for their expertise and eldritch blood. The rise and hubris before the fall, you see."

"Recruited?"

"That is correct." Bainbridge smiled. He liked to lecture, you could see. Appreciated a good, attentive student. "You see, Mr. Silver, during the Stuart era, King James I established a number of secret orders to look into witchery and magic. Amateurish stuff, for the most part—it was an enthusiasm of the monarch, and thus richly indulged. If you've ever wondered why there are three witches at the beginning of Shakespeare's Macbeth, wonder no longer. The Bard knew which side his patronage was buttered on. Anyway, a lot of innocent lives were snuffed out, witches and unversed women both. Contrary to some of the Communist cant you'll hear on street corners these days, this new century of ours did not invent senseless wholesale slaughter. But memories are short, history rapidly forgotten, and anger tends to seek local focus." Bainbridge grimaced. "And we are digressing, I fear. So yes, as I said—a great number of secret orders under royal charter. One such cabal, the King's Flame in the Forest, was charged with handling matters regarding the borders of Faerie and any leakage into our world. The Ulvers were called to it, and remained preeminent for hundreds of years. Though now that influence is faded, like the family fortunes, almost to nothing. They, at least, are a spent force, clinging to what remains of their ancestral title."

The obvious implication hung in the air between them.

"But the cabal? That's still in business?"

"Oh yes. Shrouded in great secrecy, of course. The Glorious Revolution, the Enlightenment, industrialism and modern science—these things eventually drove out the superstitions of the Stuart age, just as our culling of the great forests drove out the Huldu themselves. The amateur idiots and the sadists, the witch finders and their kind, all found themselves eventually unemployed. But the Huldu were never wholly gone, and there are those in positions of quiet power who have always known as much. The King's Flame has renamed and reinvented itself repeatedly over the past three hundred years—under Cromwell, it was briefly suppressed, but it didn't last. In fact, there are rumors that the Flame used its Faerie connections to hasten Cromwell's demise, excruciate his pains, and that the Huldu came on the wings of a mighty storm to claim his soul at the end . . . But again, I digress. The Flame is still with us. It exists within Whitehall as a sub-department in the Directorate of Military Intelligence called Section J."

"Not Section F?"

Bainbridge smiled again, convivial. "You'd think so, wouldn't you. But no—someone in the department clearly has some aggrieved sense of history. Following Cromwell's demise and the Restoration, you see, the Flame took the name the Jacobus Assembly, to honor its original founder, and it stuck until 1688 when Jacobus was deemed . . . impolitic as a choice of name. So then they became the Brotherhood of the Flame for a time, then the Honorable Society of Forest Rangers, then—well, no matter. Suffice it to say, that as their titles grew less grandiose and dramatic, so their size and influence also waned. Section J was, until very recently, no more than a small advisory group, largely voluntary, almost invisible in funding terms." The smile came back, broader still. "That's all changed now, of course."

"I'll bet."

A quiet fell in the room that was almost comfortable. Bainbridge sipped at his cordial. Duncan took a third sandwich. The fire snapped and hissed, burning low in the grate.

Duncan finished up, brushed away crumbs from his lap.

"What do you want from me, Bainbridge?"

"Ultimately?" The archmage shrugged. "Your allegiance. Though I appreciate that will have to be earned over time."

"I'm not much for allegiances. And right now, I'm busy."

Bainbridge got up and took a poker to the fire, prodded it brusquely into brighter life. Once again, as he leaned in, his eyes lit with proximity to the flames.

"You will search for the child again." It wasn't a question. "The mother, too, I imagine. Everything I have learned about you suggests as much. If the Forest held them, you would be in your element and I have no doubt you would bring them home. But Mimi and her mother are captives in the world of men. A world you have largely rejected. To operate here, you will need help."

"What makes you think I don't have help?"

The archmage straightened, put the poker aside. He faced Duncan again, head framed by the eerie Tam o' Shanter painting over the mantel at his back.

"Oh, I'm sure you do. But not at the level I can offer it. You see, I may be regarded as somewhat of an enfant terrible in polite society these days, but you'd be surprised how many elevated members of that same society owe me favors they'd rather not talk about."

Duncan nodded. "And you'd like me to owe you some favors, too."

"If you choose to see it in those terms, then I suppose—yes. That is what I'm offering. A mutual pact, for mutual advancement. These are unstable times, Mr. Silver. Delicate times. But also times of great opportunity. The Lloyd George coalition is hanging by a thread; without the dangers posed by the Forest, I daresay it would already have collapsed by now. The Conservatives sniff undiluted power on the wind, but they can't find their way to it. Bonar Law is too ill to lead them into an election, Curzon too privileged and wealthy in the eyes of voters, Baldwin, of course, too green."

"If you say so."

"You do not follow politics, then?"

"Not if I can help it."

"Well, then you must take my word for it. It is a moment in which a man with access to the right levers may rise, make great gains, perhaps even make history." Eyes still filled, somehow, with the white-hot wash of light from the fire. "And, of course, raise up his friends and followers with him."

Duncan considered. "You really think you can find Mimi Rush and her mother for me?"

"I am in absolutely no doubt that I can. I have adepts searching for them as we speak. Though, of course, what you do about mother and child once you know their location is likely to be a more . . . protracted issue."

"With which you can also help?"

Bainbridge smiled, a kindly teacher whose normally dense student suddenly sees the light. He seated himself again in the renewed warmth of the fire. He steepled his fingers.

"Leaving aside the favors I am owed, the ears whose attention I have, our brute material resources as an order are . . . not inconsiderable. Now more than ever, funds are flooding in."

Duncan grunted. He wasn't surprised. The need for answers, as the burning facade of authority creaked and collapsed in the night, was a palpable ache in everyday life. You could feel it like a bruise, laid across the whole nation.

"Yes," Bainbridge mused. "I do sometimes wonder how we might all have foundered and shrunk into obscurity without the Unbinding. But now the skeptics are thrown down, their carping modernist voices cowed. People seek meaning, *deep* meaning, and only we can offer it to them—*have* been offering it to them for decades. It is our time for the taking. I only wish Helena could have lived to see it all."

"You talking about Blavatsky?"

The archmage said nothing, only inclined his head and stared into the flames as if hoping they'd transmit a message from his old mentor.

Duncan stirred impatiently.

"All right, Bainbridge—let's allow you can help me out. What's in it for you? Why are you so keen for *me* to owe you favors?"

"Isn't it obvious?" Still gazing into the flames.

"I already told you I'm not here for guessing games."

Bainbridge looked up at him. "Why, it's the Forest, Mr. Silver."

"What's the Forest?"

"Everything. Everything to come, the new order of things. The Forest is an unavoidable feature of all our lives now, the dominant factor in all we do—as if the ocean had somehow roared in to take away vast portions of the land we previously considered our birthright. We are still reeling from the impact. But soon the time for reeling will be at an end, and we must make headway. In that at least, Colonel Hardy is correct. To make that headway, we will need men who know the Forest, who can survive there, who have the courage to face what it holds. In short, we will need men like you."

The fire chuckled to itself, as if it liked the idea. Duncan frowned into the flames.

"You think I'm not afraid in there like anyone else?"

"An American writer acquaintance of mine once told me *courage is not the absence of fear—it is resistance to fear, mastery of fear.* I think you mastered your fear early, Mr. Silver, replaced it perhaps with something else."

"I had very little choice. None of us did. Howitzers don't care about your feelings."

"Indeed, no. But I'm not talking about the trenches, and I think you know that. I'm talking about much, much earlier in your life."

In the warmth of the fireside, something chilly came to walk on the nape of Duncan's neck. He stared at the archmage.

"You don't know me, Bainbridge."

"I am beginning to."

It sounded like a threat. Duncan's voice hardened. "Is that right? Been looking in your crystal ball, have you?"

"I have been looking in a number of ways." If Bainbridge had noticed the change in tone, he appeared not to take offense. "Scrying stones are not properly part of the Order's rituals, so no, not in a crystal ball as such. Of course, I do not expect you to accept our magic as wholeheartedly as you have that of the witches. You are oriented firmly toward the feminine, that much is clear. You reek of it, in fact. And this is not surprising, given what I can surmise of your history. But the ways in which we work here under the Sword and Orb are just as effective, I do assure you."

"My history," said Duncan flatly.

"Yes, genealogy is an interest of mine. Your name, for example.

Silver, from the Portuguese *da silva*—meaning, as I'm sure you know, of the forest, from the forest. Curious, no? Not many da Silvas in this country, especially not north of the border."

Flash recall of the grubby little workshop in Shoreditch. Grime on the poky windows, sounds of drunken merriment in the alley outside. Murdoch the forger, shaking his head.

Risky, he says. *Very risky.*

What is?

Goin' for a foreign name like that. You a Scotchman an' all.

"Wouldn't know about Portuguese," he told Bainbridge evenly. "My people are from Edinburgh. I'm told Silver was a German name—Silber or Silbermann—if you go back far enough. Though we don't shout that too loudly these days."

"Understandable, yes. People are remarkably stupid about these things. Did you know they've renamed the German shepherd, of all the numbskull ideas? Apparently, people were throwing stones at the poor creatures in the streets. They call it the Alsatian now."

Duncan shrugged. "Good enough for the king. I guess dogs just have to get in line."

"Yes. Windsor, a stout English surname if ever there was one. Sounds almost bourgeois, though, doesn't it? Who knows, perhaps the shape of things to come. But do tell me, what was this family of Germans called Silbermann doing in Edinburgh?"

"Apparently, they were silversmiths." Run through the litany, the fistful of lies that Murdoch had long ago warned him to invent and rehearse. "Named for their trade, back in medieval times. Came to Edinburgh in the 1400s, by appointment to the Scottish kings. Prospered, stayed and settled. Not that anyone in the family does that now."

"What, prosper? Or work in silver?"

"Either one. I grew up a schoolmaster's son."

"Fascinating." Bainbridge, nodding amiably, like a man told a good, if obviously embellished, anecdote. "And your father, does he still teach?"

"No, he died while I was still away in France. My mother, too. The flu took both of them."

"I am sorry."

"Don't be." Duncan said, and looked the other man hard in the eye. "It's the past, it's done. I let go of it a long time ago."

TWENTY-SEVEN

R*ISKY, VERY RISKY . . .*

Murdoch is still muttering it like a litany as he gets to work, paid but unhappy. His lips purse, his glances across at Duncan are frequent. Duncan studiously ignores them, sits in a listing, damp-smelling armchair on the other side of the room. Beyond the grimed-up windows, Shoreditch carouses—voices and stumbling hilarity, the odd chime of breaking glass. Ribald shrieks of laughter. It's the first spring since the Armistice, and Forest notwithstanding, most men he's met are still walking around with a giddy light-headed gratitude at being alive. From the tavern at the mouth of the alley comes the poorly tuned *plink-plonk* of piano, some reedy attempts at song, turned up briefly loud each time someone opens the door to enter or leave, like a radio on bad atmospherics.

Finally, the forger sighs, pushes back from his desk. Props his glasses up on his balding head, pinches his eyes. Scrubs with one open hand at his stubbled jowls.

"Look," he says. "Da Silva, it's not just uncommon, it *sahnds* fuckin' uncommon. Like an aristocrat or somefink. It'll stick in people's minds, mark my words, and then so will you. You don't *want* that. An' I don't want that, if it comes back to me. You wanna sound more *ordinary.*"

"I'm used to it," says Duncan stubbornly.

But it's a little more than that.

HE DEMOBBED AS DA SILVA, had been going by it over a year before that, ever since the mix-up in the hospital. His rank was tied to it, his liaison with the Americans, the new place he made for himself in all the screaming chaos, the twist of fortune that fell into his lap that June evening with low-angled sun striping the wards through the western windows, and the starched to and fro bustle of nurses around him. The harried adjutant, advancing down the corridor toward him—*Captain da Silva! Captain Gareth da Silva?*—messy armful of paperwork, exasperated with orders he's struggling to find the officers to fulfill.

Duncan just gapes at him.

Well, are you or aren't you? I haven't got all day. We've got Yanks landing by the shipload all over Brittany, and Command is still fighting about who's going to be giving them orders, Haig or Pershing, what weapons they're going to be using, and God alone knows what else besides. Liaison is going to be a bloody nightmare. So. Do I have the right man, Captain da Silva, or not?

On some wild impulse, Duncan nods.

And are you fit for duty, Captain? Leafing awkwardly through the papers in the crook of his arm. *It says here trench fever and shrapnel wounds. But you seem able bodied.*

They dug the shrapnel out of his back and thigh a week ago at the Casualty Clearing Station. He beat the fever and shin pains two days later, here in the hospital, and he's been hobbling up and down the corridors ever since, trying to walk some strength back into his legs. He's still shaky on his feet, but—

Aye, sir. Ready to get out of here. Only my papers, sir, all my documentation was—

Don't worry about that—I'll get something sorted out. Uniform, too. Machine Gun Corps, wasn't it?

Duncan nods again, wordless, still not quite believing what he's just done.

Good. Thank you, Captain. I'll have a motor transport collect you here Monday next. You'll report to, ahhh, let's see . . . Yes, Colonel Mortimer, Kings Own Royal Lancaster, at the Naval Operating Base in Saint-Nazaire. That's four days from now. Get what rest you can, Captain, you're going to need it.

Even now, looking back, he's not sure why he did it. Like a pole-vaulter shattering some previous record, he can recall the moments of lift and free fall, the act itself, but very little of the run-up to it, the placing of footfalls that made the jump.

Then, as now, fragments come back—da Silva's soft, Welsh-accented voice and kindly face by lamplight in the dugout of the German trench they've taken, as Duncan shudders in the grip of the fever—*don't you worry, Lieutenant, I've seen this before, it's a mild dose. You're young and strong, you'll pull through*—mugs of sweet black tea he can hardly lift to his chattering teeth long enough to drink without spilling, so da Silva cups the back of his head and helps hold the mug to his lips—*soon as we stabilize that advance, lovely boy, I'll get you sent back to a CCS. They'll be able to look after you much better there*—the endless, fatherly patience the other officer has for him, though Duncan thinks he can't be more than a couple of years older—*I hear you're a bit of a terror, Lieutenant Slaven! Seen some frightful fighting, they say, and still come through it. Mentioned in dispatches, likely to get a medal before the year's out.* Duncan, feverish, can't be sure, but he thinks that'll be for the way he hacked four men to death with a trenching spade as the Germans tried to drive his party out of a machine gun nest they'd just taken at Delville Wood. Then again, it might have been something else. The rage his years in the Forest stoked in him has served him well out here, just as it did in the bullying, polish-reeking corridors of Cadogan's. He fantasizes Huldu faces on the Germans he fights, and the banked fires of his fury do the rest. *Anyway, you'd better rest up, we're going to need men like you*—the flow of mild conversational gambits to keep him engaged—*Forest of Argyll, really? Must be beautiful up there, always wanted to go, I love the forest; grew up in Cardiff myself, whole bloody life there, see, but d'you know what, my family name, it's Portuguese originally, means from the forest—silva, remember your Latin? Da . . . Silva. So maybe it's in my blood, family of Iberian foresters or something, I don't know, and I just want to get back there, to my roots like*—and Duncan shivering violently, trying to tell him to be careful what he wishes for.

HE'S ACTUALLY STARTING TO FEEL a little better by the time the Germans decide to bombard their own captured trenches and drive out the Allied advance. He hears the screaming from the sky outside, almost makes it up off his bare-boards bunk before the dugout comes down around him in a chaos of shattering timbers and choking black earth. And as it buries him, presses down on him, face and body, he feels an odd kind of letting go with the weight, something close to the feeling he had when he was shipped away to Cadogan's at eleven, a sense that nothing mattered anymore, there was nothing left for him, he could just relinquish everything and—

Man buried! Help here! Man buried!

It's da Silva's voice, and there's something flailing violently in the dirt by Duncan's upraised leg. The firm grip of hands. He's tugged at, dragged at. More muffled shouting. Someone hauls him bodily from the collapsed dugout, turns him on his side and hammers at his back. He hacks and spits up loose earth and phlegm in knots—*that's it, lovely boy! That's it! You cough up that shit!*—finally he lies panting and shuddering on the loose earthen ground. A milling of men around him in the dark, da Silva checking him everywhere for injuries—*that's fine, you go on, I've got him*—the other men recede, calling out to each other, heads turtling involuntarily as shells continue bursting farther up the line. Screams and yells and whistles, a confusion as muddy and torn and darkened as what's left of the dugout they dragged him from.

We're getting out of here, boyo—da Silva stripping off his jacket now, forcing Duncan into it one arm at a time. *That fever still got you, has it? You'd think a big bloody German shell up the arse might have cured it, now, wouldn't you?* Duncan coughs up laughter and muddy drool. Da Silva slings Duncan's arm over his shoulders, lifts him under the armpits—*can you stand?* He finds he can. *Command just called the retreat, and that's good enough for me. The Vickers are buggered anyway, Fritz'll be back up at us as soon as this shit stops. So we'd better go.*

Staggering down the trench, bits of men strewn underfoot, hung from wire where the blast has thrown the pieces high and they've caught coming down. Duncan gets glimpses of strung viscera, a grasping hand, what looks like half of a face, hooked through the eye socket—

Don't you look at that! Da Silva steering him firmly the other way, up a shambles of sloping, sliding soil where a shell has smashed the trench wall apart. *Here, this way, up you go.*

He shoves Duncan on hands and knees ahead of him, up to the crest. They crouch and look out across a darkened sea of churned mud and wire, shattered trees like the snapped-up splinters on the broken end of a plank, the same fucking ground they took with bayonets and Mills bombs, blood and rage, only days before. Shellfire lights the landscape fitfully, but the bombardment seems to be letting up.

Good a time as any, grunts da Silva, and pats him on the shoulder.

And they're off!

It's hard to run in the mud, though easier by far than it was with full pack and rifle on the way in. You lift high and stamp down, try not to snag an ankle in one of the remaining intact coils of wire, try not to slip and slide so you'll fall and land on the barbs. Duncan sees it all through the tunneled vision of the fever. He's vaguely aware of da Silva at his side, but it takes him a while to realize that they're not alone, that all along the line, men have clambered out of the trench and are sprinting alongside each other like some mad, ungoverned end-of-term cross-country event. He hears yells of encouragement, of warning as the shells howl down. Da Silva shoves him violently sideways into a foxhole—*lookout, boyo!*—and then is gone, utterly, in a shattering gout of blood and earth and steel. Duncan feels shrapnel strike home in his body, red-hot peppering pain across his back and down one leg. He just has time and presence of mind to throw up an arm to shield his face, and then he's pelted with mud and bloody fragments as what's left of da Silva rains down on him with soil and stones, and apparently one of those stones hits him in the head, and someone turns out the lights.

HE'S AWARE AGAIN OF HANDS and soft voices, he doesn't know how much later; the light has changed, the darkness is bleached through to indigo. Hands, under his arms, hauling him out of the foxhole.

Loading him onto a stretcher of some sort.

Jolting at the run across the oddly quiet ground, chased by the *crack-crack* of rifle fire somewhere behind. Maybe not chased; it's not custom to shoot at stretcher bearers, a rule that both sides largely honor. Or maybe it's still not light enough to see clearly, and all the Germans can make out is men running into the murk, back where they came from.

He thinks they must've spiked him with morphine, because he's relaxed and dreamy the whole way, even when they stumble and tip him headfirst into a sap, and he starts laughing uproariously and can't seem to stop, even when the stretcher bearers get him loaded back up.

Glad you think it's fucking funny, one of them grumbles, and of course it's not funny, not really, and he knows that, because look, here are tears, streaming like rain down his face, a shuddering release that's waited ever since he crouched on the stairs outside his parents' drawing room at Stac Dubh and understood what had been taken from him, forever, beyond anything he could ever do to get it back.

HE LIMPS OUT OF THE hospital four days later as Captain Gareth da Silva, freshly uniformed, waiting on papers, blinking in the bright French sunlight like a newborn. He seats himself in the rickety motor transport that's come for him, and is ferried, in bone-rattling discomfort, away. Off to Saint-Nazaire, off to meet Americans, off to join the war anew.

Duncan Slaven, dead-eyed, feral-nerved slaughterer of the Hun, mentioned in dispatches, has gone to his rest in the Flanders mud.

There was nothing much left for him to come home to anyway.

Later, he'll hear that Slaven was awarded the Victoria Cross, posthumous, though he'll never bother to find out which particular piece of abandoned madness in combat it might have been for.

"LOOK, WHAT ABOUT SILVER?" MURDOCH tries.

"Silver?"

"You know, like the pirate—ole Long John Silver. *Treasure Island.* It's close enough to what you want, but it *sahnds* English."

Duncan considers. He's shed Slaven like snakeskin, but he can't risk being Gareth da Silva for very much longer. As long as the war lasted, it was different. So many had died, gone missing in action, been reassigned or hurriedly promoted to fill the devastated ranks—it was a world of strangers and strange new circumstances, and Duncan now spent almost all his time among men who'd only just arrived from across the Atlantic. To the Americans, he was just another Limey officer, albeit one they got on with better than most. The chances of an encounter with anyone who actually knew da Silva from before were fleeting at best.

Families and peacetime are another thing. Reconnection, tearful reunion, is the air they all breathe these days, the desperate search for those lost, by all and any means up to and including fucking séance. Dead or alive, the vanished will be sought. Loved ones are tenacious, demob records meticulous. Passports and photographic identification, poorly applied panic measures that came in with the war and were widely expected to go out with it, too, now look like they're here to stay. He has no idea what family da Silva might have, if any, nor what their resources might be. But if they come looking, he won't be hard to track.

The new papers he's paying Murdoch for will cut the trail. But for some reason, there's something about da Silva he can't leave behind, even if it's only his name. The violent young man and the kindly Welsh officer who cared for him in the dugout—one is dead and gone now, utterly obliterated from the world, and who's to say which one it is? He has already become the other man, so completely he sometimes dreams it actually was him, Duncan Slaven, blown apart by artillery, and soft-spoken Gareth da Silva who got stretchered out.

And that this was fitting after all.

Perhaps it's that idea, cobbled together in his feverish and morphine-addled head at the hospital, that da Silva was a kinder, better man than Slaven ever could be, a less ruined man, with a better chance of a future—though what future he's going to seek is hard to see, in a world where the Forest nightmare of Slaven's childhood has erupted everywhere in the full light of day to haunt the world da Silva must step out into and survive . . .

Perhaps it would take some combination of both men to live on.

"Silver." He nods slowly. "Aye, that'll do it."

TWENTY-EIGHT

THEY DROPPED HIM IN TOWN, AT HIS OWN REQUEST, NEXT TO Consort Park, a good few streets south and east of the Doorbell. He didn't want Bainbridge knowing where he stayed, and he certainly didn't want to go back and risk another encounter with Belle D'Or this early in the day. His prick was still sore where she'd yanked it about in her cocaine abandon, he was all out of small talk, and he couldn't face drinking again just yet, at least not at flapper levels of intensity.

What he needed was time to think.

He waited until the Crossley had motored urbanely out of sight, then made his way across the street to the privet hedging and black iron railings that fringed the park. Overhead, chestnuts in autumn leaf made yellow counterpoint to the greenery. He slipped through the corner gate, into the island of manicured quiet beyond. Apart from a couple of wifeys pushing prams and a groundsman meticulously raking up the scatter of early autumn leaves, he had the place to himself. One of the black iron benches along the path beckoned; he sat on it and tried to relax. He had to keep reminding himself that his enemies thought he was dead, that no one was looking for him, that this big, brawling city had swallowed him up the way Belle D'Or would put away one of her gin martinis.

Enjoy it while it lasts, pal.

We have a breathing space, Bainbridge told him on the way out to the car. *Hardy is unaware that you survived, and that can only work in our favor. It must stay that way. In the meantime, plans must be laid if you expect to retrieve the child and her mother. I will do what I can.* He handed Duncan an embossed card. *You may contact me at this number if you wish, but you must give me time. A few days at least. I only arrived in Erlsley this morning, and there is much to do.*

You came all this way to find me?

The archmage looked at him strangely. *This is about much more than you, Mr. . . . Silver.*

And there it was. The urbane hint at disbelief, the mannered sense of some gentleman's game being played. Ambiguity, subterfuge, and masks. Duncan recalled vaguely that some scandal had attached to Bainbridge's time in America—rumors that he'd backed the German effort to keep the Americans out of the war, moved in isolationist, even explicitly pro-German, circles. Others said he'd been working for British Military Intelligence as an agent provocateur the whole time.

And now, here he was in Erlsley, building alliances for some future crisis of power that Duncan wasn't convinced he wanted any part in.

Mebhuranon up from the south, Svalenkari down from the north. Mimi Rush at the heart of it all. You are fucking involved, pal, like it or not.

In which case, the more allies in the fight he had the better, whatever their modus operandi might be. However that might make him feel.

In the war, intelligence operatives had been thin on the ground where Duncan fought. He'd met only one or two, and those passing rapidly through, there and gone too fast to form much of an impression. Which, he supposed, would go well with the job description. But once, he'd had to go out into no-man's-land by night and retrieve a spy—a pale, bony man called Ritter, apparently escaping with extensive battle plans and maps of German intentions for the Somme. The recovery went off smoothly, but later, waiting in a trench at the reserve line for motor transport out, sharing a bottle of rough brandy cadged from the local village inn, Ritter smoked in intense silence for a while, fixed Duncan finally with a bitter blue stare, and said in clipped Teutonic tones: *I envy you, Lieutenant.*

That right? Duncan poured them both more brandy. *Strange. You're the one getting a motor ride out of here.*

Ritter plumed smoke, shook his head. *You fight. That is what I envy. You fight clean, against men who will kill you if you don't kill them first. There is honor in that. I creep around, deceiving men who believe I'm their brother-in-arms, stealing their trust, so I can steal the means to butcher them when their back is turned. And then I run for cover and leave men like you to carry out the slaughter.*

What kind of man does that make me?

We've all done things we're not proud of, Duncan told him. *I wouldn't worry about it.*

But he had to wonder how he'd feel if he knew some British equivalent of Ritter was creeping around in *his* trench, setting Duncan's men up for slaughter and defeat.

And he thought that, faced with a man like that, he'd probably kill him with his bare hands.

EVENING CREPT IN, THE PARK darkened around him, some final molten fragments of sun dripping through the branches of trees at the western end. Over his head, the chestnuts shifted in the breeze in a way that started to seem like stealthy intent. He heard a couple of burrs thud to the lawn behind him. A wren popped up on the back of the bench opposite, fired streams of warbling into the gloom. A spider the size of the one he'd seen in the Forest came scuttling across the grass from the trees opposite, sidled up to him hesitantly, like a family dog looking to be petted, then pulled in its legs and cuddled itself up under the bench by his feet.

Stordalen's blood, ticking in his wrists and throat.

"All hail, Duncan."

Whispered caress to the back of his neck; it brushed every hair on his nape upright in the instant. He jerked around, found Mebhuranon crouched on the lawn behind him, five yards or less from the bench. Her eyes showed the violet center, but there were fangs in her smile. Despite the black iron latticework he was leaned against, she seemed poised to pounce on him. Beneath the partial shrouding of her cloak, she looked made of moonlight, or ivory daubed with some chemical to make it fluoresce.

"You followed me?" Wishing his voice would stay firm.

She sniffed. "You aren't very hard to find."

He supposed she could leap the back of the bench like a hurdle, claw him from his seat, tumble them both to the ground on the other side, take only superficial burns from the iron. Seasoned Huldu knew the combat tricks needed to stay untouched, had practiced and honed their skills for centuries against men with steel in all its forms. With only his hands and the sgian dubh for weapons, Duncan didn't rate his chances.

"If I intended you harm, Duncan, the harm would already have been done."

He grimaced. "I'm that easy to read?"

"Your whole species is that easy to read. And I have been doing it a long time. But you should not fear me, Duncan. There is no need for that."

Abruptly, she uncoiled, switched stance, lay back on her elbows with her legs stretched out before her on the grass, a flapper on a picnic. Her cloak wrapped her with the change of posture, rode up her thighs. She put her head coquettishly on one side, let her mass of silver and raven hair cascade off her shoulder.

It would have been a lot more appealing, he thought, if the contortions she'd just gone through hadn't been so sinuously unhuman, if they hadn't reminded him so much of the vatnalfr he'd trapped with Garner at the mere's edge in Macclesfield forest, the way it thrashed to get back into the water when he set it loose.

"I don't fear you," he lied evenly. "I just want you out of my way."

"Am I in your way?"

She parted her thighs slightly, so he glimpsed the dark-haired cleft of her sex in the scant shadow of the cloak. He felt arousal slam through him like a train. His prick strained in his underwear; the muscles in the pit of his stomach clenched. Even with Niamh, it took him a little while to get as ready as this, but he knew as certainly as he'd ever known anything in his life that the Fae queen need only curl her fingers loosely around him once and he'd come like a shaken magnum of champagne as the cork popped out.

Or not, if she chose otherwise.

He breathed with it, constructed a smile. "I'm proof against this, Meb. I have witchery, spells and wards, runes laid down."

"Yes. I feel your witch. She's . . . not much of a barrier to me."

He swallowed hard. "What do you want? You say you could have harmed me, if you wanted, but you haven't. You say you could have . . . this, if you wanted it, but you're not taking it. What *do* you want?"

"Do I have to *want* something?" Her emphasis mocked his. Her violet mock pupils vibrated. Another blink-of-eye contortion and abruptly she sat cross-legged on the grass in the gloom. The arousal puddled out of him as fast, left him with a small, throbbing ache in belly and groin. She smiled, showed him her fangs again. "We are not like you, Duncan. You should know that by now. We are willful things—capricious, itching, drawn on whim, easily bored. Perhaps I just wanted to play."

"You came a long way from the Forest for a whim."

Mebhuranon looked around her, disdainful. "Your cities hold no terrors for me. If you knew the times I have gone amid the heave of your kind in Portsmouth, Plymouth, Exeter . . ." On her tongue, in Skogurtal, the names had a curious ring, suddenly exotic. "You deaden your own senses with smolder and concrete and iron; you live and climb over each other like ants, until closing yourselves off to it all becomes your only path for survival. You are dead inside, all of you. I might walk a dozen leagues in your streets and across your roofs, and not one in a hundred would feel me, except to shiver as I pass."

"Oh, I see." Rising conviction that something was off, that he had her on the back foot. "You came all this way not to kill me, not to fuck me, but to give me a speech. Is there much more of it?"

The black slammed in across her eyes; she erupted to her feet. He readied himself, thought that in the time it would take her to pounce, he might just clear the sgian dubh from its sheath . . .

"I came," she gritted, "to warn you."

"You're a little late for that." Forcing himself to breathe. He tapped the score mark across his skull. "Had an interesting time getting out of the Forest with Mimi Rush last week."

"I had no hand in that. I told you at the time it could happen."

"Aye, and you had Hardy waiting at the other end anyway, just in case we made it through."

It was a test, and she passed it with flying colors. Her stance broke, she twitched as if from an insect at her ear.

"I don't know *Hardy*," she said irritably. "But the trees told me that your own kind turned on you. Tell me, how does that feel?"

"I spent four years slaughtering my own kind. It doesn't feel new."

She smiled. "They were not your tribe, though. I know of your Great War; every Huldu across the Continent does. We heard your screams. I have thralls who fled to the Forest rather than serve and die in the fighting."

"Smart men." Change the subject. "But if you didn't call down the Huldu on me that night—if you gave orders against it, upheld Stordalen's word—then who broke the bond? Who thinks so little of the Final Isles? Because that wasn't a few disaffected youngsters pissing on the old ways. That was a planned assault. Who called it, if not you?"

Something happened to the Fae queen's mouth—as if she held something back behind her fangs, unsure whether to chew it to death or spit it out.

"Svalenkari," she said finally.

The name, like an autumn leaf wafted from the bonfire, edged in worms of fire. The stillness in the darkening park held the syllables like perfume, and he breathed it in.

"Ahh."

"You must know how much hate he holds for you."

"Aye, I'll have embarrassed him, I imagine. Escaping the way I did."

"Embarrassed?" For the first time ever, he saw Mebhuranon at a loss. A kind of flicker went through the inky black of her eyes, brought the violet pupil back, inked it out, brought it back again. She coughed—a soft sound like another chestnut burr falling. "You think Svalenkari's *embarrassed*? Don't you *know* what you did?"

"Evidently not. Do you want to tell me?"

"You killed his grandson, Duncan."

Duncan blinked. "Stordalen? That prick was—"

"Not that preening waste, you fool! You killed *Isnorvi*! Isnorvi, son of Tragvinada, daughter of Svalenkari, future heir to the northwestern range, and you butchered him when he had barely one foot out of the cradle!"

The memory flashed forth, jagged, bloody, blue lit with the dawn, and somehow sharper than anything he recalled from the trenches—

Slashing hard, overarm, full force, back and forth, and every strike rips fresh lines of fire, fresh shrieks from the Huldu boy. Isnorvi staggers backward, both hands up now, warding, Duncan carves lines of fire across them, too. Isnorvi stumbles, goes over, falls on his side between the cairns. He tries dizzily to ward off his attacker one more time, but Duncan stomps down the arm, is on him, on top of him, punching down everywhere with the nail . . .

He shivered a little.

"Svalenkari never . . . treated him . . . like . . ." A gesture; even he felt how weak it was. "I didn't know."

The Fae queen shrugged. "Why would you? We are not like you, Duncan. How many times must you be told? We do not raise our young the same. We do not love the same. You were not with us long enough to see the nurseries, to understand. But Svalenkari will be avenged, and he is laying his plans. That is what I came to tell you."

"He's taken his sweet fucking time so far."

"And why would he not? He is immortal. Time was on his side.

His vengeance was to be fitting, prolonged, to fall on your children when you had them, for you to see and feel before it fell finally on you in turn."

"You said *was*? Time *was* on his side?"

"Until you failed the path, yes. Instead of siring heirs, you went to war. You never returned to the northern range. The arc of his vengeance withered unclaimed." Another regal shrug. "And then what you call the Unbinding came instead, overthrew everything that had been. A new era dawned, we were overwhelmed with new power, new hopes, past dreams resurrected. I would say that you were almost forgotten in the tumult—until word came from the midranges. A new figure, a woodsman consumed with rage, at ease with magic and the Forest, bringing out lost children from under our noses, leaving red ruin in his wake. It did not take long to ascertain who this was."

Duncan sneered. "And still he did not come."

"The local clan masters would not permit it. It was their territory you trampled upon, their honor you sullied. It was theirs to avenge. When none proved equal, they sent to the Final Isles for a neutral champion, and Stordalen came with his traps and plans. Svalenkari was permitted as an observer only. Now, with Stordalen slain and no satisfaction, he has faced down the clan masters, sent his own sworn clan fellows after you, taken charge of the midrange for himself."

"That must make you look bad."

"I have other concerns that press me more."

"Aye. Stealing defenseless weans out of their cradles, like every other Fae fuck that ever lived."

"Miriam is not just another human child."

"So I've heard. Ancient blood descendant of someone you know, is she?"

Something shifted in the violet eyes. "You do not understand."

"She's four fucking years old, Meb. She doesn't care about your tedious ancient blood grudges. And nor do I. You're going to live a thousand years; you'd better learn to let go of things."

"I need not go back so far. Four years past, I sat at a bonfire in the south with mortal men held high among your kind. Accords were made. A token was agreed, a symbol I might carry back to the Bright Folk as proof of the good faith of mortal men in this new age, and my standing in our relations with them. This was promised to us. *She* was promised to us."

"Not by me."

The Fae queen grinned. "And with what authority do you think you speak?"

He reached to his back, found the sgian dubh. Drew it, held it toward her, point sideways, wrist upward, unthreatening. Ceremonial. The blade glinted like a lewd wink. "The iron will speak for me. Ask your slaughtered kin at Maltby what authority it holds."

He'd known Huldu to flinch physically at the sight of an iron blade. Mebhuranon just wrinkled her nose in disdain, as if he'd flashed at her with some withered, wrinkled excuse for a member.

"I just told you—they were of Svalenkari's clan, not mine."

"You're not getting her back, Meb."

"And yet you do not have her either."

Long pause. They stared at each other. Feeling slightly foolish, Duncan lowered the sgian dubh. Mebhuranon opened one taloned hand like a blade, looked at it askance, as if unsure what it might do.

"Mimi's changeling found me," she said. "It said you named me as its sire. Sent it to me."

"Aye."

"To what purpose?"

"What purpose do you think? She was falling apart, dissolving. I thought you could do something for her."

"I did. I sent it back to the Gray."

He thought about the sad, sagging version of a child that had dragged him back out of the meadow where Hardy left him for dead.

The way it clung to Mimi Rush's rag doll when he handed it over.

"You really are a cunt," he said.

Abruptly, faster than he could react, she'd leapt the bench, landed inches from him, at his back. One hand fastened him at the wrist, turned the sgian dubh blade effortlessly away. Icy numbness raced through his flesh, outward from her grip. At his nape, by contrast, hot fingers of her breath, as she whispered to him. "And if Mimi's changeling was in rot without purpose, in hopeless dissolution, who do we find to blame for that, Duncan? Who robbed it of its reason to live?"

The sgian dubh slipped from his numbed fingers, fell away. He tried to rise, to break from her hold. Her other hand came to press hard against the side of his head. She dragged him back from the bench, onto the gravel path. More spreading chill from this new grip, enough to chatter his teeth, ache the socket of his closest eye. He felt himself robbed of will, ready to follow his blade to the ground, if she let him go. "*Who,* Duncan?"

He barely managed through gritted teeth, "Fuck . . . you."

She dumped him hard to the gravel, let go his numbed arm, slammed her freed hand against his chest instead, as if pushing open a heavy door. He felt his heart flop in his ribs like a fish in the net. Felt fingers of ice tighten around it. She hung over him with lips skinned back from her fangs.

"You," she hissed, "have mistaken your place in things."

And then she let go.

Right hand spasmed open and trembling, arm numbed to the shoulder, head chilled through with worse cold than he'd felt since winter on the Somme, an icy lump in his chest, a dull droning hum in his ears . . .

He twisted on the gravel path like a stomped bug. Mebhuranon stood, towered over him, glitter-eyed. He'd forgotten how tall she was. The spider came sidling out from under the bench, snuffled along his thigh and body, put soft forelegs and mouth palps on his chest. Not clear if it intended him harm, or, like the family dog it had put him in mind of earlier, was just worried about him because he'd fallen over.

"A wolf may be swift and strong and feared throughout the Forest, Duncan." The Fae queen's words, like dull axes falling, far off in the droning that drowned his ears. "But when he howls at the moon, the moon is not moved. Do not mistake your relationship with me again."

The spider tapped him on the chest a couple of times with one limb, as if for emphasis, or maybe just testing for hollowness, a good place to bite.

Then it spun away from him with spidery aplomb and left. From his worm's-eye view, he watched it scuttle away across the park, into the thickening gloom.

"And now, mortal, we are done." More dull axes falling, a little clearer through the now-fading drone. "I came to warn you. And so you are warned. Svalenkari wills vengeance, and he will not be stopped. With Stordalen dead and the hand of the Final Isles seen to fail, the midrange clans will no longer stand in his way. With this new age, the old order trembles, and it may yet fall."

Duncan rolled over and dragged himself back toward the bench. Maybe he could crawl under its iron rails for protection. He tried to get his arm, his heart, his chattering teeth back under control. He felt her watching, like the spike of tiny icicles all across his shoulders and nape.

"W-w-why?" he stuttered.

"Why what?"

He changed his mind about direction. Fuck this, he would not crawl and hide. Had he not done enough of that in fucking French and Flemish mud? He hauled himself instead, by crippled fractions, back up onto the bench where he'd been sitting. The stiff cold in his arm might, he thought, be thawing, one tiny, dripping fraction at a time. He rolled himself awkwardly to face the Fae queen.

"The w-warning," he shivered. "W-why t-tell me at all?"

Once again, the regal shrug. With the mess she'd made of his senses, he couldn't be sure, but he thought there was an impatience there now, and not just with him.

"The trees seem to like you," she said finally. "That has to count for something."

TWENTY-NINE

HE MADE IT BACK TO THE DOORBELL CLUB BY FITS AND STARTS. Spikes of icy pain in wrist and skull and ribs dragged him repeatedly to a halt. Forced him to lean muzzily on whatever railing or wall was at hand until the spasm passed. He tried not to let it show too much, moved on again as soon as he could. It wouldn't be a good moment to get pinched for vagrancy or drunk and disorderly and run into the cells. But whatever Mebhuranon had done to him, it was taking its own sweet time to ease. When he shoved at the buzzer by the club door, it was with a right hand still closed up involuntarily into a fist.

Arthur cracked the door, saw him and let him in.

"'lo, Campbell." Under the stiff black fakery of the wig, shiny scar tissue features creased in something like concern. "You all right?"

"Been better. Crammond show up at all?"

Arthur shook his head.

"Belle?"

"In her office. You want to see her?"

"Christ, no."

The gash mouth did its best to grin. "Probably just as well. She's in a foul mood. Time of the month, y'know."

Duncan blinked. "Woman's troubles?"

"Nah. Payroll."

He ushered Duncan down the corridor to the red-flock room, empty as yet of clientele. The barman from yesterday was there, stoking a fire in the grate. They took seats at the bar and waited until he got back to his post.

"What'll it be, gentlemen?"

Duncan eyed the bottles on the shelf behind. The Doorbell obviously catered to an exclusive crowd, but south of the border that meant blended Scotch in place of any single malt a Scottish house might offer.

"Chivas Regal," he decided. He needed something to drive out the Fae queen's shivers, and it might as well be the good stuff. "Put it on my tab."

The barman raised an eyebrow. "You've a tab? That's news to me."

"Put it on mine," said Arthur. "I'll have the same."

"Look, you don't have to—"

The fright mask turned to face him. "Yeah, I do. Any man Billy Crammond vouches for can drink on my tick all night long."

He nodded at the barman. Duncan watched the glasses laid out, the Chivas poured. He took his, lifted it in Arthur's direction, knocked it back. The polite, mellow taste smoked down his throat, made him shudder slightly, sat warm in his stomach like a banked fire. The Port Ellen would have hit harder, smoked and smoldered more, but it seemed churlish to complain. Mebhuranon's face still loomed in his head, but blurred behind the whisky the way it had blurred and wavered across the fire on the platform at Miller's Frith. Later, he'd pick apart the encounter, but right now all he wanted to do was blunt the memory.

Arthur tipped his own glass back. Signaled for refills.

"Pozières," he said. "In case you were wondering."

Duncan said nothing.

"Command was planning to wipe out this Fritz garrison at Thiepval. We thought we had a pretty good chance. Big push forward, took a lot of ground, dug in. Fritz tried to chase us out of the trenches we'd taken." Arthur staring into nothing, glass forgotten in his hand. "And they had flamethrowers. I mean, we held them off, but . . . yeah."

He gestured at his own face.

Duncan nudged the new drink toward him on the bar. "And Thiepval? The garrison?"

The harsh, gash-mouth grin again. "Nah. Ten days, and they pulled the whole division back. Lost nearly three thousand men. Course, I missed most of that. I was too busy back behind lines at a CCS, screaming with my face scorched off. Or doped out of it on morphine." He seemed to notice his empty glass for the first time, swapped it out for the refill. "Got told about it later, though."

It was a familiar enough story. Duncan sipped at his own refill, told a matching tale. Arthur caught a reference to the Americans, asked about them. Duncan yarned about Remingtons and Winchesters and slamfiring enemy trenches clean. Out of habit, he kept it vague.

"Yeah, heard about that." Arthur's enthusiasm betraying an age younger than Duncan's previous estimates. "Sweet! Germans wanted 'em banned or something?"

Duncan nodded. "Threatened to summarily execute any soldier taken prisoner with one. Course, then Pershing said they'd do the same to Germans with sawtoothed bayonets or—"

He stopped.

"Flamethrowers?" Arthur stared into his glass. "Could have gotten behind that myself."

Duncan drank for cover. Cleared his throat.

"Aye, well, anyway, that was the end of it. Storm in a fucking teacup, and the war was over a few months later anyway. I mean, don't get me wrong, it was a damn good weapon. You got to hand it to the Yanks, they know killing better than most. Jump down into that trench, slamfire three shells one way, swing and pump three more the other. You don't get much spread at close range, but it's the chaos it causes. And you can't miss, of course."

He'd seen the Remington in action a few times before he got the chance to try it for himself. Midway through an assault at Hamel, and the American shotgunner he's advancing beside gets cut down by friendly fire shrapnel ranged too short. He drags the man into a crater, sees he's missing the back of his head, and lets go. He lifts the trench gun and shell pouch, muttering obscenity and prayer, to what he's not sure, checks the load as he's been shown. As soon as the barrage is called off and it's safe to move, he charges out of the foxhole with the remnants of the American force, filled now with some trembling new rage at the senselessness of the other man's death.

Vague recollection that he was screaming—gibberish, unstrung Skogurtal syllables—as he loomed up over the German trench, fired down into it with the Remington . . .

"Awright there, lads?" Crammond's graveled tones behind them. "See youse started wi'oot me."

Duncan turned with relief. He opened his mouth to ask the question, didn't need to.

"Aye." Grim set to the big Glaswegian's pirate face, but his one eye gleamed. "We found yir Irish lassie."

THE DOORBELL CLUB HAD AN extensive wine cellar, only the front half of which served to store any actual wine. The back half, behind a cheap carpentry and plaster wall, was given over to gaudily appointed alcoves kitted out to look like torture dungeons, complete with baskets full of tasseled, embroidered whips, hanging chains, and fur-lined manacles. In the dim light of red-painted bulbs in the largest alcove, Duncan and Arthur moved a couple of bijou whipping posts out of the way, carried in a table with some odd holes cut in it, then spread and weighted an ordnance survey map of south Erlsley across its surface. Crammond brought in a hurricane lamp with the wick turned full up, hung it from an overhead bracket currently being used to dangle handcuffs and tasteful lengths of slim silver chain.

"Ingram Street." He prodded the map with a prosthetic finger. "Looks like they took yir lassie there first, fir processin', along with yir lad Gordon an' they taxi drivers. Let the drivers go soon efter, Gordon a wee while efter that. But oor guy at the station says Niamh wiz still in the cells fir the night when he left. Described yir lassie tae a tee. When he came back oan shift the next day, she wiz gone. Word is, a pair o' Branch detectives came an' took her at dawn, bundled her in a car, nae questions asked."

"Does he know where?"

"He didnae ask. Thought nothin' of it at the time. Just a bitty gossip, Special Branch showin' up like that, mystery woman o' the night, so forth." Crammond saw Duncan's impatience, held up his human hand to forestall it. "Haud yir fire, wait fir it. Ah've asked aboot the toon a bit, anythin' new or strange tae report, and there's this—parcel o' busies frae five different stations across Erlsley been reassigned tae Maunston fir quoate unquoate special duties. Hard cases, all o' them, nae the credit-tae-the uniform type. Apparently, the word wiz *altar boys need no' apply.*"

"Maunston." Duncan found it on the map, a meager once-hamlet, now cemented into the southern outskirts of Erlsley by decades of frenetic Victorian housebuilding and industrial growth. "That's right out on the edge of town."

"Aye, it is. Used tae be a big pottery works oot that way, they tell me. Lot o' they workers lived close, in Maunston. Then the Forest came, ate the pottery, so nae mer jobs, an' every cunt runnin' scairt. These days, the place is deader than yir granny's minge on a Monday night. Houses all boarded up, nae inhabitants but a few squatters. They closed doon the polis station three years ago. Asked one o' my guys, he says he thought it goat sold tae the army, but he couldnae be certain."

Something shifted and settled in Duncan's chest, something whispered and chuckled through the hollow spaces in his throat and belly and skull. Stordalen's blood, the Fae queen's touch, who could tell? Maybe it was just the Chivas.

"Has tae be it, aye?" Crammond was watching his face intently.

"Has to be," Duncan agreed, as if someone else was using his throat. And something bloomed indigo to crimson behind his eyes, like ink spilled across blotting paper. Faintly, he heard yells, gunfire, a high scream . . .

He shook himself, cleared his throat. "What have we got for wheels?"

"When ye wantin' tae dae this?"

"Soon as we can. They've had her the best part of a week already. We can't risk they move her again. Tomorrow night, latest."

Crammond glanced at Arthur. "Cobb's brother still goat that auld Vauxhall D-Type parked up over at Staid Street?"

Arthur nodded.

"Then we have wheels." Turning back to Duncan. "Ye'll love this—converted model fir ambulance service. Tough as auld boots."

"Aye, I remember." He'd been ferried wounded in a Vauxhall ambulance once, watched them in action on numerous other occasions. He'd seen them plow through mud, snow, driving rain, over rutted, shell-torn roads and ravaged fields, the worst conditions the western front could throw at them, and still, more often than not, come rattling out the other side intact. A thought struck him. "Not still painted as an ambulance, is it?"

Arthur shook his head. "Nice racing green."

"Right." He looked at Crammond. "We'll need a driver, someone to stay on the clutch round the corner until I come out."

"Ah'll pull wee Mikey Collier fir that. Think he'd be up fir it, Arthur?"

Apparently, this was funny. Arthur chuckled.

"Ye dinnae ken him, Duncan," said Crammond. "But take it fra me—boy's sound as a pound. Staff driver in the war, handles a car like he came out o' his maw wi' a fuckin' steerin' wheel in his hands."

"I'll take your word for it. Oh, aye—my Webley's still in my rooms on Skoldergate. Can you get me another one?"

"In this toon? Is the pope a fuckin' Catholic?"

"Last time I checked. All right, tell you what—if it's that easy, get me two Webleys. I don't want to piss about reloading, if things kick off. Pouch of spare ammo, too, just in case."

Arthur made an approving noise. Crammond nodded. "Nae bother."

"Dumdum load, if you've got 'em. Cross-hatched and scooped." He saw the other man wince. "None of your guys got this Maunston assignment, did they?"

Crammond shook his head.

"Good. Then we don't have to worry."

"We'll need balaclavas," said Arthur. Then, as the other two men looked at him. "What? Not like I got a forgettable face, is it?"

"Yir nae goin'," said Crammond.

Arthur bristled. "I fucking am."

"This isn't your fight," said Duncan quietly. "Appreciate the offer, but it isn't."

"That's what you think! This bloody well is my fight! You think I spent four years in the trenches, got my fucking face scorched off, all so I could come back to a land that bloody Lloyd George tells me is fit for heroes, and I have to watch British coppers act like the Bolshie secret police, just disappearing anyone they don't like off the bloody streets?"

"Anyone Irish they dinnae like." Crammond nitpicked.

"My maternal great-aunt was Irish. So—"

"Arthur!" Duncan waited until he got the burned man's full attention. Lowered his voice again. "We are going to kill men in this, Arthur. Policemen. Englishmen. Maybe more than just one or two."

"Yeah, well." Defiantly. "I killed plenty of German lads over there who deserved it a lot less than this scum. They were just following orders."

"Aye, well, in all probability so are the men holding Niamh." Duncan looked into the ruined face, the bright, desperate eyes—was shrewd enough to recognize the mirror it made. He sighed. "Look, you're welcome to ride along. Could probably use the manpower, if I'm honest. But I want you to know what you're getting into first."

Arthur nodded.

"Kind of you," he said dryly. "It's more than that fuck Kitchener ever did."

THIRTY

MAUNSTON SAT SIX AND A HALF MILES ALMOST PERFECTLY DUE south of Erlsley city center. The main London road led there, neatly bisecting what had once been Maunston's market square. On the almost-empty nighttime streets—in common with most cities since the Unbinding, Erlsley put itself to bed early—it would, Mikey Collier swore, have taken mere minutes to get across town and arrive.

Aye, well we're nae daein' that, was Crammond's response.

Instead, they stuck to darker secondary thoroughfares, passing shuttered frontages and darkened alley mouths at a quiet putter, winding painstakingly through sleeping residential neighborhoods, threading odd turns and diversions into a patchwork approach that brought their chances of being seen down near absolute zero. Duncan sat up front with Collier, who handled the big Vauxhall D-Type with the casual assurance of a man at a much-loved hobby, rarely needing to brake for corners, meshing gears with scarcely a sound, steering as if he were under no more constraint than the pilot of a motorboat out on Lake Windermere.

"Yeah, staff driver in France for a while," he told Duncan cheerily as they drove. "D-Types there, too, but with the old tourer body. Those roads, man! And always with some stick-up-the-arse colonel on your shoulder, telling you to *hurry up, dammit*! *Lives are at stake!* I mean, this? Compared to that shambles, this is a fucking doddle!"

Crammond had called him a boy and, fair enough, Duncan estimated Collier was still not yet out of his twenties. But there was a familiar quietness to him around the eyes that conveyed a greater sense of age—you saw it a lot in the men who'd come back—and his shock of thick black hair was shot through with thin streaks of gray.

For all that, he was quick with a grin and a handshake, and seemed to enjoy talking about his experiences in the war, no matter how grim.

". . . parked up by this tree in some village, Wulverjem, Wulverghem—they had a munitions dump there, but Fritz hit it and the whole place blew. So my officers were out to inspect the damage, wandering about making fucking *hem-hem* noises like there was anything they could do, and I'm sat there in the driving seat, just staring holes in the horizon, like. Suddenly, I get this hand, it comes down on my shoulder, pretty hard, and I'm thinking *blimey, that's a bit bloody familiar, innit*, so I look round—and *it's just a fucking hand*! That's all it is. Severed halfway up the forearm, all torn up and bloodied, you could see the bone everywhere. But it still had the cuff of a uniform on it, you believe that?"

Duncan nodded, unsurprised. "From the tree, right?"

"That's right! I look up at the branches and fuck me, there's bits of men and uniform draped up there like Christmas decorations. When the dump blew, it must have torn a dozen men apart and flung them up there. Hand just chose its moment, like, dropped on me. Tell you, if there's a God, he's got a sick fucking sense of humor. Anyroad, you can bet I slammed it in reverse and got out from under that tree pretty fucking sharpish. Didn't want my officers coming back, getting in the backseat and sitting down on some poor bastard's spleen! Give 'em something to really *hem-hem* about."

He barked a laugh, eased the big Vauxhall left into a downward slope and a curving avenue of well-appointed Victorian semis. Short driveways and gardens behind neatly kept hedges, upper bay windows curtained against the night. An ornate street sign announced Wardle Drive. Duncan took the map from the dashboard, applied torchlight to it.

"Bottom of this one, and then right," said Collier inconsequentially. He'd glanced at the map before they started, seemed to have committed the route to memory. "'bout a mile after that. I'll bring you by the pub. Crammond says it's all boarded up these days, and from the map, it looks like they've got a yard out back. See if we can't park in there. Puts you three corners and a couple of hundred yards from the rozzer shop. That close enough?"

Duncan nodded. He put the torch away, herded his skittering thoughts into some kind of order. Whatever was in his blood burbled cheerily to itself. The Vauxhall rolled out into the crossroads at the bottom of Wardle Drive, bent right as promised. A couple of minutes later they rattled into the drab, deserted thoroughfares of Maunston. *Deader than yir granny's minge on a Monday night,* Crammond had put it with his customary elegance. Watching the boarded-up, paint-peeling frontages glide past, it was hard to fault the Glaswegian's assessment. A couple more turns through the ghostly streets and they pulled up alongside a rambling corner pub whose weather-faded sign announced The Victoria Arms in barely legible scrolled lettering above a picture too faded and peeled to make out. Past the run of boarded-up windows, a tall wooden double gate closed off what was presumably the yard.

"Right, let's get those open," said Collier.

He slid off the driver's bench and got down, left the engine running. Banged on the Vauxhall's side panel as he walked back. Duncan followed suit, joined him at the rear. They dropped the tailgate. Arthur shoved up the canvas drop sheet and jumped down, closely followed, somewhat less elegantly, by Crammond.

"Ma fuckin' erse is sore," the big Glaswegian grumbled, rubbing the affected area to emphasize the point.

"Could be worse," said Collier brightly, climbing past him and up into the rear space. "You could be gut shot and riding eight miles of rutted road from a clearing station."

He reemerged with a pair of long-handled bolt cutters in his hand.

"All right, gents—let's get off the street, shall we?"

THERE WAS A RUSTED CHAIN wrapped around the long iron gate handles, secured through multiple links with a padlock that didn't look like it had been opened for years. Arthur held the chain taut and Collier made short work of it with the cutters. They dragged back the gates—Duncan wincing at the squeal and graunch it made—to reveal a concreted yard beyond. Clumps of weeds grew high through cracks in the concrete, ghostly in the gloom, but apart from that, the space was empty. Collier grunted, apparently in satisfaction, ran back and jumped up into the cab of the D-Type. He drove forward and slightly out into the center of the street, then reversed neatly back into the yard.

From the rear of the ambulance, they took their weapons—the twinned Webleys for Duncan, an American Colt 1911 semiautomatic for Crammond, and for Arthur a gleaming Lee-Enfield cavalry carbine that he clearly cherished as if it were a loved one. Arthur and the Glaswegian both donned the closed-face balaclavas they'd brought with them, leaving only their eyes visible in a strip the size of a post box slot. But when Crammond offered a third knitted helmet to Duncan, he shook his head.

"This is a dead man's face they're going to see," he said. "Let them get a good look."

Crammond rolled his eyes. "Fuckin' drama queen."

"Same goes for names," Duncan said doggedly. "Go right ahead and name me once we're in there. I *want* them to know it's me."

"Good fir you. Jist see ye dinnae throw ma name around in thir, but."

Duncan nodded, brooding for a minute. He looked at the weapons they carried. "All right, so you'll be Colt. Arthur, you're Carbine."

"Delightful." Arthur, hefting the long gun. "Carbine it is."

"All tooled up, then?" Collier had jumped down from the driver's bench again, come breezily back round to the rear. He took the balaclava Duncan had turned down. "I'll hang on to this if he don't want it, Billy. Just in case."

Crammond shrugged and handed the cap over. Collier stuffed it into a pocket.

"I'll keep the motor running," he said. "But don't be too long. Always possible someone hears the noise and comes for a look-see, even out here. Don't want to break any heads unnecessarily."

They slipped out of the yard like cast shadows from a searchlight sweep, skulked along the pub wall in single file, and rounded the corner. The sound of the D-Type's engine dropped off a chunk almost immediately with the turn, and by the time they'd made fifty yards and the next street corner, you had to strain to hear anything of it at all.

There was a solitary light on behind the barred glass windows of the station, but the blue Police lamp was dead on its bracket over the door, which was closed. Duncan gestured the others back, stepped up to the heavy wood paneling, and thumped on it with the butt of his drawn Webley. After the second attempt, he heard movement within, the slow steps of someone coming grudgingly to answer. Clank of iron as the barred inner gate was opened. He thumped again, vigorously. Added his voice, urgent but officer urbane.

"C'mon, man! Open up! Orders!"

" 'Oo the fuck are you?" someone wanted to know through a cavernous yawn.

"Orders from Hardy! We're to move the Irish bitch! Open up, will you?"

Keys rattled, the lock grated and turned. The door hinged slowly outward.

"Thought Hardy wanted his bloody name kept out of this. Don't know why—"

Duncan whipped him hard in the face with the Webley butt. Strangled yelp. Vague, grabbed glimpse of a police uniform tunic, unbuttoned down to the waist, gray vest beneath stretched across a burly chest. The man reeled backward, clutching at a nose spurting blood. Big guy—a handful, if he got himself together. Duncan followed him in, stomped him hard in the knee, so he went down grunting against the iron bars of the inner gate. Arthur and Crammond boiled in after him, through the gate and into the corridor beyond. Duncan pointed the Webley at the man's face.

"Look at me!" Snapping the words out—seize the advantage, seize command, and keep it. "Get that fucking hand off your face and look at me if you want to live!"

Groggily, the man lowered his hand. Blood ran out of his nose as if from a poorly closed tap, clogged in a bushy mustache below, and trickled down a chin bristly with a week's beard. Middle-aged copper, no rank, and wearing it badly. Broken-veined cheeks. Fearful eyes. Duncan thumbed back the hammer on the Webley and the man flinched.

"How many of you?"

"Five! Five!" The man lifted trembling hands, palms outward. Voice dried up, shaking, eyes taking in the balaclavas, the weapons. "In—in the cots, downstairs. Two in a room. Don't shoot me! I—I got nothing against the Micks. It's just orders."

"Get up!" Grabbing the man's flapping tunic at the collar as he tried. "Get the fuck up! You're going to show me where."

"All right, all right, I'm not—"

"Shut the fuck up! You don't talk unless I tell you to!" As the man floundered to his feet, Duncan brandished the revolver in his bloodied face. Kept his voice low and venomous. "This is going to be in the back of your neck all the way. Dumdum load—you know what that means. Anything goes wrong, I paint your face and brains all over the wall. Got it?"

The man swallowed hard, nodded. Duncan redoubled his grip on his tunic collar, got up close, pushed the barrel of the Webley into his nape, steered him past the gate like a shield. Up ahead, caged bulbs gleamed off cream-colored tiling on walls that had seen better days. Arthur held the corridor with his carbine at hip height. Closed doors on both sides, all bar one on the left where light spilled out on the passageway floor. Crammond slipped past Arthur, ducked into the room, came right back out.

"All clear in there," he murmured. "Desk, cot. Looks like we woke big man here up."

"Then let's go downstairs." Duncan shoved his captive ahead to where the stairs wound down behind another iron bar gate. "We going to need keys for this?"

The man shook his head.

"Right. Carbine, with me. Get the gate for us. Colt, you check these other doors, just in case our friend here isn't as Boy Scout truthful as he looks."

Crammond chuckled grimly, let them past. Duncan heard him start trying door handles along the corridor. Arthur eased the iron gate back—it groaned and grated with disuse, a lot more than Duncan would have liked—and Duncan steered his captive down the stairs beyond, one careful step at a time. He felt Arthur swing in behind him.

Almost at the bottom, almost—

"That you, Bennett?" Hoarse attempt at a whisper from the corridor below. "What you fuckin' creepin' around for, it's not even—"

Duncan shoved Bennett hard and the two of them cannoned down the remaining three stairs into the corridor, hit the wall opposite. Gleam of more caged bulbs off tiles. In the light they threw, he saw another man, in a nightshirt, bleary eyed, grizzled hair stuck up in clumps, three feet away. He pointed the Webley past Bennett's shoulder, hissed, "Not a fucking w—"

And it all came apart.

Bennett shoved sideways at his arm, grabbed for the revolver. The copper in the nightshirt tried to yell—it came out a strangled yelp instead. He charged forward. Nothing for it. Duncan pulled the trigger. Sharp crack as the Webley went off and the man spun with the impact, went down, nightshirt drenched in sudden blood at the shoulder. Bennett bellowed and shoved again, smashed Duncan into the wall. Duncan shoved back, got the Webley between them and fired again. He felt the shot jolt the other man off him. Bennett screamed, staggered about clutching himself and spouting blood from somewhere in his midsection. Finally, he fell down. Someone darted into the corridor from an open door farther up, had a pistol of some sort, leveled it at Duncan—

Signature whip-crack of rifle fire, faster than Duncan could get his own weapon up. The new arrival jerked and folded over himself, the pistol clattered on the cement floor. Arthur—in the corridor at the foot of the stairs, Lee-Enfield up at his eye. The man he'd shot made a plaintive sound like a smacked child, slid forward a little, then stopped. Arthur had already worked the bolt on the carbine, nodded tightly at Duncan. Clatter of boots on the stair—Crammond crashed into the corridor, Colt raised. Duncan flapped an arm at him.

"Whoa there! We're good, we're good! Ease up!"

Bennett was on the floor, still screaming. Duncan stepped back, pointed the Webley, and shut him up. Sudden splotch of blood and brain tissue across the cement by his head, and abruptly all was quiet along the corridor.

"We're good," Duncan repeated.

Crammond snorted, gestured at the mess. "Ye call this *good*?"

The man Duncan had snapped a shot at past Bennett looked to have either passed out or died from blood loss. His nightshirt was soaked through with rich crimson on the right side, gleaming slick in the low light from the corridor lamps, creeping from his body across the floor like slow floodwaters. Duncan's shot had gone in well below the right shoulder; there was no telling the damage the dumdum round had done in the chest cavity. Quite possibly it tore through the aorta, or other arteries, or both. Duncan fought off a wartime reflex to bend and attend to the man, made the count instead. Three men down, only two more remaining if Bennett was to be believed. And three shots left in the Webley. He patted the second pistol in his belt, backed up beside Arthur and Crammond, called out loud along the corridor.

"Listen to me! We outnumber you, we have you pinned down. But we're here for the prisoner, not you. Drop your weapons, get out here with your hands up; you don't have to die!"

Someone snapped a shot at him from an open door. Splintered tile jumped out of the wall over his head. Arthur put a carbine round into the doorframe the shot had come from, chased the shooter back into cover.

"Stop that!" Duncan yelled furiously. "Just stop it! Surrender, and we will not kill you! You have my word!"

In the silence that followed, suddenly he heard Niamh calling his name. Muffled behind a closed cell door down the corridor, voice cracked, desperate.

"Duncan, I'm here. *Duncan*—" She choked on his name, started coughing.

Fresh fury, storming in his blood like the churn of a dreadnought's screws.

"*I'm not fucking joking,*" he bawled. *"Count of five! Throw out your arms or we will butcher every last one of you! This is your last fucking chance!"*

Whatever was in his blood came through in his voice. He barely made it to the count of two before the pistols came clattering out onto the corridor floor.

"DUNCAN! DUNCAN, GET ME OUT of here!"

Easier said than done. The cells were all locked up, apart from the two the Maunston altar boys had bunked in. Arthur held his carbine trained on the two men who'd surrendered, made them sit on their hands cross-legged against the corridor wall, while Crammond and Duncan turned over their sleeping quarters at speed, found a set of keys. Duncan cracked the door on Niamh's cell and she fell out into his arms. He gathered her to him. *I thought you were dead,* she kept saying into his neck, *Duncan, I thought you were dead.*

She smelled of cheap carbolic soap, her skirt and blouse were grubby with her time in the cell, her hair was down, matted, tangled. She was hot and feverish to the touch. Bare, dirty feet under her skirts, and her face . . .

Duncan felt something like a vise wrap cold around his head.

They'd stripped her of any trace of makeup, left her pale and gaunt as if from some sudden famine. Her left eye was blacked, swollen and crusted. Cuts and scrapes across her cheek and forehead; it looked like damage from a ring or knuckle-dusters. Her lips were bruised in one corner of her mouth, split in two separate places. Duncan breathed deep to get a handle on his rage.

"Who the *fuck* did this?" he gritted. "Did they—?"

Bitten off. He watched as tears welled up in her good eye, leaked through the crusted slit over her left. He led her toward the two cross-legged men, indicated them with the barrel of the Webley.

"Was it either of them?"

The men looked away. Niamh peered. Shook her head.

"Are you sure?"

A press-lipped nod. Her gaze strayed on down the corridor, over the bodies on the floor. She drew a sharp breath. It caught in her throat, set her coughing violently again.

"Him," she finally managed, pointing at Bennett. "That big fucker. Him and one of the Branch men."

"Duncan . . ." Crammond's voice, warning.

Duncan went back to the prisoners, breathing hard. They tried not to meet his eye. He crouched down, dug the barrel of the Webley under the first man's chin.

"Look at her," he said very, very softly.

The man's eyes rolled in their sockets. He didn't move his head at all. His lower lip trembled. "It wasn't—it wasn't us." Desperately now. "You heard her, man, you *heard* her. *It wasn't us!*"

"I know that. Now if you want to survive the next few minutes, you're going to tell me who it was. This Special Branch cunt? What's his name?"

"You said you wouldn't kill us!"

"I'm not going to." Duncan lifted the man's chin another inch on the barrel of the Webley. He leaned in, stared into eyes clamped wide with terror. Stordalen's blood came walking in his veins. "But I am going to batter you until you tell me what I want to know. And I'm not going to be all that careful about it. You might survive, you might not. If you don't, I can always start again on your pal here. So—what's it going to be?"

Crammond tried again. "Duncan, we have tae g—"

"Give me a fucking minute!"

"Boyle!" It was the man he hadn't touched yet, yelping from dry lips he kept licking. "Douglas Boyle. He's a—he's a . . . detective inspector. Out of Belfast."

Duncan nodded. Lowered the Webley and rocked back on his heels. "Got a number for him?"

The man he'd threatened nodded brokenly. The one who'd spoken looked aghast.

"Well, but—it's only for emergency use."

Duncan gestured around at the carnage they'd made. "You don't think this counts?"

From the man's face, he judged his point made. He nodded again. "Right. So you're going to call him for me. Tell him there's trouble and he'd better get down here sharpish. Then we cuff you and your pal here to a water pipe, and you both live to tell the tale. How does that sound?"

The moment held, stretched like hot taffy before it cools and snaps—

Harsh banging on the locked cell next to Niamh's, like an ogre clamoring to be let in.

Duncan and Crammond looked at each other. Duncan put the Webley barrel back in the broken man's throat.

"Who the fuck have you got in there?" he asked.

The man flinched. "It's—dunno, some old guy. They brought him in before the girl. He was supposed to—"

"It's bloody me, Duncan!" Gruff, Lancastrian voice shouting through the plated steel of the door. "Thy bloody messenger of choice to that bastard Hardy! Are tha gonner bloody let me out of here or what?"

THIRTY-ONE

"LAST BLOODY TIME I DO THEE A FAVOR, LAD. THAT'S FOR certain." Garner glowered at him in the washroom mirror as he scrubbed his hands with a miserly remnant of carbolic soap. The water that came off into the basin was the color of dried blood. "Eight bloody days cooped up in there, food tha wunner give to a Yorkshireman, and Hardy's thugs worked me over when I kicked. And now I'm bloody constipated, too. Bloody Yorkshire—who needs it?"

"I don't think Hardy's from around here," Duncan said dryly.

"Aye, well his bully boys in blue are. Thick-as-pig-shit locals to a man." Garner rubbed a pair of now-cleansed fingers around his gums, pressing on his teeth. "Looks like they didn't do any permanent damage, though. So there's that. How's thy lass?"

"I don't know," Duncan admitted.

He'd sent Niamh with an increasingly agitated Crammond—*we've been here nearly half a fuckin' hour, Duncan, there's nae time fir this shite*—back to the parked former ambulance and away. He didn't want to think about what she'd been subjected to, and he certainly wasn't going to start quizzing her in front of an audience. Fever burned hot flushed spots on her cheeks, she had to stifle her coughing at least half a dozen times. Whatever she had, the internment had turned up the dial on it all. He masked his disquiet, held her gently, cupped her cheek, told her to go with the others to safety, he'd follow later. Garner, fresh out of his cell and simmering with undischarged rage, was adamant that he'd stay for the fireworks. Arthur wanted to stay, too, but was persuaded that he was far more vital as an escort for Niamh.

Duncan watched the three of them slip away into the early hours gloom on Maunston's deserted streets. Part of him wanted to be leaving with them, but it was a small part, and not the part that needed to be fed.

He closed and locked the station door, checked on the cuffed prisoners, and went to find Garner, who had apparently just finished in the crapper.

"You are sure about this?" he asked one more time.

Garner splashed water on his face, rubbed at his eyes, and slapped himself lightly on each cheek. He reached for a grubby towel hung on a rail beside the basin.

"Aye, I'm certain." Wiping his face dry. "Tha think I don't know I only made it out of the Forest in one piece last week because of thee?"

"You only went in because of me as well."

Garner grunted. "That . . . is true. And tha sent me to Hardy, too. But I'd be a small man to hold that against thee."

"I will get you paid," Duncan said awkwardly.

"All in good time, lad. There's more to consider for now. These bloody bastards, for a start, and what they did to thy lass." Tossing the towel into the basin. "Did tha get Miriam Rush back to her mother after all?"

"I got her out of the Forest. And then Hardy took her."

"Well, that makes no bloody sense at all." He saw Garner eyeing the scar on his skull where it peeked out from under his cap. "Tha know they told me tha were dead."

The scar itched and sparked along its length, as if something in the healed tissue had heard. "I think I might have been, for a while. It was a close call, anyway. The skogsra brought me back."

Garner looked at him for a long moment. He nodded slowly, as if grasping some until-now tenuous understanding.

"Read much mythology, lad?"

Duncan shrugged. "Aye, the usual. Greek stuff at school."

"Norse? The Edda, the sagas?"

"Not so much."

At Cadogan's, they'd covered both, but he'd shied away from the Viking myth base. The Huldu were in there, of course, albeit distorted, and he wanted no part of that. By contrast, the Greek myths felt safe—mannered, arid tales and heroic deeds from hot, bright lands far, far away, the polar opposite of the damp, dark nightmare memories he carried from his time in the Forest.

"But tha know who Odin is?"

"Course."

"Well, they say Odin hung dead and pierced with his own spear on Yggdrasil—that's the world tree—for nine days and nights, all to learn and bring back runes of power. When he was done, he came back from the dead with those runes, brought back power and wisdom both. Tha have to wonder—I always wondered—back in the times it comes from, if that's not a tale about skogsra healing."

"I'm still working on the wisdom part."

"Probably so is that one-eyed bastard." Garner stirred from his thoughts, clapped Duncan on the shoulder. "C'mon, let's go bait this trap of yours."

In the office space where Bennett had been on watch, the two prisoners were handcuffed either side of a big cast iron radiator. Duncan took the telephone off the desk, freed up some cable, and brought the device over near the two men. He set it down on the floor in front of the man he'd broken. Drew his Webley again.

"Here's how this is going to work," he said quietly. "You're going to call Boyle and tell him there's an emergency. Then you'll give the phone to me. You'll say nothing else. You don't try to warn him, and you'll both live. You have my word. We'll cuff you downstairs, and the day shift will find you in good health. You do anything else, you fuck things up for me in any way at all, and I will shoot both you and your friend here dead. Is that clear?"

The man nodded, hypnotized with fear. Duncan looked at his companion on the other end of the radiator. He was already nodding in time with his comrade.

"Good." Duncan lifted the receiver. "Then dial."

He watched as the man dialed the number with a trembling hand. He listened as the phone rang, heard it picked up at the other end, and held it to his prisoner's ear. A clipped voice snapping down the line, expletives and a question.

The man cleared his throat. "Yes, I know sir, I know. But we have an emergency here, sir."

Crackle and snap.

"It's, uh, it's better if you just see for yourself, sir."

Duncan took back the receiver, put it to his ear. Put on his best officer's voice. "Detective Inspector Boyle?"

"That's right. And who the bloody hell are you?"

"I'm from Hardy. Captain John Craigart, late of the Argyll and Sutherland Highlanders. Directorate of Military Intelligence now. Section J."

He felt down the line how the name set a stir in the other man. There was a pause. Boyle came back measured, outrage quelled.

"It's almost three in the morning, Captain. Do you mind telling me what Section J is doing in Maunston at this hour?"

"I'm afraid, Inspector, that's largely classified. I can give you some information when you get here, but it will be limited to what you need to know in order to help me clear this mess up. Now, I'm loath to involve Colonel Hardy at this point. He certainly won't thank me for dumping it in his lap, and as I'm sure you know, he doesn't suffer fools or failures gladly. I'm told by Constable Bennett that you were responsible for the young Irishwoman's interrogation."

"Myself and Bennett, yes." Stiffly. "That is correct."

"Then you and I definitely need to have words, Inspector. In private. Now, please. Be as quick as you can."

Duncan hung up on Boyle's protestations.

WITH GARNER'S HELP, HE TRANSFERRED the prisoners one at a time to the cells downstairs. There, in separate cells, he cuffed them again to a convenient radiator pipe and told them not to make any noise. He closed the door on each cell. Back upstairs, he installed Garner in the office and gave him instructions. When he heard a car pull up in the street outside, he closed the office door to a crack and went to the front door to open up. A ruffled-looking man in his fifties stood on the step in a crumpled raincoat, unshaven, battered fedora crammed on his head. There was a stubby Hillman tourer parked behind him, canvas cover up, one front wheel bumped recklessly on the pavement. A similar restless lack of kilter in the way the man stood. No attempt at pleasantries.

"Boyle. You're Craigart?"

"I am." Duncan gave him a genial officer-class smile. "Excuse the mufti, we try not to draw attention to ourselves in the Directorate. Please come through."

Boyle followed him in, peering around. "It's just you?"

"My sergeant is in the office, trying to sort out medical support." Duncan gestured at the cracked-open office door, through which Garner could be heard, busily talking down the phone to himself in tones carefully shorn of Lancastrian countryman brogue. *I don't really care about that; how soon can you have him here; yes, it's bloody urgent—I see—all right, I'll hold while you ask.* Duncan pulled an apologetic face—*awkward business this.*"

"Where's Bennett?" Boyle asked warily.

"He's downstairs with the others. Please." Duncan waved him ahead, toward the opened gate and stairwell beyond. "I'd ask you not to blame Constable Bennett too much, any more than you'd blame yourself. I find it's not productive to—"

Boyle turned back at the top step, gave him a hard look. *"Blame?"*

"Yes," Duncan said precisely. "Blame."

The Special Branch detective flushed. "Listen, all we did was rough this Fenian bitch up a bit. Nothing excessive. You know how it is—a few backhanders and slaps, a few hands where she didn't want them to go. Throw a scare into her, shake her up, make her think about what worse we *could* do. Standard operating procedure."

"Oh, I'm sure." Duncan lifted his hands, placating. "It is not my intention, Inspector, to criticize your methods. But, as you'll see, we do have a problem now."

"Yes, so you keep saying. What problem, exactly?"

Duncan pulled the apologetic face again. "I don't mean to be vague, Inspector, truly. But it's perhaps better if you see for yourself. Get an unbiased detective's eye on things." Another gesture, urging the other man down the stairs. "Please."

Boyle rolled his eyes, grunted, and took the stairs. "I don't know what experience you've had in interrogation, Captain, but this kind of—"

Three steps up and back, Duncan braced on the walls with both hands, stomped forward as hard as he could. He hit Boyle low in the spine, sent him flying, like a man tied across the mouth of a cannon and blown away. Boyle flew out ahead of his own legs, went tumbling awkwardly down the angled curve of the stairwell, hit wall and floor at the bottom with a thump. High, wrenched scream that Duncan guessed meant a broken bone.

Duncan drew the Webley and went down after him.

"What the fucking hell do you think you're playing at?" All civility shredded from Boyle's voice, but the rage died in his throat as he saw the gun in Duncan's hand. He scrabbled backward in the confines of the corridor, one tweed-trousered leg dragging awkwardly.

He bumped into Bennett's corpse.

Jerked around, saw the other blood-drenched body as well.

One slow moment, as it dawned on him. Then, breathing hard, he turned himself back to face Duncan. Lifted himself as well as he could on his elbows, glared defiantly upward.

"What are you then—fucking IRA?"

"No," Duncan told him. "This is personal. You don't lay hands on my woman."

The two men stared at each other across the gulf of what had been done.

"You'll hang for this," Boyle spat.

Duncan had planned to shoot him in the belly and let him linger. But something in the gritted courage he saw staring back at him, some Welsh-accented tracery of compassion, shifted his aim at the last moment. He shot Boyle in the face, watched him jerk back slumped against his fellow interrogator's already cooling corpse.

He stood over his handiwork for a long moment.

But the thing that now lived in his blood only bubbled and chuckled and turned over endlessly on itself, like an increasingly smooth-running motor, and was not even close to satisfied.

"WE'VE GOT A RIDE OUT," he told Garner, upstairs. "Hillman tourer, parked right outside. You want to go and crank it up?" He hesitated. "You do know how to do that?"

Garner gave him a look. "I don't *like* motorcars, lad, and I don't want to *own* one. Doesn't mean I don't bloody understand how they work. I ran a bloody farm, for Christ's sake!"

He went out into the street. Duncan descended the stairs once more, stepped over the dead men. They lay there in the narrow corridor space, like abandoned sacks of some crop no one cared about anymore. He went into the first cell where he'd handcuffed one of the prisoners. The man huddled into the radiator he'd been cuffed to, looked up fearfully.

"We're done here," Duncan told him. "And my word holds—you

will not be harmed. But when Hardy gets here, I want you to give him a message for me. You tell him Duncan Silver is back from the Forest, back from the fucking dead, and I'm coming for him next. Duncan Silver. Got that?"

From the man's face, he judged that he did.

Upstairs, he reloaded the Webley from the pouch Crammond had given him, pocketed the spent shells. He ripped the phone cable out of the wall—why make Hardy's job any easier—killed the lights in the office, and joined Garner on the pavement outside. Boyle's Hillman was all started up, puttering quietly to itself in the predawn gloom. Duncan puffed out a long, relieved sigh. The air was just cold enough to put ghostly scraps of frost in his breath as it blew away. Autumn's fair warning, the first of the season.

"You don't want to drive, then?" he asked Garner with a sidelong glance.

"Do us a favor and shut thy trap, lad, I'm in no kind of mood. Just get us out of here."

Duncan obliged. He'd not had to drive in quite a while, and the Hillman was a little stiff in the gears. But it ran smoothly enough once they were rolling. He felt himself beginning to relax as they threaded through the empty streets.

"I'll need to call the White Mare," Garner said somberly. "Maggie Worrart's a good woman, she'll have fed and stabled Mabel for me the while. But I conner expect her to keep it up forever without word."

"We'll find a call box." Duncan remembered belatedly that he'd been meant to call the witch. "Saw a couple on the way here."

"I saw one just now." Garner turned in his seat, nodded back the way they'd come. "Down that last right turn back there. You got coin?"

Duncan nodded, took the next right, and brought them back round through the southern end of Maunston, searching for the box. He found it at the end of a street that looked out directly on the Forest across a scant sixty yards of scrub-grown waste ground. Beyond that, he saw the bricked rise of the pottery's bottle kilns above the canopies of the trees that had drowned them. At the tree line, someone had abandoned an AEC Y Type with full load, and with the cracking and lifting of the concrete as the new growth erupted, the lorry had sunk at the back and tilted, spilling crates through the canvas cover and over the side. In the shrouded moonlight, it looked like a black-and-white illustration from some Vernian tale of submarine horror, as if something dreadful and tentacular was trying to drag the vehicle down and back into the trees.

"Nice spot," grumbled Garner.

"Aye, you can see why nobody was keen to stay. Sit there a minute, will you. Got to make a call myself."

Duncan jumped down from the Hillman, dug coins from his pocket on the way to the call box, heaved open the weighty latticed iron door. The hinges protested with years of disuse, gave grudgingly and quite noisily, did not piston closed afterward. It left him with a chilly sensation of exposure at the back of his neck as he dialed.

"Duncan!" She always knew it was him, before he even spoke. He was almost used to the faint slither of unease it always gave him. "This is a *very* liberal interpretation of the words *not early.*"

"Aye, sorry. Got caught up, busy all day, there wasn't—"

"Well, you'd better come and see me anyway." Riding down the apology, impatient. "Tomorrow. Soon as you can, darling."

"Look, that's what I was calling about. There's no need to go magicking after Niamh. I already found her. Problem solved."

"Well, that's just as well, because I hadn't even started scrying. But that's not why you need to come and see me. Something else has come up."

He hesitated. "I'm kind of pinched right now, Sal. It's not—"

"This is for your benefit, Duncan, not mine. Have you ever known me to waste your time?"

It didn't need a reply.

"Then get here as soon as you can."

She hung up.

For a moment, Duncan stood like an idiot with the warmed Bakelite of the receiver still at his ear. Blink. Not what he'd expected.

But then—odd spells and torrid, drunken sex, disembodied voices and half-seen shadow figures in the hall, the luck of a barnyard squabble and the still-beating heart of a Final Isles Huldu prince—when had Wolfbane Sally Bethune ever delivered him anything approaching the expected?

He went to put the receiver back on its cradle, jolted rigid before he could complete the motion.

In the pit of the receiver's speaker, down at the limits of hearing on the empty line, he caught the whisper and chime of high, sibilant voices chanting his name.

Duncan . . .

Come back, Duncan . . .

Did you think it was over, Duncan, did you think you could just walk away . . .

Did you think it would be that easy*?*

Duncan!

A taloned hand, falling on his shoulder . . .

"Duncan?" No talons, just Garner and the edge of worry on his voice. "Lad, what are tha playing at? We don't have the time for clagging about!"

Duncan blinked again. Shook himself. He turned in the confined space, squeezed out past the other man, handed him the receiver.

"Sorry," he said vaguely. "Just thinking about something." He dug around in his pocket for more coins, handed them over. "Here. I'll wait in the car."

But as he walked back to the Hillman, he looked out at the Forest edge sixty yards off, the scrub-grown concrete ground between, and wondered with a shiver what kind of sly, slim roots might have wound undetected beneath that surface without showy cracking or rupture, found the cabling of the modern age, and somehow—*what? spliced with it? infested it?*—made connection.

And he wondered where else in the places men built over and thought safe, the same thing might be happening even now.

GARNER WAS A COUPLE OF minutes. He came hurrying back from the call box, shoulders hunched more defensively than you'd expect for the mild chill in the air. He climbed into the car, looked at Duncan strangely.

"Line all right?" Duncan asked neutrally. "You get through?"

"Aye. She'll feed and water Mabel for the duration. Stout lass, Maggie is. Always has been. Said I'd pay her soon as I'm back."

"You can't go back to Macclesfield right now." It jerked out of Duncan before he'd realized what he was going to say. "Not with that fuck Hardy still in play."

"Aye, well, I'm not the only one. Don't see thee or thy Irish lass safe to walk the streets of Erlsley for the time being either."

They both sat in silence while the truth of it soaked in.

"Bit bloody complicated, aye?" Garner said finally. "Looks like fighting the bloody Fae was the easy part."

Duncan nodded, wordless, weighed down with new concerns and complex fears he had no way to name. He stared out at the tree line, the dark spaces below the canopies, the broad stretch of the Forest beyond.

This time, he did not shiver.

This time, he felt the deep, eerie call, and it was like the voice of some dark, unnerving lover, calling him home.

THIRTY-TWO

THEY DUMPED THE HILLMAN IN THE EAST OF THE CITY, ON A Zeppelin bomb site that was still awaiting cleanup. Duncan drove in over the unreclaimed brick rubble, wove past low stubs of walls the bomb had here and there left intact. He let Garner out, then front-ended the car in a shallow crater at the center of the site. Cut strips from the Hillman's canvas awning with the sgian dubh, uncapped the petrol tank, soaked the rags for a crude fuse, then lit it.

They beat a hasty retreat.

The crump as the tank blew was undramatic, would not trouble anyone sleeping in the vicinity. Flames rose cheerily in the body of the car as they watched, the windscreen splintered and cracked. Shadows danced on the ruined walls as the vehicle burned, soft and cozy, as if from a campfire for Gypsies out of a tale. They put their backs to the glow, walked westward.

A cold, gray dawn crept across the city at their heels. Had almost caught up with them as they slipped into the Doorbell Club through the service entrance at the side, and shut the door on the waxing light of day.

Entering the red-lamp gloom and slightly stale warmth of the club felt like an escape of sorts.

Or maybe just a postponement.

THE MAIN BAR WAS STILL doing business, but only just. A well-fed, suited man in his fifties with an immaculate shave and a neatly kept mustache sat in one booth, bookended by two blond girls half his age clad in scraps of translucent silk and not much else, who seemed intent on cleaning out his ears with their tongues. At the bar, a gaunt young man in an army captain's uniform leaned over cocktail glasses and rubbed noses with a dark, voluptuous woman visibly stark naked beneath an open French army greatcoat she wore. Farther down, Belle D'Or held court in her usual spot, sipping from her jade cigarette holder and talking quietly to the barman. Blackout curtains on the windows kept out the pale axe of day.

Neither clients nor working girls paid Duncan the slightest attention as he led Garner to the back of the room, where Crammond and Arthur sat in the last booth, sharing a bottle. Belle glanced his way as he reached her, a speculative look, but she said nothing, just plumed smoke out at him and switched away with chin and shoulder like an offended cat.

"Take it I'm not as popular with our hostess as I was a couple of days ago?" he asked as he and Garner slid into the booth with the other men.

"None of us are," said Crammond. He pushed glasses at them, poured from the bottle—some generic Scotch Duncan had never heard of. Their Chivas Regal days appeared to be behind them. "Ye can see her point. Lassie agrees to hide one fugitive fir me, suddenly she has two on her hands. Three, if yir friend here frae across the Pennines needs shelter, too. And it's aww gaunnae get a lot worse when the news comes oot about whit we did in Maunston." He raised his glass. *"Sláinte."*

They drank reflexively.

"News may not come out," Duncan tried gamely. "Maunston's a ghost town, we all saw that. No one outside of Special Branch or the

Commission is going to find the bodies. And I can see Hardy slapping a D notice on everything anyway, at least for now."

"They're still gaunnae turn up the heat, Duncan. Word'll get oot, folk'll get scairt, hiding will get harder. Belle and I have a good working relationship, but I cannae push it."

"Aye." Duncan sipped his drink again. "Fair enough. Where's Niamh?"

"Put tae bed. She wanted tae wait up with us, but Belle wouldnae have her in the bar with her face the way it is. Givin' the wrong impression, she said."

"Yet here I sit," said Arthur mildly. "Can see that Mrs. Pankhurst having some issues with that."

"Shut yir hole, Arthur, ye're part o' the furnishings here, and ye know it. Listen, Duncan, she's been well taken care of. Belle had one o' the girls draw her a hot bath, dose her wi' aspirin and somethin' fir that cough. They put her in a good room on the third floor, 307, end o' the corridor. Ye should gae up and see her."

Duncan nodded. "Garner here can't go back to Macclesfield the way things are. He will need a place, at least for now."

"Ah wiz afraid o' that. This is getting oot o' hand, Duncan."

"Agreed."

He heaved himself back to his feet, drained his glass, and grimaced—the Scotch was some rough old stuff. He put a hand on Garner's shoulder.

"Sorry about this. Didn't see it coming at all."

Garner shifted uncomfortably under his grip. "Tha're alreet, lad. Go see thy lass."

He went—out through the discreet dark velvet curtain at the back that led directly to the Doorbell's broad red and gilt carpeted staircase and the rooms above. No one on the stairs as he climbed, no one on the landings, or the red-flock-wallpapered branching corridor he took on the third floor. The cream-paneled doors to the rooms were all drawn closed and silent, the carpet underfoot deadened his footfalls like walking on moss. Up all night, the whisky and the men he'd killed—it piled up behind his eyes, gave everything the detached sensation you sometimes got after the shelling let up and you were stumbling around a trench trying to work out who'd died and who hadn't.

He turned a corner, passed a single door that stood ajar near the end of the row. The oversweet reek of cannabis smoke, wafting into the corridor. Duncan glanced in, caught a glimpse of one of Belle's girls flat on her back in bed, staring at the ceiling. She was naked to the waist, breasts pooled on her chest, a fat roll-up slanted between her lips, hair a soft blond halo. Smoke hazed the whole room dreamlike.

As he hesitated, the girl rolled her head to the side and looked out at him. He thought she made a faint snorting sound, a laugh so tired it never made it fully past her lips. Her eyes on him were as empty as a Huldu's stare.

A second girl peered round the edge of the door. Saw him, pushed it firmly shut in his face.

He moved on, knocked gently at the door of 307. No response. He turned the doorknob gingerly, eased the door open, and slipped inside. Big velvet curtains at the window, the room sunk in gloom. A narrow apron of daylight seeping through onto the ceiling above the curtain rail. Niamh was a huddled shape under the covers, face turned away, black hair combed out loose on the squashy white pillows. He knew instantly that she was not asleep.

"Duncan?"

"Aye, it's me." He closed the door gently, went and sat on the bed at her side. She didn't turn to face him. "Just wanted to see how you are. I didn't want to wake you."

"I'm fine, I'll be fine." In a low, shaky voice that said she was anything but. "Thanks—I mean, thank you. For coming to get me out of there."

He put his hand on her shoulder, tentatively. Couldn't tell through the bedclothes if she felt too hot or not. "You had to know I would."

"They told me you were dead." He felt a faint shudder go through her. Now she turned, awkwardly in the tight covers, showed him her face. She'd been crying. "I thought you were dead, Duncan. How are you not dead?"

He crinkled a grin he didn't really feel, touched the scar along his skull. "Nothing kills me, girl. I'm like your old Irish hero there, what was it? Cuckoo Lane?"

She snorted a broken laugh. "That's not how it's pronounced!"

She fought free of the covers, sat up and put her arms around him, hugged him to her. Someone had lent her a long white nightgown, a little frayed in the collar he noticed, looking at it from a couple of inches away. She breathed deep, and he felt it catch again, felt her strain against the cough. It came out anyway, but better, he thought, than before, less harsh and hacking. He held her, stroked her hair. He felt how the tension ebbed from her body like collapse. He held her some more. *I was so scared,* she whispered into his ear. *They said they could do anything to me if I didn't cooperate.* He held her. Her voice grew smaller. *They . . . did things, Duncan, they . . .*

He held her.

Finally, she pushed herself free from his grip, held him at arm's length. She wiped at her face with the blade of one hand, sniffed.

"Did you kill him?" she asked.

He nodded.

"Billy Crammond said you would. He said there's no stopping you once you start." She stared at him as if seeing him for the first time in her life. "Christ, Duncan. What are we going to *do*?"

"Right now, what we're going to do is sleep. Both of us, because we both need it. After that—" He shrugged. "We'll see. Tomorrow's another day."

She tilted her head at the curtains, the apron of gray light on the ceiling. "Tomorrow's already here, Duncan."

He grunted. "Don't remind me."

THEY SLEPT SPOONED IN THE big bed, under heavy covers, seven hours straight, according to the Mappin & Webb. He dreamed of dead men reaching for him from the branches of nighttime trees, spiders promenaded on leads by old-fashioned Victorian matrons in the park, Mebhuranon looming fanged and grinning over him like some ship's figurehead smashing into the room ahead of the prow she jutted from. Vague memory of sounds from the street outside, the soft insistent patter of rain at the windows, of stirring to change position once or twice, stroking Niamh's face, planting a kiss on the nape of her neck, of soothing her when she coughed in her sleep, but these could have been dreamed, too. When he woke for real, the apron of light from over the curtain rail had brightened and spread into long blurred fingers, reaching across the ceiling almost to the door. The pattering at the windows had turned heavier. The rain, at least, had not been a dream.

He lay looking up at the radiating pattern for a while, listening to the rain and feeling Niamh breathe rasping into his side. Hungry, he realized. He was hungry. He twisted and fished the Mappin & Webb from the bedside table, held it up to see the time.

Nearly two in the afternoon.

Fuck.

The witch.

Duncan eased himself out of bed, trying hard not to disturb Niamh. She mumbled and shifted, but didn't wake. He carried his clothing from where he'd left it strewn on the floor, seated himself in a big red velvet upholstered armchair on the far side of the room. He dressed as quietly as he could, watching Niamh sleep. His thoughts churned like the wheels of an ambulance stuck in mud. Flashlit recall, no more coherent than his dreams.

Boyle's death—the detective's face, mottled with rage and fear, just before Duncan put the dumdum slug through it, turned it to senseless clay—*you'll hang for this*!

The wink of light from across the river, the brutal slap of the sniper shot as it scorched his skull.

Another kind of war—Hardy, officer-urbane over tea and cake—*with new enemies and rules we have yet to learn.*

Enemies he now seemed to be stacking up like sandbags on a redoubt.

Svalenkari wills vengeance, and he will not be stopped. Mebhuranon's warning while he twisted and crawled on the park path at her feet. *And so you are warned.*

Right now, it was the least of his worries. He had enough to deal with right here in the realm of mortals. His apartment watched by the police, his bank accounts unsafe to access, his face no doubt about to be printed out on a thousand wanted posters in police stations across the city. Garner and Niamh hunted by Hardy and the Forestry Commission, and now by Special Branch, too. Crammond and his associates, dangerously exposed the longer they insisted on helping Duncan out. His welcome at the Doorbell Club wearing out faster than the barrel of a Vickers on the Somme.

And lost somewhere in the midst of it all, who knew where, Mimi Rush, whom he'd promised to bring home, and the mother he'd promised it to as well.

You will search for the child again. Bainbridge was apparently certain. Nice of him, that. Strong vote of confidence. But where and how he'd search, and with what desperate scavenged resources, were questions Duncan had no answers for.

This is gettin' oot o' hand, Duncan.

True enough.

Sitting with his boots still unlaced, watching Niamh sleep in the rapidly eroding island of safety he'd brought her to.

Christ, Duncan. What are we going to do?

The two Webley revolvers gleamed darkly on the floor by the bed, partly shrouded in the folds of his coat where he'd dropped it. He retrieved them with stealthy care, stowed them either side in the long pockets of the coat, and slipped out of the room with the garment over his arm.

What are we going to do?

For now, he was going to see the witch.

HE WENT DOWN THE CORRIDOR to the landing, found Arthur seated there on the floor at the top of the stairs with the casual lack of concern for clothing or available furniture that you saw in a lot of men who'd come home from the trenches. There was a folded copy of the *Manchester Guardian* beside him on the carpet. He looked up as Duncan approached.

"Afternoon. Your girl all right?"

"I think so. She's still sleeping." Duncan sat down next to him on the stairs. "Nice shooting last night. Meant to say."

"My pleasure. Been a while. Was worried I'd lost the knack."

"Sharpshooter, were you?"

"Tried out for it. Waiting on orders when this happened." He gestured, almost apologetic, at his fright-mask features. "Never got the chance after that."

"What I saw, you'd have made the grade for the Lovat Scouts, no problem."

Arthur approximated a smile. "Thanks."

"I've to go out for a bit. You mind keeping an eye out for Niamh when she wakes?"

"Consider it done. More or less what I was doing up here anyway."

"Man, don't you ever sleep?"

"Not well." Another gesture at his fire-ravaged face. "Not since this. Got a couple of hours after you left, been up since about ten. I'll tell you what, though. If you're going out now, you're going to want a hat."

Duncan looked up at the skylight in the ceiling above the stairs. It was awash with rain. "Any chance I could borrow one?"

"Sure, we'll find you something. Belle's got a wardrobe for the girls like you wouldn't believe. You want to grab something from the kitchen before you go?"

"No, I'll get something on the way. You seen my Lancastrian pal?"

"Garner? Yeah, he already ate. Breakfast with the girls in the back dining room, a while ago. Think he's still down there reading the papers."

"I'd better go talk to him. Is Belle about?"

Arthur chuckled. "Now you want unicorns. Belle won't be up for at least another two hours. Creature of the night, she is, just like Carmilla in that Murnau movie. You seen it?"

Duncan nodded. "Greta Schröder. I think Schröder's got a bit more meat on her bones than Belle, though."

"All that bloodsucking, I expect. Can I give her a message? Belle, I mean."

"Aye, well, just wanted to apologize to her for the inconvenience. Tell her we'll be out of her hair as soon as I can organize something else."

"Have you got somewhere in mind?"

Duncan grimaced. "Not really. Got some ideas, a favor I might be able to call in. But it'll take some putting together."

"My advice? You need to get your girl out of town. Maybe down to London."

"Aye. Maybe."

"Or out somewhere remote, fringes of the Forest where no one'll dare come after you, but not too far in. They say there's still some Gypsies living that way. Garner's a woodsman, too, isn't he? Could he live like that?"

Duncan said nothing. He'd left the Forest running on basic goals—find out why he'd been betrayed, pay it back with interest. When the phone calls he made from the Turk's Head in Maltby went unanswered, he'd understood there would be more to do, and the bad news on Skoldergate just drove the point home. To the list of what had been taken from him, he added Niamh and shoveled a fresh load of fuel onto his rage. But it was only now, in the cold, rainy light of this new day, that he grasped how completely, in little more than a week, the life he'd built for himself here in Erlsley had been blown apart.

"Think about doing that myself sometimes."

It took a moment for Duncan to realize that the other man had spoken again. "Sorry, what?"

"I think about heading to the Forest fringes sometimes. Maybe even the Forest itself." Gesturing at his fright-mask features. "Y'know, when this just gets too much, I wonder about it. Being alone out there, if it'd be so bad. Spent a year sleeping rough in London after demob, didn't really want to be with people, and I was drinking a lot. That wasn't so bad. I mean, nothing is, after what we went through over there, right? You're not scared of much anymore. You can take the cold and the rain—at least there's no fucking mud!—and the busies, they mostly leave you alone. People were actually kind a lot of the time. You know, they'd see the face, they knew. They'd give you money. I just wonder how bad the Forest can be, is all."

"It can be pretty bad," Duncan told him grimly.

"Well, so can I. You don't think I'd scare the Huldu off, looking like this? They're supposed to love beauty. They say they only take the most beautiful children, say they look beautiful themselves, that beauty is the only thing they value."

Duncan thought about Mebhuranon. "It's not beauty, exactly. It's . . . hard to explain. And anyway, they can shape-shift into things you should be glad you'll never have to see. Believe me, Arthur, the Huldu aren't anything you want to be around. You're better off sticking with what you've got here. Paid work, bed and board, the girls. Is it so bad?"

"Belle pays her girls to fuck me." Trying hard for lightness of tone, not quite making it. "Sometimes I suspect there's a morbid curiosity in it for them, too, but that's about the best I can hope for. Even with the kind ones, it's more pity than anything. You know, you get tired of seeing that in people's eyes. You wonder whether you'll ever belong again."

There was a short answer to that, but Arthur didn't deserve it. Duncan settled for a noncommittal grunt. The other man barely noticed. His voice grew musing.

"They say that when the Huldu revel, they do it with the abandon of beasts, whole writhing masses of them across the floor of Forest clearings, that their women use human thralls for their pleasure in those ceremonies as happily as their own kind, and do not care what they look like, how they're made. Is that true?"

True, to a point—though thrall involvement was a lot less common than the Russell Maynard Dalton Faerie romance crowd liked to believe. Duncan had seen it only once or twice, each time through the eyes of a child, for whom it was a sight more terrifying and incomprehensible than arousing.

He shook his head.

"You don't want to be a thrall to the Huldu, Arthur. Really. You think you're not scared of much anymore? There are whole levels of fear in the Forest you haven't seen."

Arthur stared away down the staircase. "Sounds like a challenge to me."

He wouldn't be the first, Duncan knew, to head into the Forest with a headful of inchoate longing and misconception and death wish daring, never to be seen again. Tales of demobbed, damaged, and rootless men *last seen entering woods near X* were rife, so common in the first couple of years after the war that in the end the papers gave up printing the stories.

You could, Duncan supposed, blame the myth base—knights, warlocks, poets, and dreamers down the centuries, riding off into the realm of Faerie in search of some heart's desire or other, sucked in by the promise of abandon, escape from the harsh gray strictures of the world and the affairs of men. Or you could just blame the times, the war, and the general sense of despair, the keenly felt hollowness of things.

But in the end, it came down to a fairly basic truth—when you've charged across no-man's-land into scything machine gun fire and lived to tell the tale, the foundations of your relationship with mortality shift. Survive the same thing enough times, and something structural gives way in your sanity, too. You hear siren calls you were once deaf to. Your fear is a floppy, unreliable thing, no longer fit for purpose.

And a walk in the woods, however haunted, might well seem like a good place to finally make your peace.

Few attempts were ever made to track and bring back the men who disappeared. Where family or local well-wishers did organize to search, the searchers almost always came back empty-handed or, on one or two famous occasions, did not come back at all. It was not long before a general acceptance set in that such departures were no more admitting of remedy than those involving a pistol to the mouth or pockets full of stones and the jump off a high bridge.

Duncan looked sideways at his companion. Arthur's gaze was lost somewhere far beyond the stairwell walls of the brothel they sat in.

"Do me a favor, man," he said.

Arthur stirred. "Hmm? Yes, of course. If I can."

"Come down and talk to Garner with me. He's a woodsman from way back. He'll set you straight."

"IT'S THE BLOODY CINEMA, THAT'S what it is," was Garner's unexpected opinion. "If tha ask me. Never had that to contend with when I were a lad."

Arthur blinked. "Come again?"

"Cinema!" Folding his newspaper closed, putting it flat on the long wooden dining table with a thump. Warming to his theme. "All sitting there in the dark, staring into that light like it's the door to another world. It's not healthy."

"Ah, come on," Duncan protested. "It's only like theater on a screen."

Garner snorted. "That's what tha bloody think, lad. Theater's physical, it's a thing, it's *real.* It's carpentry, and paint, and flesh-and-blood actors right there in front of thee, living and breathing just like thee. Tha have to make the effort to forget they're actors. But what's up on that screen, that is another bloody world. Eternal faces and bodies that tha conner touch, that'll never age. *It's just like Faerie.* And we've made a bloody industry out of selling it to people, a dream they can never have, a place they'll never go, people they can never be, but they'll spend their whole bloody life yearning for it. No wonder they run off into the bloody Forest!"

Duncan and Arthur looked at each other, wordless for ticking moments.

Finally, Arthur shrugged.

"Problem solved, then," he said. "I guess I'll just go to see *Carmilla* again."

Duncan was silent a moment longer.

Then, abruptly, he chuckled. Arthur made his approximation of a smile. Duncan chortled again, louder. Arthur joined in. Garner looked from one to the other, as if they'd both gone barking mad.

"Oh aye," he said testily. "What's so bloody funny?"

Arthur closed his ruined mouth with a snap. Shook his head. But the damage was done. Duncan tried to clamp his own mouth shut, couldn't prevent a silly smirk spilling out. The laughter bubbled inside him like a witch's spell out of control, rancid old tensions clamoring for release. Arthur snorted, made a noise like a choked belch, and that was funny, too . . .

And then, suddenly, the dam burst and they were both cackling like fishwives, nothing really to do with anything that had been said, roaring with laughter for its own sake that built and built, squeezed tears from their eyes, ached their sides, robbed them of breath and still scaled upward, until the cook and a couple of Belle's girls looked round the dining room door like small, wondering children—a sight that started Duncan and Arthur off again—and finally came in to demand, along with Garner, just what the bloody hell all this unlooked-for fucking hilarity was supposed to be bloody about, then.

THIRTY-THREE

IT WAS STILL RAINING WHEN DUNCAN GOT TO CRAWGATE, HARD enough that he held on to his hat and ran splashing through puddles from the tram stop to the pie shop's awning for cover, in hopes that he could shelter there until the worst was past. True to his word, Arthur had found him a broad-brimmed gray fedora from somewhere in the Doorbell Club's dressing room, a little bent and battered and smelling suspiciously of French perfume, but it did the job. His hair, at least, stayed dry.

Safe under the awning, he took the fedora off, shook the excess water from brim and crown, glad that Arthur had prevailed upon him to take it after all. Coarse, abrasive drumming on the angled canvas over his head, as if it were gravel being poured there, not water. The rain sluiced and curtained off, hit the pavement in sheets, splattered back up. He moved farther in to avoid getting splashed. A couple of customers came out of the shop: a young shopgirl in some liveried apron he didn't recognize, a big, untidy man in a workman's jacket and boots, and an elegantly dressed old woman whom Duncan thought at first might be a witch come down for a late lunch, until she bumped against him and he felt not even a hint of the faint sensual charge that witches, in his experience, tended to carry around with them.

"Oh dear! I am sorry, young man," she excused herself, brushing lightly at his sleeve as if she might have stained it. "I was just trying not to get splashed. You know, I think this is the worst rain I've seen since the Forests erupted. We had storms like this back then as well."

"Too bloody right!" said the workman, angling for some attention from the girl at his side. "You know who I blame? That lot up the hill."

The shopgirl said nothing.

"You know who I mean, love, eh?" He jerked his head at the upward slope of Crawgate. "Bunch of twisted old women squatting up there, cooking up their potions and strife. No offense meant, ma'am."

"Oh, I don't live around here," said the elegant old woman vaguely.

"What happens if you don't settle and have a family, like. Get a good man to provide for you, have some kids. It's what women want, you know. What makes 'em happy."

The shopgirl looked resolutely out into the rain.

The scruffy man pressed on, undeterred. "Too much gallivanting these days. Those flappers don't know it, but they're playing with fire. It's all fun and games, innit, until suddenly it's not and you're on the shelf and it's too bloody late. That's how you end up like them up there, all bitter and dried up. Know what I mean, love?"

The shopgirl looked now as if she were contemplating a headlong dash out into the thick of the storm. Duncan took pity on her.

"You ever met a witch?" he asked loudly.

The workman swung on him. "Eh?"

"I was just wondering if you've spent time with witches." He met the man's stare amiably. "You seem to be a bit of an expert."

The man's mouth flapped soundlessly. Out of nowhere, something electric came scuttling down Duncan's nerves with the hunter speed of Mebhuranon's spider in the park. The muscles in the pit of his stomach twinged, a faint shiver of mauve light seemed to blast outward in his field of vision, wash over everything, put a momentary sparkle on the rain before it faded down the street.

"I expect you'd better be going," Duncan murmured. "No time to stand around."

The man's mouth twitched at one corner. His eyes seemed to defocus, lose their heat. "I'd best be going," he agreed in slurred tones. "No time to stand around."

He backed away from Duncan, out from under the awning, got hit in the face by the sluicing rain off its edge, barely seemed to notice. He turned away without even wiping his face, blundered off across the street, weaving slightly. Duncan blinked, still trying to rid his vision of the afterimage of mauve radiance. He looked at the shopgirl, the old woman, saw they were both staring oddly at him.

"Well," he said breezily. "Doesn't look like it's going to stop anytime soon. Maybe our eligible friend had the right idea. Ladies."

He fitted his borrowed hat back onto his head, turned up his collar, and stepped out into the downpour. The two women watched him go without a word. He tipped his hat to them, then set about trudging up the hill toward Sal's place, buffeted by sweeping, wind-driven curtains of rain.

He was pretty much drenched by the time he reached the witch's door.

He hit the buzzer, waited for the door to yawn magically open, squelched irritably up the stairs. The customary black cat showed up on the first landing with its inscrutable jade gaze, but he stared it down with such malevolent intensity that it hissed and slid back into the shadows, out of his way.

"You took your sweet time."

Sal, leaning over the landing banister rail, bundled up in a black and dark green gown he hadn't seen before, hair up and sloppily pinned. It gave her a faintly oriental air.

"Storm held me up." He'd called ahead to her from a phone box in the street before he took the tram, and by rights should have been there a while ago. "It's fucking biblical out there. Whole city's drowning."

"Well, you certainly seem to be." Squishing one arm of his coat in her fingers, wrinkling her nose at the water that oozed out of the fabric. "Nice hat, by the way. Come on, get in, get that off, get your coat off, too. We'll see if we can't warm you up. Got visitors. We've all been waiting for you, darling."

She bustled about him as they went into the apartment, helped him shrug himself out of the coat, noted the weight of the two Webleys in its pockets with the faintest raised eyebrow but no comment. She hung the coat, ushered him forward down the hall and into the living room. Every lamp in the room was on, cheery pools of warmth and radiance on walls and side tables to push back the miserable gray rain-light seeping in from outside. There was a good fire crackling in the grate, and from some gathering of bowls and paraphernalia on the low lounge table, a curious sludgy popping sound Duncan had never heard before. A faint odor permeated the room, sweet but not entirely pleasant, and maddeningly familiar.

"Duncan, this is Nimble Shanks Annie Spence." Sal gestured at a gaunt, long-limbed woman of about fifty, who sat folded on the sofa in ankle-length black lace skirts, a grubby white men's shirt, and a waistcoat. She was stirring the contents of a tiny steaming cauldron with a long steel fork. She nodded at Duncan without speaking. Sal pivoted about, gestured again. "And of course you'll remember Jeremy from before."

Duncan looked at the ex-apprentice warlock impassively. "Hello, Jerry."

Ewart bobbed his head, shifted in his armchair, and swallowed. Sal went and sat on the sofa beside Annie, waved at the remaining free armchair. Duncan lowered himself into it, eyes mostly on the cauldron, which he now saw was suspended on an iron tripod over a small alcohol burner. As he watched, Sal picked up a small slab of something yellow and dropped it into the pot. Nimble Shanks Annie stirred, the slab began to soften and melt into the mixture.

"What is this?" Duncan asked suspiciously.

"This is fondue," said Sal. "It's from Switzerland. Would you like some?"

"You'll want a bit more wine in it," Annie opined. She had an oddly soft, melodic voice that didn't suit her appearance at all. "Really."

Sal picked up an uncorked bottle from the table, sloshed a measure into the tiny cauldron. Annie withdrew the implement she was stirring with, spiked a small cube of what looked like smoked ham from a plate on the table. The mixture in the pot bubbled sluggishly, the largest bubble popped and released the maddeningly familiar odor into the room again. *Cheese,* Duncan realized suddenly. They were melting cheese.

"You're hungry," said Nimble Shanks Annie with no hint of a question in her voice, and plunged the ham cube on the fork into the melted cheese mix. "You want to try?"

"Look, I didn't come here for dinner, I—"

Sudden blotch of hunger in his stomach. He had not, after all, found time to eat on the way across town. He sighed. Annie smiled and hauled out the cube of meat, now wrapped around with a thick coating of cheese that trailed long tendrils back into the pot. She wound these up by twirling the fork handily round three or four times, then reached across the table toward Duncan.

"Open wide," she said, and he did.

The ham-and-cheese combination, spiced with wine and other elements he couldn't quite make out, exploded in his mouth, put an itch in the hinge of his jaw and a desperate squirt of saliva onto his tongue. He chewed and swallowed in a kind of rapture.

"Good, isn't it?" said Nimble Shanks Annie placidly. "Gift from a customer of mine a few years ago. He said he thought it suited me. Are you going to tell him the bad news, Sal, or am I?"

Duncan looked from one to the other of them. "Bad news?"

"Yes, I'm afraid we have some new information for you, Duncan." From somewhere, Sal found another long steel fork, spiked a small cube-cut piece of bread from another bowl, and dipped it into the cheese. "Regarding your new Sword and Orb allies."

"It is not the Order," Ewart said weakly from his armchair. "Our founding principles are sound and just. I myself . . . the vision is transcendent . . . this is not . . ."

He faltered to a halt as Duncan nailed him with a stare.

"Bainbridge intends to betray you." Sal, nibbling on the cheese-coated bread. "It seems he has a working relationship with Colonel Hardy and the Forestry Commission after all. And is playing both ends against the middle, so to speak. Jeremy here was kind enough to bring us the news."

"And you know this how?"

Ewart gulped again. "When, uh, when I first received orders to watch Irene Rush and her daughter, I was given the address by a man named Oakley. At the time, I, well, I thought he was an adept. The seniors at the temple treated him that way; how was I to . . ." He caught a glance from Nimble Shanks Annie, stumbled on. "Anyway. Oakley came to see the archmage—Mr. Bainbridge—at the new house yesterday. I spotted him arriving, overheard them talking as I went past the drawing room. Talking about—well, you, for one thing, Mr. Silver, and from what I heard them saying, they—"

"I really think it's best if Mr. Silver hears this direct from the horse's mouth." Annie rose from the sofa and crossed to her former acolyte with a soft brushing of skirts and a speed that wouldn't have looked amiss on a warrior-caste Huldu. She raised one hand with fingers splayed. "I'm sure you won't mind, Jerry."

"Oh, again, mistress? Well, it's just, I don't—"

He fell abruptly silent as the witch's fingers made some unfeasibly flexible motion in the air in front of his face and ended with a thumb printed firmly onto his forehead. He fell back slack in the armchair, eyes glazed but still open, mouth slightly agape. Nimble Shanks Annie muttered something under her breath, made a couple more passes with her hand. The light from the lamps flickered, vibrated for a moment, and then dimmed to nothing. A cool, gray gloom soaked into the lounge, in which the tiny alcohol flame from the burner seemed suddenly piercingly bright. Annie tightened her fingers into a loose fist, made a tugging motion back toward her breast.

. . . and any further changes to our arrangement, said Bainbridge recognizably into the gloom. Duncan jerked a glance at Ewart, saw his mouth making shapes for the words. His throat lumped and contorted in eerie fashion, as if it contained an unfeasibly large parasitic worm.

Another voice, less urbane. *That will be for Colonel Hardy to decide.*

Ah, no, in fact, it won't. This—all of this—will be for me *to decide, Captain. And I'm not necessarily inclined to the colonel's view that this is what has to happen.*

For all that Ewart's mouth moved, the voices barely seemed to issue from it. Instead, they fluttered and swooped about in the dimmed room like echoes, like spooked birds seeking an exit.

We gave you Ada Endershall! We told you where she was!

Only, I think, because you knew they'd engaged a competent woodsman. You were scared that with Silver involved, things were sliding out of your control.

We had Silver handled.

Really? Is that why you let him steal back the child and bring her almost all the way home?

We stopped him when it counted.

Yes, so I hear. However—

I don't care what you've heard, Bainbridge. Silver is off the board. You don't have to worry about him anymore. He's dead.

Quiet fell on the last word. Then stretched. For a moment Duncan thought the hearing—séance, eidetic recall, whatever you wanted to call it—was over. But when he looked at Ewart, the ex-acolyte was still slumped in the armchair, head tilted back, mouth open, like a man fallen asleep midjourney in a train carriage seat. Duncan almost expected to hear him start snoring . . .

Yes, well. Even through the filter of the hearing, the delight in Bainbridge's tone was evident. *There again, I'm afraid you are quite wrong, Captain. Duncan Silver is very much alive. And, unless I'm much mistaken, about to cause you even more trouble than before.*

Another silence, shorter this time.

What are you talking about? Oakley snapped.

I'm talking about the man you very sloppily failed to shoot dead a few nights ago. Duncan Silver survived your attempt to kill him. In fact, yesterday afternoon, he was sitting exactly where you are now, telling me all about it. He's understandably aggrieved. I'd advise Colonel Hardy to start locking his windows at night if I were you.

Raw silence.

Oh, and Silver will come after the child again, believe me. Where is she, by the way?

Somewhere safe.

Fine, don't tell me. I can very likely scry the details myself. But! Voice suddenly raised, as if the captain had leapt to his feet or offered some other threat. *I won't need to.*

What do you mean?

I mean that while it might please me to rub Sir Michael's disdainful noble nose in his own ignominious failures, helping Silver rescue the mother and child and spirit them away somewhere does not in fact serve my interests any more than yours. I propose an alternative arrangement.

Which is what? Suspiciously.

Which is for Colonel Hardy's ears, not yours. Tell him he's invited here Friday night for dinner, say about nine. He can bring you, too, if he likes. In the meantime, I'm bringing someone he'll want to meet, someone with what you military types would call vital strategic intelligence. *I'll happily share it with the Forestry Commission, for a consideration.*

Still trying for a seat at the table, are we, Bainbridge? Brusque contempt in Oakley's tone.

A small, icy silence welled up in the wake of the words. Nothing but Ewart's breathing to be heard. Then Bainbridge again, in chilly, measured tones.

Captain, I don't expect someone of your inferior rank and limited outlook to understand this, but what I am trying to do here is build *the table that we will* all *need to sit at, if we are to survive these times. That includes your much-vaunted new and clueless Forestry Commission; it includes superannuated stuffed shirts like Sir Michael Endershall, sadly; and it will need to include men like me, because we are the only ones who have a hope in hell of understanding this new age and bending it to our will. Sharper minds than yours, Captain, have already grasped this, in Whitehall, in Oxford and Cambridge, and in other places I have no intention of even mentioning to an underling such as yourself. I have conversed with these men, and the necessary furniture is already being moved into place. My seat at the table, as you put it, is already assured. Now. You will convey this, all this, to Colonel Hardy, and I suggest you recommend to him that he bring a less insolent tone than yours to dinner this Friday night.*

This time, the quiet that fell was electric. Even through the eavesdrop spell, you could hear it crackle between the two men.

Is that clear enough for you, Captain?

Oakley cleared his throat, awkward. *And Silver?*

You let me worry about Silver. He may yet prove an asset, if I can keep him onside. There is more to Duncan Silver than meets the eye, and I, for one, believe we . . .

Voice fading out, like a radio program turned rapidly down. Ewart sat, flop mouthed, glassy eyed, and motionless in the chair, like some particularly gormless stuffed ape exhibit in a museum. A thin line of drool shone down his chin like snail track. Duncan looked at the witches. Nimble Shanks Annie shrugged.

"That's all there is. Apparently, someone else came down the corridor and Jerry was forced to beat a hasty retreat. Lucky he wasn't caught, to be honest."

"What do you think, Duncan?" Sal, still stirring the cheese pot.

"I think I'm going to feed Bainbridge his own fucking entrails."

"Yes, darling, understandable. But that's not really what I meant. I mean—does this make any kind of sense to you?"

Duncan brooded.

"It makes sense that Hardy was watching the mother all along," he said finally. "I got back from meeting her Tuesday afternoon, and he'd already dropped his card off with Niamh at Skoldergate. Irene Rush called me on the Monday. Most likely someone followed her to the call box, then rang the operator to check the number after she'd gone. I get assessed as a threat, Hardy makes his pitch to get me down to London and out of the way. What's not clear to me is why they'd share their information with that magicking cunt Bainbridge." He paused. "No offense."

The two witches looked at each other.

"Yes, I think if anyone could lay claim to the title *magicking cunt,* it would be us," said Sal dryly. "Though I'll admit Bainbridge does have some raw talent. It wouldn't do to underestimate him, Duncan. One or two of the sisters have made that mistake in the past."

She looked pointedly at her colleague.

"All right, all right." Nimble Shanks Annie, grumbling crossly as she dunked a fresh piece of ham into the cheese. "So I let him steal Jerry when I wasn't looking. It's not like we took those phallus-obsessed fuckers seriously back then."

Wolfbane Sal muttered something under her breath. Duncan cleared his throat into the silence it left.

"Well, he seems to have found his way back to the fold." He nodded at Ewart, still slumped apparently entranced in the armchair. "Nice of him to have an attack of conscience like that."

This time Sal cackled, very witchlike, then put fingers over her mouth and stopped. "Sorry. But you say the cutest things, Duncan."

He looked at her, uncomprehending.

"He didn't have an attack of conscience," Annie said indistinctly through her mouthful of ham and cheese. "He had an attack of patent Wolfbane Sally Bethune loyalty invocation. Nice binding spell, too, Sal, very subtly done."

Flash recall of Ewart and the witch at the top of the stairs. Sal and her dabbing, maternal fingers, her muttered hiss-click litany of half-sounded syllables under her breath.

Annie would never forgive me if I let a former apprentice of hers walk out of here without so much as a care spell. Look, I'll just . . . There! All done!

Duncan stared at Ewart's slumped form again. "You . . . you *bound* him for this?"

The witch made a modest face. "Wasn't that hard, honestly. There's a big part of Jerry that isn't at all sure he made the right choice when he quit Annie here for the Orb. Easy to work with that. I just had to tie it specifically to you and the current situation."

"In some ways," said Annie, wiping her mouth daintily with a crumpled napkin from the table, "Jerry wasn't such a great loss to the coven. Very . . . bendable."

Duncan eyed her with distaste. "So you just bend him and use him and then throw him away?"

Annie raised an eyebrow. "Says the man who hit him in the face for walking too close behind you in the street."

"That wasn't—"

"Anyway." Shooting a lascivious look across at her fellow witch that put a quiver in the pit of Duncan's stomach. "Not like young Jerry didn't get his reward from us both earlier this afternoon, am I right, Sal?"

Wolfbane Sal grinned. "He certainly seemed to be enjoying himself."

"Do you think we worked him too hard, though?"

"Well, I didn't hear him complain at any point." Sal pretended to consider. "Though I suppose his voice *was* a bit muffled now and then, so—"

"Aye—look." Duncan made a fending-off gesture. "Ladies. Could we talk about your conquests some other time? Is there—"

"Are we embarrassing you, Duncan?" Nimble Shanks Annie spiked a fresh piece of meat and lowered it into the cauldron, turned it this way and that in the bubbling cheese. "You really only have yourself to blame, you know."

"And how's that?"

The witch pulled out her piece of meat, offered it to Wolfbane Sal who leaned in and tugged it off the skewer with her bared teeth, winked sidelong at Duncan as she did it. The room felt stuffy and heated, ripe with torrid implication.

"Jerry came to see us last night with this news," said Annie. "Very eager, he was. We asked him to come back bright and early this morning so you could meet him, and, well, we've had him here all day twiddling his thumbs waiting for you. We had to do *something* to keep him entertained. And ourselves, come to that."

"Good for you," said Duncan curtly. "I got here as soon as I could. Now—this meeting tomorrow. Is there any way we can get Jerry here to eavesdrop again? Listen in on it the same way?"

"The same way?" The witches exchanged another glance, no longer lewd. As if someone had opened a window, let in sudden cold air. Sal shook her head. "There's no way the Order is going to let him hover in a corridor outside a meeting that important. Especially after he's been unreachable for most of today. He'd just get caught. We need something else."

"Perspicacious water?" Annie offered.

Sal pursed her lips. "Could be made to work. But not at much distance."

"Do you have some?"

"No, not bottled up and ready to go. Ziroonderel downstairs might."

Annie snorted. "That old fraud? 'Derel's selling to credulous new agers, not actual witches. There's less magic in that place than there is up a black cat's arse."

"You're being unkind. She's still—"

"What's perspicacious water?"

Both women looked at him. Then at each other. Sal sighed.

"It's water that . . . Look, it's complicated. You know how water refracts light?"

Duncan groped in dim memories of his physical science classes at Cadogan's. Nodded, unsure.

"Right, well there are ways to make it not only refract, but, uhm—*resonate,* if you like, communicate with . . . other bodies of water the same. You could say they get, uh . . . tangled up. There are angles we're not privy to here in the physical world, bonds we cannot see or even calculate well, but they work to connect . . . uhm . . ."

"It can carry vibrations, too," said Annie helpfully. "So speech, most noises if they're loud enough."

"We ask Jerry to place a carafe of prepared perspicacious water in the room before the meeting. And we give you the rest in a Kilner jar about this big."

"But you'll have to be within resonance range."

"Which, for a volume that small, is about . . ." Sal raising eyes to the ceiling as she muttered something—invocation, calculation, maybe both—under her breath. "Sixty-five feet."

Duncan thought about the drawing room he'd talked with Bainbridge in, the bay window, the garden outside. The room couldn't be more than about fifteen feet across, wall to window. And beyond the glass, the lawn stretched a dozen yards at most before the bushes and trees began along its edge. He could huddle in the brush line unseen easily enough, for as long as the meeting with Hardy took. Under cover of night, especially in weather as wet and murk-ridden as they seemed destined to suffer, the chances of anyone from the house stumbling on him were pretty low.

"I can manage that," he said.

Wolfbane Sal beamed like a schoolmarm at a favored pupil.

"Can he, though?" asked Annie sharply. "Bainbridge knows him already. He'll be attuned. And by the sound of it, he's already picked up on resonances from this Fae heart's blood trick Duncan here somehow survived. *There is more to Duncan Silver than meets the eye.* Well, quite. Even if Bainbridge doesn't know exactly what it is, what caused it, it's obviously made an impression. He may not spot the tangled water—especially if we tincture it with some basil or lady's mantle—but even at sixty feet, he might be able to sense that Duncan is around."

"Duncan is Tyche-warded; I gave him the full deck a week ago—luck in stealth, evasion, chance encounter, prowess. That ought to be enough."

Nimble Shanks Annie grunted, unconvinced. But she didn't push the point.

Duncan nodded at Ewart, who had begun to snore lightly. "Does he have to report back in at the house today?"

"Not necessarily," Annie said. "He can always tell them he went down with a head cold or something, didn't come in because he was worried it was the flu."

"Aye, that's a decent enough excuse."

"Sal here can even give him a case of the sniffles to fit. Right, Sal?"

Wolfbane Sally picked at her teeth with one witchy fingernail. "Can do, yeah. Elf bolt ague and drip ought to be about right; I can do that spell in my sleep." She saw the look he gave her. "Not *actual* elf shot, Duncan, it's just what they call it in the trade. Easy enough to cook up. He can go home with it tonight."

"He'll need to take this perspicacious water with him, too," Duncan said somberly. "We can't risk him coming back here tomorrow, same day as he plants it. Can you get it made in time?"

"If we can't just get it from downstairs, yes, no problem." Sal gestured toward a door on the other side of the room, a sanctum Duncan had never seen inside. "I've got all the makings in there. Annie, you'll stay and help?"

"Wouldn't miss it for the world, dear." Annie was still watching Duncan with a gleam in her eye that he didn't much like. "This is starting to look like a legend in the making."

THIRTY-FOUR

THE STORM HUNG GRUMBLING OVER ERLSLEY ALL AFTERNOON. It spiked the gray horizon with wires of white fire, lashed the city unmercifully with rain, dimmed down the light to a premature evening gloom. The witches busied themselves preparing their perspicacious water—Ziroonderel, it seemed, had none in stock downstairs—while Duncan went out to buy a map and make a couple of phone calls that couldn't be overheard. It earned him a freshly drenched hat and coat, but by then he was beyond caring. On the Somme, he'd not infrequently been wetter than this for days at a time, and basted in cold mud into the bargain. You got used to it.

You got used to anything in time.

First call—the Doorbell Club. They found Arthur for him, brought him to the phone.

"Trouble?" the sharpshooter asked warily.

"Not exactly. But I could do with the use of Mikey Collier and that ambulance again. It's for tomorrow night. Local stuff only. Think we can swing it?"

"Sure. I can ask Cobb. Doubt his brother's using it at the moment. Bloody thing's more like a family heirloom than a means of transport, spends all its time parked up under tarpaulin in that shed of theirs. Neither of them really likes to drive."

"And Collier? He likely to have any other commitments?"

Arthur snorted. "Any chance to get behind a wheel, Mikey Collier is in. He'll need paying, of course. So will the Cobbs. You want me to speak to Billy?"

"If you see him. But I'll try him myself, too."

"Right . . ." An odd hesitancy on the line. Duncan felt a premonitory chill down the back of his neck.

"Is there a problem, Arthur?"

Awkward pause.

"Hope not," the sharpshooter said. "But your girl's been coughing pretty hard. Belle wants to call the house doctor. She's worried about her girls catching something."

Duncan weighed his options. They weren't many.

"Fair enough," he said finally. "But Niamh already saw a doctor in the summer. I don't think it's anything infectious."

"I'll tell them that."

Duncan rang off, dialed Crammond's home number. A chirpy female voice answered, turned abruptly frosty when he identified himself.

"He's gone out, Duncan. You know how it is. And I don't think you should be calling here like this."

"Believe me, May, I wish I had another choice. Can you tell him I need a little help? If he calls round tomorrow morning, I'll hash it out with him."

"You mean to that . . . club?" Ice on the line. "I don't like him spending time there, Duncan."

"I won't keep him long."

Silence, more ice. Duncan waited for a cable to snap somewhere under the weight.

"Well, then, I'll tell him," she said stiffly. He heard her gather breath for her parting shot. "But I'm going to tell him what I think, too."

"Tell him whatever you want, May. Just give him the message."

In the faint hiss on the line, he could feel that she still wasn't done. He didn't want to antagonize her, for Crammond's sake and his own. He waited.

Rain drummed audibly off the roof of the call box. He turned his head to watch it stitch and trickle down the fogged glass panels.

"You're ill luck, Duncan," she spat out at last. "You know that? Ill luck and a crow's shadow at noon, my mother used to say. I see it in you, I feel it like creeping cold on my nape. There's something black and twisted following you, Duncan, and I don't want Billy anywhere near you when it catches you up."

She slammed down the phone.

He rolled his eyes. Tapped for the operator, gave her the region and number for his final call, the out-of-town option, the long shot.

"Capstone Park House," said a mannered male voice.

"This is Duncan Silver."

Slight shift in tone, perhaps a faint warmth, though nothing you could warm your hands at. "And how may we help you, Mr. Silver?"

"It's complicated. Would you please inform the viscount that I'd like to speak with him at his earliest convenience?"

ACCORDING TO THE ORDNANCE SURVEY of east Erlsley, Adept House backed onto woodland that sprawled the best part of a mile north before it ended beside a canal. Eastward, it ran sparse between factory sites that had mostly been abandoned on general principles since the Unbinding, but which, at least to Duncan's knowledge, were relatively untroubled by Huldu incursion. The deep Forest didn't begin for another five or six miles to the east.

"I can get through on this side," he said, pointing at the eastern approach and the lack of contour lines. "It's flat ground; it's why they built there. Going to be a lot more overgrown now than it shows here, but it's still better. North is going to be too steep, up from the canal and then down again. Going to be slipping and sliding on my arse the whole time if I try it in this weather."

"Our arses," Nimble Shanks Annie corrected him. "I'll be coming with you."

"You will not. This is likely to be dangerous."

"Oh, dangerous, is it? You don't say! Pan's aching balls, Sal, these woodsmen really are something, aren't they?"

She looked at Wolfbane Sal, who shrugged with uncharacteristic awkwardness. No help there. Annie rolled her eyes, turned on Duncan again.

"Listen, sonny, you think *going to the Forest* is something you people invented in the last five years? People like me have been *going to the Forest* for spells and woodcraft, for witchery and ancient wisdom, for bloody fucking *centuries* before you were even born! I was facing down the Fae over woodland spell songs while you were still in short trousers."

Sal snorted. "Lot less facing down, more top-to-tailing, as I recall."

"You shut up."

"What, you're going to pretend—"

"It doesn't make any difference, ladies!" Duncan waited until he was sure he had their attention. "I'm going alone. That's the end of it."

Annie set her jaw. "Remind me again whose perspicacious water this is?"

"That's not the point!"

"That is entirely the point. You think you'll just pick up that jar and shake it and that's all there is to it? Scrying through elemental tangle isn't something you learn overnight. You are going to need guidance, young man, whether you like it or not."

"She's right, Duncan."

"I notice you're not volunteering," he retorted.

Sal smiled and popped a last remaining cube of ham from the cooling fondue into her mouth, chewed it down with gusto. "Mhmm, well. Scrambling around in the wet and dark really isn't my forte, darling. I'd just slow you down. Annie here is quick and . . . nimble. Famed for it, in fact."

"Legs on me like you wouldn't believe," Annie agreed, grinning. "Like a girl half my age. Have a look if you want."

Duncan grunted, defeated, and went back to the map, while Jeremy Ewart watched from the sidelines with fairly obvious envy and chagrin.

THEY SENT EWART HOME NOT long after. He took his share of the tangled water in a tightly sealed Kilner jar about the volume of a battlefield canteen, strapped into a leather carrying satchel he said he could bring into the house the next day with no problem.

"You don't have to get it all into the carafe," Annie told him. "It can take dilution up to about a third. But anything more than that, and we'll struggle to get a connection. Just watch your back, Jerry. Don't get caught. If you do, it's all for nothing."

"They won't catch me, Mistress Spence." Ewart blew his nose into a tattered handkerchief with the Order's mark on it. He was already in the grip of Sal's elf bolt ague and drip. "You can depend on me in all things."

He walked out of the apartment with a shiny cannon fodder look on his face that gave Duncan more of a wrench than he'd want to admit. It was an expression he'd seen too often on young faces in the trenches in the early days. He listened to Sal wish him well in the hallway, watched Nimble Shanks Annie sit on the sofa and pick absently at the long stringy leavings of melted cheese from the fondue cauldron.

"It doesn't bother you?" he asked. "Sending him out into the firing line like this?"

The thin witch shrugged. "We're all in the firing line on this one. Thought you'd be used to the idea, a man like you. Did you worry so much about the men you led into machine gun fire on the Somme?"

Duncan said nothing.

"Besides which." Licking cheese grease from her fingertips. "Little fucker ran out on me for his phallus-obsessed masters. I confess I'm feeling a limited sense of responsibility for how his choices have worked out. I'm not his mother, you know."

"Evidently not."

"It's what a lot of them are looking for, of course. Acolytes, apprentices, herb runners—for a lot of them, it's just a second shot at the womb. But then, of course, boys will be boys, and boys must tear free of Mother's apron strings in order to become men, so it's a bumpy ride at the best of times."

"You could stick to female acolytes."

"Yes, some of the sisters do that." The witch sniffed. "Girls are great to train, it's true. I just don't really like fucking them as much."

Wolfbane Sal swept back into the room, retying her gown under her ample chest, grinning toothily. "Well, guess who was *very* uncomfortable leaving Duncan here alone with us both."

They both looked at him intently, like a couple of crows eyeing up a tasty piece of carrion.

"You're sure Jerry's going to hold up?" he asked deflectively.

"I think he's had his faith in the Order of Prick and Pussy sufficiently shaken, yes," Annie said with relish. "Then again, wouldn't be the first time he's reneged on an allegiance to us, would it?"

"Oh, stop your gnawing, both of you. He's going to be fine."

"Aye, Sal, so you say. But what if he starts acting suspicious, or leaves that water somewhere it gets found? Bainbridge gave me the impression he can sense—"

"Don't you worry about Bainbridge." Sal flopped onto the sofa beside her colleague. "He's your typical belle epoque upstart—pushy bourgeois aspiration laced with delusions of aristocrat grandeur. He's too self-satisfied by half to be much good at magic. Or, more important, to believe he could ever be penetrated." Seeing the other witch's smirk. "Oh stop it, what are you, twelve?"

"Annie." Duncan, hurriedly quelling his own smirk. "Do you have weapons you can carry?"

"Weapons? Well, there's this." Annie split her long lace skirts demurely, sat forward, and spread her legs akimbo. Strapped to the top of her right thigh, a six inch serpentine-edged iron blade topped with ornate ivory grip molded for the fingers that would hold it. "Will that do?"

"In a clinch, it would." She'd been right about her legs, he saw. "If we get into a serious fight, or a chase, not so much. I was thinking more of a gun."

"Oh, I don't like guns, Duncan."

"No one likes guns," he said irritably. "But they clear a path when you need one in a hurry. Maybe Sal's right and Bainbridge is an arrogant prick with shite magic and he won't realize we're there. But if he does spot us, I want to be able to punch holes in whoever he sends out to get us."

Nimble Shanks Annie put her legs away, smoothed her skirts over again. She gave him a secret smile. "Oh, I think you like guns a lot more than you let on, Duncan. I think you like the damage they do. I'd watch that if I were you."

"Annie." An oblique warning note in Wolfbane Sal's voice.

The thin witch sighed. "All right, all right, yes. The hero of the hour come round, he must carry thunderbolts of course. Doesn't mean *I* have to. I really thought you were too old for this nonsense, Sal. I thought we both were."

"He ate the heart," said Sal quietly. "And is still standing."

Nimble Shanks Annie pulled a face. "You know as well as I do that could mean any number of things."

"Oh, come *on*!"

An elaborately innocent look. "Come on what?"

"You're digging your heels in, Annie, and you know it. A live Huldu heart, fed on in the moment of freeing it from the chest. Look at every rooted legend we've got. Look at the lore. You know what it says."

Duncan, with an effort, stopped himself switching back and forth on the exchange like a cat watching lawn tennis.

"What does it say?" he asked.

"It says you should be dead," said Nimble Shanks Annie shortly.

Sal tutted. "It says you are probably from a mixed bloodline. There are only a handful of figures in legend who were apparently able to do what you did and survive. Arthur Pendragon is the most celebrated, but there are a few others—Weylund, Beowulf, Havelok the Dane. In every case, there's reason to suppose they were Faerie kin. The legends hint at it, or sometimes just claim it outright."

"See, we're not the only ones who fuck Faeries, Duncan." Annie's eyes glittered with sardonic humor. "It's just not as fashionable as it used to be, that's all. Fallen out of favor. But never fear—the weird sisters keep the flame of tradition alive."

Duncan frowned. "Bainbridge said something about this. He said Mimi Rush—the child I went to the Forest to get last week—he said she was a direct descendant of a Fae noblewoman, and that's why they took her."

The witches exchanged a thoughtful glance.

"He's dug deeper than I'd have thought, then," said Annie. "Not bad for a—what was it, Sal?—a belle epoque upstart. Maybe we've underestimated Bainbridge after all."

"He's guessing, Annie. Stabbing in the dark."

"Could it be," Duncan, slowly, working the concept through, "that *all* the children they take have Fae blood to some extent? I mean, they're long-lived, right? Eternal, some of them. Thousand years is nothing, gone in an instant. They still blame us for the trees our ancestors cut down and burned in the Neolithic. Are they just trying to claim back something they think we took from them?"

"Does it matter?" asked Annie.

"Well . . ."

"She's right, Duncan. Would that make you feel better about your years in the Forest, about what they did to you? They held you as a thrall, after all."

He felt the old rage simmering. Held it down. "It doesn't change how I feel, no. But it's like the war. If there was some way to *understand* the whole mess, to make it make sense . . ."

He petered out. Gestured helplessly.

"Might make it easier to deal with," he said.

The two witches looked at him. Nimble Shanks Annie made a soft shape with her mouth, the awwwing of a mother to a flustered baby. Wolfbane Sal shot her a warning glare and cleared her throat.

"If you're looking to me for an opinion," she said slowly. "I'd say Bainbridge likely has something there. But it's nothing you could build a house on. Did the Huldu steal babies because they were of Fae blood? Probably. Some of the time. It's pretty clear we have interbred with them, time and again—all the legends talk about it, and there's sisterhood lore from last century, too. Recent cases, unreported, where they called a wise woman to help sort out the mess. The odd comely milkmaid goes missing, comes back pregnant, and when the little bundle's delivered, it has eyes of ink or fangs. Although, from what I know, I think it's probably not that easy to conceive across the species line."

"Not for want of trying, eh?" Annie, grinning.

Sal rolled her eyes. "So when it comes to reclaiming what they saw as their bloodline descendants, maybe centuries down the line, yes—it makes some sense. But over time? I think it's just become custom, something they do out of habit, because they always have—because they *can.* In the end, what might have started in ritual and purpose ends up just another whim, an urge to be satisfied."

"You're as well not looking for too much sense from the Fae," Annie muttered. "It's not exactly their stock in trade. Magic seals them off from the need to be rational, the need to *behave,* and what's left is just a whole lot of dark abandon."

"*Dark abandon,*" mimicked Sal, evidently amused. "First time I've ever heard you say it like that."

"Nothing wrong with a bit of dark abandon now and then." Annie flashed the grin again. "Within reason, as long as you can get away safely afterward. But creatures who *live* by it?"

She shook her head, oddly sober again. The grin decayed into a kind of wince.

"You can get hurt," she said.

"It's what that prick-obsessed idiot Bainbridge doesn't get," Sal said, "with all his *the will is divine and all of the law* bollocks. Humans aren't built for that manner of abandon. They shrivel in the force of it, or they rise up as tyrants. I tell you, Duncan, seriously—you open the door fully to what the Fae and the Forest represent, it'll make what you went through over in France look like a picnic on Blackpool beach."

THIRTY-FIVE

DUNCAN LEFT SAL'S PLACE AROUND SIX. NIMBLE SHANKS ANNIE said goodbye from the sofa with a wolfish grin, Sal saw him to the door and pecked him on the cheek for farewell.

"What do I owe you for all this?" It suddenly occurred to him to ask.

"Oh, more than you can possibly ever repay." She saw the look on his face. "I'm *joking,* Duncan. We're witches, not the hosts of hell. I'll talk to Annie, work something out. You can settle up once all this is done."

"You know I'm good for it, Sal."

"Oh yes. Now go on with you. Stay out of the rain. See you tomorrow evening. Bye." She closed the door with what felt like unseemly haste.

Duncan stood listening for a stupid moment, ear tilted to the panels of the door. Heard nothing at all. If the two witches had any immediate gossip about him, they were clearly sharing it at volumes too low for eavesdropping to work.

Presently, the black cat came soft-footed up the stairs, took station just beside his left foot, and stared up at him curiously. Duncan shook his head at his own idiocy, prodded the cat out of the way with the toe of his boot, headed down the stairs, then out into the rain. He got lucky with the trams, was back at the Doorbell Club before seven. He fended off a pointed comment from the doorman that Miss Belle D'Or would like to speak with him *urgently,* went straight up to the third floor instead. He found Arthur in the dim, red-flock quiet of the corridor outside the door to Niamh's room, straddling an obvious boudoir chair in reverse. A couple of Belle's girls floated about him like attendant nymphs with some grim, monster-headed demigod.

"Doctor's in with her now," the sharpshooter murmured. "Said he wouldn't be long."

"I guess we'll wait, then."

The doctor was as good as his word. Duncan had barely managed to peel off his soaking coat and hand it off to one of the girls, who said she'd hang it for him—he warned her, as mildly as he could, not to go into the pockets where the two Webleys were still pulling the lining out of shape—when the door of 307 opened and a small, neat man, impeccably dressed and clean shaven but for a small, neat mustache, stepped out. His expression was grave.

"You are the . . . husband?" he asked Duncan in a surprisingly deep voice. His tone was dubious on the last word.

Duncan nodded. It was easier than explaining. "Aye, that's me."

"Then I am very sorry for you, sir. It's my opinion that your wife has an uncommon species of cancer in her lungs, and there is very little to be done about it. The recent, ehm, privations I understand her to have gone through will have done nothing to improve the situation, and may have triggered these worsening bouts of coughing. But the condition itself is not new. It is many months advanced."

It was nothing Duncan hadn't been expecting deep down inside, but still, he felt himself go cold as the disease was named. As if he stood in an elevator whose cables had been abruptly cut and it dropped out from under his feet.

"She gave up smoking months ago," he said numbly.

"Yes, so she tells me. Of course, it's by no means clear that there is any link between the habit of smoking and this disease. You shouldn't believe every alarmist pamphlet you read, hmm? But even allowing such a link, perhaps owing to her weaker feminine constitution, I'm afraid ceasing to smoke once the cancer is extant would not be of much help."

"There must be something you can do." Duncan, bargaining desperately.

The doctor shrugged. "There are some experimental treatments with radium, and with X-rays of course. But success rates are low. The techniques are in their infancy, and the treatments often cause a great deal of suffering for what is, in my professional opinion, very little reward."

"You're saying she's going to die?"

"I am sorry. But I would be remiss if I gave you unfair hope of some miraculous cure, some arcane ritual with radiating crystals or other such nonsense of this new age. I deal in medicine, not magic and superstition, and even in these times, it is to medicine that we must cleave."

"How long?" Duncan asked flatly.

"A year, maybe two. Rapidly worsening health within eight to ten months. More than that, I'm afraid I cannot usefully predict. Beyond those eight to ten months, she is in God's hands."

"I thought we were cleaving to medicine, not superstition."

The doctor looked at him reproachfully. Pursed his lips.

"If you'll excuse me, sir," he said in measured tones, "I have done what I can. I must see the mistress of the house now. It is she who is paying."

SHE WAS SITTING IN AN easy chair in the corner, facing the door when he let himself into the room. Soft yellow light; she'd lit the lamps. She still wore the nightgown Belle's girls had loaned her, had combed her ink-black hair out long over the white cotton, let it lie past her shoulders onto her breast. She watched him out of her one good eye as he closed the door, locked it, and turned to face her.

"So now you know," she said brightly. "All that sucking woodsman cock for nothing."

"Don't say that!" Biting back the rage as soon as it flared. He stood, desolate, marooned in the middle of the room. "Why didn't you tell me before?"

She looked steadily at him. "What difference would it have made, Duncan?"

"I—" He shook his head.

"Sure, you already knew anyway. I've seen the way you look at me when you think I won't notice. How gentle you are with me." She got up out of the chair and went to him. Put both hands on his arm, leaned into him. "I'm sorry about that woodsman's cock line, that was a bitchy thing to say. It's just . . . the way I feel, I want to smash something, Duncan. Upset everyone, break things, scream. I want to be fucked. I want—"

She put her wide open mouth into his upper arm, below the shoulder, bit into the damp cloth of his shirt and the muscle beneath. She made a muffled, high-pitched wailing sound into his flesh, put a chill on the nape of his neck and tears in his eyes.

He held her while she did it, as best he could.

Finally, breathing heavily, she lifted her face to him.

"I want you to fuck me, Duncan," she said. "Please. Fuck me, make me come. Make all this go away."

He thought at first he wouldn't be able to—there was a weight like a sandbag in his belly, an aching in his throat. But some vestige of the sultry atmosphere at Sal's place, the interplay of carnivorous looks and lewd allusion, seemed to have found its way home in his pocket. He looked down at the shape of her breasts under the nightgown cotton, felt the way she pressed one thigh between his legs, and abruptly he was hardening. She felt it and laughed, eagerly, reached down to rub her open palm across the swelling, fumbled at his fly. He was rock hard now, straining at the cloth. She worked the buttons, got her fingers inside, then her whole hand. She cupped the top of his prick with her palm.

He grunted, shuddered, took the nightgown in both hands. Pulled down hard, popped the fasteners down the front, and tugged the fabric down her shoulders, exposed the tops of her breasts, pale white, stuffed together in the clasp of the paler white cotton. The sight spiked through him, electric. He tugged again, harder, tore the thin cotton somewhere, he heard it, felt it give. She laughed again, gabbling *yes, Duncan, yes, yes,* had by now unfastened his belt and trousers, was working his prick slowly in her fist. One more yank on the nightgown and it dropped, puddled around her feet. He lowered his face, pressed it between her breasts. She made a soft sound, let go his prick, clasped both hands on his head. He drove her back to the edge of the bed and she let herself fold at the knees as she hit it, fall backward loose across the coverlet. Her legs stirred languidly apart. He dropped to his knees, buried his face between her thighs, breathed her in.

LATER, WHEN THEY WERE BOTH fully spent, when soft mouthings and rough handling alike failed to rouse either one of them to any further passion, and Niamh's breathing finally deepened toward sleep, he eased himself carefully out of the tangle of their limbs under the covers. It was close to midnight by the Mappin & Webb. The tiny radio-static crackle of the breath in her lungs caught at the lower edges of his hearing as he kissed her throat. He went around gathering up his clothes from where they'd been flung, dressed to shirtsleeves and stockinged feet, then let himself quietly out of the room, boots in hand. The crackle of her lungs went with him, tangled in his ears, caught in the crimp of his mouth at one corner, the light gritting of his teeth behind the grimace . . .

The boudoir chair was still in the corridor outside, pushed tidily to one wall. He sat on it to put the boots on. Midway through the process, the door of the next chamber cracked open and one of Arthur's nymphs from earlier peered out with a roll-up in her mouth. She grinned when she saw him.

"Ooh, you're a noisy one, Mr. Campbell," she giggled, and breathed copious cannabis smoke out into the hallway.

"Arthur still about?" he asked her.

The girl drew on her roll-up, gestured downward at the floor with it.

"Try the bar," she said in a voice high and squeaky from holding the smoke in, then plumed it out at him and spoke normally again. "He's usually there."

But he wasn't.

Belle D'Or was. Seated in her usual spot at the bar, black flapper dress half open down the back, jade cigarette holder loaded and smoldering, gin cocktail at her fingertips. Traffic was brisk around her, the usual coming and going of the girls with clients in tow, a couple of sporadically noisy groups drinking and fumbling at each other in the booths. Belle lifted an imperious hand at him as he came in, didn't quite snap her fingers, but might as well have. He mustered some calm. Pushed through the distracted clientele and seated himself on the barstool next to hers.

"You wanted to talk to me?"

She looked narrowly at him a moment. Nodded at the barman, then sideways at Duncan. The barman turned and took down a bottle. The Chivas Regal. He poured a generous measure and set it in front of Duncan on the bar.

"On the house," said Belle in her smoky voice. "I am very sorry about your girl."

He raised the glass to her, knocked back the whisky in one chunk. "Appreciate it."

"However, I'm afraid that—"

"Three days," he said.

"I'm sorry?"

"Three days and we're gone. Me, the girl, my other friend, too. I need tonight, tomorrow night, to organize it, maybe Saturday night as well, if things don't go as planned." Duncan forced himself to stop gabbling, because even to his own ears, it sounded altogether too much like pleading. He spaced his words. "Sunday evening at worst, we're out of your hair for good. You have my word."

The steady, narrow gaze on him again. "You're not IRA, are you?"

"No."

"Billy did promise me you weren't. But I get the impression he'd have no problem lying to protect you. You seem to mean a lot to him. And I know he's a Catholic himself."

"So are a lot of people. It's not a crime, last time I checked."

Coming back from the Forest at eleven years old, Duncan had missed Christianity as a feature of his upbringing, and the dose he was given at Cadogan's never really did stick. Even now, as an adult, he found the rituals and schisms and paraphernalia of the faith weirdly arid and bookish and beside the point.

"Not a crime, no." Belle sipped at her cigarette holder, blew thin smoke along the bar. "But it is a crime to give comfort to Irish Nationalists, and I don't want to find out that's what I've been doing."

"That's not what you've been doing. You have my word."

"Please understand, I have nothing against the Irish themselves. And I think the reprisals policy over there has been a national disgrace. But it's awkward enough to keep the Doorbell safely open as it is, without giving the authorities political ammunition into the bargain."

"You have my word," Duncan repeated.

There was a slight pause, almost as if she was writing it down. "Well, then," she said brightly. "Another drink?"

He shook his head. "I was really looking for Arthur."

"Arthur has gone out. On an errand, he says." She shrugged. "Well, of course, he wouldn't have much other reason to go out at this time of night, not with what I allow him on tap here."

Duncan said nothing. She smiled sourly.

"It's not an errand for me, I might add, which rather leads me to suspect he's doing something for you, Mr. Campbell. And he's not a man who takes on friendship or obligation lightly." Belle smoked meditatively for a moment or two. She gestured elegantly with the cigarette holder. "So—Billy Crammond, and now Arthur. You seem to have something of a glamour about you. Something that hard men will follow without question." She grinned down into her drink. "Hard women, too, even if I do say so myself."

Duncan shifted on the barstool. "I think I'd better go and check on Niamh again."

"Really? From what the girls tell me, my impression was that you've checked her pretty thoroughly tonight as it is."

He got up to go. She put a hand on his arm.

"I'm sorry, that was overly forward of me. Rude, even. It's just the snow talking. Stay and have another drink with me, Mr. Campbell. I don't bite. Not unless invited to, anyway. I won't try to make you do anything you don't want to. Arthur will doubtless come back, but in the meantime, a little conversation can't hurt, can it?"

He looked into the cocaine-blasted eyes, saw an odd need there that felt too much like a reflection for comfort. He settled back to the stool, nodded at the barman, and watched the Chivas catch the light as it poured, like a ribbon of water transmuting into molten gold by some alchemy long suppressed and now let loose upon the world once more.

BELLE D'OR PROVED SURPRISINGLY GOOD company now that she wasn't trying to nibble various parts of his anatomy. They talked, increasingly easily, about the state of the world—the war, the peace, the stuttering economy. The inevitable counting of the dead, the holes in life they had left. The Forest, and what it might contain, what it might portend. Duncan stayed quiet about his work as a woodsman. He trusted this woman to a point, and they'd be gone soon anyway, but Hardy and the police might well come sniffing around in the future, and the less Belle knew about her impromptu guests, the better for all concerned.

They talked, and they drank, and he just about held his thoughts about Niamh at arm's length, staved off the need to scream that she had given up into the muscles of his upper arm.

What Belle D'Or was staving off, he never discovered.

Sometime after one in the morning, Arthur showed up in a soft cap and coat that had seen more than their fair share of rain. He greeted them both, apologized to Belle for his absence, then gestured Duncan to an empty booth at the end of the room.

"Got news," he said. "If you don't mind, Belle?"

"Oh, he's all yours." She raised a hand in slightly slurred imperial largesse, waved it at the Chivas bottle on the bar. "Here, Duncan's been cutting quite a swath in the top-shelf booze. No reason to stop now. Take the bottle with you."

Arthur nodded his thanks, swiped the bottle and a glass from the barman. Duncan followed him to the booth and slid in. Arthur got straight down to cases.

"Spoke to the Cobbs and Mikey Collier. All good for tomorrow night. You want Collier to swing by and collect you here?"

Duncan thought about Belle's misgivings for the club, the risk of exposure. "Best not. We should keep this place out of it as much as we can. Look, I'll give you an address for him to meet me at. Up on Crawgate."

"Crawgate, eh?"

Even on Arthur's inexpressive features, the surprise was stamped clear. But he made no further comment, and Duncan made no effort to enlighten him.

"Aye, I'll need to be over there to collect something anyway. And it's a lot closer to where we'll be going." Abruptly, the whisky and everything else crashed in on him. He felt as weary as he could ever remember. "Look, we can hash out the details tomorrow. Are we going to need money up front?"

"No, I spoke to Billy earlier. He'll front for you. It's not as much as I thought it might be anyway—Collier's doing it for next to nothing." Arthur paused, poured himself a drink, and knocked it back with a grateful shudder. He was still in his wet coat, had not taken the soaked cap from his head. Duncan imagined he was not wearing his wig. "I think our Mikey's taken a shine to you."

You seem to have something of a glamour about you. Belle's words, floating back through his drink-misted mind. *Something that hard men will follow without question.*

In his memory, the natter and rattle of the Maxim guns along the German line. Men falling around him like heavy coats flung down, to the ground or to hang folded over the barbed wire, with fatally astonished looks on their young faces.

He drained his glass, shivered a little.

"Billy may not need to front me after all," he said. "We'll see tomorrow. Now I've got to try and get some sleep."

Arthur poured himself another generous measure from the Chivas bottle. Touched a finger to his waxy brow in salute.

"Good luck with that," he said, and drank.

THIRTY-SIX

IN THE END, HE DIDN'T SLEEP VERY LONG OR WELL. THE WHISKY AND the crackle in Niamh's lungs kept him from any clean rest, left him tossing and turning beside her, forced on him a state of groggy semiwakefulness shot through with sour dreams that tipped only grudgingly into deeper sleep as dawn began to stain the ceiling above the curtain rail once more. He woke a couple of hours later. Gifts from the night before—the hangover he deserved like an iron spike through his head, and a bladder strained to bursting. Niamh snored gently beside him. He went in underwear down the corridor to relieve himself, came back and climbed into bed again, but was by then too viciously awake to do more than lie on his back and sift his throbbing head for anything that wasn't rage or bitterness or despair.

Get up, Duncan. Get up and find a way to fucking fix this. You're talking to witches this afternoon. Maybe they can do something. Maybe—

He got abruptly out of bed. Niamh moaned and turned over, but did not wake. He dressed properly, mouth of the man in the mirror a thin, tight line, and went down to the dining room the girls used at the back of the club. He found Crammond and Arthur sitting at one of the spartan tables over demolished breakfast platters and mugs of tea. They appeared to have been waiting for him. Arthur got up to greet him as he came in, ducked into the kitchen, and ordered another plate, some more tea. Duncan sat down opposite Crammond.

"Morning," he croaked. Cleared his throat and tried again. "Morning. Thanks for coming over. Sorry I had to call the flat like that."

"Ah, dinnae pay any attention tae May. Ye ken whit she's like."

"Still."

"Arthur telt me ye've had the doctor oot tae Niamh? She awright?"

"Not really."

Crammond looked down at his plate. Was silent. Arthur came back and sat down at Duncan's side.

"Eggs and bacon," he said. "They'll have it straight out to you. Fresh pot coming, too. Oh yeah, and this came for you first thing by courier."

He handed over a thick and waxy foolscap envelope with an ornate, wine-colored wax seal across the closing flap. On the front was written in an elegant hand *Sworn Documents Included—For the Private Attention of Duncan Campbell Esq*. Duncan slid a finger under the seal and broke it, lifted the flap, squeezed the envelope from the edges so he could peer inside. He nodded to himself.

"Sworn documents?" Crammond wondered quietly.

"You could call them that, aye." Duncan fished out one of the big white sheets between his fingers and put it down on the table in front of the other man. Crammond gaped at what was printed on it.

"Ten fuckin' pound?" He looked at the envelope with fresh respect. "How much is in there?"

"Three hundred. Some of these are fifties."

"Fuckin' *fifties*?" Crammond leaned in closer, dropped his voice to a corrosive hiss. "*Three hundred fuckin' pound?* Ye mind tellin' me whit the fuck this is for?"

"It's for you."

A serving woman came out of the kitchen with a tray. Duncan slid the ten-pound note back into the envelope, closed the flap, and handed the package across the table to Crammond. The Glaswegian held it as if in a trance, waited until the woman had laid down the tray with its steaming teapot and filled plate, then retreated again to the kitchen.

"Duncan, I—"

"I owe you, Billy. For all this." Duncan gestured around at where they sat. "For taking me in and squaring it with Belle. For Mikey Collier and that ambulance ride. This one coming, too. For the Webleys. Most of all, for the risk you took, for standing by a dead man walking like it was no big fucking deal. Is it enough?"

"Is it . . . ?" Goggling at him as if he'd just sprouted fangs. "Is it fuckin' *enough*?"

Despite the dull ache of the hangover and everything else that hung over him now, Duncan felt himself grin. He couldn't help it. He reached for the plate of bacon and eggs, felt something rising in him that he recognized from his time in the trenches. Not hope, but a gritted hilarity and sense of purpose that somehow made hope beside the point.

"Tell you what," he said, deadpan. "If there's any left once you've squared everyone, buy something nice for May, and tell her it's from me."

NOON FOUND HIM BACK ON Crawgate. Bacon, eggs, and several mugs of strong tea laced with aspirin had his hangover down to levels where it more resembled focal competence than pain. It was the simple engine that kept him moving forward.

See the witches.

Find out what Hardy and Bainbridge had planned.

Get out of town.

Three more days. Blank out detail and consequence beyond that, because right now none of it mattered. His plans were laid. Crammond and Arthur briefed, Niamh and Garner reassured that rescue and fresh refuge were coming soon—all they need do was sit tight. Niamh was disgruntled and foul mouthed about it, small glints of the woman she'd been before her abduction starting to reemerge, and his heart took a tiny tick upward to see it. Garner just grunted phlegmatically and nodded.

Be careful out there, lad was all he seemed prepared to say on the matter.

Taking it to heart, Duncan stopped off at a tram change on the way, found coins and a call box, rang the number on the card Bainbridge had given him. An anonymous voice at the other end took his name, went away. The archmage picked up the phone a minute later.

"Mr. Silver. Good afternoon, this is a pleasant surprise. But I'm afraid if you're calling for news of Mimi Rush and her mother, I am no further forward."

"Well, how long is it going to take?" Ironing his voice of all tone other than brusque demand. The witches might not rate Bainbridge's scrying abilities, but better not to give him any reason to apply them in the wrong direction. "I don't have a lot of time."

"Believe me, Mr. Silver, I appreciate the urgency of your situation." Urbane, soothing. "And to a very real extent, it is my situation, too. But we cannot afford to move too hastily. If Colonel Hardy and the Commission were to discover that we are allied—"

"We're not allied yet, Bainbridge. Don't jump that gun."

"That is not my intention. But were the colonel to be aware that we are even in contact, the results could be catastrophic for any hope of resolution. You are a woodsman and will doubtless have told your clients on occasion that they must be patient and let you work."

"You're not a woodsman."

"No, of course not. But, like you, I am concerned to find Mimi Rush above all, because she is the key. And the arena I operate in is, in its way, just as fraught with dangers and complications as the Forest. You must give me time to work, Mr. Silver."

"How much time?"

"Contact me at the beginning of next week. Monday or Tuesday. Better to make it Tuesday. By then, I should have some news at least."

Duncan said nothing for a couple of seconds. He let the silence hang. Let Bainbridge squirm.

"Tuesday," he said finally. "You'd better have something pretty fucking concrete for me, or this partnership is dissolved."

He hung up. Hoped he hadn't overegged it.

At the bottom of Crawgate, he stopped at the pie shop again, got Cornish pasties this time, and trudged up the hill, trying to shield the package from the worst of the rain with his arm. The Webleys weighed heavy in his pockets, his hat brim dripped in sullen symphony with the rhythm of his steps, and Niamh's breathing clawed at his heart.

"Don't they do that witch's pie anymore?" asked Nimble Shanks Annie as they unwrapped his offering in the kitchen. "Would have thought that'd be an obvious choice. Good, spicy mix they put in those, really warms your belly for you."

"I'll ring and take fucking orders next time."

Pin-drop silence. The two witches paused and looked at each other. Annie raised an eyebrow elaborately, then busied herself with her pasty. Wolfbane Sally reached across the table and put a carmine-nailed hand on Duncan's arm.

"What's happened?" she asked gently.

HE ARGUED IT WITH THEM like a bull terrier, jaws clamped and worrying at prey. Got nothing for his pains but weary head shaking and increasingly irritable responses.

"But you're witches, for Christ's sake!"

"Witches, yes. Not gods." Nimble Shanks Annie wiped flecks of pastry from her lips. Brushed her fingers together to rid them of grease. "Magic has no recourse against the Black Crab. It's written. How many times is it written, Sal? Tell him."

"She's right, Duncan." That awful compassion in Wolfbane Sally's face again, in her low voice. It floored him like a punch to the sternum. "Perhaps if you'd brought her to us when it first began. But even then. The Black Crab—the body turned against itself, against its owner's will, against life itself. Like trying to persuade men not to go to war. In the end, there is no magic for that."

"The doctor said there are treatments! Experimental processes with radium—"

"Try them, then," said Annie.

"There must be something you can do!"

The thin witch turned on him, bright eyed. "Listen to me, woodsman. I have seen the Black Crab, I have stood in its path and tried everything in me to break its will. I was at Charlatan Nell's side in the Gloaming Chapel, long before the Unbinding, long before magic was suddenly *so fucking fashionable* again. I spent my talent and my will, I gave up my blood on iron, I pledged years of my youth to any dark thing that might want them. I foraged day and night for every herb and bark scrap that might infuse a healing spell. I begged favors from the Bright Folk when I could find them and whore myself to them. And you know what? Charlatan Nell still died! The Black Crab would not be denied. Will not be denied. *There is no fucking path to this!*"

She flung herself to her feet and stormed out of the narrow kitchen space. Angry heels across Sal's wooden board floors, the slam of the front door. Duncan and Sal sat quiet in the wake of her departure like men after the burst and dirt shower of a near-miss shell.

"Who's Charlatan Nell?" Duncan asked eventually.

"Her mother."

More quiet. Duncan traced a pattern absently with his index finger in the pastie flakes and crumbs across the kitchen table. The rain insisted at the windows, *tap tap-tap tap tap,* senseless lack of rhythm, an inexhaustible natural chaos that did not care.

"She'll get drenched if she goes out in this," Duncan said.

"She'll have taken a coat. I know Annie, she's not stupid, even in anger." Sal looked sadly at him. "I'm so sorry, Duncan. You bear enough as it is."

"It's fine. We all die of something."

"I would hope—" The witch stopped and cleared her throat. "I hope you won't be stupid in anger. I know it's a lot to ask, especially of a man, especially a man who's seen what you have. But take a leaf out of Annie's book. Mine, too." An unconvincing attempt at a smile. "We're wise women, Duncan, after all. Weird sisters. Take it from us. Stupid in anger serves no one."

Duncan forced a thin smile in answer. "Aye—wise and weird, that's you, right enough, Sal. And tell me, are you happy?"

The witch shrugged. "We reach an accommodation with things, I think. A knowing balance. So yes, near enough."

Duncan nodded. Stared at the pattern he'd drawn in the flakes and crumbs on the wood of the table.

"Wisdom," he repeated. "A knowing balance."

But he said the words as if naming some exotic land overseas he would never afford the tickets to reach. And when the witch heard him, he saw her turn away, swallow and clear her throat again, thumb small tears from the corners of her eyes.

ANNIE CAME BACK LATE IN the afternoon with most of the day's light already drained from the sky, and the rain still at the windows in soft but implacable assault. She banged about in the hall, made a lot of obvious noise with the door and taking off and shaking out her coat and hanging it up. She came into the living room and found Duncan seated in a chair near the window, eyelids heavy, a borrowed book in imminent danger of slipping from his hands. She put a hand on his shoulder and Duncan blinked, looked up.

"Sorry," she said succinctly. "Where's Sal?"

The book fell from his fingers, hit the floor with a clunk. She bent and reached down with a lithe grace that belied her years, scooped it up again. Duncan gestured at the door to the inner sanctum he'd never seen.

"She went in there to do some . . . preparation, she said?"

"Oho, did she?" Annie nodded, looked absently at the book. "Prufrock? Eliot? Never heard of him. Any good?"

Duncan shrugged. "It's poetry."

"Well." The witch pulled a face. "Sooner you than me."

She turned and went to the door Sal had retreated behind. She knocked, a bit diffidently, Duncan thought, and Sal's voice called her in by name. She gave him a witchy parting smile, opened the door a crack, and slid inside. Billow of some faintly sulfur-scented fumes, an odd blue light, and then the door was closed tight again and Annie was gone. Duncan sat up straighter on the sofa, rubbed his eyes, tried to rouse himself from the stale late-afternoon neurasthenia that had stolen over him. He took out the Webleys, one by one, and checked the load. He walked about the living room a bit. He picked up the Prufrock again. Put it down. Finally, inevitably, he found himself standing in front of the window, staring out at the rain and the gathering murk. The witch's home muttered to itself around him, rush of water in plumbing, floorboard creak, other, less easily explainable sounds . . .

Some unreckoned space of time later, he was roused from his doze by the self-important, ratcheting blurt of a car's klaxon in the street outside. Nimble Shanks Annie came back out into the living room, smelling strongly of woodsmoke and sulfur. Over the threshold of the open door, weird shadows played on the floor at her heels. Still the faint bluish light from within.

"Well, that's us," she said brightly. "The hero's hour come around. Get your coat. We'd better go down."

Sal appeared in the doorway behind her, smoke apparently writhing directly from her hair in half-suggestive forms.

"You be careful, both of you," she said maternally. "I'll keep exhorting the storm at this end, but it's a ticklish thing to get right. Should stay murky enough to cover your approach, but I make no promises for how long it'll last. Duncan, you let Annie handle the water tangling on her own, she's very good at it. Don't interfere."

Annie smiled brilliantly at him. "She's right, I am phenomenally good."

Down in the street, the converted Vauxhall ambulance stood in the rain like a patient draft horse. For all its flanks were no longer daubed with the red cross, the vehicle gave Duncan's memory a sharp kick, back to an evening near Dernancourt, another ambulance getting rained on, the bitten-off groans and curses of injured men within, someone yelling orders, distant rumble of artillery like thunder across the sky . . .

As if some vast, unsuspected force tore a hole in time, merged memory and present in a hallucinatory fog for him—rip and roll of thunder in the sky over Crawgate. Sheet lightning flickered on gray behind the tall tenement roofs. The rain redoubled its drenching efforts.

"You getting in or what?" Mikey Collier, leaning across the driver's bench with a broad grin as he shouted. "Better out of sight in the back, I reckon. The lady there can ride up front if she likes."

It made all kinds of sense. Duncan pulled open the door and handed a very amused Nimble Shanks Annie up onto the bench. She settled there with the poise of minor royalty being given a tour of a battlefront.

"Hello, young man. Anna Spence. But you can call me Annie."

Collier's grin turned appreciative. "Mike Collier, at your service."

"Collier." Duncan, snapping his fingers for the other man's attention. He had to pitch his voice over the drumming of the rain on the Vauxhall's roof. "Mike! You know where we're going?"

"Arthur said the East End? The old industrial strip?"

"Aye. The munitions works. South entrance. Just take us up to the gates, we'll go on foot from there."

"In this rain?" Collier saw the look on his face and shrugged. "As you like. Sooner you than me. Oh yeah, Arthur's in the back. Brought you some toys."

"Arthur came with?"

Collier laughed. "What, you thought he wouldn't?"

AT THE HEIGHT OF THE war, Duncan knew, the Erlsley Number One Munitions Plant was turning out ten thousand shells a week, employing over fifteen thousand workers, almost all women, and sprawled over a couple of hundred acres including a working dairy farm. Accidental explosions killed more than three dozen in the course of the conflict. Production all but stopped with the Armistice, and the factory would likely have been mothballed altogether with the signatures at Versailles, if the Forest hadn't come and eaten much of it in the interim. As with Maunston, as at ten thousand points across the whole country, managed shutdown gave way to panicked retreat. The whole place had lain abandoned ever since.

"Dairy farm?" Arthur wondered, bemused.

"Aye. Offsets the effects of cordite, apparently. You work with that shite for very long, your skin starts turning yellow. Drinking milk fixes it."

"Is that right? Learn something new every day."

The Vauxhall bumped to an angled halt and Collier banged on the panel between them. They rolled up the canvas drop sheet, dropped the tailgate, and climbed out into a mercifully mild drizzle. Murky light all around and the looming, prison bar silhouette of the factory gates. Heavy-duty chain-link fencing ran off to either side, reinforced by the bushes and small trees that had grown there, intermingling with the metal. Dimly, through the murk beyond the gate, you could make out the angular lines of the armory buildings, the long, low run of railway loading quays between. There was scrub growth almost everywhere; some of it looked pretty high. Trees fringed the far borders of the site, and here and there you could see where fresh Forest growth had erupted like smallpox across the previously cleared ground. Tall stands of ash and elm and yew, one corner of a storage shed shattered as if by bombardment, a tentacular oak waving thick triumphant arms in the gap.

Moonlight slipped between separating clouds for a scant few moments, put a hard gleam on a generous heaping of padlocked chain around the closed gates. Collier ducked into the back of the ambulance to find his bolt cutters. They took the chain off in sections. Duncan draped a half-yard length around his neck under his coat collar.

"Never heard of the Huldu making incursions here," he said when the others looked at him askance. "I guess there's nothing much to interest them, and too much abandoned iron lying around. But I get the feeling that times are changing, for us and for them. As much as we can, we'll follow the rail lines and the buildings. But sooner or later, like it or not, we're in the woods." He patted the length of chain. "Never hurts to have the extra iron."

Arthur had brought him the trench knife, the McCulloch in its sheath, an ammunition pouch of extra shells, and a box of dumdum .455s for the Webleys. Through the thin cotton of his shirt, the wet, cold iron links on his neck felt forced and needlessly dramatic, and maybe they saw that doubt in his eyes. Mikey Collier took another length, but he let it hang diffidently from one hand.

"Going to be parked here in a metal box anyway," he said apologetically. "Iron gates, fencing's chain-link, too. Think I'm safe. Maybe I'll keep it on my lap, like?"

Arthur said nothing. But he fished up another slightly shorter length of the discarded chain, put it over his shoulders in imitation of Duncan. Nimble Shanks Annie just snorted and shook her head.

"I'm a witch, Duncan, not a gladiator. I'll be all right."

Duncan shrugged. The chain's links shifted against his neck, already warmed by contact with his body's heat.

"Hope you're right," he said curtly. "Maybe you can scry ahead a little for us anyway, just to be on the safe side."

"If you ask nicely."

"Thought I just did."

They forced the left-hand gate, dragged it open together against grating, stony resistance, made a gap wide enough to pass. Then, one by one, they slipped through, into the quiet of the rotting dead industrial landscape beyond.

THIRTY-SEVEN

THEY REACHED ADEPT HOUSE WITHOUT INCIDENT.

The woods turned out surprisingly sparse, wide-spaced young beech and birch, not much brush between the slim trunks, and no nasty surprises. Easy enough to navigate, even by night, even in the rain. Here and there, faint rustling or the call of a night bird tripped Duncan's senses, but it was momentary, quickly dismissed. For the rest, the witch had made a rapid scrying cast in a puddle on cracked concrete outside one of the factory sheds, ascertained that there was nothing in the woods that wanted to stop them, and if they were watched, then the watchers did not make themselves known. The house loomed out of the murk unexpectedly fast, a cheery assemblage of warmly lit window rectangles through the trees.

They skulked along the edge of the bedraggled lawn, got as close to the house as they could without leaving the trees. Crouched there under a halfway-decent beech crown that kept the worst of the rain off. At ground level, rhododendron bushes dominated the brush like some Wellsian alien growth. It gave them ample cover. Duncan peered out between fleshy, bruise-colored leaves, spotted the ground-floor bay and French windows into the drawing room. Still no curtains hung; you could see right to the back wall, make out the lit fireplace, the painting hung over it, the door left ajar.

"Is this close enough?" he asked the witch.

"Oh, I should think so, yes. We can stay right here in the trees."

Duncan checked the Mappin & Webb. "Right, we're early. Arthur, you want to slip round to the front, check for arrivals?"

Arthur nodded, hefted his carbine. "Back soon as anybody shows."

He scuffled back through the bushes, slipped away in a broad arc around the right flank of the house. Duncan unshipped the carrying satchel for the perspicacious water, opened it, and drew out the Kilner jar. It looked dull and unremarkable in his wet hands, a workaday Victorian artifact for more convenient living, nothing more.

"Right, let's see this work," he said.

Nimble Shanks Annie settled herself cross-legged at his side. She took the jar from him, seated it upright in her skirted lap. She bowed her head. Rain-draggled hair fell forward to shroud her face. She made flat palms, pressed them to the sides of the jar. Inflected droning noises came from within the black shroud of her hair, interspersed with small, tight cries like the calling of birds of prey. Her palms moved in circular soaping motions on the glass, her fingers splayed and flexed, seemingly independently of each other, faint, eerie clickings and crackings of cartilage . . .

At the heart of the jar, a tiny spot of blue brilliance sprang up, like the cone of a Bunsen flame on full air. It stuttered a couple of times, then appeared to turn over in the water and swell into something like an amoeba seen under a microscope. The radiance dimmed rapidly out of it as it grew. Nimble Shanks Annie made noises akin to choking. Words surfaced from the glottal noise, or at least syllables, but in no language Duncan could recognize. The dim glow filled the Kilner jar, became a small, wavering image of the room they could make out across the lawn. The witch cooed with audible delight, caressed the jar like the face of a much-loved infant. Finally, seemingly content, she let go the vessel, leaned back on her hands like a girl out at a picnic, tossed her hair out of her eyes, and lifted the jar with a tilt of her hips.

"There you go," she said proudly. "Textbook water tangling. Feast your eyes. I doubt you'll see it done better this side of the Brocken."

Duncan peered closer, saw that the image in the water was not a stable vision, like a movie projection. Instead, it swirled and rippled like reflections in a nighttime lake. The corners of the room he remembered came and went; the view seemed to rotate slowly about a center that was perhaps the low table between the two armchairs at the fireplace. And the flames in the grate wavered through colors from mauve to green and back, passing through a truthful ruddiness only for a few moments at a time.

Annie wiggled her hips a little—gratuitously, he thought—and the Kilner jar wobbled in her lap. He blinked and looked up at her. She gave him a brilliant, girlish smile.

"You're probably better not to stare too much," she said. "It'll make you dizzy."

"Already is," he grumbled.

"Don't focus so much on what's in it. Just let the whole vision wash over you, like a sunset." The hips tilted again. "Like any thing of beauty you can't touch. Oh, look."

For a mistrustful moment, he stared at her, wondering if he was going to have to fend off her advances. She didn't seem any less highly sexed than Sal, but surely out here in the rain and woodland wet, she couldn't . . .

A slow smile twisted her lips. She nodded down at her lap. "I mean—look, we're not the only ones who came early."

He peered at the wavering image again. Disturbance now in the wobbly view, a figure striding into the room, followed more hesitantly by another.

"You'll need to put your hand there," the witch told him. "Palm flat to the glass, to feel the vibrations. Like this."

She shifted her stance and pressed her own hand to one side of the Kilner jar. Warily, he did the same. Instantly, a familiar voice rinsed into his ears.

". . . set everything out, have you?" Bainbridge, uncharacteristically brusque, looking around him. There was a sharp, crystalline tone to the way his words came through in Duncan's ear that made it almost painful to listen. "Whisky, soda?"

"Water as well," said Jeremy Ewart, audibly diffident. "All there on the table, Luminance."

Nimble Shanks Annie snorted. Mouthed the word *Luminance* with broad derision.

"Yes, well." Bainbridge paced about. "I don't think Colonel Hardy is the sort of gentleman who'd simply water his whisky. But you never know. And as for Miss Freeman, who can tell? She's not the most stable of females, yes, perhaps just water for her—" He came to a halt. "Jeremy, what on earth is wrong with you? You're as jittery as a princess with a navvy's privates. If you're still not feeling well, perhaps you should go home."

"No, Luminance—I'm fine. I just . . . I worry about our dealings with the secular authorities."

"The secular is always with us, Jeremy. I have taught you this. We cannot transcend it, in this life at least. We must deal with it as best we can. You let me worry about Colonel Hardy."

"Yes, Luminance."

"In fact, you'd better get out front, ready to greet him. I sense his approach. He's come early, it seems. Something serious must have happened. Show him in here as soon as he arrives. But see to it he is alone."

Ewart nodded jerkily—or that might have been the limitations of the scrying vision—and backed toward the door. He stared nervously for a moment, as it seemed, right out of the Kilner jar and into Duncan's eyes. Then he was gone. The witch took her hand away, rolled her eyes.

"Oh, Jerry. Princess with a navvy's prick, indeed. Why don't you just *stare* at the bloody water and give the whole game away for us!"

"You think he has?"

They both peered at Bainbridge's lone figure in the glass for a moment, but the archmage didn't deign to glance their way. He seemed, as near as Duncan could tell, to be looking at the Tam o' Shanter painting over the mantelpiece. Heavy sigh of relief from the witch.

"No, we probably got away with it this time." She snorted again.

"Calls himself a luminance? A master mage? I've seen more sensitivity in carrots."

Then they both heard it.

The sound of a car coming up the long drive to the house.

HEADLIGHTS SWEPT PALE, COLD FINGERS across and through the trees. Duncan fought off a trench-bred instinct to duck. The growl of the motor shifted, grew less intense, as the car made it to the top of the rise. He caught a couple of brief glimpses as it swept round the final curve—not enough to recognize make or model, only the limousine silhouette—and then the bulk of the house blocked his view, muted the sound. Duncan heard the engine turned off, an exchange of voices too faint to make out words. Doors slammed.

"Here we go," he muttered.

"Here we go," agreed the witch serenely.

They watched the glass together, saw Bainbridge turn about to face the door. Duncan put his palm to the glass just as the door flew open. Confused tumult of muffled voices from the hallway, like the splintering of crystals in his ear, nothing coherent he could catch. Hardy stood in the doorway as if propelled there by the force of the uproar.

"Did you tell him, you jumped-up, traitorous oik?"

Bulky figures crowding behind him. Bainbridge appeared to wave them off.

"Come in, Colonel," he said mildly. "Jeremy, close the door, please. No, Compton—it's fine. Really. Leave us alone, all of you. This is just a disagreement between gentlemen. We'll sort it out. Isn't that right, Colonel?"

Hardy stood a moment, visibly rigid with rage. Then—an officer calm descending. He turned his head.

"It's fine, Captain," he said, in clipped tones. "I'll be fine. Please wait for me out front."

He took a couple of steps into the room. Movement behind him in the hallway. Figures moving back. Someone pulled the door quietly closed.

"Now then, Colonel." Bainbridge turning away, apparently toward the low table Jerry had positioned the carafe on. "Let me get you something to drink, and you can explain what you mean. Did I tell what to whom, exactly?"

"Don't play the fool with me, Bainbridge. You know damn well who I'm talking about."

The archmage poured whisky into two glasses, turned and handed one to Hardy. "I can perhaps guess. Here. Have a calmative. Chivas Regal, twenty-five years aged. It's really very good. Your health, sir." Raising his glass, sipping delicately. "We're talking, presumably, about the illustrious Duncan Silver. Or, as I'm beginning to believe we should call him, Duncan Slaven of Stac Dubh."

Hardy glared at him over the rim of his glass. Tossed back the contents.

"I don't care what his fucking name is. Silver murdered four policemen last night. Men with families. One of them was a Special Branch detective inspector."

"Impressive." Bainbridge sipped at his drink again. "You must have really upset him. I'm not entirely sure, though, why you think this has anything to do with me."

"You're talking to him, aren't you? He stormed the holding station where we had his Irish chippie and his friend from Macclesfield."

"Yes, that makes sense. I can very easily see the man doing something like that. However, I don't know where this holding station of yours is."

"You could have found out. You could have"—Hardy gestured angrily—"*divined* it, I imagine."

"Perhaps I could. I'm not sure. But the fact remains, I didn't. And I certainly wouldn't have told Mr. Silver, if I had."

"So you say."

Bainbridge sighed weightily. "Colonel, I am attempting to keep

Duncan Silver onside, because what I *have* divined is that he likely has a major role to play in this dawning new age of ours. There is an aura around Silver, a frisson of potential, the likes of which I have rarely seen. That doesn't mean I would assist him in committing mayhem of this sort, or indeed thwarting any of your wider plans. You did have a plan, I take it, for these people you imprisoned?"

Hardy opened his mouth. Closed it again.

"We were responding to circumstances," he said more calmly. "It was a fast-developing situation, and I'll be the first to admit it got messy."

"Indeed." Gesturing toward the armchairs and the fire. "Why don't we both sit down? It's going to take intelligence to see our way out of this. Intelligence and cool heads. Help yourself to another drink, please. There's soda or water, as you prefer. Please, Colonel. Sit."

Crash of undergrowth behind him—compared to the shrill, tinny crystalline sounds in his ear, it was coarse and deafening. Duncan jerked his hand off the glass, whipped around. Saw Arthur, rain-streaked face, crouched with the carbine across his knees, breathing hard.

"Four men." Jagged between caught breaths. "Driver. Gorilla. Two officer types. Driver stayed. With the car. Other three are inside."

Duncan nodded. "Hardy and an aide. We've seen them. Adding the gorilla means he doesn't trust Bainbridge at all."

"Looks like a bloody sergeant major I had. For basic training, at Salisbury plain. Big, untidy bastard, he was, just like this one." Breath mostly recovered, Arthur goggled in fascination at the blue glowing Kilner jar in Annie's lap, the dancing cameo images within. "Is that . . . ?"

"Yes, it is," said the witch shortly. "Now be quiet, please."

She grabbed Duncan's wrist, pressed his hand back to the glass.

". . . called you here to meet her." Bainbridge was at the door of the room, leaning out into the corridor. "Compton—would you be so good as to go up and ask Miss Freeman to join us now? Thank you. And Compton—treat her kindly, please. She's been through a lot."

He made his way back to the fire.

"Poor girl, she's still not fully recovered from her ordeal, even now. What it must have taken to escape from her Huldu masters, with the Forests the way they are now, and when she could remember nothing of her life before them."

"You're quite sure she's genuine?" Hardy's skepticism was clear even across the tinny crystalline version of hearing it was strained through.

"Oh yes, Colonel. There are ways to tell."

"But you haven't matched her with records of the family she was abducted from?"

"No. Freeman is her own choice of surname. We estimate she's about thirty years of age, and she was traded as a thrall from one region of the British Isles to another at least twice that she can remember. It would be almost impossible to pin down her point of origin. We have explained this to her. She is . . . starting afresh with the Sword and Orb, you might say."

A muted knock at the door and a pale, dark-haired woman was ushered into the room, dressed plainly in white blouse and dark skirt. Both men rose reflexively to greet her. Bainbridge grew effusive.

"Ah, Rachel. Thank you so much for joining us. Come and sit by the fire, please. This is Colonel Hardy. He'd be very interested to hear what you told me about the Huldu nurseries."

The woman called Rachel moved hesitantly to the armchair Bainbridge had been using. She perched on the edge of the seat, as if poised to flee at a moment's notice. She tugged a hank of her long black hair continuously through the fingers of one hand after the other, as if endlessly searching the tresses for nits.

"They are not like us," she husked, so low that Duncan could barely make out the words.

"In what way, Rachel?" Bainbridge, prompting from behind the chair like a doting father helping his infant daughter with a learned recital. "How are they different?"

"They *leave* them."

Something so stark and desolate in the way she said it that Duncan felt a chill blow through him. Felt Nimble Shanks Annie looking at him, met her gaze. She frowned a question. He shrugged. Shook his head.

Rachel started up again, like a freshly wound clockwork toy. "I saw it, in the glade by the old father oak. Where the tree thief church is standing still, with the cross god looking on over the door. The mothers come to give them suck, but not often. And they leave them again, even when they weep, they leave the babe with the . . . they call it *eilsinni.*"

Now Duncan frowned. He knew the word in Skogurtal, had heard it enough times for it to fix in his mind, but now, reaching for meaning, he found nothing, just a vague sense of dread . . .

"Companion?" mouthed the witch, shooting for translation. He nodded doubtfully.

"Rachel has made drawings for us," said Bainbridge, now at the table, shuffling papers. "And these correspond to other little-known accounts out of legend, tales told by other supposed returnees from the Fae realm over the centuries, though these have been only whispers and closely guarded arcana."

For one moment, he looked up and out of the window, across the rain-drenched lawn and into the trees and bushes beyond. Duncan felt a weird, disorienting wrench—the tiny figure in the water image staring away, the man himself simultaneously right there large as life, a couple of dozen yards away and seemingly staring right at him.

"Bloody Section J, I suppose," Hardy said. "From their archives?"

"I do not yet have access to Section J's archives," Bainbridge said absently, shuffling the papers together. "Though I have begun negotiations in Whitehall that I hope will bear that fruit, among others. No, these accounts are from other sources."

He came back to the fireplace and took station again behind Rachel's seat. Held up some of the papers for Hardy to see. The scale of the tangled water image was too small for detail.

"As you can see, Colonel, eilsinni appear to mutate as they grow, much like the Huldu child itself. But I think what we're dealing with here at base is simply a highly evolved kind of placenta."

A deep shudder ran through Duncan, enough that he almost let go the Kilner jar. He knew the witch was staring at him, frowning. Bainbridge's voice wavered and almost went out, came back as Duncan pressed the glass again.

". . . begins as not much more than a living cushion for the newborn, a warm bed. There are these nubs, which I think must serve as nipple substitutes, rather like a modern pacifier. Perhaps they even supply some form of nutritive. But in any case, as you can see from Rachel's drawings here, these nubs begin to elongate, become more like tentacles. And they are, apparently, mobile, prehensile even."

"They turn the babes," Rachel mumbled. "Like snakes, they turn them. Prodding, touching, turning over."

"Are you really quite certain about this?" Hardy, appalled, almost outraged by what he was hearing. "Can we honestly take this—this fantastical narrative seriously?"

Rachel's voice rose. "I'm not a liar! I have seen them!"

"And we believe you, Rachel, of course we do." Bainbridge put a soothing hand on the young woman's shoulder. "Might I remind you, Colonel, that right here in our own country less than six years ago, entire forests erupted from the bowels of the Earth in the space of a single night. England transformed by forces beyond our understanding in a matter of hours. You yourself admit you have seen soldiers struck down with elf shot, a Huldu prowling the trenches of our army after its victim. Do you really now balk at this?"

Hardy cleared his throat. "It seems . . . fantastical."

"Yes, so you have said. But I ask you—frame this in another way. Do you think that, if asked to, we could not imagine a future in which the human race will build machines to take away the daily drudgery of child rearing in just this way? If our very own Mr. Wells were to write it in one of his futurist romances, would we not entertain it as entirely possible?"

"That's not the same! You're talking of machines, devices. Not . . . living things."

"The Huldu do not appear to have any use for machines. They are shape-shifters, bodily self-sufficient. Where else, then, would they go for such technology, if not into their own bodies, the wombs of their own women, where life itself is made, to find the necessary resource?"

Hardy made a noise. Unclear what it was meant to convey. It didn't matter; Duncan was lost, locked into flash recall of *a darkened forest glade, faint mewlings, soft movement, and something equally soft and sticky he's just stepped on with his bare foot. He looks down—not far, he can't be more than three years old—and sees something that makes no sense . . .*

Jellyfish, Duncan realized, as the memory unlocked. It looked like a huge pale jellyfish, like the ones that used to wash up on the beach at Cadogan's, but far bigger—

And a baby lying asleep upon it, sharp Fae features glistening and dreaming . . .

His own scream, high and shrill—

And from the jellyfish, somewhere near the baby's head, a slim tentacle uncoils, rises like a cobra to the sound of a snake charmer's pipe, and turns, questing, in his direction . . .

Cool, Fae hands, grabbing him from behind.

They bear him up, away from the glade and what it holds. A sibilant voice, snarling in his ear, until he is set down again, slapped repeatedly back and forth across the head and face and arms, until his whole body is trembling and his face is stinging sore and ribboned wet with tears, and he's told never, ever, ever, *to walk there again . . .*

Duncan surfaced, panting harder than Arthur had when he arrived. The witch and the burned man, both staring at him in the rainy dark. He swallowed, hard, pressed again at the Kilner jar's smooth glass side.

". . . as they become mobile, so the eilsinni learns motion, too.

Look, as you see here, it's more amoeboid than anything at this stage. But with more time—see, limbs, arms and legs, and finally, a near-perfect copy of the emerging child, a caring twin endowed with preternatural intelligence and instincts to protect. Can you imagine? The first coherent memories that a Fae child will make *are of its own face looking back at it*!"

The fervor in Bainbridge's voice was almost religious. Hardy, clearly uncomfortable, cleared his throat again.

"Are you saying . . . that this is where the changelings come from?"

"I think it very likely, yes. Not the same eilsinni as are used to raise their own offspring, of course, but I dare say that Huldu females would be able call forth similar placental growth, more or less at will—perhaps over a period of days or weeks, as the plan to snatch a human child is laid? Once delivered, what we call magic would be used to mold the creature to resemble the child it will replace. It makes perfect sense, does it not?"

A long, quiet pause.

Hardy picked up his drink, set it down without tasting it. He put the same hand to his brow. Made an obvious effort. "Miss Freeman. A question, if I may. What happens to these . . . eilsinni, once the child is grown?"

"They fade." Even allowing for the crystalline rinse, Rachel's voice was one of the most brittle, empty sounds Duncan had ever heard. "They corrupt, they stumble, they die. I have watched them. All go back to the Gray."

"Their purpose is, after all, served." Bainbridge, explanatory, almost lecturing. "We know that if a changeling is discovered and taken from its adoptive family, it sickens and dies fairly fast. From the eyewitness accounts I have read, it's a very similar process to what Rachel here is describing for us. Without purpose, the eilsinni simply . . . runs down, like one of the Wellsian machines we were just discussing. From what Rachel says, it seems to occur once the Fae child reaches one or two years of age. But Colonel, I feel that we are digressing well away from the main point here."

"Which is?"

"Which is that Rachel here can pinpoint, with some degree of accuracy, where these nurseries lie. You heard her description—a great oak, a church long abandoned, with the Christ figure over the door. She has been a very special type of thrall for the Fae, rewarded, I can only assume, for long and faithful service. For many years, in at least two different parts of the country, she has acted as a kind of watchman"—a rich, avuncular chuckle—"well, watch*woman,* I suppose we'd have to say, at least if we want to keep Mrs. Pankhurst happy. A watchwoman, then, for the Huldu's offspring and their nurturing. And there is more. There is reason to suppose that these are ancestral sites, knowing what we do of the Fae's deep conservatism, and it seems to me that with modern mapping techniques, they would be relatively simple to locate. Would you not agree?"

"I suppose so, yes." Hardy, grudging.

"Yes. And, Colonel, if we know where the Huldu's offspring are nurtured and raised—well, then, is it not reasonable to assume, using artillery charged with all manner of iron shrapnel, that we can stand off at a comfortable distance outside the Forest and annihilate them with long-range bombardment?"

THIRTY-EIGHT

Duncan and the witch stared at each other over the blue glow from the Kilner jar, like witnesses at some awful locomotive smash. Like outriders come across the early signs of a new war machine on the field of battle, the fresh horrors it could inflict.

Apparently, they weren't the only ones.

"Excuse me?" Hardy leaning forward in his armchair. "You, of all people, want to bring modern warfare against the Huldu? You want to slaughter their children with artillery?"

"I want to offer them the threat of it, yes. And I need you to do it for me, so I can mediate."

"I don't understand you, Bainbridge. A couple of months ago, they tell me, you threw Sir Michael's offer of employment back in his face. You told him he was part of a dying culture, could not possibly grasp the subtleties of what the new age would bring or need. You told me much the same, to my face."

"Yes, I know."

"Rational modernity is dead, you told me."

"And, substantially speaking, it is. Certainly people don't want it anymore. And it appears the Earth and its powers have responded."

"You don't consider shrapnel shelling with long-range artillery to be modern?"

"I certainly don't consider it to be hugely rational." Bainbridge prowled the room. "And to be completely honest, I don't really want to have to carry it out. But the Huldu must understand the need for rapprochement. If we are to have diplomatic relations, then they must be based in strength. And I need to have distance from the threat, so that it is not seen to come from me, so that I can offer alternatives."

"You could have broached this in concert with Sir Michael's initiative."

"And why exactly should I do that?" Sudden edge on the archmage's voice. "Endershall vilified me in the pages of the national press when I returned from America. He called me a traitor. He upbraided me in public at my club and in the street. Did you really think I was going to cooperate with a man like that?"

"He's not the only one to level those accusations."

"He has been one of the few to pursue them, even when he received assurances from within government that they were unfounded."

"Assurances from close friends of yours," said Hardy sardonically.

"The accusations are unfounded!" Raw fury for just a second. Rachel quailed visibly in her seat. Perhaps Bainbridge noticed; as abruptly as the rage had risen, it ebbed. The archmage grew calm and even toned again. "Every action I took in the United States was at the behest of His Majesty's intelligence services. I feigned my allegiance to the pro-German initiative to better infiltrate their agents. I passed back information that—"

Hardy held up a hand. "Save your protestations for someone who cares, Bainbridge. The war is over. Whatever minor part you may or may not have played in it no longer matters. But *this* war—the war against the Huldu—is yet to be won. And I won't fight it alongside a man who has more sympathy with the enemy than with his own species."

"I do not sympathize with the Huldu, Colonel. I simply understand what they represent far better than you, or any of the men whose will you serve."

"We are all striving to understand what we face, Sir Michael included."

Bainbridge shook his head emphatically. "Endershall is a superannuated fool. Less relevant with every passing day. Like so many of our so-called ruling class, he believes himself still in control of something that is tilting far beyond any skill or power of his or his kind to rebalance."

"And what do you believe, Bainbridge? No, don't tell me—let me guess. That you should be the next king of Elfland by government decree."

"Would that be so bad? You sneer, but would it? Consider—a strong human conduit through which the atavism that has returned to haunt us can be mediated. Think of it as appointing a governor to a troublesome, benighted imperial province. An officer of empire with the vision and experience to deal with the shape of things to come."

"Bainbridge, I wouldn't appoint you to govern a brothel in Port Said."

"Then what are you doing here, Colonel?" The archmage left his position behind Rachel in the armchair, moved to stare out of the window again, back turned pointedly to the other man. The silence yawned. "No answer? Let me tell you, then, why you are here. You have come because you know that I am right."

Hardy snorted derisively, but still he had no response. Bainbridge gestured, out to the view beyond the glass. His voice was soft, almost entranced. "Look out there, Colonel. The woods beckon, and once again we are afraid of what they hold. Fearful, emasculated, and confounded. The Forest encroaches, a new and terrible era dawns, and you and our rulers are out of ideas. Our current overture—gifting of a single human child of Fae lineage whom our ancient neighbors were able to take at their leisure anyway—has failed at every level. As it was doomed to from the start, as I could have told you, had anyone taken the trouble to consult me at the time. It was at best an attempt at abject appeasement, at worst an admission of both historical guilt and weakness. It is not the way forward, and I think by now that even Endershall and his cohort can see this."

Hardy had evidently had enough. He stood abruptly up. "I came here to tell you that Silver has to be stopped. That is all. Bad enough that he has interfered in these matters of state, but now he is a murderer, too. A killer of men, not Huldu."

"Mr. Silver has been a killer of men for almost a decade. His country was pleased to provide him with the practice."

"I'm not talking about Germans, Bainbridge. I am talking about Englishmen. Our own compatriots, and policemen to boot."

"German, English, Irish." The archmage made a throwaway motion with his hand. "Perhaps these distinctions, too, are becoming superannuated. From what I hear, the Forests of Europe teem with these same terrors as ours. The enemy we face is a common one. And Duncan Silver, whatever his . . . excesses, remains a seasoned warrior for our cause. Perhaps Achilles sulks in his tent—but can we forgo him at the siege?"

"I will not give the wink to a man who has murdered officers of the law!"

"That's very honorable, Colonel Hardy. Though, as I heard it, you did see fit to try and shoot him dead when he was in your way."

"That was a tactical decision, and I won't—"

"Colonel, enough!" Bainbridge turned away from the window, faced back into the room. "Even if I wanted to, I could not give you Silver. I have no idea of his whereabouts. He may have left Erlsley altogether for all I know—though I doubt that. He wants the child, and he is tenacious to a fault."

"You listen to me, Bainbridge." Hardy was still up out of his chair, irate. "I demand an undertaking from you, right here and now, that you will help me bring Silver to heel. The Commission will not entertain further association with you unless you agree. Your negotiations with Whitehall will come to nothing, that I can promise you. His Majesty's government will not tolerate anarchy in the ranks."

Bainbridge shrugged. "Well, we can argue about this once the man is in custody. For now, it's an abstract concern. But if you really want Silver, there is a simple way to achieve this. Where are you keeping Ada Endershall and her daughter?"

"We're keeping them safe. Somewhere I have no intention of revealing to you."

"You don't need to. You merely need to let Silver know, and he will come for them. For that matter you could supply a completely false location, as long as he trusted it to be the true one. If you wish me to facilitate that, of course I can."

It spiked through Duncan like ice—like a smoother, more benign version of the sorcerous blast Mebhuranon had laid on him in Consort Park. He let go the Kilner jar, was rising from his crouch almost before he realized it. The witch looked up at him in surprise. He turned to Arthur.

"I'm going to need cover," he said tightly. "Back shortly. If anyone comes out after me, you put a bullet right through them."

Arthur nodded, sliding prone amid the wet earth and tangle of rhododendron roots. He cuddled the carbine stock to his cheek. Duncan stood and tugged one of the Webleys from his coat pocket. Nimble Shanks Annie put a hand on his arm.

"Duncan, what are you—"

"I'll be back," he repeated, and strode out onto the lawn.

IT WAS MERCILESS OPEN GROUND—he was in clear view for anyone who cared to look out of a window overlooking the lawn, and there were quite a few windows—but he crossed it uncaring, fleet and silent as some vengeful ghost. He barely felt his feet in the soaked grass, the steps he took. Something at his back blew him onward like a leaf on a gust of autumn wind.

He reached the French windows, risked a moment to try the ornate outer handle, found it locked. He stepped back, stomped hard at the frame with his boot. Musical chime of glass as it broke, shattered, fell out of the frame on either side in jagged puzzle pieces. The doorframes, lighter than Victorians would have built, splintered and cracked, smashed around the lock, then rebounded outward. Duncan toed the right-hand frame wider open and stepped through the gap into the drawing room beyond. His boots crunched on glass. He pointed the Webley.

"Colonel Hardy," he said. Tight, combat grin gripping his face. "Did the Maunston survivors not carry my message to you?"

"You!" Hardy, abruptly rage pale. "You murderous *bastard*!"

His glance sideways was for the fireplace, the ironmongery beside it, a trench impulse, maybe dart for the poker, grab and swing—

Duncan crossed the space between them faster than the other man's thought. Whipped the butt of the Webley hard into the colonel's temple, floored him. Hardy went to his hands and knees, dripping blood from the wound. Duncan swung his arm like a weathervane, pointed the gun at Bainbridge and Rachel.

"I'd sit this one out if I were you."

He grabbed Hardy by the collar, dragged him more or less back to his feet. The colonel was groggy from the blow to the head, offered little resistance. Blood down his forehead and face, probably in his eyes.

"Colonel Hardy and I are going for a walk in the woods. You or anyone else comes after us, you will be shot dead. Hardy here doesn't have the monopoly on snipers."

"Mr. Silver, this won't—"

"Think yourself lucky, Bainbridge." Duncan already backing out, dragging Hardy with him, grinning hard. "I don't have the time to deal with you too right n—"

The drawing room door burst open, banged back on its hinges. Bulky figures, a raised weapon. A lick of witch's luck blew Duncan's way; the door slammed the wall, bounced back again, caught the aiming arm. A shot went wide. Duncan shot back, twice, saw his target stagger—

Bainbridge crashed into him from the side, fists and tangling legs.

A real handful despite his age and build and airy archmage demeanor, who'd have thought it, treacherous, mannered piece of shite didn't look like he had it in him . . .

Duncan rode the first blow, hooked a vicious elbow into the other man's head, knocked him aside. Hardy summoned some trench thuggery, clawed at his face. Someone else came through the door. Duncan barged Hardy aside, swung and shot—saw a head snapped back—swung back again toward Bainbridge, fired twice, blind. High cry—Bainbridge went over, but it wasn't his voice. Bolt upright in the chair, Rachel stared back at him out of shocked dark eyes. Time slowed; his vision went acid clear. Blood drenching her blouse down at the waistline. Perhaps she saw him stare—she looked down, saw the blood, too, whimpered and pressed both hands to the damage. The blood welled up over her clutching fingers, sluggish pulse. Bainbridge, struggling to rise, clutching at his thigh—

One shot left in the Webley. Shuddering sense of things falling apart . . .

You will not heal this way—fucking *Meb's* voice, of all things, jumping into his head when he least fucking needed it.

Club Hardy in the head again for good measure—

The door hinged back open. Duncan yelled, wordless, pointed the Webley, and whoever it was quailed aside, arms flung up vainly for protection. He held his fire. Later, he thought it might have been Ewart . . .

Bainbridge stumbling, slipping over in his own blood on the boards . . .

Rachel, whimpering, bleeding—

Snag fucking Hardy by the collar again, haul him grunting and flailing weakly to the shattered French windows. Webley trained on the doorway in case someone else fancied their chances. Summon your voice—bellow it out for all of them to hear—

"Do not follow us outside!" It came out a hoarse and grinding roar, someone else speaking for him surely, the voice of a murderous bastard if there ever was one. *"You will be shot dead if you do!"*

You will not heal this way.

He got Hardy through the shattered portal, dragged him out into the wet and the dark.

THE FRENCH WINDOWS CAST WARM lamplight in angled blocks onto the darkened lawn. He hauled Hardy left and out of their reach. Odd sense of relief creeping in his nerves with the shift to shadow. Through the grip he had with his hand, he thought he felt the other man's resistance rising again—tough bastard, you had to give him that. He jammed the Webley barrel hard into the base of Hardy's spine. Snarled in his ear.

"Don't test me, Colonel!"

"You won't . . ." Slurring, panting. "You can't . . ."

"I just fucking did, so stow your shite."

He made the tree line, pulled Hardy unceremoniously through the tangle of bushes, crashed him face-first flat to the ground. He put his own weight on top, jabbed the revolver into the man's lower back again. Put his mouth to Hardy's ear again, hissed through gritted teeth. "I've seen men shot through the spine before, Colonel Hardy. They can live long lives in wheelchairs and nappies, unless they get up the courage to end it themselves. I need you alive, but that's about it, *so don't fucking test me*!"

Flat whip-crack report of Arthur's carbine, off to the left.

Duncan got to his knees, hauled Hardy up in front of him. They crabbed through the undergrowth, lurched between the trees, working a wide, careful arc back to where Arthur and the witch waited.

Two more reports from the carbine.

"All right?" he asked as he collapsed Hardy again beside them.

"Yeah, they've got the idea." Arthur, laconic, not lifting his eye from the rear sight. "Might try to circle round from the front of the house, but unless they do it from both corners at once, I can hold them as long as I've got bullets."

"Good man." Duncan clapped him on the shoulder. "Won't need

to do that, though. Just hold here about five minutes, then fall back, follow us out."

"Sweet."

"Duncan, what in Hecate's fuckworthy name do you think—"

Duncan cut across her protestations. "He knows where Mimi and her mother are being held. He's going to tell me. Now come on, let's get out of here."

The witch muttered something under her breath, but she got up, stowed the Kilner jar back in its satchel, slung it nonchalantly over her shoulder.

"I'll carry it," she said. "You've got your hands full."

They skulked away from the house, lost its lights rapidly in the trees and murk behind them as they straightened up and moved faster. Hard to tell under the canopies, but the rain seemed to be tuning up, from drizzle to something more driven—ought to make pursuit even more of a nightmare for anyone who might come after them. Duncan forced the pace as much as he dared in the low light and the uneven ground underfoot. He drove Hardy ahead of him with cuffs across the head from his free hand, prods with the barrel of the Webley in his back. A few minutes on, Duncan heard the carbine again, a single shot, then more silence. Another two minutes, another report. No answering fire. It didn't look as if Adept House contained men with the weapons or stomach to rush Arthur in his sniper's hide.

When they reached the thinning fringes of woodland at the edge of the munitions plant, he grabbed Hardy to a halt, raised a hand to Nimble Shanks Annie.

"We wait here for Arthur."

"Gets my vote," panted the witch. She'd been struggling to keep up. She unslung the satchel, dumped it on the ground with evident relief, braced hands on her widespread knees and bent over, working at getting her breath back under control. "That's about enough—soldiering—for one night."

Duncan surveyed the darkened loom of the abandoned factory buildings ahead, the low brush and the scattered copses that grew between, the open ground. Beyond the tree that sheltered them, the rain slashed down with increasing vigor, murking the view. "You want to try scrying the way through again, make sure we've got no nasty surprises waiting for us?"

Still bent over, she gave him a sour look. "You want to give me a fucking minute?"

"You bloody fools," spat Hardy meanwhile, glowering, clutching at his head. "You'll hang for this! Both of you! Your sniper friend, too!"

"Shut up, Hardy," Duncan told him tiredly. "You're in no position to be making threats. And, since you failed pretty fucking dismally to kill me with a sneak sniper bullet yourself, you'll forgive me if I'm not too impressed with promises of due process."

"I don't . . ." Maybe there was something in his face, because Hardy turned away, looked to the witch. "Perhaps you can make him understand, madame? You are interfering with *matters of state,* matters you cannot possibly—"

Duncan stepped in, stomped him behind the knee, dropped him face-first in the dirt at her feet. A thin, rising fury like a scream, seething in his inner ear . . .

"Madame?" The witch wiped sweat and rain off her face, straggled back her hair. "I like that."

Duncan kicked his tumbled prisoner savagely in the belly—trying to drive out harsh visions of Rachel's bloodied, frantically clutching hands, the stealthy welling-up pulse of her lifeblood running out . . .

You're ill luck, Duncan. You know that.

Aye, well. Hold it together.

He crouched at the other man's side, snarled in his face. "You think four scrape-the-barrel scum coppers killed is a big fucking deal, Hardy? I'm just getting started. You have no fucking idea what I'll do to anyone who gets between me and Mimi Rush now. I'll gut Sir Michael fucking Endershall himself, balls to breastbone, if he stands in my way. And you, you faithless cunt—"

"I won't talk, you know." Breathy voice and a defiant bared-teeth grin raised toward him. "You think you can make me?"

"I know I can." Duncan tossed the Webley aside, grabbed Hardy's head in both hands, twisted it roughly. "You see where we are? This is off the fucking map for you, Hardy. But for me, it's close to home. You tell me where Mimi and her mother are, or I'm going to take you into the deep Forest and introduce you to some of the things that live there."

Hardy spat at him, thick, bloodied spittle that barely made it past his lips, then hung slick and drooling from the corner of his broken mouth.

But Duncan saw the terror awake in his eyes, and something in him sang at the sight, sticky black joy through his veins.

"Sweet, you waited!" Arthur hurried up, out of breath, carbine still unslung. "Wasn't looking forward to crossing all that open ground alone."

"Aye, we'll get Annie here to scry it again in a minute. Get your breath. Like the man says, more haste, less speed. You have to shoot anyone?"

"Not yet. Warning shots only."

"You! Listen to me!" Hardy, trying again with the new arrival. "You've served your country, that's clear enough. You cannot permit this! You have a duty to king and country to stop these people."

Arthur spared him a glance. "You're joking, right?"

"Duncan." The witch, straightened up now, frowning, some urgency creeping into her tone. "There's some—"

And blood erupted from her throat.

THIRTY-NINE

DUNCAN GAPED, PARALYZED IN THE COLD WRAP OF SUDDEN nightmare, the serpent hiss of rain.

Like some awful price exacted for the murder of Rachel—Nimble Shanks Annie, right there before him, close enough to touch, clutching suddenly at her throat. Splattering of lifeblood over her frantically gripping fingers. Her eyes clawed after his, she tilted on her feet. Tried to say something. More blood bubbled out over her lips, she coughed it up, choked on it, staggered and fell.

It was only then he saw the arrow.

Black, somehow viscous looking along its edges, jutting a handbreadth out of her throat, the spike that stopped her hand clapping flat to the wound it had made. As her legs tangled and folded, as she tottered and tilted and fell, he saw the rest of it, more than two feet of the same black, drip-spined greasy shaft protruding from the back of her neck.

She was dead before she hit the sodden ground, eyes staring into nothing, while Duncan, numb in nightmare, went right on gaping at what had been done.

Arthur to his credit, was faster to react.

"Archers!" In the same moment he yelled, he swung—Duncan would later realize—to face the direction the back of the shaft had pointed.

Something flitted between trees. Arthur threw up the carbine, snapped off a shot. No sooner loosed than on to the next—work the bolt, eject, combat rapid, mad-minute-drill style. The carbine barrel tracked left an inch. He fired again. Duncan thought the flitting figure maybe stumbled, but—

Standard jacketed load—lead and cupronickel, trace iron content in the jacket at best. It would punch a hole right through the Huldu, if it hit square.

And Fae flesh, steeped in Forest magic, would heal the wound back up in minutes or less.

Duncan tore the McCulloch from its sheath, pumped a shell into the chamber. Behind him, Hardy, still on his knees, stared in transfixed horror at the shaft through the witch's neck. His nightmare from Mons, come calling after all those years, like the death he eluded in the trenches and must have thought put behind. Duncan could almost feel sorry for the man. Hardy's voice scaled to a cry, almost ecstatic in its terror.

"Ohhh, Christ! They're coming!"

Duncan fired into the trees and rain, three shells on general principles, roughly where the flitting shadow had gone. He'd brought no Kegg bombs, and against this foe, the Webleys were useless, even the dumdum rounds could only gouge and stagger . . .

"Fall back!" he bellowed. "Arthur! Get to the sheds! We've no chance here!"

"I hear you!" Cool, clipped, not looking round. Eyes still on the trees, carbine cuddled tight to his cheek. "That's a lot of open ground!"

"We've no fucking choice!"

Another black shaft came out of the woods, slicked through the air between them. Arthur tracked it, fired back.

"Get going!" he yelled.

Duncan spared one more look for Nimble Shanks Annie, her violated throat and bloodied mouth, black in the low light, her shocked open staring eyes. He took the fuel and fury it gave him, then he was moving, weaving, out across the brush-grown, rain-flogged open spaces of the munitions plant. The nearest built structure was over a hundred yards off, a pair of long, low storage sheds he'd spotted when they first arrived at the fringes of the woods.

Too far off, if the archers wanted them. If the Fae wanted to make a quick end of things.

Closer in—*there!*—a decayed flat wagon, rusted to the tracks that led across the site, about halfway to the sheds. Duncan clipped his course, darted for the wagon, flung himself into the scant cover it offered, twisted about to see what had happened to the others. Hardy was only a few dozen yards behind him, but groggy and stumbling. Arthur brought up the rear, still in cool, sharpshooter command, turning every few seconds to scan for targets. As Duncan watched, evidently he saw one. He dropped to one knee, the carbine snapped up. Thin crack of the bullet on its way. Up again and moving.

"Arthur!"

The sharpshooter hooked a look, saw him, changed course. Hardy came blundering with. Last few yards . . .

Arthur spun and dropped again, cracked out another rapid-fire pair of shots, shoot-strip-the-bolt-shoot. An arrow shaft came hissing out of the rain-filled gloom, went right over his head. Punched Hardy in the back, hard enough to throw him forward to his knees, came out his chest at sternum height. Arthur went over backward on his arse with the shock of the near miss. Duncan tore the remaining Webley from his pocket, charged out of cover firing, emptied the gun into the tree line, threw it away. Hardy crawled about on hands and knees, coughing blood. Duncan darted past him, grabbed Arthur under the arms, hauled the sharpshooter backward toward cover.

They collapsed together in the lee of the flat wagon, hunkered down, shoulders to the iron bogie.

"Thanks, man!" Arthur, panting. He still had the Lee-Enfield in his right hand, had never let it go when he fell. "I owe you one."

"On the house." Duncan unsheathed the McCulloch from his

back. Inched an eye round the cold, rain-beaded iron molding of the bogies, scanned the tree line for movement. "We're in luck. They're not coming out to play just yet."

Arthur recovered a two-handed grip on the carbine, held it to his chest like a lover. "Swear I scored hits at least a couple of times."

"Aye, you probably did. Jacketed load, no iron. You'll stagger them, but it won't do much more than that."

The sharpshooter grimaced. "Good to know."

A dozen yards out, all the while, Hardy made choking, mewling, pleading noises—from the sound of it, elf shot through the lungs, he was going to be a while dying. The two men listened to it for a minute, recall of a hundred deaths on the wire, like barbs dragging embedded in the brain.

Arthur slanted Duncan a look. Duncan hesitated. Nodded.

Arthur worked the bolt on the Lee-Enfield—fresh brass gleam of the shell as it jumped out—listened a moment with bowed head, for position. Then he swung up over the top of the flat wagon, pulled the carbine in to his cheek, and fired.

Flat crack of the single shot in the rain, across the deserted night-time spaces of the munitions plant.

Hardy fell silent.

Arthur dropped back into cover, glanced at Duncan again, and nodded.

And there goes my best chance of finding Mimi and her mother.

Absently, he checked the load on the trench gun, caught the two shells in his cupped hand as they popped out. Fed them mechanically back in through the McCulloch's receiver.

Assuming either of us live that long.

He could feel the tilt of the moment, the slow sinking sense of everything sliding from his grasp, falling to pieces, falling away. He stared out across the remaining half mile of abandoned industrial plant that separated them from the gates and escape in the ambulance. Impossible to cross that ground in one piece with the Huldu in pursuit.

One way or another, this was it.

At least you won't die in the fucking Forest.

"How many you reckon?" the sharpshooter asked him quietly.

"Archers?" Duncan held down a shudder, frowned into memory. "Not many. Two or three, maybe? They're not common. It's something they learned from us, back in the Neolithic, and they haven't handled it all that well."

Arthur grunted. "Wasn't my impression. They killed the witch first, for safety. They spiked Hardy and left him for bait in the open. They know what they're doing."

"Not what I meant." Duncan was in no mood to explain. "Listen, the damage you can do with that carbine is limited, and they'll heal fast from it. You reckon you can make head shots?"

The sharpshooter gave him a ragged grin. "Pale-as-fish-belly bastards like that? Ask me for something difficult."

"Right. So you hang dark, cling to cover as much as you can, put out eyes." Duncan patted the McCulloch. "I'll handle the closer-in stuff."

He let himself settle against the molded iron of the wagon bogie. Tugged the iron chain from around his collar by inches, laid it in a coil within easy reach. He laid out the sgian dubh next to it. Rain speckled and splattered them both. Breathe deep, compose yourself. The jolting change of gear—killing Huldu now, not men. He let the banked, familiar fires of his rage come on, comforting as the fireside childhood memories he'd never been given the chance to make. He held the McCulloch across his chest.

THEY DIDN'T HAVE TO WAIT long.

Across the brush they came, three pallid, hurrying figures—two Huldu scouts and the taller, more angular form of an archer behind. Duncan snarled a silent grin. It was the old hunting party standard, a formation so ingrained and traditional among the Fae that seeing it felt almost like a reunion with some old school bully—one you now knew how to handle perfectly.

He turned his head to Arthur, whispered barely louder than the hissing of the rain. “Leave these to me. There’ll be plenty of work for you soon enough.”

The scouts wore their cloaks dulled down to something that glinted like the dark kaleidoscopic swirl of oil on water. Their fangs and talons were combat grown, anticipatory. Nothing he hadn’t seen or killed before, but the archer . . .

He’d seen them as a boy only once or twice. They were not common around the Huldu camps, a deformed and reclusive elite, and what the Huldu children whispered about them was vague, contradictory, the fuel for myth even among a mythic folk. The ancient Huldu saw Neolithic hunters with bows, grudgingly took note of the upstart innovation, shape-shifted their way to a response. But such extreme shape-shifting was no easy thing, even for the Fae. The transformation needed for this was radical and, it was whispered, difficult to undo. *They just stay that way,* Drasvinad said once, in hushed tones a million miles from her customary whimsical cruelty and laughter. *It hurts too much to make the change, or to change back. Only the strongest are chosen.*

The archer stood seven feet tall, long limbed and heavily muscled like all his kind. But he moved with less grace, made a more careful, lopsided figure when set against his comrades. Where his left hand and wrist had once been, a gnarled, bifurcated growth sprouted from the brutally muscled forearm, curved upward a yard, downward a yard to match, gleaming like wet bone in the night, wrapped tightly about with what Duncan assumed was sinew. It formed the undeniable outline of a long and powerful recurved bow, strung tightly from top to bottom with what had to be another single strand of yet more sinew.

Somewhere up on the creature’s hunched right shoulder, Duncan knew, would be a hole, wet and gory deep through the archer’s body, into which shafts of hazel or birch or pine were fed to marinate and steep in body fluid, to grow their dripping fletches and spines and bladed heads. *They soak them in their darkest hates,* one Fae boy said airily one night around the fire. Looking balefully at Duncan across the flames. *All the hate for the tree thieves, all the vengeance feelings and hurting for the Forest.*

In the murky light and rain, as the party drew closer to their hiding place, Duncan thought he spotted a dozen protruding fletched shafts over the archer's shoulder. But none were yet drawn or nocked in the bow.

Last fucking mistake you'll ever make, sunshine.

He rolled out from the flat wagon, came up on one knee, slam-fired into the approaching Fae. Three shells, midsection height. The scouts went down, shredded and screaming, the archer staggered and howled and reached up and back for a shaft to load his bow. Duncan popped to his feet, two steps in, fast, lifted the McCulloch to shoulder height, and put a shot through the Huldu's head. Blue-green flash and explosion, upward, outward splatter of blood. The archer stood, skull like a cupped piece of crockery from some archaeological dig, still guttering faintly with flame, then tumbled ponderously into the brush.

"Duncan!"

The yell and the crack of the carbine hit at the same time. Head yanked around—pale forms rising wet and muddy from the brush on the far side of the flat wagon, at least a dozen. And two more archers. They must, he thought jaggedly, have crawled for hundreds of yards through the low growth. Arthur was up on one knee, firing, ejecting, firing, ejecting, the mad-minute drill again, as fast as Duncan had ever seen it done. Fanged heads jerked, figures spun and stumbled, some of them fell.

But they got back up, *they got back up again.*

Duncan raced back to the other man's side. Three shells left in the McCulloch—he chose the archers for targets, put two shots into the first, saw him go down in ruin, spent the last shell to stagger the other. He threw down the emptied trench gun, grabbed up chain and sgian dubh from where he'd left them, leapt up onto the flat wagon with a howl. Leapt down and ran right at the staggered archer, chain arcing through the rain over his head.

He got lucky, hit the Huldu in neck and shoulder. Iron links, sinking in, sparking smolder and green fire. The Fae archer shrilled and twisted. Duncan swung and lashed again, across the face this time, a blinding stroke. Then he closed with the sgian dubh, reverse grip in his left hand.

Into face and neck and chest. Screams and flailing, smolder and rain, the archer's deformed bow arm battering awkwardly at him, the talons on the other hand slashing like razors. He rode the blows, deflected the talon slashes most of the time, kept on hacking. Behind him, the steady crack of Arthur's carbine. He saw an opening, stomp-kicked into the wounded Fae's knee, felt it give and buckle. The creature finally went down. He flogged viciously at it with the chain, opened smoking trenches across its chest and belly and throat . . .

The carbine fire, choked off.

He spun about, saw Arthur, up out of cover and wrestling against a Huldu scout, carbine rammed crossways at the Fae's chest. Flash and smolder as the length of the barrel made contact. The Huldu shrilled, but did not give ground. Seasoned iron fighter, then—warrior caste. Duncan came at the run. Maybe Arthur heard him, he turned his head, eyes wild, panic printed clear, even across those rain-soaked, fire-ravaged features. Snapshot split second—the Huldu seized the moment, worked some rough-and-tumble wrestling trick, learned on the Forest floor with other young males, who knew how many centuries gone—the bracing barrel slipped and flipped, Arthur staggered sideways with the force of it. The Huldu stood strong, chest still licked with tiny green flames and smolder into the night air, struck with one after another taloned hand . . .

Duncan roared, leapt back up onto the flat wagon, launched himself feet first. He hit Arthur's attacker full force with both boots, knocked the Fae backward to the ground. Landed, rolled. Came up in a muddy crouch, just as the Huldu scrabbled upright and lunged at him with its bloodied talons. Duncan, desperate, fell back the way he'd rolled. The Huldu's slashing hand missed him, went too high. He lashed out with the chain, got lucky again, caught the arm. The links wrapped around, sank sizzling into Fae flesh. He yanked savagely, pulled the Fae down on top of him, screamed into its face, put an eye out with the sgian dubh, then sawed the knife blade raggedly across its throat. Blood exploded across the space between them, splattered on his face like fresh, hot rain, cardamom spiced. He spat it out, shoved the hemorrhaging scout off him and away. He scrabbled back to his feet and to Arthur.

Was just in time to see the sharpshooter die.

One or other of the Huldu's talon slashes had ripped open his neck at the side, taken most of an ear with it, severed the carotid. Arthur lay propped at a crazy angle against the flat wagon bogie, painted with his own blood. He stared at Duncan oddly, as if they'd only just run into each other. He held one hand pressed hard to the damage the Huldu had done, but seemed to have forgotten it.

"Now *that*," he said, in a bubbling voice, "was a mad minute!"

"Oh Christ, Arthur . . ."

The sharpshooter frowned, took the hand away from his wound to study it, peering at his blood-buttered palm in puzzlement. "Oh . . ."

The hole in his neck filled up with blood, pulsed over the ragged edges of the wound, spilled all down him. He tried to turn his face down and look at it, then hung his head in silence instead. His arm and the bloodied hand he'd been wondering at went limp. Rain dripped off the fingers. He did not move again.

You're ill luck, Duncan. You know that.

Fresh, stealthy motion, off to the side.

Duncan swung around, blade and gore-dripping chain, crouched at bay as a ragged line of scouts moved to encircle the flat wagon with wary care. He counted seven, no, eight, padding closer, some of them still with misshapen, damaged heads from Arthur's fusillade. The holes the sharpshooter had punched gave them an awkward, listing aspect, as if they were blinded—some looked as if they might actually be, eye sockets glutted or torn open—and now had to listen intently for their enemy before they moved. There'd be more like this out there in the brush, downed, but they, too, would shortly heal and get up . . .

No time to get to the McCulloch, certainly no time to load it. They'd be on him the second he moved. You could see in the way they were poised, all they needed was to see him flinch or turn.

"Come on then!" he screamed at them in Skogurtal. *"Who's fucking next?"*

Blank black stares, lips peeled from fangs. He nerved himself for their rush, he drew a deep, shuddering breath that seemed to set tiny fires burning along his veins, under his nails, in his teeth. He bared his own snarl . . .

"Enough!"

Her voice hit him a heartbeat before she did, the low, luxuriant tones warped into a cry that seemed to float on the night air somewhere between anguish and rage, and he knew instantly, despite all distortion, whose voice it was.

Mebhuranon!

She came like a stooping bird of prey, cloak wrapped, trailing long dark and silver hair, cannoned into him with shoulder and arm, knocked him flat to the ground, stood over him, fanged and taloned and staring blank as a black stone angel. He had no idea where she'd come from, from what cover among the buildings or the trees, whether she'd simply dropped from the fucking sky . . .

"Stay down," she snarled in English, and the sudden, stabbing shock of that alone was enough to hold him where he lay.

Then she rounded on her fellow Fae, made a cat's hiss sound, and they bent their heads, abandoned feral crouch for obeisance in the scant second it took Duncan to prop himself up and see. Her voice raged in Skogurtal, but it was an ornate, antique form he struggled to make sense of, fenced around with formulaic phrasing and allusion to things that, in his rattled state, made no sense, had no grounding in anything he knew. The best sense he could make of it was that she had come just in time and that they, all of them, ought to be ashamed, and so should Svalenkari, their master . . .

He gave up trying to keep pace.

"Is this a [hunt? offering?] worthy of the One Who Watches?" She stormed on. "Must Svalenkari [feed?] like a [???] with belly grown pendulous as a [???] who came before? What will your [fetches? guardians of?] in the Final Isles and End of Days say of your [???]? Where is [honor? name?], where is memory, where is [???] back to the Beginning?"

One of the uninjured Huldu bared fangs, started to say something—

Mebhuranon was on him before he got three syllables out. She slammed him to the ground, crouched and cracked her jaws wide, made a sound like a buzzard's cry, showed her fangs to him, let him scrabble backward away from her on his hands and arse. Then she straightened, looked around at the rest of them, made a sound this time like the rushing of a hillside stream in spate. She gestured angrily toward the woods.

"Go, all of you! Now! Slope away, the way you came here, no better than creeping [???] or tree thieves, no more [worthy?] than [???] in the eyes of the One Who Watches and Her [brood? beloved?]. Go and [pray? desire?] only that the Final Isles shall not know this sorry, bitter tale!"

Someone dared speak up, spat out the name Svalenkari—

"Svalenkari," she snarled back, "will have his [day? appointed hour?]. But he will have it as we have [lived? honored?] these hundred thousand [returns? losses?]. He may besmirch himself, but he will not besmirch the [name? realm?] of the Bright Folk, I will not permit it, not now, not while the moon is in the sky and the ocean in its bed, nor ever after! Now *go*!"

Slowly, then, very slowly, they dropped their stares, turned, and began to leave. The fully hale among them paused in the brush to help their head-shot comrades to stand and lean on them and limp away, too.

They left their dead where they lay.

They left Duncan and the Fae queen silent in the gloom by the flat wagon. They faded across the rainy open ground in ones and twos, and into the tree line once more.

Presently they were gone.

"They came for you," said Mebhuranon finally.

Duncan got himself to his feet with an effort. "So I gather."

"Svalenkari will not be denied." She was, he realized, still speaking English to him. She stared down at Arthur's body, out across the brush to where Hardy lay with his head shot through and the elf bolt shaft still in his chest. "Were these your friends?"

He thought about it. "This one, yes."

"Then I am sorry for this loss."

"So am I."

Perhaps she heard something in his voice. She turned more fully to face him—she topped him by a good six inches—put one taloned hand on his chest. It was like being touched by something out of Milton's vision of hell.

"A reckoning has come," she said, still in English. "Svalenkari demands, and the clans will hear him. I cannot balance this. So tell me, Duncan, what will you give up, for the child to be saved, for Mimi and her mother to walk free? How far will you go?"

Rain hissed in the brush, like soft radio static.

Across the desolate industrial landscape of the shut-down munitions plant, through the eager woodland waiting at its fringes, a vast silence bent inward behind the sound of the rain, as if to hear what his best offer might be.

He stared into Mebhuranon's pitiless black gaze.

"You already know," he said.

FORTY

HE MADE THE MUNITIONS PLANT GATES AND THE WAITING AMbulance after what seemed like an eternity of sodden footfalls in rain that pelted his naked head and the drenched shoulders of his coat like punishment. He slipped numbly through the iron gap they'd opened on the way in, a lifetime ago. He stood drenched in the downpour and the wet yellow gleam of the head lamps.

Mike Collier got out in a hooded army-issue rain cape, came round the front of the vehicle to meet him. Stared past him, out through the gates to the abandoned plant beyond.

"The others?"

Duncan shook his head. Rain trickled down his cheeks, dripped off his jaw.

"Fucking hell, are you sure?"

"I'm sure. Get us out of here."

"But—"

Duncan looked at him. Collier flinched.

"It's over," Duncan told him. "Nothing we can do is going to change anything that matters now."

CODA

BACK TO THE GRAY

And what rough beast, its hour come round at last,
Slouches towards Bethlehem to be born?

—William Butler Yeats

FORTY-ONE

OCTOBER DAWN.

In the uncertain blue-gray light as the day hesitated on the brink, Capstone Park House bulked more like an outcrop of million-year granite crags than anything men had built by hand. Later, sunlight might creep down the southern facades, gilding the somber gray stone, putting flashy puddles of reflected brilliance on the serried ranks of windows, picking out the detail of dressed stone and crenellated battlement lines. But for now, the house dreamed itself timeless, geological and blunt. It stood like a promise made, like a rampart and refuge against the turbulence of shattered norms and hoary old confidences cast down.

Duncan stood on the battlemented balcony roof of the south tower and shivered in a cold wind that had blown up out of the west overnight. Implication held him stiff at the parapet, thoughts of the road that had led him here, the final steps still to take. The final signature he had given to underwrite the Fae queen's compact, the balance of payment, the choice. And yet, he'd given it readily enough. Could not regret it, even now. Had perhaps always known, somehow, that it must come to this.

It's fine. We all die of something.

He put both hands on the stone balustrade, stared at them intently for a moment, then looked up and outward.

From up here, you could see right over the sprawling lawns and gardens of the great house, see the long glinting run of steel mesh fencing that closed them in, and beyond that mile after unending mile of tree canopies nodding in the breeze, copper and golden brown with the autumn die off, massed across the southern expanse of the estate, like some encamped army at siege, waiting for the order to attack before winter could fall.

He heard slippered feet slap time up the steps of the spiral staircase behind him in the corner, the huffing of someone badly out of breath as they leaned on the propped trapdoor at the top. He didn't look round, didn't want to embarrass his host while he was getting his breath back. He leaned his hands on the parapet again and looked at them like tools he was no longer quite sure how to use.

"They told me you were up here," said the new arrival gruffly. Footfalls across the rooftop, a bulky presence at his shoulder, faint and somehow comforting odor of pipe tobacco. "I suppose you couldn't sleep either?"

Duncan shook his head.

The other man joined him at the parapet. Viscount Savin of Askerndale cut a commanding figure at forty-seven years old, even here in pajamas, dressing gown, and naked, slippered feet. He was tall, with the build of a man once proudly athletic, handsome in a way that hinted at his rumored eastern European ancestry. His neatly kept beard and thick head of grizzled hair gave him a vaguely naval air, as if he'd just doffed a captain's cap and stepped off the bridge of a dreadnought. Duncan supposed it was appropriate—much of the wealth that made Savin the twenty-fifth richest man in Britain had been made by his family from the ocean. Savin Line vessels might not be spoken of in quite the same breath as those of Cunard or White Star, but they plied the same routes, and by all accounts they provided some solid competition in both comfort and speed. A Blue Riband award was anticipated soon.

"They will come, you know," Savin rumbled kindly. "I don't like

Sir Michael very much, but he is a man of his word. Bainbridge, too, in his own way."

"Let's hope so."

"In any case, you and your friends are welcome here at Capstone Park for as long as this may take. And there is no question of the police or anyone else intruding uninvited. I will not permit it. I hope you know that."

Duncan smiled to himself. Over the phone to Erlsley, later at the door of his family's hereditary seat when their car arrived, Savin had been emphatic verging on profane.

"Aye, you made it clear enough. I'm not sure I've thanked you properly yet. It's been a rush."

The viscount grunted, turned to lean with his back to the view and the Forest. His voice grew gruff again.

"There is no need for thanks, as you well know. My boy is safely home. Every night before bed, I hug him to me and I give thanks—not to God, Mr. Silver, but to you. In your accounts with me, rest assured, my side of the ledger will forever be in red ink."

Duncan inclined his head, said nothing. Held down another shiver. Savin watched him for a moment, then clapped him on the shoulder with awkward camaraderie.

"It is overly autumnal up here, is it not? Perhaps we should go down and see if Barton can scare us up some breakfast, hmm?"

Duncan nodded, put the Forest at his back for a while, and followed the viscount to the stairs.

He wasn't hungry.

But with what was coming, he couldn't afford to skimp on fuel.

NINE DAYS.

Nine days since Collier dropped him, drenched head to foot and daubed with Huldu blood, at the rear entrance of the Doorbell Club. He looked back now, and it felt like time lived by some other being he had only the most tenuous connection with, an automaton out of something by Wells maybe, endowed with his basic reflexes and memory, but otherwise detached.

Or perhaps a changeling.

Jagged snapshot recall of actions taken, decisions made, the impact of consequences he trailed behind him like a Huldu cloak in vivid colors of blood and dark—

Belle D'Or's face when he told her about Arthur, the way her catlike poise skidded away from her, as if she'd slipped abruptly sideways on a snapped heel. The way she slapped him full across the face with all her force and stalked away, shoulders tight and trembling, before he could see her weep.

Crammond, summoned to the club, grim-faced as Duncan explained quietly what had happened, where he would now have to go with Niamh and Garner.

What promises he would have to keep.

Niamh and Garner, subdued, in varying degrees of shock. *Lad, what have tha bloody done?* Garner kept repeating, like some kind of litany. *Do tha realize what tha've done?* By contrast, Niamh said nothing at all, only sat pale and intent, looking at him out of one hollow eye and the swollen slit that masked the other, and reached out to hold his hand, very tightly.

Savin's voice, grave over the phone.

The car came for them early that evening, gleaming black and pearled with rain, driven by a chauffeur in full uniform—not, in fact, something entirely out of place for the clientele the Doorbell Club was known to service. It collected them from the rear entrance in failing light, took them out of Erlsley with the fiery leavings of sunset still layered across mauve clouds in a western sky that looked as if it'd been torn apart by shelling.

THE PAPERS.

SLAUGHTER AT MYSTIC RETREAT: TWO SHOT DEAD, OTHERS WOUNDED

was the *Yorkshire Evening Post*'s phlegmatic accounting. The girl, Rachel, had died, together with one of Bainbridge's men. *Nice shooting, Duncan.* Bainbridge himself and a second man were being treated in hospital for gunshot wounds, both expected to survive. Witnesses at the retreat were oddly vague. The identity and motives of the intruders remained the target of an ongoing police inquiry and a subject for speculation.

The Times correspondent in Erlsley was evidently prepared to indulge in said speculation and to dig a little deeper in the process. ABDUCTION AND ROBBERY OF ARCANE ARTIFACTS SUSPECTED: SCANDAL STALKS THE MOST HATED MAN IN BRITAIN ONCE AGAIN. Someone on staff at Adept House had either slipped up, or just been slipped enough to talk to the man from London. *And London,* Murdoch the forger had once told him, *sucks like that maelstrom in that Verne book. Bad old town, she never lets go.* Duncan remembered Bainbridge's furious protestations and rancor at Endershall, wondered if Sir Michael and the new owner of *The Times* shared a club.

The next day, *The Manchester Guardian* had INNOVATIVE POLICE DOG UNIT TRACKS SWORD AND ORB INTRUDERS; MORE BODIES FOUND AT DISUSED MUNITIONS PLANT; SWORD AND ORB MYSTERY DEEPENS. Two dogs, from a new experimental patrol force based out of Hull docks, were apparently on loan to Erlsley police and had made short work of the trail through the woods, to find the bodies of Hardy, Arthur, and Nimble Shanks Annie. Much was made in several publications of the witch's involvement, the magical wounds she had received, and there were some lurid allusions to her past, but there the detail died. Arthur was named, curtly, as Lieutenant Arthur John Brightwell, ex of Kitchener's 12th, mentioned twice in dispatches, invalided out following the battle of Pozières, of no fixed abode ever since. No mention of Hardy by name, rank, or more recent assignment. He remained an *unidentified associate* of Malcom Bainbridge.

Section J, roused from slumber, come north and wielding D-notices in both fists, was Duncan's best guess. Staying ahead of them was the first order of business.

Hardy was gone, but someone else would be picking the bones out of the Maunston police station raid. Even if Bainbridge chose to stay silent—and depending on what bargains he needed to strike, what ambitions he still maintained, that seemed unlikely—Duncan's return from the dead had to be known by now. They would be searching for him, unofficially for the time being, full national police involvement soon on tap if that failed.

And only a matter of time before someone went back to his rooms on Skoldergate, went through his client notes, and made the connection to Viscount Savin.

Niamh coughed insistently through the nights. He held her, soothed her back to sleep as best he could.

Even here, behind the fortress ramparts of wealth and exception, time was running out.

DISGRACED MYSTIC DISCHARGED FROM HOSPITAL, blared *The Times* the following week. REFUSES TO ANSWER QUESTIONS FROM THE PRESS, RECOVERING AT HOME.

No specific address or even city was mentioned, but Duncan was willing to bet the archmage had returned to Adept House.

He talked to Savin; he talked to the others.

He rode roughshod over their protests, made light of what was coming, understated it as much as he could without making it obvious that he was lying.

Then he picked up the phone in Savin's study, held it for a long moment in silence, until the operator came on the line, and he asked her to connect him with the number Bainbridge had given him.

GARNER WENT HOME THE FOLLOWING day.

"Safe enough now," Duncan told him as they walked out to the car in the late-afternoon sun. "Maunston's buried, apparently. No one wants to talk about it anyway. Too many awkward questions going unanswered. Looks like Hardy overreached, even by his masters' standards. They're drawing a line under the whole thing."

He handed the other man a thick envelope. Garner rolled his eyes.

"I don't need paying, lad. Not after all this."

"Well, the widow at the White Mare will. She's had that bloody horse of yours for the better part of a month."

Garner turned the envelope in his hand, gauged the thickness. "There's a lot more here than a couple of weeks' feed for Mabel."

Duncan shrugged. "Treat her to something nice, then."

"Oh, aye?" An unwilling grin crept out onto Garner's face. "Mabel, tha mean, or the Widow Worrart?"

"Both. Either. Whichever takes your fancy. I know which I'd choose, but then I don't like horses."

"Aye, well, they don't bloody like thee either, lad."

Both men stood quiet, hovering on the verge of something neither was going to say. Savin's chauffeur stood waiting, rear door held open for his passenger. Duncan looked down at the waxed manila bag in his left hand. Hefted it. The McCulloch's blunt, utilitarian lines, softened in the wrap of the cloth. He drew a deep breath and—this bit cost him more than he'd show—offered it on both open hands to Garner. The Lancastrian looked steadily at him.

"Are tha sure, lad?"

Duncan nodded. "Aye. *Bring blade and body only to the glade*, same as it ever was. There's no other way this works."

Garner took the bundled trench gun awkwardly, as if gathering up a swaddled child. He swallowed hard. Searched grimacing for words like a man trying to force shreds of meat from between his teeth with his tongue, until Duncan took pity on him and clapped him on the shoulder.

"It'll be fine," he said. "Nothing I haven't done before."

But as he watched Garner driven away, the smile faded slowly from his face and so, drowned behind sudden cloud, did the sun.

THE CARS ARRIVED IN A convoy of three a little after lunchtime, rolling sedately up the long gravel drive like toys and then round onto the forecourt of the house. Bainbridge's Crossley in pole position, followed by a gleaming blue Rolls Royce Silver Ghost and then a nondescript little red and gray sedan Duncan thought might be the new Austin 7 the drivers at the Erlsley Bird taxi rank had been chirping about all fucking year long. Two fairly obvious plainclothes police officers sat in it, looking cramped and irritable as they drew up in the fumes of the Rolls' exhaust.

Duncan and Savin watched the convoy arrive from the first-floor study window. The plainclothesmen got out first, unfolding themselves with visible relief from the car, stretching the kinks out of their limbs as they looked around. From each of the limousines sprang a liveried chauffeur to hold open the rear door, and the passengers stepped out onto the gravel of the forecourt. Curiously, Bainbridge emerged from the Rolls, not the Crossley, limping visibly on his sphinx-headed cane, and just ahead of another man in his late fifties with thick iron-gray hair and a Kitchener mustache.

The Crossley disgorged a thin-looking woman wrapped in a long gray coat and matching beret, and a small child in a floral print dress who clung to her side like a limpet. It took Duncan a blank moment to recognize Mimi Rush and her mother, then Susan's sturdier figure as she climbed out behind them. All three of them stood apart from Bainbridge and his companion, even after they'd all alighted, and when the man with the Kitchener mustache tried to say something to them, Mimi hid her face in her mother's coat, and the mother turned her head angrily away.

"That's Endershall?" Duncan assumed.

Savin nodded. "That is Sir Michael, yes. Shall we go down?"

They met the visitors in Capstone Park House's marble-flagged main atrium, where Savin's staff were helping them out of their coats. Mimi spotted Duncan as he came down the broad staircase, and her face lit up as if at fireworks.

"Mama, it's *Duncan*!" she squealed, tugging at her mother's sleeve, even as a manservant was trying to take said sleeve and the coat it belonged to from its owner. *"Look!"*

The woman he had known as Irene Rush met his eye. Her lip trembled a single moment, then firmed again as she forced a thin, tight smile. Mimi tugged at her again, pulled at her arm so she bent down, and then whispered excitedly in her ear. The mother nodded, and Mimi tore free, raced across the marble flooring like an unleashed greyhound, and, as Duncan reached the bottom step, flung herself at him full force. He just about got his arms out to catch her in time.

"You came!" she said fiercely into his chest. "I told Mama you would! I told her you'd come to get us."

He hugged her back, crouched to her level, and set her back on her feet again. "Well, really, you two came to get me. Because look—here you both are."

"No, but—" Face creased up with sudden confusion. She looked back doubtfully at her mother for guidance, but Ada Endershall-Ulver, more slowly and deliberately than her daughter, was already closing the gap between them. She put her arms around Duncan, held him tight to her, and whispered, *thank you, thank you,* over and over again, pressing her face to his. He felt the sparse, hot smear of tears against his cheek. Beneath the coat, she was thin and frail, worn down with the waiting and not knowing . . .

"I think that is quite enough! Unhand my wife at once!"

Peppery, baritone voice, educated and used to command. Duncan felt how the woman in his arms shuddered at the sound of it. He set her gently to one side. Looked to where Sir Michael Endershall stood bristling a handful of paces away, restrained only, it appeared, by Bainbridge's hand on his shoulder. He felt his lips peel from his teeth.

A fresh mottling rose in Endershall's cheeks. His voice scaled upward. "How dare you grin at me, you *insolent baboon*!"

Duncan looked at Bainbridge. "Does he hold any sway in this?"

Bainbridge shook his head. He seemed amused.

"I have come here," snapped Endershall, "out of duty to—"

It was as far as he got. Duncan hit him with the hardest right cross he'd ever thrown at a human being. Wet, gristly crunch as the other man's nose broke against his knuckles. Endershall staggered back on the marble flags, pinwheeling his arms, found no balance, hit the floor flat on his back. Duncan glided after him, fists up. He caught movement from the two plainclothesmen out of the corner of his eye, a twitching forward. He angled a couple of inches toward them. Looked them in the eye, one after the other. Whatever they saw in his face, it stopped them dead in their tracks.

No one said anything at all. Savin's staff were frozen in place, the gathered coats of the visitors still over their arms. Sir Michael Endershall flailed on the floor like a man fallen through ice, managed to gain purchase and prop himself halfway up, eyes blazing with rage. He seemed not to feel the blood streaming down into his Kitchener mustache and over his lips. His mouth worked.

"You get up," Duncan told him grimly, "and I'll break your fucking jaw for you, too. I'll cave your ribs in, I'll puncture your fucking lungs. I'll put you in hospital for a solid month, if I don't kill you."

Maybe it was the mustache.

Behind him, he heard Mimi Rush whimper. His fists loosened a fraction at the sound. He leaned over the downed knight of the realm. His voice dropped to a corrosive hiss.

"You threw away the only thing that matters," he said. "And you did it for *politics*. You are everything that has gone wrong with us. You belong nailed to a tree on the Forest fringe, offered up to the powers there you prostrated yourself to."

He leaned in closer. "I'd put you there myself, but I don't have the time."

"I AM SORRY ABOUT THE police. They were at Endershall's insistence." Bainbridge, gesturing idly with his brandy snifter as they sat in the south library. Soft autumn afternoon sunlight suffused the room, painted itself richly on walls of neatly shelved leather-bound books.

"I tried to dissuade him, of course, but Mr. Silver's record has not encouraged him in such matters of trust."

Duncan grunted. Buried his face in his own drink.

"I trusted Mr. Silver to bring my daughter out of the Forest," Ada Endershall-Ulver said coldly. "And he did. I would trust him with my life."

Bainbridge smiled. "Oh, I agree entirely. Don't misunderstand me, Lady Ada. I am here unaccompanied, without forces, because I know Mr. Silver to be a man of his word. I know he will fulfill the terms of our agreement, just as I hope he—and you—have faith in my will to do the same from my side. Funds have already been transferred to the viscount's credit, though I understand there may be a few days to wait before confirmation goes through."

"Funds were not required, Bainbridge. I'm not a shopkeeper." Savin turned away from the archmage with disdain. He faced Ada and a sudden warmth flooded his voice. "At my order, my lady, you have a first-class cabin reserved aboard the RMS *Northern Light*, departing November 7 for New York. Tickets for yourself, your daughter, and your maid, Susan. There will be no charge."

Tears welled in Ada Endershall-Ulver's eyes.

"You are very kind," she said softly.

Savin bowed stiffly. "We are kindred spirits, my lady. The same nightmare visited upon us, the same salvation delivered, and by the same man. How could I not make every possible provision for your comfort?"

Bainbridge cleared his throat, clearly none too pleased with being excluded. "Yes, well, anyway. You will be met in New York by arrangement with some friends of mine, and accommodated at their home in Manhattan until you find your feet, so to speak. A stipend has been agreed with Sir Michael; I think you'll find it generous. To continue after the divorce is finalized as well, of course."

"Of course," she repeated dustily.

"Yes, well, then." Fumbling a bit. "It only remains, my lady, to wish you every happiness going forward, for you and your daughter. I think you'll find America . . . invigorating. Brimming with potential. It really is a new world." A sour glance at Savin. "It is not haunted by the same phantoms and failings that plague us here, you see. Perhaps that's why the Forests have not stormed it in the same way."

"Yes, thank you, Mr. Bainbridge. I'm sure we will make a go of things there." Ada Endershall-Ulver looked across the room. "And you, Mr. Silver?"

Lost in the warm march of sunlight down the library shelves, Duncan took a moment to notice she was talking to him. "Hmm?"

"I'm not a fool, Mr. Silver. I know the way this world works. What have you done to win this future for us? What was the—the *trade*? What is your side of this agreement?"

And across the leather spines, something seemed to happen to the light, as if the afternoon lost faith in itself, staggered by the onset of evening and the promise of winter to come. The tinker's daughter's words rose in his mind.

There's something black and twisted following you.

Duncan forced a smile.

"It's a small matter," he said.

FORTY-TWO

ONE LAST THING.

He lay on his back in the bed next to Niamh, listening to the rasp and bubble of her breathing, watching the high, shadowed ceiling over their heads as if something fanged might come at him out of it. Weariness was bone deep in him, but undercut by something else—a tiny, trickling electric current in his fingers and teeth and skin that seemed to press him hard into the mattress and hold him immobile. It had taken until past midnight before Niamh settled properly into sleep, and even now, he knew, her lungs might tip her back into hacking wakefulness at any moment.

It was time.

He slid out of bed with painstaking care, padded naked across the palatial bedroom to the balcony windows and the heavy purple floor-to-ceiling drapes that curtained them off. He slipped between the drapes, stood close up against the glass. Felt the chill from outside coming off the pane. He opened the catches, pushed the windows wide. Stepped out onto the cold stone flags of the balcony beyond.

There was a waning moon high up over the Forest to the west, bobbing through wind-driven cloud that gave it a sense of rushing, dizzying motion all its own. Soft pewter light across the lawns and gravel driveway of Capstone Park House, blotched now and again with the racing shadow of a cloud. Cool night air from the breeze ghosted his naked skin, not quite wintry enough yet to be unpleasant, but it was getting there.

"Are you ready, Duncan?"

Echoing his thoughts as if reading them. For all he'd expected to hear it, her voice put ice water down his spine. He turned about, tipped his head back.

Mebhuranon crouched on the narrow stone portico above the window, apparently as comfortable and at ease as any raptor on a branch. She leaned slender arms on knees, tilted her head at him, wolflike, as she stared down. The breeze stirred her silver and dark hair, picked at the folds of her cloak where it hung down either side of her crouch. Looking up, he could see the prehensile grip her feet maintained on the stone, could see between her legs to the delicate cleft of her sex, revealed with no more thought than the haunches it separated . . .

He swallowed hard. "Yes. I am."

She executed some kind of boneless tumble dive, dropped through the four yards of night air, and landed with no more sound than a shadow. She rose upright at his side. Loomed amiably over him.

"Then show me," she said.

He led her inside, through the drapes and into the center of the room. She stood poised, staring at the woman in the big bed. For just a moment, it seemed as if the grand dimensions of the chamber had been built for her, and he and Niamh were just some interloping race of smaller, grubbier beings. She tilted her head again, seemed to be listening for something. She bared her teeth, hissed.

"Ahhh, this. The Eternal Unwarded unleashed, the Chaos Dance," he thought she said. "This we have seen before." The faintest crease of a frown across her broad, pale forehead. "Though not here, in the lungs. This is new. A new curse."

A sudden terror stalked him. "Then—"

"No." As if she had already heard his fear. "Oh no. It merely makes it simpler."

She folded herself onto the bed at Niamh's side—Duncan, for one mad moment, recalled Murnau's *Carmilla*—floated one splayed hand over the Irishwoman's face and breast, muttering almost inaudibly, sibilants that nonetheless bit into him like winter cold. Niamh stirred, not restlessly, sinking languidly somehow into the pillow. A faint smile bent her mouth at the corners. Her lips parted.

Snake swift, the Fae queen snatched her by the back of the skull. Put her own mouth to the parted lips and breathed in hard. Her back arched with the force of it. For a second, the seal of her lips with Niamh's bulged and flexed impossibly, as if a dozen eels roiled around in the space between their mouths. A grunting, growling noise emanated from Mebhuranon and her unpupiled ink-black eyes widened. Then she whipped her hand from the back of Niamh's skull, pressed it instead to the mortal woman's forehead, and pushed Niamh down into the mattress. Duncan caught, or thought he caught, a glimpse of something like a long dark ragged tongue recoiling back up into the Fae queen's mouth . . .

Then it was done.

The two women, Fae and mortal, parted. Niamh turned over in the bedclothes, snuggled down into the pillow, breath suddenly inaudible. Mebhuranon gagged, turned aside, spat hard into her hand, like a Shoreditch streetwalker voiding her mouth of come. Her tongue came out, inhumanly long, and she scraped it back into her mouth under her teeth. Spat again, less violently.

She sat for a moment, contemplating what lay in her palm.

Duncan moved closer, but as he did, she closed up her hand into a fist, made a flexing, grasping motion, and all he saw was a splatter of viscous black dripping off her palm and fingers, dissolving into tendrils, then into threads, and then into nothing at all. Mebhuranon wiped her hands together, palm across palm. Stood up.

"Done," she said. "All is as you asked."

He nodded, wordless. Did not trust himself to speak.

"We come for you at dawn," she said. "As agreed. Oh, what *now,* tree thief?"

He cleared his throat. Gestured at Niamh. "Can you . . . is there a way she can sleep until I'm gone?"

The Fae queen raised an elegant eyebrow.

"Never bargain with tree thieves," she muttered cryptically, and he thought from the words she used that it had the ring of proverb or cant. "Well, then."

She gestured, peevishly, a single pass over Niamh's sleeping face.

"There. She will not wake until the sun reaches its zenith. The rest will do her good. Now ask me no more boons, my part is complete. Only be ready to render yours."

There's something black and twisted following you, Duncan.

"I already am," he said.

And felt, somewhere dark in the roots of his being, that it was the simple truth. He was tired, he was out of options, a kind of trench daze was on him for the first time since the war.

Let it all come. He could not fault the bargain he had struck.

Mebhuranon grunted, brushed past him, and then through the thick drapes at the window, almost, it seemed, without disturbing them as she passed. Duncan barely noticed.

He knew he would not sleep.

He sat beside Niamh, waiting for the hour to come around, listening to her breathe.

It was enough.

AN HOUR BEFORE DAWN, HE put his iron rings on one by one, went down and breakfasted with Savin and Bainbridge. Bacon and eggs, blood sausage, kidneys, buttered beans, and toast. Once again, he wasn't really hungry, but he forced himself to eat. The three men sat over their food in near silence, broken only by the chink of cutlery on plates and the viscount's soft words of thanks whenever his serving staff brought anything to the table.

"No Endershall?" Duncan asked finally, when it was clear no one else would be joining them.

Bainbridge gestured with his fork. "Sir Michael prefers not to involve himself with the grubby detail of magic. I suspect he feels it makes him look foolish."

"You'd think he'd be used to that."

Strained smiles from the other two, but no laughter to match. The atmosphere was too maudlin, too heavy with preparation for loss. Savin had been increasingly withdrawn the last two days as Duncan's inevitable departure drew near. *Are you certain,* he asked repeatedly. *Are you certain you must do this, man? Is there truly no other way?* And he paced restlessly as he talked, like the lions Duncan had once seen at Edinburgh Zoo, pacing out the boundaries of their enclosure, powerless to go beyond. It was the same way he'd paced three years ago when his son was in the Forest and a mysterious, unproven woodsman called Silver his only hope of getting him back. It was the same dreadful admission of forces beyond his command, the caged anger of a man used to calling the shots, who could now only wait and hope and pray.

It was the war, the trenches, and the waiting, all over again.

Oddly, Duncan found himself feeling sorry for the viscount. The complications, the intricate constraint, the diplomacy and delicate patience required to navigate these things—he felt as if they were drifting away from him, distant as the sounds of fighting somewhere a long way down the line, a messy, endlessly inconclusive battle he would not now be called to, not his problem anymore.

He felt himself filling up instead with the raw, violent simplicity of the Forest's call.

Where Savin was withdrawn, Bainbridge was merely guarded. Duncan caught him once or twice in a calculating stare when he thought no one was looking, guessed that he was checking and rechecking the forged links in this chain of undertaking he had staked his current position and future on.

"So what is it for you now, Bainbridge?" Duncan asked him. "Filling the vacuum at Whitehall, spearheading the charge at the behest of your good friends in government? They make you head of Section J yet?"

"Something like that, yes."

Duncan saw the grimace at the corner of Savin's mouth. He raised his coffee cup in ironic toast. "Here, then—to the man of the hour."

Bainbridge shrugged magnanimously and reached for more bacon. "Someone has to be."

THEY WENT OUT TO THE fence line and a carefully made high iron gate, in front of which Savin's groundsmen had already built the summoning fire to Bainbridge's instructions. The flames crackled and leapt, cheery orange against the gray-blue dawn.

"You are quite certain about this?" Savin asked Duncan one more time.

Duncan smiled. "We're beyond that now. Don't worry about me. You have given me all the help I need, all that I could ask. Tell the truth, I think it was always going to come to this."

"Destiny." Bainbridge nodded sagely. "She overmasters us all."

Duncan held his smile frozen, made an effort not to roll his eyes. Savin cursed under his breath. Bainbridge dug in his pockets, brought out an ornate amber vial. He unstoppered it, walked widdershins about the fire, gibbering something that might have been Latin.

Then he upended the vial over the flames.

Quick, eager rush of purple light, shooting jagged through the fire. A small puff of greenish smoke rose and rolled away eastward.

They stood and waited.

The Huldu came.

SIX OF THEM, SLIPPING ONE by one from the gloom under the trees beyond the fence. Powerfully built warrior caste, honor guard brawlers, haughty with affected disinterest as they quit the tree line and came through the iron gate, but Duncan saw that they had already extruded fangs and talons way past the norm. Savin swore when he saw them, staggered involuntarily back a step.

"Duncan . . . !"

"It's fine," Duncan said sharply. "Stay calm. They'll harm no one so long as this is honored."

The Huldu formed up in two ranks, turned inward to face each other, and Mebhuranon came down the file between them. Her hair seemed to burn in the dawn like black and silver flame around her face. Her naked form slipped in and out of view beneath her cloak as she walked. Savin swore again, this time at different register. Bainbridge faced the Fae queen and bowed deeply from the waist.

"My Lady of the, uhm, Boughs," he intoned in really pretty shaky Skogurtal. "I have, as agreed, the supplicant. He has, as agreed, come willingly to, uhm, this place of invocation. He has, uhm, as agreed, undertaken—"

"Yes, very good." Mebhuranon waved a hand irritably. "Shut up now. Stop talking. Our agreement stands. We give up claim on the child and undertake, as before, to talk further of coexistence between our kinds. It is peace between us for now."

"I—"

"That is all." She snapped her fingers and turned about. Duncan stepped forward to join her. He'd thought it would cost him a large portion of his will to do it, to take the step, but in the event, it was almost easy. A vast, black anticipation was filling him up, seething in his veins, lapping at his jaw like small waves, seeding an urge to snap and snarl and bite. He felt the honor guard gather at his back, put his hands on his belt, one touching the hilt of the trench knife sheathed there, felt how they recoiled the faintest fraction as he did, and he grinned.

Then he let the Huldu lead him into the Forest and away.

HE COULD NOT TELL HOW far they traveled, or in what direction, because on the way something happened to time and the light. The thin blue dawn stayed blue, did not give way to paler shades. No low, angled sunlight broke through the thinning autumn canopies over their heads as they trekked on a bearing Duncan could not ascertain. They walked in permanent twilight, feet almost soundless on leaf mold and black mud paths between the trees. Birdsong faded out, was lost to distance and then to any hearing at all. Once he saw a raven perched on a branch over the path, but it made no comment, only turned its beak and watched the procession on its way with a beady eye. A bleak stillness held the Forest in its grip, silence pressed into Duncan's ears like cotton wool wadding.

They came finally to a broad clearing, slim young beech and elm and a single ancient oak with roots grown out like the gnarled arms of thrones sunk deep into the ground around it.

In front of the oak, Svalenkari was waiting.

The cloak he wore was soft blue to match the twilight, shot through with restless black lightning and kaleidoscope sparks that moved on the fabric. His hair was long and black to match his eyes, and had been braided intricately in four places. In his right hand, down at his side, he held the saemdil blade. He turned, fang-grinning, at Duncan's arrival, lifted both arms in mock greeting.

"Hello, tree thief, life thief, mortal scum. You've grown, haven't you?" Stropping the blade back and forth on the air with casual ease, so it made a faint, hollow whoop on every stroke. "Barren, they tell me, which is a shame, but at least a decent kill in your own right. Do you have a valediction before I take you apart?"

Take you apart. In Skogurtal, there was a cadence to the phrase that rang ornate, carried echoes and significance, dark taste of horror, almost an incantation. But Duncan felt no fear at all. He had no room for it anymore.

"A valediction? How about 'Keep an eye on your grandchildren, they die easier than you know'?" He bared his teeth back at the Huldu. "You know, I always wondered why Isnorvi was such a twisted little fuck. But now, knowing his bloodline, makes a lot of sense."

A new stillness gripped the clearing. A score of Fae gazes bent on him in glowering disbelief, lips peeled back from fangs. Svalenkari made a noise deep in his throat, moved away from the oak. He lifted his arm and pointed at Duncan down the length of the saemdil blade.

"Make ready, tree thief," he snarled. "Your doom is on you. With blade and body only, I come to the glade. I shall need no more."

"Aye." Duncan, grinning eagerly as he shrugged his way out of his coat. "That's what Stordalen told me. And I ate his fucking heart."

He pulled the sgian dubh out from its sheath in the small of his back, settled it into his right hand. Drew the trench knife in his left. The hate came seething upward in him, a tension, a dark drug spiking through his veins like some new species of cocaine, a thundering river that would carry him, as he let go, to whatever end this was.

There's something black and twisted following you, Duncan, and I don't want Billy anywhere near you when it catches you up.

Well, Billy was away. Niamh was away, too, breathing easy, soft and warm and safe in her bed as sunrise approached. And one day quite soon, Mimi Rush and her mother would stand on the deck of the RMS *Northern Light*, steaming steadily west to better things.

He'd done what he needed to, his promises were kept.

All that remained was this.

Svalenkari will not be denied, the Fae queen had told him. *And I must have order among the Bright Folk once more, no matter the cost.*

He hefted the two iron blades, met Svalenkari's ink-black stare. He bared his teeth again.

"Come on, then, you Fae fuck! Let's get this done!"

He thought he saw sudden lightning spike in the empty black of the Huldu lord's eyes, mauve and toxic green, some veinous paroxysm he'd never before seen in any Fae. Svalenkari's jaws opened, his fangs lengthened visibly by fractions. He gave out a deep, coughing bark.

"Do you hear the tree thief?" He exhorted the other Huldu. "He thinks this will be quick? Ohhhhh, Duncannnn, you have no idea what awaits you before I finally send you back to the Gray! Once, the hand of the Bright Folk reached out to you, would have lifted you up beyond the muck of your miserable mortal count of days! But you—"

"Come on!" yelled Duncan. "I came to slaughter Fae, not listen to them make vapid speeches! Enough stroking yourself, Huldu! *Let's get this fucking done!*"

He rushed the Fae lord with twenty years and more of hatred pumping through his heart. Lashed out with one booted foot, slashed high and low with his blades.

Svalenkari was not there.

Gone, flinched aside in a flicker of pale limbs, striking back left-handed at Duncan's breast as he moved. Duncan felt a spike of numbing cold over his collarbone, the same blow Mebhuranon had dealt him in the park. Any lower and it would have stopped his heart. As it was, he staggered, felt tendrils of ice reach down and touch the ventricles. He swung himself clumsily around to find the Fae lord, to face him at least . . .

Svalenkari stood a short distance off, still in front of the ancient oak, fangs half shrouded in a downward curving sneer.

"You thought perhaps that Stordalen *was* somebody?" he asked mildly. "A pampered princeling with the name of the Final Isles in his mouth every second breath?"

"At least," Duncan said, panting, pulling air into his chilled lungs as best he could, "he knew how to keep his word, and theirs."

"His word?" A deep, mirthless chuckle, as if the oak itself laughed. Svalenkari seemed to shoot a look at Mebhuranon. "The word of the Final Isles? Of a dream five thousand years dying? The word of a corpse walking?"

The Huldu stalked closer. Duncan raised his knives, readied his guard.

"Do you know," Svalenkari asked him, "what they have in the Final Isles?"

Duncan feinted with the trench knife, swung, whiplash swift, with the sgian dubh. Trying for the Fae's throat, but Svalenkari flowed gracefully with the strike, caught the small knife across his shoulder instead. Sputter of green fire, he fell back a long step, made a hissing noise through his teeth.

The wound smoldered into the twilight air.

Svalenkari pressed his face closer to it, breathed in the smoke as if it were perfume. He grinned skullishly at Duncan.

"Oh, well done. But you see, for the Old Ones like Meb and I, iron is not quite the ward you tree thieves like to believe. Isn't that right, Meb?"

Across the clearing, the Fae queen said nothing, only watched with blank black gaze.

"So you see, little Duncan. You'll have to do better than that."

Duncan rushed him again, trench knife up like a shield, sgian dubh looking for a low slash to belly or thigh. Almost absently, Svalenkari tilted and kicked him in the chest. Knocked him back ten feet and onto the Forest floor. Jarring impact, right down his back to the base of his spine.

It was all he could do to keep hold of his blades.

"But you interrupted me," the Huldu lord rumbled, ambling toward him, shoulder wound still fuming faintly. "You know what they have in the Final Isles, Duncan? They have *cities.* Just like you, just like the tree-thief scum, they live under roofs, behind walls, like creatures frightened by the majesty of the Forest that enfolds us, that gives us life. They *hide*, Duncan! Is it any wonder they find time to spin their webs of law and rule and given word, till we all are bundled and bound like spiders' prey?"

He reached down with big, pale, taloned hands. Duncan slashed desperately from the ground. Svalenkari laughed, blocked the trench knife, and seized the hand that wielded it at the wrist. Savage, biting cold, deep into the bone. He took another gash from the sgian dubh, this time across the ribs, rode it with a grunt. He lifted Duncan effortlessly off his feet by the arm he held, hurled him casually across the clearing. Duncan hit and tumbled, over and over, lost the trench knife from fingers gone numb, barely avoided stabbing himself with the sgian dubh as he rolled.

Laughter around the clearing, like the burble of some dark brook he couldn't see.

"Did you think you were the hero of this tale?" Svalenkari asked him, circling around Duncan, not even in a fighter's crouch. The wound in his ribs smoked faintly, but his voice was untroubled, musing. "Because you bested a Final Isles princeling and tasted Fae blood? Did you think you were Pendragon returned, perhaps, the once and future king of mortal mud piles, the champion of tree-thief men?"

He stepped close. Duncan slashed with the sgian dubh, tried desperately for an Achilles tendon. Svalenkari danced aside, stomped down hard on his right arm, pinned it to the ground. Ice flowed up and down the limb, numbing to the shoulder, down to the fingertips and there, the sgian dubh trickled away from his grip. He flexed his ringed fingers desperately, both hands, working to get feeling back. Without feeling, there was no—

"Let me tell you a secret," Svalenkari said amiably. "One you won't read in your mortal legends. We took Arthur Pendragon when his power grew troubling among our own kind as well as yours. We took him into the west, we took him to the Final Isles, and there, for his insolence, *we took him apart.*

"And now, pinned to this great oak, that's what's going to happen to you."

The Fae lord bent over him, dodged a weak punch, and took the rings on his forehead. Flash of green fire, he grunted again, shook his head, and blinked to clear his vision. He struck Duncan hard across the face in turn, bloodied his mouth and nose with the blow, turned his head. Duncan jolted and flopped like a landed trout. His vision shattered apart in tiny points of light like the pattern on Svalenkari's cloak. The Fae lord grasped him by the collar, dragged him bodily, blood dripping, across the clearing to the oak. He raised the saemdil blade for the first time since the fight began. He held Duncan pinned against the rough gnarling of the bark with his free hand.

"Would you like to beg?" he wondered.

But Duncan just grinned at him through bloodied teeth.

Spat blood at the ground between his feet.

"Get it done," he snarled. "You faithless Fae cunt."

HE CLAMBERS UP NEXT TO his mother on the sofa, with the big book under his arm. He opens it and pushes it into her hands. Snuggles against her soft warmth.

But Duncan . . . Something close to horror in her tone. She shrinks from him. *This is a fairy tale. You're eleven. You're too old for fairy tales.*

He looks into her face for a long moment, sees nothing there he can call on, hold to, make his own again. He sits solemnly a long moment, blinking into the firelight.

You're too old for fairy tales, Duncan, she insists.

Tears well up, balance on the lids of his eyes.

He turns away from her to hide them.

He scuffles off the sofa again, walks away, leaves the book, the warm fire flicker and lamplit haven of the room. He stands a moment in the gloomy corridor outside, back pressed to the wall as if pinned there, as if held against some immovable ancient oak.

You're too old for fairy tales.

He's come home. He held on to desperate memory and fought his way here. He is done.

There is no more.

He climbs the darkened stairs to his room and to find sleep, as he has always been, alone.

FORTY-THREE

OVER HIS HEAD, THE GREAT OAK SPLIT APART.

Creaking, cracking, tearing—later he would wonder if it was the same sound the citizens of Britain had heard in 1918, over and over, across the whole nation, as the great trees erupted from their tamed landscapes overnight.

Fresh, green, sappy scent.

Svalenkari—saemdil blade raised level to drive right through Duncan and into the wood behind—recoiling now in sudden shock.

The McCulloch fell out over Duncan's crooked right arm, fell into his fumbling, half-numb grip.

Too old for fairy tales? This is no fucking faerie tale.

Almost, he dropped the gun—

This a human story! And a human's going to fucking finish it!

Reflex from the trenches saved him—chilled fingers forced to function, to grasp. He leveled the shotgun at Svalenkari from the hip. Clamped the trigger and fired.

Slamfired three shells into the Fae lord.

The trees seem to like you. That has to count for something.

Svalenkari staggered, stumbled, dropped the saemdil blade. Chuckling, hissing green fire at the edges of the sudden damage to belly and breast. Smoke poured from the holes the iron had made. He gaped down at himself in disbelief. Tried to turn away, to retreat, perhaps, to the ranks of his fellow Fae. No one else moved, the Fae queen least of all.

Duncan lurched away from the oak that was holding him up. Somehow he stayed on his feet unaided. He followed the stricken Fae lord's stumbling progress across the clearing.

He will impale you against the great oak. Mebhuranon's matter-of-fact words as they stood at the top of the south tower together in the cold October dawn. *He will tear you apart with his bare hands. You cannot defeat him with blades, no more than you could defeat me.*

No wonder he'd shivered in the autumn wind, had still been shivering when Savin came up and found him later.

But with the speaking iron, you may yet send him back to the Gray.

From Garner's carefully instructed hand to the Fae queen on the fringes of the Forest, from Mebhuranon to the skogsra and into the bole of the oak, and now from the skogsra into his iron-ringed mortal hands. Around the clearing, the Huldu stood frozen, staring at what had just been done. None moved to intervene. None moved to help Svalenkari as he heard Duncan's footfalls and turned to face his executioner. His gaze swung wildly about, perhaps lit on Mebhuranon, where she stood silent among the others, face impassive.

"You—" He coughed, and thick smolder curled from his open mouth. "I planted spoiled seed, I—"

Duncan stared at him. "No. What you did, you and Isnorvi and all the rest of you Fae fucks, you built a machine. And you built me to last."

He slamfired the McCulloch dry.

Watched Svalenkari torn through with the iron load, set afire, murdered where he stood. Watched him crumple in ruin and blue-green flame.

FOR WHAT SEEMED LIKE AN eternity, no Huldu uttered a sound.

They stood and stared in silence at the smoldering, green-fire-eaten carcass in the center of the clearing, the hunched and shivering mortal stood over it with the speaking iron in his hands.

Until the mortal spoke.

"The word of the Final Isles," Duncan enunciated, the recitation Meb had given him, "will not be flaunted. The old paths will not be forsaken. This is what waits, if ever they are. Mortal chaos, an Unbinding. The speaking iron will be waiting, *I* will be waiting—for you all."

Angry murmuring, like a vast serpent through the gathering. Duncan clung to the emptied McCulloch and hoped they wouldn't call his bluff.

Mebhuranon stepped forward. The murmuring ceased.

"We have all seen where Svalenkari's path leads," she said loudly. "And it is not our path. Will any among you still walk it?"

There was some muttering, but low, and it petered out pretty fucking fast. The Fae queen inclined her head.

"Then come. Four among you who were close with him, take up Svalenkari, for he has gone back to the Gray. We will honor his passing. Even for renegades, even for the failed and forsaken, there must be ritual and what is right to do. The word of the Final Isles, the word of the Bright Folk, the word of the Forest itself is unbroken in all things, across all time."

After an awkward pause, four Huldu came forward, pushing through the spectating ranks. The colors in their robes were damped down and muddy, they crouched like fighters, peeled lips back off fangs as they approached Duncan.

But they left him alone.

He watched numbly as they gathered up the still-smoking corpse and carried it away between the beech and elm.

The others filed away after them, fading one by one into the twilit gloom.

Last to go was Mebhuranon. She turned at the fringes of the clearing and looked back at him. Duncan nodded at her. For a moment, it looked as if she might leave without a word.

Then her lips peeled back. She let her fangs show.

"I do not like machines," she said.

Duncan shrugged. "I don't like being one. But what's done is done."

They stared at each other.

"Your mother," said Duncan suddenly, impulsively. "Do you—"

The Fae queen shook her head.

"I had the eilsinni," she said. "My own face bent over me, caring for me, nourishing me, falling away to let me flourish. We are not like you, Duncan."

"Guess not."

"Well, then." She stirred impatiently, looked up at the tree canopies, where the gloom was bleaching out, whatever glamour that had held here for the duel now giving way to the daylight it had denied. "You will have to find your own way out. I imagine you'll manage."

He swayed a little on his feet. "I imagine I will."

The Fae queen twitched, made as if to step into the trees, hesitated a moment more.

"I remember few mortals," she said. "They wash away like foam on rapids. But I will remember you, I think."

Somewhere, a wren warbled from its perch, greeting the freshly unleashed day. Duncan's gaze flickered reflexively to the sound.

When he looked back, Mebhuranon was gone.

HE FOUND HIS KNIVES WHERE they'd fallen, wiped them and stowed them securely.

He went and seated himself in the sunken throne arms of the old oak's roots, pressed his back into the bark, put his knees up in front of him and rested the emptied McCulloch across them. He thought he heard a tiny, girlish giggle trickle down from the fresh wide crack in the trunk where the trench gun had fallen out into his arms.

He waited.

But the sound did not repeat, and the skogsra, if it was there, didn't show itself to him.

He shrugged. They were, he reminded himself, flighty, flirty things at the best of times.

In a few minutes, he knew, he'd have to get up and start pathfinding, working out compass points and the best way to get himself home.

Instead, somehow, he sat there in the oak root arms of his sunken throne and watched, unhinged from time, as filtering rays of winter sun came probing, then filling the clearing, lancing it with light, then tracking, sweeping, finally ebbing as the sun moved round between autumn branches and then sank, diminished, choked off, gone to molten embers in the black twig mesh at the limits of visibility to the west.

He watched the twilight come on once more.

HE FEELS STORDALEN'S BLOOD RISING in response, ticking in his veins again with the gloom, shivering his skin, itching in his fingernails and teeth.

And then, abruptly, the whole Forest lights itself for him, like a field of votive candles, soft bluish glow away between the trunks, along the ground like mist, and a warm green-gold pulse at the heart of every tree.

Presently, the skogsra emerges from the bole of the oak over his head, bark-paper skin all sticky with secretion, and twines herself about him, sprig haired and nut brown and giggly.

Treefuckah, she teases him.

The nearly wolf-sized wolf spiders come out one by one to scuttle and play around at his feet. He grins at the sight.

Feels how his teeth lengthen softly to bared fangs in his jaw.

ACKNOWLEDGMENTS

No Man's Land is something of a departure from previous books, a bit of a leap in the dark, and therefore a risk taken. And it is a lot easier to take risks when you're not painfully concerned with pleasing an existing market, nurturing an existing revenue stream, living by deadlines rather than creative delight. Thanks are therefore due first and foremost to all those who facilitated this particular leap—

To Laeta Kalogridis, who set me free and gave me the ride of a lifetime into the bargain.

To Vlad Korolev for friendship, faith, and generosity with both time and the best set of toys I've ever been given to work with.

To my long-suffering editors, Gillian Redfearn and Anne Groell, who wore the long delays and spasms of creative doubt with infinite patience, and still signed enthusiastically on the dotted line when their flagging author showed up with a whole new direction and a set of as-yet wholly unbaked ideas. I could ask for no finer professional backing.

And thanks to all those readers who made it clear they would far rather have the book I wanted to write than one I felt constrained to put out, and encouraged me to take all the time I needed to produce the former rather than the latter.

On the research side of things, two particular resources were invaluable in creating the world of *No Man's Land*, and I returned to them time and again.

Somme Mud by E.P.F. Lynch is a sanguine but unremitting first-person account of what it was like to be an infantryman in the trenches of Flanders and France during the First World War. Much of the in-your-face detail of Duncan's wartime memories is borrowed from or otherwise rooted in the real-life experiences of Private Edward Lynch, as detailed in this book. It deserves to be read by anyone who wants to grasp the flavor of those desperate times.

The Long, Long Trail (longlongtrail.co.uk) is—no other words for it—a labor of love by freelance military historian, researcher, and author Chris Baker, hosting an immense treasure trove of logistical detail and data about the so-called Great War. In many ways, this resource was the perfect hardheaded companion to the more anecdotal and impressionistic storytelling of *Somme Mud.* If you have even a passing interest in the period, you really should drop by and sample the site.

Special thanks also go to the very erudite and accomplished Adam Roberts, professor of literature, SF author extraordinaire, and all around polymath, for agreeing to read the manuscript with an eye to telling period detail. Adam has saved *No Man's Land* from multiple embarrassing anachronisms and honed its historical accuracy for me with razor-sharp aplomb. Any such errors left in the text are mine alone.

Closer to home, also invaluable in research terms was the advice and training of my Krav Maga instructor, Jack Gunton, who has, over the last several years, really tuned up my appreciation of what makes a good fight. A number of the combat sequences in *No Man's Land* would have been considerably less compelling without Jack's input and critique.

And a quick shout-out to Beth and Ellie at the Unthank Arms, where a quite surprising amount of *No Man's Land* was written, with the help of splendid table service.

Finally, my deepest thanks go, as ever, to my wife, Virginia, and my son, Daniel, for bearing with me once again during the long process. Together you are, and will always be, the engine of all I do.

ABOUT THE AUTHOR

RICHARD K. MORGAN is the acclaimed author of *No Man's Land, Thin Air, The Dark Defiles, The Cold Commands, The Steel Remains, Thirteen, Woken Furies, Market Forces, Broken Angels,* and *Altered Carbon,* a *New York Times* Notable Book and winner of the Philip K. Dick Award. His dystopian thriller *Market Forces* won the John W. Campbell Award; *Thirteen,* a meditation on genetically engineered humans, won the Arthur C. Clarke Award; and his revisionist fantasy *The Steel Remains* won the Gaylactic Spectrum Award. *Altered Carbon* has been in feature film development since publication and is now a two-season series on Netflix.

richardkmorgan.com
Bluesky: @quellist1.bsky.social

ABOUT THE TYPE

This book was set in Baskerville, a typeface designed by John Baskerville (1706–75), an amateur printer and typefounder, and cut for him by John Handy in 1750. The type became popular again when the Lanston Monotype Corporation of London revived the classic roman face in 1923. The Mergenthaler Linotype Company in England and the United States cut a version of Baskerville in 1931, making it one of the most widely used typefaces today.